I0787962

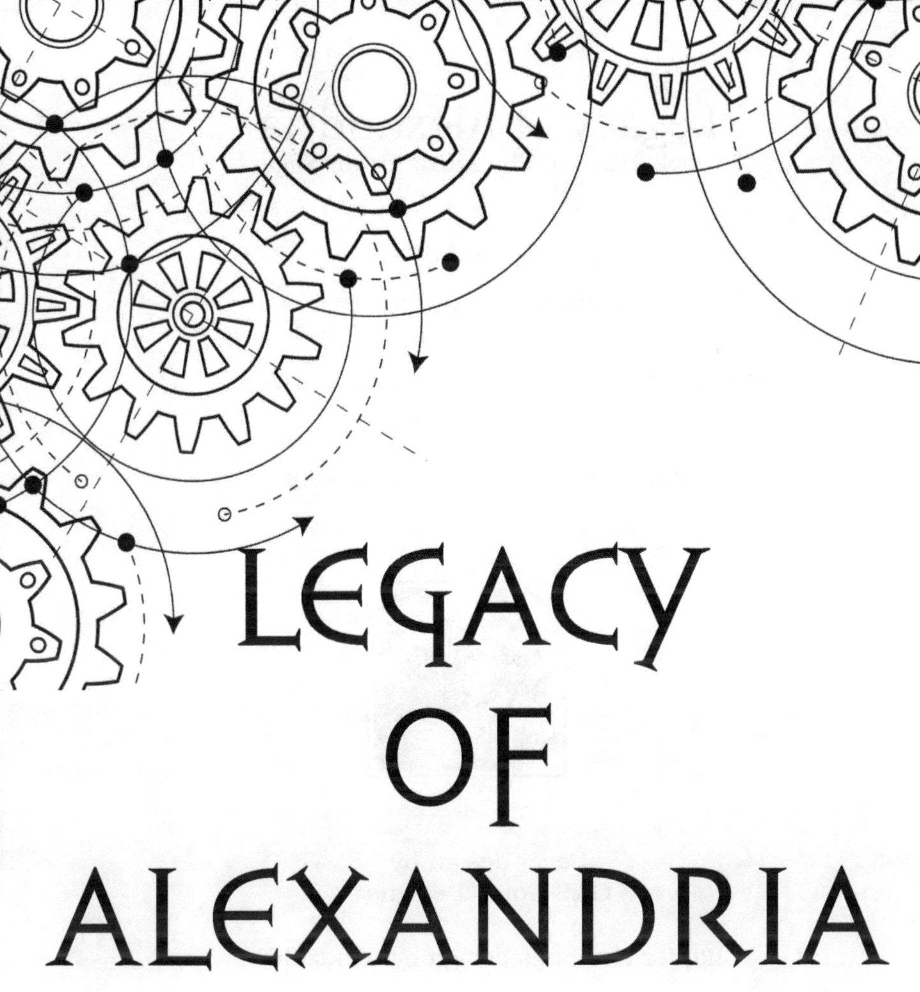

LEGACY OF ALEXANDRIA

Book Three of The Alexandrian Saga

Thomas K. Carpenter

Legacy of Alexandria
Book Three of The Alexandrian Saga

Hardcover Version

by Thomas K. Carpenter

Published by Black Moon Books

Cover design by
G&S Cover Designs

Chapter Headings design by Aleks49011

Discover other titles by this author on:
www.thomaskcarpenter.com

ISBN-13: 978-1-958498-13-2

ALEXANDRIAN SAGA

Fires of Alexandria
Heirs of Alexandria
Legacy of Alexandria
Warmachines of Alexandria
Empire of Alexandria
Voyage of Alexandria
Goddess of Alexandria

Other Books by Thomas K. Carpenter

The Dashkova Memoirs
Revolutionary Magic
A Cauldron of Secrets
Birds of Prophecy
The Franklin Deception
Nightfell Games
The Queen of Dreams
Dragons of Siberia
Shadows of an Empire

The Kingmaker Saga
The Stone Tree
The Crystal Bard
The Ghost Tower
The Champion's Prophecy
The Shadow Labyrinth
The Autumn Empire

The Hundred Halls Universe
SEASON ONE

THE HUNDRED HALLS
Trials of Magic
Web of Lies
Alchemy of Souls
Gathering of Shadows
City of Sorcery

THE RELUCTANT ASSASSIN
The Reluctant Assassin
The Sorcerous Spy
The Veiled Diplomat
Agent Unraveled
The Webs That Bind

GAMEMAKERS ONLINE
The Warped Forest
Gladiators of Warsong
Citadel of Broken Dreams
Enter the Daemonpits
Plane of Twilight

ANIMALIANS HALL
Wild Magic
Bane of the Hunter
Mark of the Phoenix
Arcane Mutations
Untamed Destiny

STONE SINGERS HALL
Song of Siren and Blood
House of Snake and Tome
Storm of Dragon and Stone
Sonata of Shadow and Thorn
Well of Demon and Bone

THE ORDER OF MERLIN
The Order of Merlin
Infernal Alliances
Tower of Horn and Blood

LEGACY
OF
ALEXANDRIA

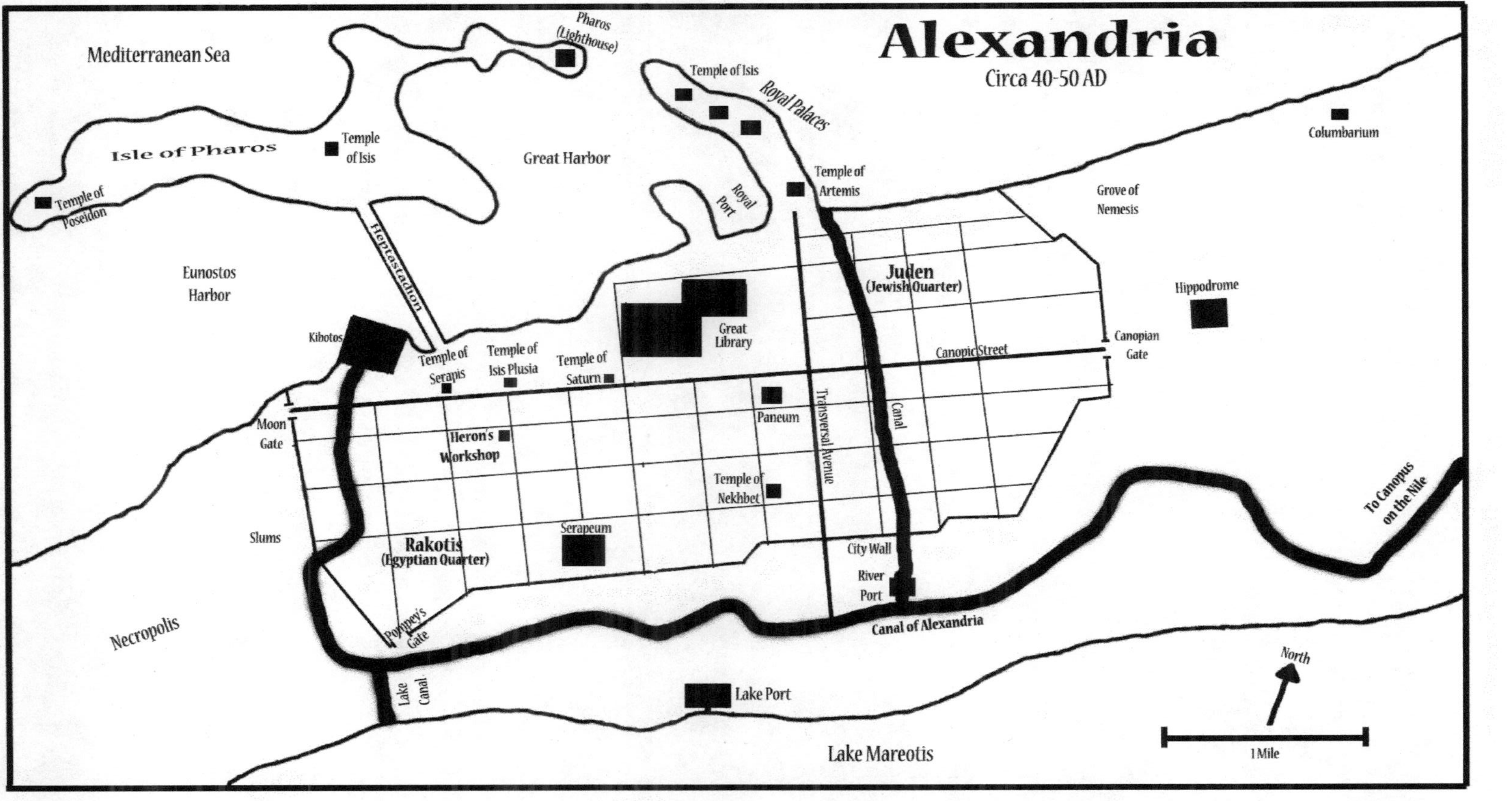

Alexandria
Circa 40-50 AD
Mediterranean Sea
Pharos (Lighthouse)
Temple of Isis
Royal Palaces
Columbarium
Isle of Pharos
Temple of Isis
Great Harbor
Temple of Artemis
Grove of Nemesis
Temple of Poseidon
Royal Port
Juden (Jewish Quarter)
Hippodrome
Eunostos Harbor
Great Library
Canopic Street
Canopian Gate
Kibotos
Temple of Serapis
Temple of Isis Plusia
Temple of Saturn
Paneum
Transversal Avenue
Canal
Moon Gate
Heron's Workshop
Temple of Nekhbet
To Canopus on the Nile
Slums
Rakotis (Egyptian Quarter)
Serapeum
City Wall
River Port
Necropolis
Pompey's Gate
Canal of Alexandria
North
Lake Canal
Lake Port
1 Mile
Lake Mareotis

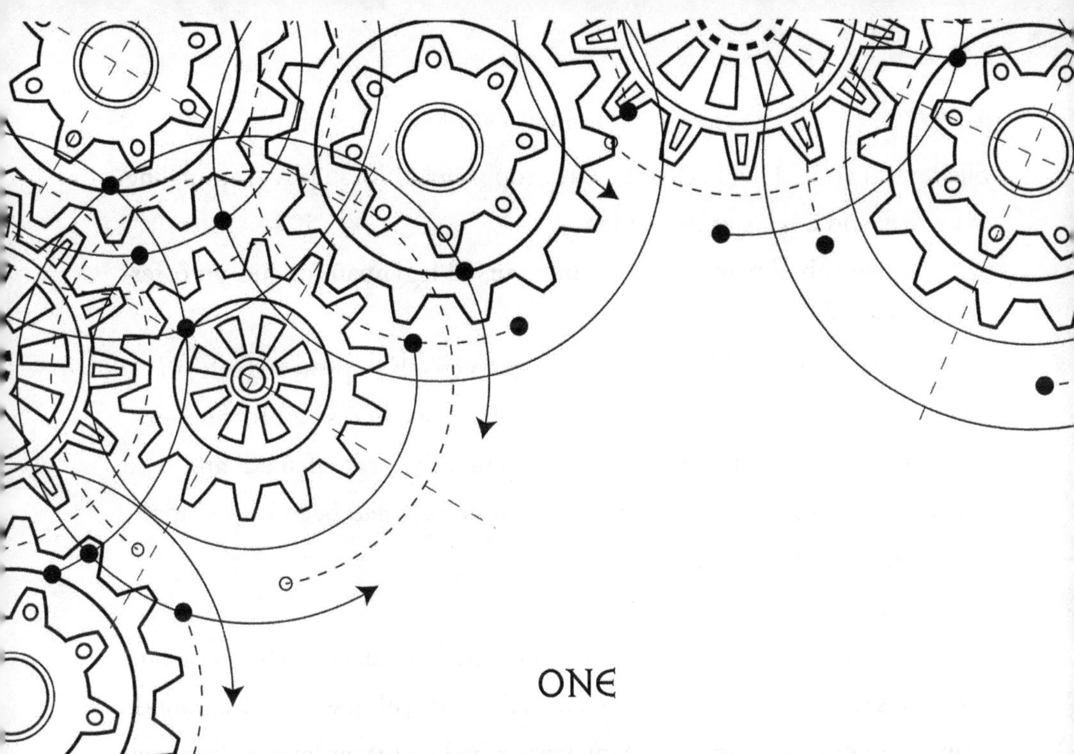

ONE

In the temple of reeds, the bound man waited for the tortured cries of the fallen antelope to grow silent, signaling his turn to die. Plants snapped like thin bones while the restless beasts splashed amid the brackish waters, reflecting the uncaring sky.

The thrashing stilled and a chorus of insects resumed their dirge. Biting flies feasted on his flesh, already knotted with scars and pinkish wounds. The walls of the temple refused to hide him from the glaring sun, so he squinted away the light in hopes of witnessing his fate.

The priest and priestess of Sobek had left him on the stone slab.

Slick moss cooled his backside. Bark ropes held him in place, strangling his wrists and ankles as they dried.

Bait, they had named him in their cursed Egyptian tongue, an offering to their vicious god.

The stone was wide and tall enough to give him protection from all but the most determined crocodiles. They seemed sated from their energetic feasting. The bound man imagined the orgy of teeth and hard, green, lumpy flesh tearing apart the antelope that had been loosed in the walled garden of the temple.

Bait.

Bait for a living god. The one they called Petsuchos, who lived on the cool sands of the island. A terror adorned with jewels. The bound man could not imagine how many priests had lost their lives to fix those valuable baubles on the great Nile crocodile.

A dragonfly landed on his nose. Shimmering wings dried themselves in the morning sun. The bound man held still, for the appearance of the dragonfly had banished the biting insects from his face.

Beyond the walls of the temple garden, the bound man heard children playing. Singing even. Playing games in the white chalky streets outside.

The words of the song crawled in through his mutilated ears like a snake and curled around his thoughts, squeezing them until there was nothing left but remembrances of pain. Pain in the dark. In the deep of the temple where only the priest and priestess entertain.

Sobk. Sobki.

The names they bade him to use. Not the others, not the one from before when he was...

No. He wasn't supposed to think of that. Not their names, not their lives, not his, either.

Sobk. Sobki.

They were his gods, now. He whispered their priestly names and the dragonfly took flight.

Bait.

Low and go, the crocodiles lurk. Chomp!

He cursed that he ever knew even a word of Egyptian. He imagined their slight, brown arms snapping together in homage to the crocodile god Sobek as they danced outside the walls.

Tooth and jaw, the crocodiles snap. Chomp!

The priest and priestess had left him on the slab before. Many times. Too many. They whispered to him that one day he would give himself willingly to Petsuchos, the avatar of Sobek.

Spin and turn, the crocodiles roll. Chomp!

The bound man tried to flex his hand, a ghost memory. There was no hand. Only a raw stump when he'd reached out to Petsuchos and the green monster had taken it clean off.

Bait. He would give himself to the crocodile god, one piece at a time. They told him that on the first day when he'd come to the temple of reeds. He didn't believe them. He thought he was stronger than them. His hands had tormented hundreds before them. The price of pain was well known.

Snap and rip, the crocodiles feast. Chomp!

The day he lost his hand he knew the limits of his will. Though he had not reached it yet, he could see the day clearly in his mind. They would let him into the garden, unbound. He would wade through the insect-ridden waters, a feverish glory reflecting on his face, the smaller beasts waiting like deadly, submerged logs.

The sands of the island would squish between his toes. The beast Petsuchos would lumber from his sandy throne and he would kneel before it, knowing the brief terror would be worth the release.

Toes. The bound man giggled, a kept madness bubbling up through his lips. He'd forgotten about his toes. Only six of them now. Memory of the day he'd offered his foot to one of the smaller beasts came back to him. Only a gristly end toe remained.

How long had he been in the temple that he could not remember when he lost part of his foot? Would he even be able to wade through the water to the sandy island by then? Or would the great beast meet him in the water?

The bound man shuddered. Not in the water. He didn't want to meet his end there. His body would spin and spin and spin. A drowning death, full of terror.

Bait. Sobk. Sobki.

Bound together. Bound like the bark ropes on his arms and legs. Just enough slack that he could stick his head over the edge and offer it to one of the beasts. Not enough slack that he could even scratch his nose.

Chomp!

The children wandered away from the temple walls. The song lingered in his flayed ears.

Bait.

The waters at the edge of the island splashed as a massive body pushed into it. A thick, earthy smell of rich mud filled the air. The bound man imagined powerful clawed feet pushing through the water, spinning eddies of blackish water behind.

Petsuchos. The avatar of Sobek was coming.

His heart laboring in his chest felt like a beacon for the watery monster. Sending out pulses, drawing him in. The thudding in his ears reminded him of a different time. A forbidden thought, one he tried to shake free.

In the deeps of the temple, the priest and priestess always knew when he was thinking of *before*. They smelled it on him. Maybe Petsuchos smelled it now and was coming to punish him.

He remembered the thud of feet on the wooden box. The sightless terror of grasping for a lever that was not there. The *woman* who had bested him. Taken everything from him, including his name, and given him to the priest and the priestess. Sobk and Sobki.

The other crocodiles fled from Petsuchos. Watery noises fleeing to other parts of the temple. Reeds bent and crackled away from the beast.

A low grunt thrummed, part breath, part growl. He caught sight of a ridge of jewels, sparkling in the sunlight, tramping towards him. The splashes turned to sucking mud sounds. The fetid breath of a meat eater washed over him.

The bound man lay still. A rumble echoed in his breast like a drum answering the call.

Insects fled the approach of the monster; the once buzzing reed temple now a mausoleum. Even the city outside grew quiet as if it waited for the consent of the crocodile god to resume its clatter.

The bound man knew he was in the Egyptian city Shedyet. South of Memphis along the Nile and often called Crocodopolis by the locals and far, far from the white walls of Alexandria. He'd been an important—

Thump.

The monstrous tail of the beast slammed into the stone slab. Rattling his teeth in his jaw. The cold eyes of the creature were upon him.

The bound man took a breath and tried to remember his place.

Bait.

I am an offering to the god of the Nile. The silent death in the reeds. I keep the people safe.

He remembered the whispers of the priest and priestess. Teaching him with their knives and cruel implements with even crueler names. The Death Spin. Snapping Jaws. Thousand Biting Flies. Iron and flesh and darkness and a fear that went on forever.

Breath heaved like a great growling bellows blowing his unkempt hair into his eyes. He would only have to push his head over the edge for his pain to be over.

Sensing his fear, Petsuchos pushed its snout onto the edge of the slab. The head was turned so he could see the dead eye of the beast. The stink of rotted meat was overwhelming

Bait.

The bound man reached. His fingers caressed the leathery snout, right above the white angled teeth. The mouth waited like a trap.

The creature only had to lunge with its back legs and it could crush his head. Yet, it hadn't. The bound man found his fear drained. He was mesmerized by the beast, much like the day he'd offered his hand as sacrifice.

He placed his good hand inside the beast's mouth. The air was warm, pleasant. He took a breath and slipped the bark rope around his wrist over the tooth. As the rough rope touched the yellowish flesh at the base of the hard, white incisor, the beast jerked off the slab, nearly taking his arm with it.

Petsuchos angrily slapped its tail against the stone and lunged over with its mouth, barely missing his head. With a free hand, the bound man tugged at the remaining rope. He was able to slip the other side from his other arm, because the hand was missing. Sitting up, while the beast scrambled at the edge of the slab, he yanked on the loose ropes on his ankles and around his middle until they came undone.

The bound man stumbled off and into the mud, hitting face first, as the Nile crocodile climbed over the stone. He crawled forward, trying to push himself up, but the missing hand and partial foot kept him off balance.

Mud splattered his backside as the bulk of the crocodile hit the spongy ground. He limped as fast as he could, trying to circle away from the water. The beast thundered behind, roaring and corralling the bound man back to where he didn't want to go. The small crocodiles swam away, splashing him with their tails. Reeds smacked him in the face as he sunk into the mud.

He threw himself forward, swimming rather than fighting the muck that threatened to trap him. He'd never been a great swimmer, only daring Lake Mareotis when he was a youth.

Slapping at the surface, unbalanced, he propelled himself in fits and starts. He kept waiting to hear the heavy splash of Petsuchos entering the water, but his ungainly thrashing probably covered up the great, silent beast.

Before he knew it, he found himself crawling onto the wet sands. He barely climbed to his feet, feeling the wet sand squish between his toes, just as he'd dreamed about on the stone slab, before the giant crocodile came lunging out of the water after him.

He stumbled and half ran, keeping steps ahead. On the back side of the island, there was a tree. Using his remaining hand, he scrambled into the lower branches, expecting the sharp pull of teeth on his leg the whole time.

Petsuchos ran right into the trunk, shaking the drooping limbs and nearly knocking him from his perch. The tree listed backwards, as the sandy soil was a poor base. The beast pushed again and the tree tipped backwards, throwing him into the water.

Branches clawed and slapped at him. The tree was drowning him as Petsuchos gnashed at the tree. He pushed at the branches and held his mouth above the water. The trunk snapped as the great crocodile climbed over.

White teeth snapped at his legs. He scrambled through, expecting jaws to yank him back at any moment. In the water again with the beast, he paddled hard with his feet. There could be other crocodiles ahead but he couldn't tell. There was mud in his eyes.

He reached the other side near the wall. A stubby tree without low branches was his only chance. Petsuchos was swimming toward him, its powerful tail propelling it away from the submerged tree.

On the third try, his fingers grasped the lowest branch. He wedged his feet against the wet bark and pulled, willing himself upward. His muscles felt ready to explode from effort. Toes caught enough purchase to help him climb. He hooked his arm around the branch and lifted his feet up as teeth snapped like a great trap.

Petsuchos muscled into the tree, but this one was on solid ground. Still, it shook as he climbed. The bound man found a branch that leaned out toward the wall. He edged onto it, praying to his Sobek that it would not break.

The wood creaked and bent. Petsuchos stopped bumping the tree and moved beneath him, mouth open. The jewels on the back of the beast still shimmered in the sun.

Feeling like he couldn't go any further out on the limb without it breaking, he half-stood and leapt toward the wall. He hit the top halfway, knocking the air from his lungs and scrambled up before Petsuchos could take his feet.

He looked around to make sure no one had seen him. The priests and priestesses of Sobek were the highest members of Shedyet society. If he was seen escaping, they would hunt him down and give him back to the temple.

With no one watching, he dropped into the dirt outside the temple. The street was empty enough he could hear the rattling of a wagon wheel and the clop of horse hooves around the corner.

Free. He had escaped. Bait no longer. His limbs trembled with effort. It took many long breaths before he could calm himself enough to think.

He would need to find food and clothing. In a city of Egyptians, he would stick out. But he'd learned much in the temple of reeds. The crocodile waited, submerged like logs, until prey came along. He could be like one, gathering strength. He needed to be ready for the priest and priestess. And then, Alexandria.

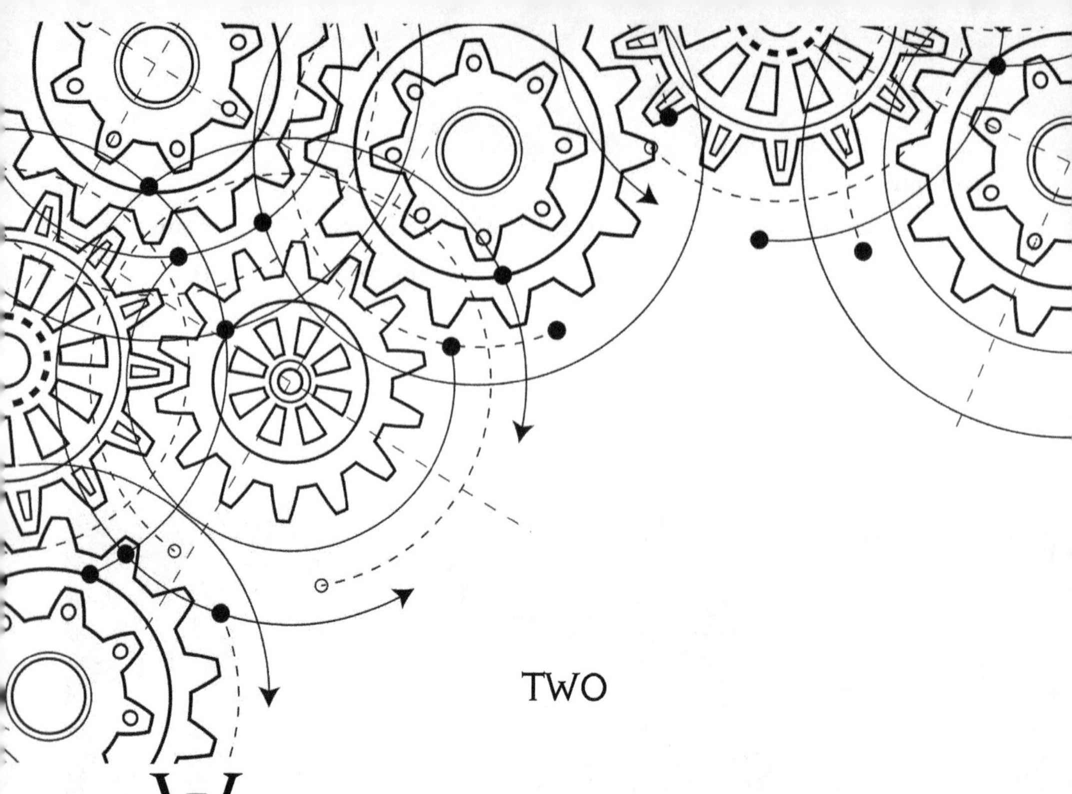

TWO

Wind whistled across the beacon level of the Lighthouse of Pharos. The structure rose high above the city, higher than any other building in the known world. Even the famed Colossus of Rhodes would barely reach the lower level, if it were still standing.

Heron, the Chief Engineer of Alexandria, squinted into the distance beyond the city walls. Plutarch had placed a bucket of pitch in the sands to the east of Lake Mareotis, the most likely approach of the Roman army.

The keepers of the beacon flame watched her from the safety of the inner ring. Even at the outer edge, Heron could feel the heat. Pullies squeaked with effort, bringing wood to keep the fire burning. The lifts were in constant motion, straining the arms of the beacon keepers. She made a mental note to donate a steam mechanical to the Lighthouse for the pulley system.

Her invention had been disassembled and hauled to the top. She'd reassembled it herself. A tripod frame held a curved piece of glass, bound by copper. The angle and direction of the glass could be adjusted using her tools.

The strange glass was one of many objects she'd pulled from the Curiosity Rooms in the Great Library. After the naval battle with the Romans using the magnetite stones to coordinate their attacks, Heron wondered if there were other items in the Great Library that could be put to use.

None of the scholars knew what to make of the head sized piece of glass. Nor did they know where it came from. The glass was curved on both sides and distant objects seemed larger when viewed through it.

Heron had written extensively about optics in her book *Catoptrica,* advancing the theories of Euclid and Lucretius. Once she saw the glass object, she thought about Archimedes' heat ray.

"Heron of Alexandria?" The heavily accented voice startled her.

A beautiful Kushite woman in colorful robes stood at the top of the stairs. Her hair was bound by golden threads. Tiny jewels around the woman's eyes sparkled in the sunlight.

Heron nodded. "You are Bani, daughter of King Natakamani and Queen Amanitore. Apologies that I have not properly thanked you for your assistance with my daughter. You risked much when you helped Sepharia."

The woman took measured steps toward Heron. Her pleasant smile hinted at mischievous thoughts. "It is I that should apologize. The *Michanikos* is more handsome than the descriptions. I should have introduced myself much sooner."

"You flatter me," said Heron, bowing. That the disguise fooled the Kushite princess pleased Heron.

Bani slipped her hand around Heron's arm. Musty perfume reminded her of Hoth the Black. She quickly glanced at the harbor to see if the *Mars Valiant* had returned, knowing well that he wasn't due for weeks. As infuriating as he was, she missed his company.

"What strange device is this? It looks like an eye," asked Bani.

"An astute observation," said Heron. "Maybe we should be inviting you into the Library for consultation."

Bani leaned in close. "Your rules forbid me. As the weaker sex, I would only taint your writings."

Heron withheld her comment. An ache formed in her chest.

A soft hand touched her face. Bani demanded her attention. "You haven't told me about your invention."

The pull of the woman's beauty affected even Heron. Bani's ebony skin glowed with an inner light.

"A weapon, maybe." Heron pointed to curling black smoke rising from numerous buildings. "The city's workshops are busy making weapons of war to fight the Romans. I seek other ways to gain advantage."

"You scholars never speak directly. Always round and round the target," prodded Bani.

"Truth in every word," said Heron. "I desire to focus the power of the sun through this optic. Using its energy we might be able to destroy siege weapons from a distance."

"Does it work?"

"Let us find out," said Heron.

Bani released her arm and Heron finished adjusting the lens, pointing it towards the bucket in the distance. Plutarch waved flags to signal her adjustments. When the white flag appeared, she set the screws.

"And now we wait," said Heron.

"For what?" Bani asked.

"If Plutarch shows us a red flag, then the pitch caught fire. A blue flag means the test has failed. If we cannot burn even that which lights easily, then wood is out of the question," said Heron.

A gust of wind slammed into them. Bani stepped close again and captured Heron's arm.

"Is war the only thing you men think about?" asked Bani.

Heron sighed, the Kushite woman's words cutting her keenly.

"I would think of other things if the Romans would give consent to peace," said Heron. "But we must be ready to defend ourselves."

"And when you have won, won't you need to maintain your superiority?" asked Bani.

"You will make a great Queen," said Heron. "Your wit slays my feeble arguments."

The Kushite woman squinted. "Not many men would admit such a thing."

"I am not like other men," said Heron. "Thoughts are the gears of my success. If I cannot admit plain truth then I will never see beyond my own faults."

"So your optic has other uses?" Bani stroked the copper bindings around the glass.

"Perhaps. It can be used for seeing distant objects and maybe as a communication device. If only there were more hours in the day," said Heron.

"My mother Queen Amanitore believes that power derives from the perceived value of an empire," said Bani. "For that reason, we cloak ourselves in gold and jewels to remind others the value of our friendship."

"A wise course." On the sand east of the city, Plutarch still waved the white flag. If the bucket of pitch did not burn soon, the experiment would be a failure. "Freed from the trappings of war, I would do the same to this city. This City of Wonders is nothing compared to the vision in my mind."

Bani took delight in her words. "Then make it so. As you said, the workshops are busy with the chariots of war. There is never time, except for what we take."

The loadstone of responsibility weighed on Heron's shoulders. "I have neither the gold nor the men to spare and the Satrap would not support it."

Bani's smiling eyes hinted at secrets. "I came to see you for two purposes. The first, a message from my mother Queen Amanitore. To subdue the savage lands around our kingdom, she wishes to build an automata that rivals the fabled Colossus of Rhodes, gilded in gold from head to toe."

A short laugh slipped Heron's lips. "An automata that large? Even if I could make one, the gilding would take a decade to plate. The process of hammering it on is laborious to the point of madness."

Bani massaged Heron's arm lightly. "If you can make this, my mother promises her support of Alexandria *and* whatever the *Michanikos* desires. The resources of our country could free up one as skilled as you."

Heron shook her head. "I cannot. I know the mind of the Satrap on this matter and the automata would take too long to build. The fate of our burgeoning empire might already be sealed before the ink on the plans was dry. What is the second request? Maybe I can be of service."

Without warning, Bani leaned against Heron and pressed her lips against Heron's surprised mouth. Heron let her lips respond, tasting sweetness on her tongue. Warmth sprung up in her chest. *Would this be what kissing Hoth or Jarngard would be like?*

A hand snaked down her backside. Heron pulled away, untangling herself from the Kushite princess. "I cannot."

Bani's eyes flickered with annoyance. "This I offer freely. I would warm your bed tonight and ease your troubles."

The shock and anger Heron imagined when Bani undressed her brought a twitch of humor to her lips.

"Apologies," said Heron, "work is my mistress."

With her feathers ruffled, Bani lightly stomped her foot. "Real men do not turn me down. It must be as they say, that you are truly a machine and not a man. The offers remain though I cannot say for how long. Who can say how long the flame of passions stay lit."

The Kushite princess left the beacon level, as proud as a gilded peacock. Despite the heat of the fire, the air became surprisingly chill. Heron crossed her arms.

"Her bed will soon be warmed while mine remains empty," said Heron, leaning on the rail.

She could have her workshop or indulge the passions of her body, but not both. Was she truly a machine man destined for a life of erudite celibacy?

The white flag was replaced by the blue and Heron felt a moment of relief that her experiment had not worked.

"If there was a god of irony I would believe in you," said Heron to the pale sky. "My inventions can light neither my passions nor a bucket of pitch."

Was it as the Kushite princess said? Her inventions would be a never ending succession of war machines to keep Alexandria in power? How droll and tasteless a life that would become. She would deserve the moniker of *Michanikos* then.

Heron gazed at her city. Alexandria. The City of Wonders. The City of Miracles. This place was her passion.

The grand steepled buildings of the Great Library made her heart thrum with pride. Though the city was contained within walls, Canopian Gate on one side, Moon Gate on the other, Heron imagined the trails of thought and word streaming out to cities across the known world. To Heron, Alexandria sat within a great web of human invention.

A black haze drifted from the Rhakotis District. Workshops filled with hammering and the belching sparks of foundry fires. High upon the Lighthouse, she could smell the pungent iron ore mixed with the clean salt air.

The harbor was filled with white sails and black hulls. Trade flourished after the defeat of the Roman navy. Ships brought more books to the Library, a well of knowledge so great she would never read even a thousandth of the books.

To the east of the harbor, jutting out toward Pharos Isle, the royal pier glittered in the sunlight. Even from this distance, she could see white togas passing the golden mechanical lions of her creation. Their throaty roars were lost amid the noises of the industrious city, but Heron heard them in her mind.

Ambassadors from every nation flooded into the city. A new empire had risen to oppose Rome. Kingdoms came to measure the might of the Satrap. The Kushites, though a power in the south, were not the largest suitors. The Parthians had sent their favored son Vima with a large contingent of elephants and soldiers. Heron heard they wished to trade war elephants for steam mechanicals, a deal Agog would have to carefully decline.

Lastly, her gaze fell upon the Soma of Alexander. The mausoleum of her ancestor set a heavy stone in her chest. To the ends of the earth, Alexander wished to define his empire. Heron felt that feverish desire, as well.

Heron glanced shamefully at the glass optic. What a small and pitiful invention. Alexander would laugh if he stood with her on the Lighthouse. He was a man who founded cities and conquered nations.

She lost all taste for her work and resisted the urge to throw the tripod from the Lighthouse. Only her scholarly habits stayed her hand as she would be remiss to damage such an artifact from the Library.

How could she return to her workshop? Her greatest inventions paled against Alexander's accomplishments. Her work was like the shadow of a simple man beneath the Lighthouse of Pharos.

Alexander's words from the lost temple cave came back to her like a conflagration of the northern forests. Seized by an ache she had no name for, she repeated the words written on the stone. The words left her lips like an offering, spoken to the muse of her city.

"I, Alexander the Macedonian, son of Zeus-Ammon, and the one named in the greater destinies, do hold myself, or whoever comes after me, to change this world, from the farthest sea to the farthest sea. For flesh is weak and men need a shining light like a beacon in the fog."

The infinite sky caressed her with a breeze. The Mediterranean suddenly felt as small as Lake Mareotis. Heron gripped the rail. She could see as far east as the Indus River, as far north as the lands of the eternal night, as far south as the deepest jungles.

"Like a beacon in the fog..." the words trailed from her lips.

A vision consumed her, great stones as large as her workshop, climbing an impossible stair. The world needed a beacon. This discovered truth made her chest want to burst with exhilaration. In that moment, she felt a true kinship with Alexander. His were eyes that saw the whole world. She, too, must learn.

Heron took to the stairs, images whirling in her mind. She must get to the Palace. Speak with Agog and enlighten him with her vision. There would be no denying her now. No matter what he said, no matter how he argued. Even if it meant she tore her garments in protest and took her promises to greater powers, whoever they might be.

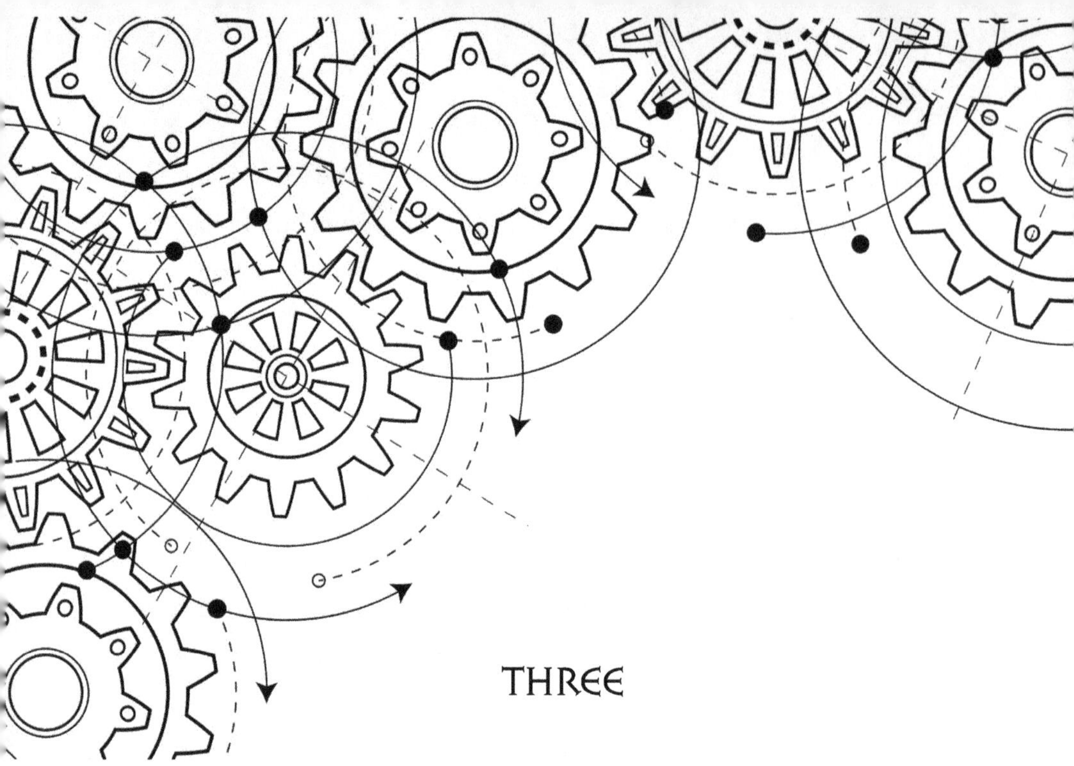

THREE

In her haste, Heron marched across the city, discontent to wait for her horse to be saddled. The road across the Heptastadion hunched in the water like a bouldery serpent scaled with cobblestones, splitting the harbor between the Eunostos and the Great Harbor.

Alexander had once marched across a similar road during the siege of Tyre. For a year, his engineers built the mole, throwing rock and timber and earth into the water. Alexander himself spent months with his men, laboring along side of them.

For him, the construction wasn't a theoretical exercise as so often seen in the Great Library. His efforts conjured reality from his visions.

The marble halls of the Great Library overlooked the harbor like a scholar speaking to the assembled. Heron was surprised at the distaste that filled her when she glanced at the hallowed buildings. Never before had she seen them in that light. What was knowledge without action? What was thought without sweat?

The runners along the docks called her name. Her thoughts were so tightly wound, she feared to even gesture or the rehearsed speech in her head would come tumbling out without an audience.

The city shrunk and her steps grew, bringing her to the Palace before she even realized it. Footsore and coated in a light sweat, Heron practically knocked Agnar from his feet when he moved to stop her.

"Machine man! Your timing is like a victorious battle to a flowered maid," said Agnar anxiously.

"Speak quickly, I must see the Satrap," she said.

"It's Jarngard. He needs your help," said Agnar.

Heron searched for someone else to take his complaint. "Must I be of service every time one of you Northmen can't wipe your ass? It's no wonder that Rome thrashed you at every battle in the north. What now?"

The words flew from her lips faster than she could reign them in. Agnar took no insult, in fact, he seemed to relish in her verbal flaying.

"That's why we came to you, Machine Man," laughed Agnar, "cause we spent too much time in the mead hall to fend off the Romans."

"I need less talking and more explaining," she said. "What is wrong with Jarngard?"

Agnar towered over her like a mountain. Not quite Agog's girth, but near his height. But the barbarian suddenly seemed like a child asking for an extra piece of bread, shifting on his heels. "Agog wants to kill Jarngard and he might when he finds him."

"Why? Quickly, quickly." Heron snapped her fingers.

"Jarngard insulted the Parthian Prince, Vima. The Prince was showing off his favorite war elephant and Jarngard called it an overgrown dog with a penis for a nose." Agnar chuckled.

"Has Athena cursed him? What set him on this path of insanity?" she asked.

"He's drunker than a jarl before he has to sleep with his ice wife," said Agnar.

"What did the Satrap do?"

Agnar held his hands out and made fists. "Threatened to rip him apart with his hands if he didn't get out of the city. Told him to set sail for the North."

Heron sighed, feeling the burden of Agnar's problem suddenly shifting to her. She wondered if Alexander had ever had to deal with drunken Northmen with a sailors' mouths. Heron was about to ask where he was when she heard singing. The guttural language of the Northmen had a certain warlike poetry and it carried for a long way in the marble halls.

"Why didn't you just drag him out by his tunic?" she said, marching toward the singing.

"Not as easy as it sounds, Machine Man," said Agnar. "The man wrestles like the kraken after a ship full of fat sailors. That, and well, you'll see."

She didn't walk much further before she did. It was Jarngard. His fists were clenched into balls. He stumbled past the palm fronds as he sung. Heron didn't understand the song, nor did she care. He was also naked.

It was not uncommon to see a man naked in Alexandria. Sporting events were sometimes performed in the nude. On the rare occasions she attended these events, the combatants were too far away to really see.

Beneath the taut bindings, her nipples strained. So soon after she'd been kissed by the Kushite princess Bani, she imagined herself pressed against the naked Northman.

Desire was as unfamiliar as falling and just as exhilarating. In spite of the faint scars kissing his back and the matted hair across his chest, she wanted him.

"Magic me a great whale made of steam, *Michanikos*," said Jarngard, "his royalness bids me to haunt his Palace no longer."

"I might make you a donkey cart instead and haul you off to the dung fires." Speaking slowed the thumping in her chest.

Jarngard grabbed his cock and wagged it at her. "Or maybe I'm an elephant and that prissy Prince will ask me to spray him with water."

Heron kept her gaze level. Jarngard stumbled against the wall. His eyes were unfocused, his tone a maudlin slur.

"Men in useless silks come this way," said Agnar, glancing down the columned hall. A distant doorway blurred with movement.

Jarngard wavered before Heron. He pushed his finger against her chest, right on an aching nipple. "At least you have purpose, *Michanikos*. You are the Satrap's conjurer of magics. His master of tricks."

Footsteps and chattering approaching. The guards at the end of the hall slapped their gladius against shield in salute.

"Yes, just a conjurer of tricks." The words lay ashy in her mouth. She gave him her best master's stare, but she felt defanged by his words. "Best get you out of this hall before the Satrap has me conjure you a rope to hang by."

Jarngard put his hands on her shoulders. The heat of his body warmed her. She could tell he'd been drinking honeyed mead.

"Give me purpose like you did Hoth," he said.

"Whatever you want, just get out of this cursed hallway." She was torn between wanting to push him away and leaning into him.

Agnar spoke roughly through gritted teeth. "By a jarl's boots, *move*."

Heron hooked her arm around his and dragged him from the hallway as the procession burst through the opposite door. Jarngard did not resist her direction. They were near the Green Room so she took him outside to Sepharia's apartment. The girl was with Polyxena's guests, so she knew it would be empty.

A quick shove sent him stumbling into the couch. Heron pulled fabric rolls from the closet and motioned for Agnar's weapon. Using the blade she cut a sheet for Jarngard.

"Wrap yourself Roman style before you visit the dream gods," she said sternly.

Jarngard pulled the sheet over him like a blanket. When it was clear he had no intention of following directions, she took Agnar's sword and slapped him on the top of the head with the flat of the blade.

"By the gods of the underworld, what was that for?" He held his head.

"I'm not your..." She had to catch herself from saying 'mother'. "—father."

"And I'm not your wife," he said rubbing what would probably become a knot. Agnar laughed heartily, standing guard in the doorway.

When Jarngard looked up to her, she was run through with pity. His bloodshot eyes seemed to peer into some stygian darkness.

"What ails you, Northman?" she quietly asked.

"Aye, *Northman*," he repeated. "That's what ails me. I rot in this city without purpose. Playing messenger for Hoth or nursemaid to your daughter is the only thing the Satrap sees fit for me. Better to put my traveling boots on and head east, see this Old Babylon I have heard so much about with its great walls and Hanging Gardens. From there I could strike out to places unknown. I'm sure I could bring back a thing or two for your Curiosity Rooms."

"Come to the workshop tomorrow," she told him. "I must speak to the Satrap today, but tomorrow I will have work for you."

Jarngard growled. "I don't want work, I want purpose! Even a man like you knows the difference."

"I do," said Heron. "Tomorrow. In my workshop."

She didn't give him a chance to respond. Heron slapped the hilt into Agnar's hand. "Make sure he doesn't leave before he's sober or I'll make surc you carry tomorrow's load of wood up the Lighthouse by hand."

Agnar grinned.

She took a circular route towards the Satrap's private quarters. The words that had formed so easily in her mind earlier were now as faint as morning mist at midday. Coupled with the lack of momentum was the ache of her womanhood. Seeing Jarngard naked had stirred something in her. A passion that would have to be quenched by her work. Her vision from the Lighthouse required absolute servitude to purpose. She hoped Jarngard wouldn't complicate that.

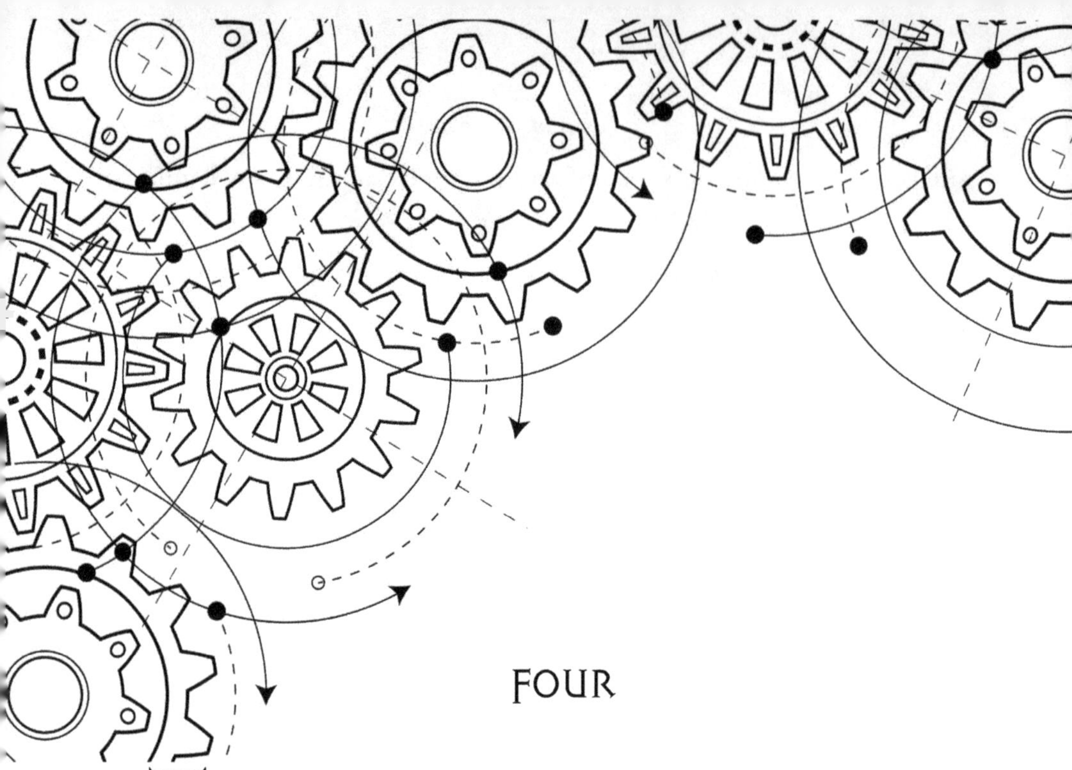

FOUR

The Royal Port was an inlet nestled up to the Royal Pier. A great chain, raised and lowered, kept unwanted boats from the docks that led to the Palace. A servant directed Heron down to them. Agog was reviewing a new type of boat made by one of the city's workshops.

Climbing down the steep stairs that ran jaggedly across the stunted cliff, Heron could see the broad shoulders of the Egyptian Nektam standing with the Satrap. The former blacksmith, her peer in the workshops, was a towering behemoth of muscle, but stood no taller than Agog.

Heron shivered, thinking about meeting Agog in the North, dressed in black furs and surrounded by screaming Northmen, wielding blades glinting brightly against the snow. He was a great black bear dressed in the guise of a man.

Both men stared at something dark and low in the water. There was no sign of this new kind of boat the servant warned her about.

"Greetings, Satrap and friend Nektam," she called.

Nektam was first to turn. He seemed less than pleased, the edges of his mouth tugging downward. Agog did not bother with subtle gestures with arms crossed and brow hunched.

"Why are you here?" asked Agog.

"I—" The words in her mouth lost their luster. "...need to speak with you about a project."

"I hope it is as wondrous as this iron boat of Nektam's." Agog gestured to the water.

Standing away from the dock, Heron could not see the boat, except for the gray edges poking above the wood. She'd thought it a simple oared fishing boat, slathered in a dull pitch, but as she moved closer, she realized it was nothing of the sort.

Nektam's rich voice sang out his words, "Not iron but steel."

Crouched on her heels, Heron ran her fingertips along the top. The craft was the size of a simple boat, but made of steel. Cross beams kept the hull rigid.

"By Archimedes, what a wonder," she exclaimed.

"Aye, by Archimedes is right," said Nektam. "His theories of displacement proved my design before it first touched water."

The calculations ran like a river through her head. "The weight. This steel must be so thin."

"His workshop is making the best steel in the city now," said Agog, his gaze flashed in her direction. "I think you have competition for Chief Engineer."

She snapped up like a rod. Nektam's bronze skin glowed with pride. She nearly reminded Agog that Nektam's foundry had been rebuilt under her direction after the explosion and supplied with the newest and best steam mechanicals. Nektam could make the best steel only through her inventions.

She held her tongue. Pointing out the obvious seemed petty. Nektam had turned that steel into a new invention, one they would need in the coming war with Rome.

"He can have the title if he wants," said Heron. "With it comes endless requests to fix the sewers and roads."

"See," said Agog. "Heron already plies me with excuses in preparation for disappointment."

A pair of fishing boats tacked past the port. Sailors called to each other in Greek as they scrambled amid the sheets and lines. Heron turned her back on Agog.

"How large a vessel can you manufacture?" she asked.

Nektam flexed his arm while absently rubbing a whitish scar that ran the length. "Plans are drawn for a boat three times this size, including powering it with a steam mechanical. Without wood to worry about, I can freely keep the fires glowing hot."

"How will you push the craft through the water?" she asked.

"My thoughts run dry there. I imagine a water piston of some kind, but I fear my designs will be artless," mused Nektam.

"Take inspiration from the water wheel at the head of Lake Mareotis, or maybe the oared vessels of your pharaohs," said Heron.

"There are no pharaohs unless you're speaking of me," said Agog, agitated.

"Have I wronged you in some way with something I have done, Satrap?" Heron held an open hand to her chest.

The big man bristled like an overgrown porcupine. "It's not what you've done, but what you haven't done. Your workshop has been idle, or making farces that even the temples would have rejected. Rome will not wait for us to be good and ready."

"I have not been idle," Heron snapped back. "I search for advantage against the Romans. Was it not those magnetic rocks that helped us thrash their navy? I seek more of the same, so that like Alexander, we may beat them with unconventional tactics as well as our skill."

Agog clucked his tongue. "Are you suddenly a master strategist prepared to lead us in battle? I need more steam mechanicals, not tricks. The Romans have more men than the sky has stars. Yours is one of the biggest workshops in the city and it has made me practically nothing lately."

Nektam stepped to the side and bowed. "I return to my workshop, Satrap. I will send a man to retrieve the boat later."

Neither Heron or the Satrap acknowledged Nektam as he left.

"You do not chastise him—" Heron pointed to the Egyptian, climbing the cliff stairs. "—for creating this boat of steel?"

"That's because his workshop has created more steam chariots than any other in my city," said Agog. "I will win the war on the backs of men like him."

Words choked in her throat. The passion that she'd carried with her from the beacon level of the Lighthouse had been blown clear like morning mist during a summer storm.

"You wound me..." she muttered.

"Stop your bleating like a woman," said Agog. "Now is not the time for hesitation."

Heron felt the sting of his words keenly. How like a woman he would never know. Standing on the Lighthouse, feeling bigger than the pyramids, she'd felt herself, a woman destined for great things. Now, she was an imposter again.

"What is with everyone?" asked Agog to the sea. "First, Jarngard, now Heron."

"We seek purpose," replied Heron.

"I've given you purpose," he said. "You just won't listen."

"Purpose like a master with his slave? Does a bound man ever look truly happy? Look instead to the craftsman laboring in his endeavors.

Though he sweats and aches the same as any slave, he is in glorious ecstasy for his efforts," she said.

"The Romans will care little of your desires if they take the city," said Agog.

"You said it yourself. The Romans have an immense, well-trained army. The greatest military since Alexander the Macedonian." Invoking his name bolstered her will. She took a deep breath and continued into the breach. "You need more than just steam chariots and steel boats. You need a freed people driven with purpose, even if that purpose is the defense of the city."

The Satrap ground his teeth. He held his fists before him and squeezed. "I am the Satrap! May the gods have mercy on you if I hear any more about freeing the slaves or the joys of your craftsman. I need weapons and men. Where are those great metal soldiers you promised me last year? That is what I need more than anything!"

"What about the Parthian prince? You need him," said Heron.

"Because he has war elephants! And many men, more than even we can muster. And because most of all, Rome wants him. If he sides with them, they will have an army the size of the Mediterranean Sea!" said Agog.

"Then give him what he wants and you'll have his army," said Heron.

The great man turned away shaking his head. "I don't know what he wants. He's playing a careful game for his father. For all I know, he's here scouting for the Romans and I have already lost. But I do know he's a proud and vain man, and when Jarngard insulted his war elephant, I wanted to tear my hair out."

"He just wants purpose," said Heron quietly.

Agog put a hand to his head. "What is this project that will bring me my victory? The one you came all this way to tell me about. If it will win me my victories, or assure me the services of this Parthian prince, then I will assent."

"It can," said Heron, realizing that she'd never put form to her ideas. She knew she needed a monument to show the world that Alexandria was different, but she hadn't the foggiest idea of what it was.

"Speak, Machine Man. Amaze me with your miracle. Conjure me a victory," said Agog, dryly.

Heron closed her eyes and took a deep breath. She let the vision from the Lighthouse creep back into her limbs. The Satrap's gaze felt hotter than the sun. Her mind was blank.

"I..." Words trailed from her lips. She knew that her creation needed to be the talk of the world. That it would even give Rome pause in its audacity. Heron thought back to Alexander's words in the cave and let them burn into her flesh.

She said the words even before she considered how impossible her task would be: "I will build the greatest pyramid the world has ever known."

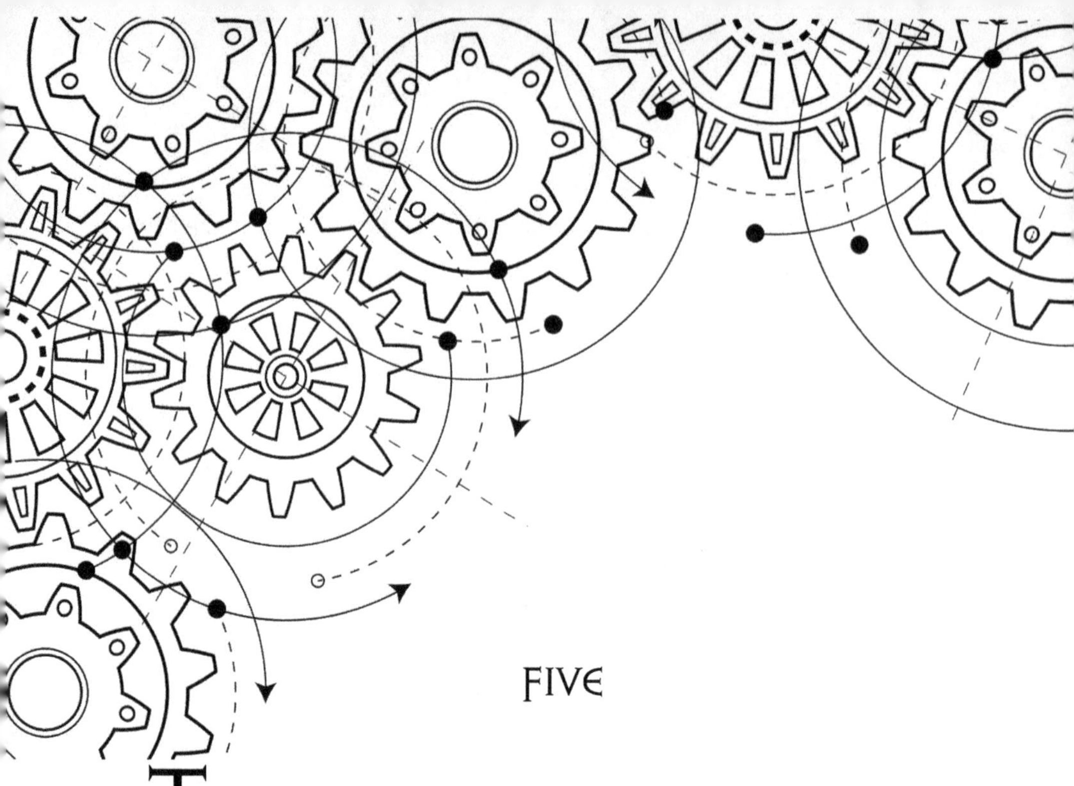

FIVE

The leisurely pace of the pleasure barge slid through the waters of Lake Mareotis past the white walls of Alexandria. Sun shades ruffled in the seaward breeze. Sepharia lounged on a silken pillow, fingers entwined with another. The fingers were delicate like a child's. The hand belonged to the Satrap's wife-to-be, Polyxena.

Sepharia leaned toward Polyxena. The lilac perfume enveloped her, concealing the sea air. "Must men always compete?"

Polyxena smiled. Her sunburst brooch glittered in the sun. "As women do. We just play a different game."

On the mid-deck of the barge, under the watchful gaze of the Satrap, the Parthian prince Vima preened with a javelin in his hand. The Northman Agnar held his own javelin. The two men were laughing.

A slave tossed a painted, wooden disc high into the air over the water. Both men blurred into motion. Javelins speared the disc. When it fell into the water, a slave swam out to retrieve it. Vima's red tasseled javelin was closer to the center mark.

"He moves with supple grace," said Sepharia.

"They call him Vima the Viper for that reason," said Polyxena. "He's quite pleasing to the eye, isn't he?"

Sepharia smiled and glanced away, feeling Polyxena's gaze upon her. "I've heard he is a hero to his people. Their version of Alexander."

"Every land wishes to claim some of Alexander's glory." Polyxena patted her hand.

"And only you have that right," said Sepharia.

When she looked into the older woman's eyes, she found herself imagining what it would have been like to know Alexander. Polyxena shared the same blue and green eyes as he.

"If only you were my daughter," said Polyxena, "then we could match you with this Vima and tie our two empires together against Rome."

"I wish that were true as well. Doesn't he have a wife already?" asked Sepharia.

The Macedonian woman nodded toward the prince's wife. Zenobia was attended by slave women. She sat demurely on a bench near her husband, who was now demonstrating his skills with an axe.

"I invited her to sit with us, but she declined," said Polyxena.

Sepharia leaned into the cushions and sipped cautiously at her wine. The soothing cadence of the oarsmen made her sleepy. The barge circled around the west side of the lake near the Therapeutae village.

Two half-naked men stood waist deep in the lake and beat dirty robes with rocks. Baskets perched on their heads, filled with laundry. With one hand they held the basket while the other thrashed the floating garment.

Women moved between the thatched huts along the water's edge. Children's voices could be heard from further in. Dung fires left black marks against the sky.

"What primitive beasts are these?" asked Polyxena.

"Jewish ascetics," said Sepharia. "They live simple lives without pleasure."

Polyxena wrinkled up her nose. "How terrible."

The barge moved near the men in the water. Vima, whip in hand, directed the oarsman. As the craft drifted past, the Parthian prince shouted something at them in his native tongue. Agnar and the Satrap seemed confused by the sudden change in tone.

When Vima hefted a javelin, Sepharia found herself standing. The Parthian prince threw it towards the men in the water. The Jewish ascetic went under and Sepharia expected to see a wooden rod sticking from the man's chest.

A host of laughter went up in the middle of the boat. Even Agnar and the Satrap joined the prince. Anger rose in her chest. Polyxena gripped her fingers tightly.

Floating in the water, the basket lazily spun away with a javelin sticking through it. The ascetic splashed after it to retrieve his laundry. Sepharia heaved a sigh and sat back down with Polyxena.

"Men play such strange games," she said.

"He's testing us," said Polyxena. "Seeing how much we need him."

The barge turned back towards the city. The men ended their games. Food on platters was brought out. Sepharia picked carefully at the rich foods - the honeyed grasshoppers, salted antelope, spiced palm nuts - her stomach ached from too much wine.

Vima appeared at the edge of the sun shade. His crimson tunic rested comfortably on his lanky frame. The Northmen carried their muscles in the chest and arms. Vima had a sinewy grace.

"The Satrap should not hide such stunning creatures away from my eyes." Vima spoke in a lyrical accented Greek that brought a blush to Sepharia's cheeks.

Polyxena inclined her head slightly, the half-smile on her lips imparting a regal air. "It was our honor and delight to watch you practice your javelin throws. You were the victor by far."

"Like your Alexander, I have not been bested in battle. Either single combat or full scale war," boosted Vima.

"My ancestor is the mark by which all men should be measured," said Polyxena. "Though such a height is a long fall."

Vima took a goblet from a waiting slave. "I heard as much. This news travels quickly. Sure to give Rome pause. Though it's a travesty that you did not reveal yourself to me. I would have made you a Parthian Queen."

"I could still be one yet," said Polyxena.

Vima stiffened almost imperceptibly. Sepharia held her breath at the implied threat. The prince smiled and laughed while his eyes did neither.

Polyxena spoke less harshly. "But Alexandria is the true birthplace of Alexander's greatness. It is fitting that I should be Queen here."

Vima smirked. "So you'll throw off the Satrapy and take the mantle of the pharaohs?"

"If we are to do battle with Rome then we will do it with the full might of the south behind us," said Polyxena. "But not until after the wedding."

Vima's gaze flickered to Sepharia. Standing so close, she could smell his sweat. Her blush deepened.

"I did not know you had such a beautiful daughter," smiled Vima.

"If only it were so," said Polyxena. "This is the Chief Engineer's daughter, Sepharia."

"What a high station you Alexandrians give to the common born," smirked Vima. "Do you bestow titles on your horses?"

Sepharia lifted her chin. "Alexandria is a city of the mind. A city of wonders."

Vima leaned his head back and laughed. "I jest. I came to see the wonders of this Machine Man as much as the Satrap. Is your father really made of these machines? Does he have brass legs as the stories say?"

The splashing of a nearby waterwheel echoed over the smooth oar strokes. The barge neared the city canal. A towering bronze statue of Anubis stood over the spinning device, swinging its staff in halting motions.

"*That* is an automata," said Sepharia, "to help ward off the evil lake spirits. The wheel provides energy for its motion and for the mill inside the walls. My father is nothing like his automatas. He is flesh and blood like you and I."

An air of contemplation settled on the Parthian prince before turning to a secret smile. "I am not simple flesh and blood, girl. I am a scion of the gods. A direct descendant of Ormazd the Good."

"Apologies, Prince Vima. I did not mean to imply otherwise," said Sepharia.

He laughed off her explanation. "Your eyes were not meant to see my greatness and if you could, it would drive you mad. That is why in battle, I am unstoppable."

Polyxena interjected, "Together our two empires could topple Rome and split the world in two."

The prince ignored Polyxena. "Where is this famed workshop? I want to see how these machines are made."

"Of course," said Polyxena. "We shall take you to visit in a few days, maybe a week. First we must discuss the needs of our empires."

Vima became visibly annoyed, glancing sternly into the distance. "These are topics I will discuss with your future husband, not his wife. Tomorrow I wish to see this workshop after I visit the temples. My eyes wish to know the secrets of these wonders. Tell me, Sepharia, can your father make a metal soldier to fight for him? What wonders is he creating in that workshop right now?"

A well-spring of guilt filled her when she realized she had not visited the workshop in months. She spent the bulk of her time with Polyxena.

"I cannot say," said Sepharia. "One never knows."

Vima winked. "Secrets, I understand. Still, I would see them. If the Satrap wants me as his ally, then I must see how wondrous these machines really are. Or are they just tricks to amuse the masses?"

Vima did not wait for an answer. He returned to the center of the barge and clasped Agnar on the shoulder. Polyxena's worried glance filled Sepharia with unease. She'd heard that Agog and her father had an argument the day before. A note to Heron might warn her of the implications of the visit, but she knew her father could be intractable when angry. It did not portend well for the future of the Alexandrian empire.

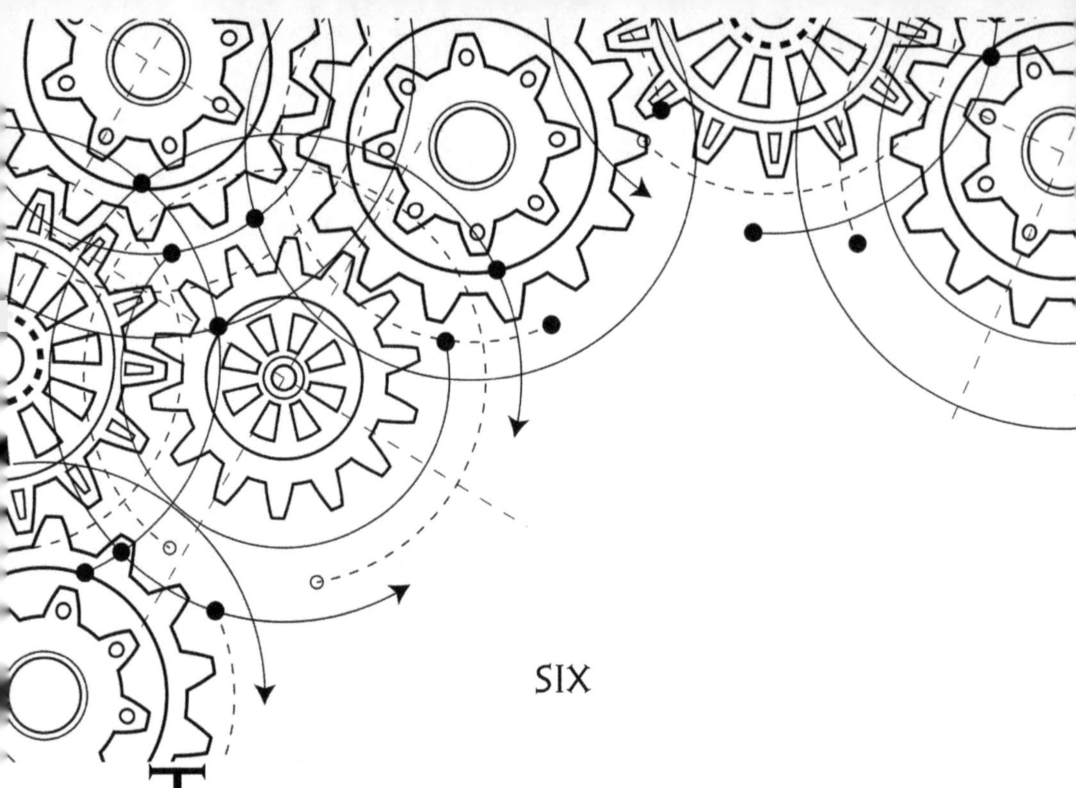

SIX

The laughing of the Satrap lingered in her ears, stinging like a thousand gnats. She had never laughed at his requests. Called him mad or an idiot, yes she'd done those things, but never laughter.

Heron rotated the ink well between her fingertips. She straightened her quills, aligning the shanks to the frayed edge of the papyrus. These acts did nothing for her mood, nor did they dismiss the baritone voice from her mind. In a rush, she knocked open the ornate box and scooped up a spoonful of the violet powder.

The shivers went bone deep. Heron ran a hand through her short black hair. She'd given him the inventions to steal an empire. Found the source of the fires and the pretense to name Polyxena the heir. Now he forbade her from leaving the city or for working on anything but more steam engines.

To make matters worse, the Parthian prince would visit soon and inspect her like a potential buyer might scrutinize a slave.

"I am nothing more than a tool," muttered Heron. "Not even worthy to be an heir of Alexander."

Sparks sputtered from the foundry fires listlessly. Hammers thudded dully against wooden scaffolding. The normal banter had been strangled into silence.

The Satrap's demands were not equal to her efforts. Freedom from her debts and the Alabarch had been traded for servitude to another. She'd built her workshop to pursue her interests, not to become a factory of war.

Heron blinked away the exhaustion and stared at the neat, careful lines on the papyrus. She barely remembered drawing them. Each time she thought about stopping, the Satrap's words echoed in her head, propelling her forward.

"If it doesn't help me beat the Romans, I forbid you from working on it. Strike this foolish notion from your mind. A pyramid? Really, Heron? Are you mad? And I don't want you leaving the city either. I was a fool for sending you to Old Babylon. Rome would have you captured or dead if they could."

He'd said more. The words had gummed up her thoughts and during the long night, chunks of them broke loose and flew through her head like diseased bats.

Now the man they called Vima the Viper would visit. Sepharia had sent a note warning her. Heron smiled, thankful her daughter was still on her side. The warning had been enough time to get Jarngard out of the workshop. She sent him to the Emporium with Punt for foundry supplies.

The sounds of speaking carried from the entryway. Heron dusted herself off, smearing new stains across her tunic, eyeing them with as much interest as a cat might give a mathematical equation. Plutarch marched into the workshop with Vima and Agog. An unfamiliar woman held Polyxena's arm while Sepharia trailed behind. Heron assumed it was Vima's wife by her brown, lustrous skin. She was beautiful like a quiet, secluded forest pond. Zenobia was the name she recalled from Sepharia's note.

"The Man of Machines!" called Agog without a trace of their argument in his voice. "The city's greatest inventor and Chief Engineer."

Heron bowed in the manner of her station. Her knees wobbled as she bent.

"Greetings, Prince Vima. My humble workshop is yours to inspect." Heron kept her head inclined and waited for the Prince's greeting to resume standing.

Vima examined her leisurely, a slight tick forming at the corner of his mouth. The prince turned to Agog.

"Such an ordinary looking man. Are you sure this is the *Michanikos*? I see no gears or metal parts as the stories tell. And this workshop looks like every other one I have ever seen," said Vima.

"I assure you there are no other workshops like this in the known world," said Heron as politely as she could through gritted teeth.

Agog stepped up and clasped Vima on the shoulder. "I assure you he is quite remarkable. It is what goes on in his mind that is so valuable."

Vima shrugged and wandered into the workshop. Heron straightened.

"I see no great works? Not even one of these famed steam mechanicals I have examined," said Vima with arms wide. "Those chariots alone will not conquer the Romans."

Heron had instructed her workers not to look at the Prince and focus on the task, but even a sideways glance told her the problem. As she'd told the Satrap, she'd been working on smaller inventions and ideas, nothing grand like a steam mechanical or a steel boat. To placate the visitor, she made Plutarch pull out a dusty unfinished miracle from the storage room. The brass legs of Horus barely filled out the scaffolding. Even her men knew the project was purposeless and mimed their way through the construction.

Agog sensed her discomfort and cleared his throat. "Show Prince Vima your newest designs."

Her gut twisted. In her frenzy of all-night work she couldn't even remember what she'd been working on, but it couldn't have been for the Satrap. Anger blurred the lens of her memory.

Heron glanced to Sepharia for support, but her daughter and the Satrap's future wife had wandered away and were showing Zenobia a table of measuring instruments. The Parthian princess held an iron ruler for angles up to the light streaming in from a high window.

"My designs?" she asked the question to herself as much Agog.

"Yes, your designs, what else would I mean?" Agog turned to Vima. "The *Michanikos'* mind works always. I have come to visit and found him wandering through his workshop, lost in thought. Then days later, a miracle appears!"

Vima leaned over the papyrus, studying the drawings. Agog's welcoming face turned into a glare. He motioned toward her to join the Prince.

"Explain your newest miracle," commanded Agog.

"Yes, *Your Grace*," replied Heron.

Before Heron could join the Prince, he turned to them with a bright smile on his face. "So you can make giant metal soldiers. I knew you could."

"Wha—?" said Heron.

Agog stepped to the table. Heron followed.

The previous night's frenzy of sketching formed out of the fog of delirium. "I'm afraid that design isn't ready to be seen yet."

Heron removed the stones at the corner of the papyrus and let the sheet roll up, not even caring if the ink had fully dried. She turned away from Agog's questioning eyes, feigning at difficulty in putting the rolled papyrus into a wooden travel case.

Prince Vima was partially right about the drawing. It was a giant metal soldier, but just not one that could move. She was designing the statue requested by Bani's father. She remembered that much now.

There was a second papyrus beneath the first. Heron ticked off the number of days in her mind. It could possibly have been two days, but she wasn't quite sure. Her stomach grumbled in punctuation to the previous thought.

Vima had soured at the removal of the drawing. She recognized her error by the stoning look she was receiving from Agog.

"Apologies. This drawing will be of more interest to you. It's a new weapon in defense of the city." She cleared her throat. "Good Prince, your keen eyes lifted the purpose of the last drawing quite readily. Do they tell such a truthful tale again?"

Spurred by the challenge, Vima seemed to forgive, and poured himself into examining the drawing. Heron resisted the urge to move Vima's arm when he ground his elbow across the papyrus, creasing it in his enthusiasm to understand. Agog waited cautiously by Vima's side, more intent on conveying his displeasure than investigating.

"The markings of your steam mechanical is quite apparent to me. But the rest looks like one of my elephants nailed to your cart." The intelligent sparkle in Vima's gaze gave her pause. He understood more than he was letting on.

"It's a steam pump and the analogy to the elephant is quite apt. The great belly is the steam chamber and the long tube vomits the steam out. It's a modification of my water pump."

"And what does it do?" asked Vima.

"It's for repelling invaders trying to break down a gate, or climb ladders," explained Heron.

Vima crossed his arms. "But why not pitch? Or burning arrows?"

"A good turtle can protect a ram with wet hides. Even pitch will burn too slowly to matter. Steam fits through any opening and burns like the hottest fire," said Heron.

"Then I would knock down your gate with catapults from a distance," said Vima. "What good is your steam pump then?"

Heron shrugged. "For every strategy there are a dozen to counter it. But more options leads to an unpredictable opponent."

With his back to Agog, Vima winked at her. "Unless you can out think your enemy and neutralize all his options, or overwhelm them like Rome—"

A dreadful clatter ended the discussion. Zenobia stood a few paces away, hand to mouth. A basket of bronze tubing lay scattered on the floor. She'd clearly knocked it from its perch.

"Apologies, I should not have placed—" Heron began to say, but as the words left her mouth, Vima moved like the viper he was named.

"Clumsy woman, how you embarrass me!" Vima swatted his wife to her knees with an open hand across the jaw. Heron was accustomed to seeing women punished for their mistakes in Alexandria, but the speed and ferocity of the Parthian prince stunned her into immobility.

Zenobia cowered on her knees as Vima repeatedly struck her. After the first few blows, Vima grabbed a bronze pipe and hit her across the shoulder. The pipe bent like a heated rod. He kept swinging, his arm rising and falling a piston on a steam engine.

Her hysterical screaming filled the empty workshop. Work halted and the men, some who had probably hit their wives, gaped open mouthed. Sepharia crept backwards, face ashen with fear. Polyxena's face blanked, eyes staring lifelessly into the distance. A nearly imperceptible twitch at each blow told Heron much about the Polyxena's past.

Heron threw daggers with her eyes at Agog, pleading with him to stop the beating. When his jaw grew resolute, she knew he would do nothing. Anything for his empire, those would be his thoughts.

Without concern for her own safety, Heron marched to Vima and grabbed his raised arm before it could strike again. The Parthian prince was considerably stronger than her, but the angle of his arm and the unexpectedness of her action kept him from striking Zenobia again.

"Not in my workshop," said Heron, barely containing her ire. "Not in Alexandria."

The cold, hatred in Vima's eyes almost made her let go of his arm. The man had never been defied before. She could feel the straining of his limbs. He yanked his arm away from Heron. The previous pleasing slant of his face now the mask of the underworld. He marched from the room and a tangible doom seemed to flood in behind him.

Zenobia sobbed at her feet, broken and bloody. Before Heron could move to comfort her, Polyxena appeared and helped the woman up. Heron expected some manner of thanks, but Polyxena only whispered, "You fool."

Heron reached out to Sepharia, but her daughter moved to help Polyxena. A look of confusion crossed Sepharia's eyes as she left.

Her workers resumed their farcical tinkering, leaving the workshop to sound like a graveyard full of dull bells. Heron crossed her arms defensively as Agog loomed.

"Even when Alexander the Macedonian killed his closest friend, Clitus, no one uttered a word otherwise, and the *man* had saved Alexander on the battlefield twice. Vima has three wives, even if he killed this one, an attractive but clumsy woman at best, he would still have two more. Don't throw away my empire for a woman."

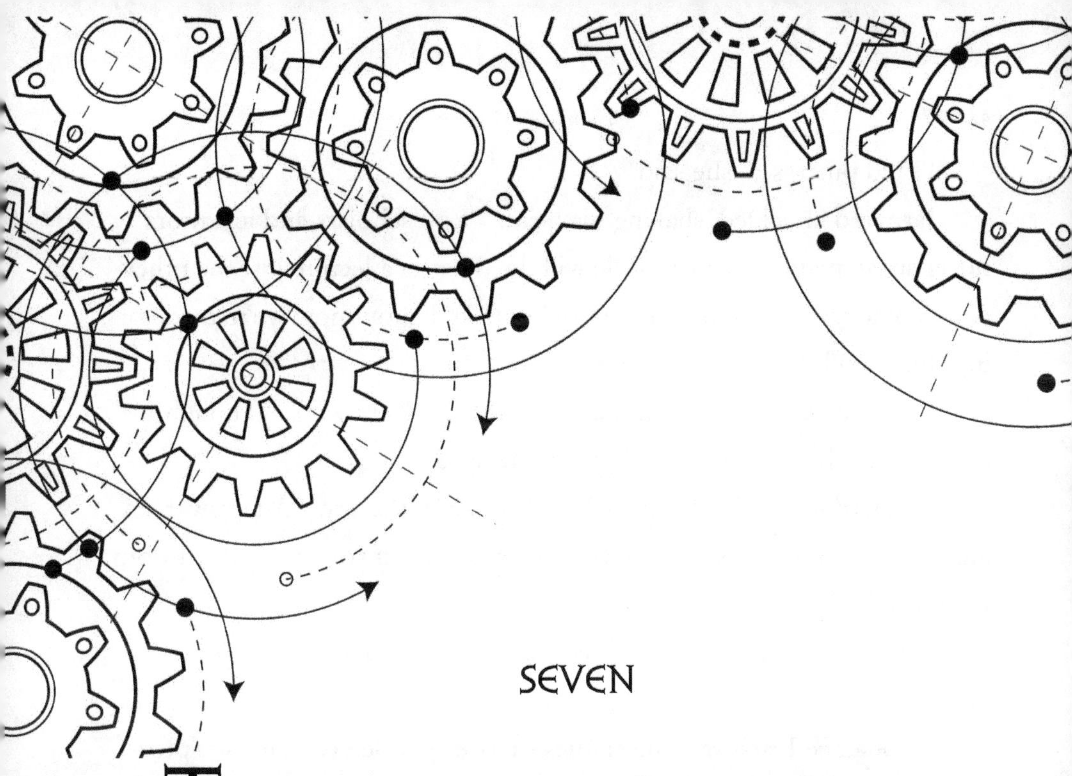

SEVEN

The steady clopping of horse hooves rang against the stones. Peddlers called out their wares in dozens of languages. The greasy smells of boiled meat mixed with the press of human sweat. Heron rode with her hood up, dressed in traveler's clothing. She leaned back against her saddle as the street sloped toward the docks.

A brown mare pulled aside. The rider had a soldier's presence, an easy rhythm with his mount, the wary, never resting gaze. Even without a single weapon, Heron knew him a fearsome foe.

"Ave, Jarngard," she said.

"He'll come around. He always does, though I was surprised he stripped your title of Chief Engineer," he said.

Heron angled around a wagon filled with vegetables on its way to the Emporium. "I gave him no choice. He had to repair the honor of the Parthian Prince. In truth, Nektam is a better Chief Engineer now. I tire of making his war machines."

"What will you do now?"

"Find purpose," she said.

Jarngard chuckled, shaking his head. "You scholars and inventors never speak plainly when a riddle will do. I sat in a lecture just the other day to practice my Latin and the teacher talked about how we're made of invisibly small things called atoms."

"Or maybe the truth is not easily explained," she said. "Though I envy those who find the world easy to navigate."

Jarngard leaned his head back and spoke to the sky. "An answer, an answer. All I ask for is an answer. Oh, Athena can you pry such wisdom from his lips?"

The smile came easy. "Athena? Do you not call on your northern gods?"

"Not since I first saw the statues of your goddesses. Our sculptors in the north are thick of hand and blurry of eye. I was an easy convert." Jarngard stroked the neck of his horse. "And still, he does not answer."

"I'm visiting an old friend," she said. "I have a favor to ask. Without the funds of the city at my disposal, I must pursue other means."

Jarngard nodded. "Mind if I join you? I lack a reason to be in the city."

She agreed and they let their horses plod towards her destination. Heron was in no hurry to get there. The urgency she felt on the Lighthouse had been quenched by the Satrap's decision.

The gentle breeze and fresh, salty air lured her to a calm state. Jarngard's quiet companionship was soothing. He'd been thrown from the Satrap's favor just as she had.

"I'm unused to this," she said as they cut along the edge of the docks. Runners for the Library scampered across the long wooden fingers, arms stuffed with papyrus.

"Riding?"

"Breathing." He gave her a nod that said he understood.

"You should come to the north when it snows. It forces you to do nothing but keep warm and drink mead. By the time the snows melt, the desire to do anything, no matter how stupid or outrageous, fills you, and you strike out without delay," he explained.

"That sounds terrifying," she said honestly.

"Most of our adventures can be blamed on not seeing the sun for a couple of months." Jarngard craned his neck at the buildings. He kept his hair shorter than before but it still blew into his eyes. "Where does this adventure take us?"

"Right here," she said and dismounted.

A wooden sign bearing the name 'Cassandra's Tavern' swayed in the breeze. Flickering oil lamps reflected through the distorted windows. A boy with two papyri tucked under his arm pushed past them and into the tavern.

Behind the counter a handsome, raven-haired woman wiped clean a mug. A few patrons were seated at the wooden tables. They appeared to be scholars from the Great Library by their disheveled robes and blank, introspective stare.

Taut bark-ropes suspended brass implements in the rafters. A finely crafted astrolabe hung above Heron's head rotating slowly in a breeze from a sea-side open window.

Heron forced herself to relax by taking a deep breath. The intervening years could have changed much. Her request might be completely pointless now.

Jarngard made a sharp intake of breath between his teeth. Clearly, he'd just noticed how beautiful Arethussa was. Though the lens of her memory had dimmed, Heron thought Arethussa might have grown more lovely since she had seen her last. The freedom of her careful position providing bounty.

The woman glanced up and gave them a practiced, welcoming

smile, but not one with any recognition contained within. Heron's pulse skipped a beat from disappointment.

"Please tell me this is a secret lover of yours, I should want to hear the stories," Jarngard muttered under his breath.

When Heron pulled back the hood of her traveler's cloak, Arethussa's eyes flickered with thought. The woman set the mug and rag onto the counter.

"Good Heron?" asked Arethussa.

"Apologies, I know I promised to visit, but the coin of my name had been tainted and I did not want to cause you harm," said Heron.

Arethussa rushed up and embraced Heron, much to the delight of the Northman. By the sparkle in his eye, he assumed much. The faint brush of soft lips against her cheek made Heron blush.

"I would have gladly risked harm for you. Without your intervention so long ago I never would have built all this." She gestured to the room.

Jarngard spoke in a hushed voice with a secretive glance over his shoulder at the two scholars, seated together, but clearly lost in their own thoughts. "But I thought a woman could not own property in these lands?"

Arethussa paused and gave the Northman an appraising look. Heron quickly introduced them.

"Do not worry about them," said Arethussa. "Tiramisus and Phillip are gas sniffers. They catalog the smells of the world and some, I think, have sunk too deeply into their memory and they cannot shake them loose. So do not worry about speaking freely around them. After their studies in the Library, they often sit like this until mid-afternoon before they realize they are here."

Their blank gazes were more recognizable now from her explanation. Heron had seen the same on men who had been hit in the head during battle or by the unrestrained hoof of a wild horse.

"I do not really own this building, though for all practical purposes it is the same. Heron found me a patron to attach my name so that I might practice freely," said Arethussa.

Heron relaxed into an easy smile. "I had forgotten my own cleverness. Arethussa married a Roman man in absentee and everything she does is in his name while he possibly still lives in Rome unaware."

"How could such a thing be done?" asked Jarngard.

"The gears of the Empire are much like a machine. Push the right levers and you'll get the result you want. It only took the right documents and a little seed money. Look how large her tree has grown," said Heron.

"And you are Chief Engineer of Alexandria," said Arethussa brightly.

Heron grabbed Arethussa's hand and examined it. Ink stains shaded the palm. "I see you still keep up with your studies."

"Yes, and the business has grown." Arethussa entwined their fingers and pulled her forward. Through a door on the back of the room, a table full of scribblers worked busily at scrolls.

The scribes were young and the short hair deceiving. Heron might not have seen it except she was fluent in this type of deception. She hoped Arethussa couldn't see the same in her.

"Young scribes learning the arts?" asked Heron.

"I offer freelance book copying services. The Great Library isn't the only one who can do it. Nobles pay good coin to enlarge their libraries," said Arethussa.

"And you make copies for yourself," said Heron. "Plus your *scribes* get practice and possibly learn something from the work."

A hand squeeze told Heron she was right. The warm smile in Arethussa's gaze told Heron that the woman had long harbored feelings.

Arethussa showed them another room, though they did not enter. It was a private lecture hall attached to the back of the tavern. The stone seating wrapped around in an oval shape. The lecturer had a high lilting voice and spoke in Latin. He was explaining a mathematical proof. The open door was barely paid any attention. Once they had seen their fill, Arethussa brought them back to the tavern.

"When my charges are complete with their work," Arethussa explained. "They often sit in the room next to the lecture hall to listen."

"You've done quite well."

"My thanks to you, Heron. Even from afar, I was inspired by your legendary efforts and sought to better myself. Your past kindness was a constant reminder not to let the burdens of my gender stop me."

Arethussa released her hand and poured them each a cup of aromatic, blackberry wine. The woman gave her a glance filled with longing and ache. "But you did not come here to visit me after so many years. Or you would have done so long ago."

"Apologies, Arethussa. My debts kept me chained to my duties." Even back then, it had hurt not to reveal herself to Arethussa as a fellow woman. She had a bright mind and at the time, only lacked the means. Heron had encouraged her, though it seemed she needed little, even as a young woman she had been stealing books from her master Philo.

"I would have given what I could to ease your burden if only you would have asked," said Arethussa.

"Entangling you in Lysimachus' grasp. The better course was to act as if we'd never met, especially given the connection with Philo," said Heron.

Arethussa spoke sadly, "And now you come back, but I can see it in your eyes that it is not to see me. You need something. Is it the clay pots?"

The regretful nod weighed Heron's heart. It was clear that Arethussa had been waiting for her to return. The repercussions of her deceptions could sometimes be quite cruel. "Know that it brings me joy that you prosper, but yes, I need to know about the clay pots."

The Northman had been quietly observing the exchange. His fingers rested on the leather bag around his neck. As he caught Arethussa's gaze, he gave her a roguish smile. "I am not so weighed down by duty at the moment if you need a companion."

"I heard you Northmen make your companionship with sheep and other livestock." She winked at him.

"What other men do in the cold, sunless nights, it's not for me so say," laughed Jarngard. "But I never found my furs without warmth."

"Now you sound like Hoth," said Heron. "Enough banter, I do need to hear about the clay pots."

The admonished Jarngard took a place at a table and propped his feet onto a railing. He closed his eyes and feigned at sleep.

"I'm afraid my memory is weak on them, but I will tell you what I can. What do you wish to know?" asked Arethussa.

"Everything."

Heron questioned Arethussa for a couple of hours. When scholarly patrons arrived, she would stop and serve them wine or bits of fruit and nuts, but she returned after each. Jarngard waited patiently, even appearing to listen at times.

When they left, Arethussa gave her a hopeful peck on the lips. The misplaced feelings tugged heavily on Heron's heart. Even if she had time for emotional entanglement, letting Arethussa have her way would only end in disappointment. Unlike her ancestor Alexander, Heron knew she would never have time for love.

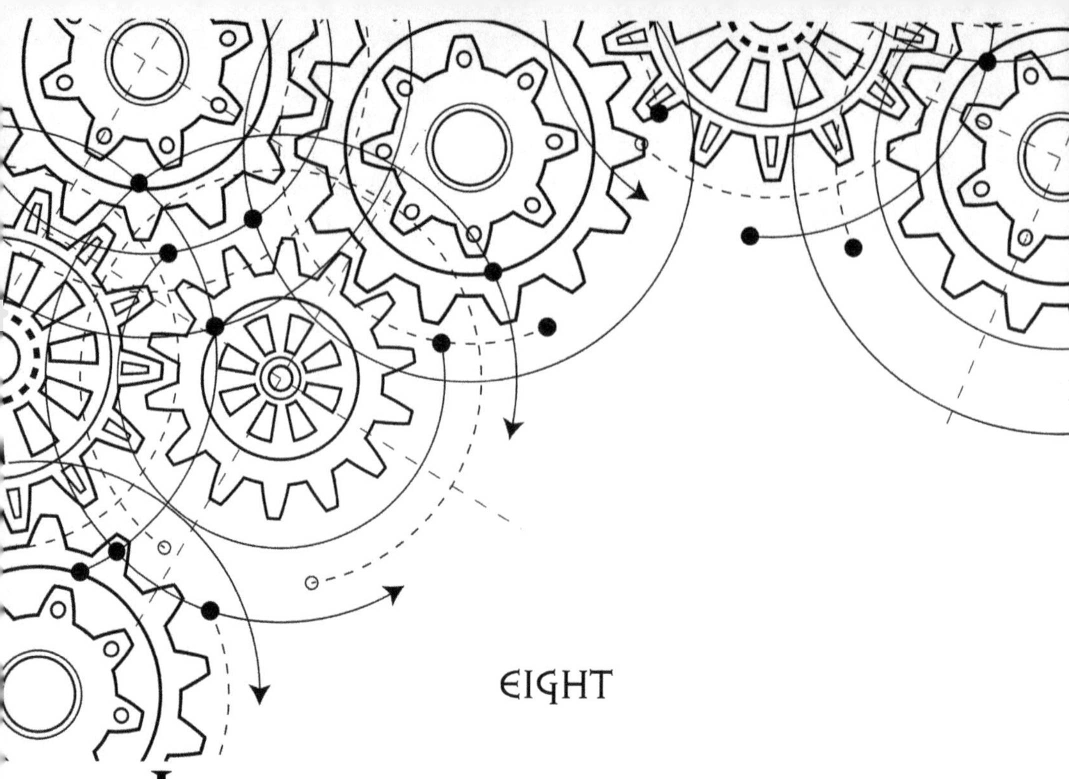

EIGHT

Jarngard sat in his window, sipping watered down wine. The brief storm broke into scattered clouds, headed south toward the desert. Mist rose from the streets amid the morning travelers that called out to each other in strange languages. The rumbling clank of a steam mechanical thundered down a nearby street. Alexandria was busy shaking off the rain. Soon the smells of baking bread and ore fire would be thick on the southern winds. He coughed away the thick, moist air and refilled his cup, returning to his spot in the window.

White sails drifted past the island of Pharos, carrying cargo and ideas. In the distance, more ships receded toward the horizon. From his perch, Jarngard couldn't see the Great Harbor, though he knew it was choked with ships flocking to the great city.

A heavy thump from the workshop shook the walls. Jarngard glanced in that direction, but did not stir. He smiled, remembering the first time he'd run into the workshop expecting destruction only to find the workers lifting the statue's thigh into place.

He sighed. His lands would be buried in snow now. He imagined smoke twirling from chimneys, great shaggy dogs romping through the snow, the warmth of furs, and the cold kiss of frost. The *Nereid's Song* waited in the harbor to take him back. The captain would depart at the setting sun with or without him and he'd given the man a large sum to extend his trip to get him back. While Hoth and his fleet patrolled the Mediterranean, once into the choppy seas beyond, dangers lurked. Reports of piracy further west sounded suspiciously like the Romans.

Jarngard left his room. He had not told Heron yet. The man was his friend and he deserved to know. Jarngard found him in the back of the workshop near a stack of crates.

The inventor hunched over a wooden basin. A dozen clay pots lay scattered around the inventor. Thin copper ribbons ran into the basin, connected to the pots.

Heron, who had not yet noticed him watching, stood as still as a statue, hand to chin, clearly observing something that only he could see. Then decisively, he moved to another location and adjusted the ribbon on one of the clay pots before falling into a motionless state again.

While the name Machine Man meant nothing to Jarngard, he found himself quite fascinated by the inventor. When he watched Heron, and he had quite often since coming to the workshop, he found the inventor to be much like a military leader.

Wanton, recklessness only got a man killed in battle. Or half his face taken off like Tormod. The best commanders observed the flow of men and horses before leaping into action, but once decided, then threw themselves into battle and could not be dissuaded.

Except that wasn't completely true of Heron. The inventor was different. Not quite a battle commander, but something greater. Jarngard told himself that's why he'd been watching the man work these last few days.

In battle, two sides competed for domination. What he observed from Heron was an inevitable motion. His efforts did not stop when he was complete, but carried on like an avalanche tumbling down a mountainside.

"What do you see in your basin? Wood-witches in the north are said to see the future in their cooking pots," said Jarngard.

The unamused stare he received from Heron was worth the comment. Jarngard chuckled and sipped his wine.

"You speak of needing purpose, yet all you do is consume fermented grapes and sit in your room."

"You promised purpose, good Heron. Here I wait, full of vigor, ready to be thrown like a spear at your target," replied Jarngard jovially.

The inventor allowed himself a crack of a smile. "Truth, I promised as much. Apologies on my inattention, I've been busy on a puzzle with no time for giving direction."

"Lend me your problems then. At the very least I can feign at thinking about them while I drink more wine." Jarngard held his cup high in salute.

Heron straightened and indicated the scaffolding behind Jarngard with his outstretched arm. "See that cylinder, that is a thin slice of the statue Ammon's leg."

"His leg? That statue must be huge," exclaimed Jarngard.

"My plans make him around two hundred feet tall which is twice the size of the largest statue ever constructed, the Colossus of Rhodes. He will wield a great golden staff and his arm will move after a heavy rain, indicating good fortune to the people of Kush," said Heron.

"Can such a thing be done?" he asked.

"There are details still to be worked out, but I believe it is possible," Heron explained.

Jarngard set his cup onto the nearby table. Fathoming the construction made him reel. Such a thing was like the Lighthouse on Pharos, which despite his knowledge otherwise, Jarngard considered that the gods had designed it rather than a man.

"How will it move? Or know when it rains? Are you sure you do not toil for the gods themselves?" asked Jarngard, nearly exasperated by wonder.

The great inventor laughed, a sweet melodic sound that was pleasing to his ears. "It is not so unbelievable. Rain catchers will fill at the top of the statue, inside its hollow body and when they are full, they will fall, pulling the gears that wind the arm. At the bottom they will empty and rise again to be filled once more."

Jarngard shook his head. "The Satrap will pay for this?"

"No, he will not, but Queen Amanitore of the Kushites will since the statue will stand there. And for this effort they will supply men and gold for a different project, one I will need your help on, if you so choose. For the Satrap has released me from his service, so that I might bring the Kushites to his cause."

The sounds of the workshop suddenly filled his ears. He'd come to tell Heron that he was leaving the city. It pained him to even think about saying the words, so he delayed, hoping to find a more appropriate time.

"And what of this other project? Is that what those basins will help you achieve?" asked Jarngard.

Heron shook his head. "No. But I will tell you about the basin. It's that puzzle I was getting ready to explain." Jarngard came closer and Heron continued. "If you remember a few days ago when we visited Arethussa."

"How could I forget? She haunts my dreams still. I should wish to visit her," said Jarngard. "Which reminds me, how did you come to meet her?"

"Good of you to ask, that tale serves two masters," said Heron.

"She once worked for my rival, Philo. He tortured her for the amusement of his clients, so I freed her from his service, hiding her in a different part of the city until he thought she had run away or been killed. He soon forgot, since women were nothing to him."

"If he was your rival, how did you come to be involved?" he asked.

"There was a death, a Roman citizen of some importance, and I was asked by the Magistrate of this district to help. We learned the death was accident, though it involved these clay pots that the uninitiated say contain the deadly flames of ghosts," explained Heron.

Jarngard stepped gingerly away from the clay pot near his foot.

"Don't worry, friend. For them to kill you, you would have to make a special effort," said Heron, clearly amused.

"What are they?" Jarngard frowned at the pottery.

Heron sighed regretfully. "In truth, I do not know. They were made by a man who died before I could speak to him. The technology comes from the east, maybe even Old Babylon. So the secret of their making is lost to me. But I can use the ones that the Magistrate confiscated and stored in a Roman warehouse."

The stacks took meaning for Jarngard. There had to be hundreds of clay pots in the crates. "If you do not know, then how will you use them? You inventors are curious folk."

"Yet you swing a sword and I doubt you could make one," said Heron. "These clay pots are known to the Great Library. Scholars muse upon their uses and one of them is the plating of gold onto other metal objects. Normally, it would take a blacksmith weeks to hammer gold into foil and attach it well enough to stay. And then the gold might fall off later, bringing much shame to the blacksmith. Also, they could only do a small portion. I need to plate the entire staff of Ammon and his ram's horns. There aren't enough blacksmiths in the world to accomplish this task in the time I need it completed."

Jarngard stared into the basin. A hunk of metal was submerged in a foul smelling liquid. Bubbles formed on the hunk and occasionally one released itself and floated to the surface.

"Does it work?"

"Not yet," said Heron. "But I have time. This construction will take me a year or two to finish."

"The Romans will invade before then," said Jarngard.

"All the more reason for the Kushites to support Alexandria."

Jarngard nodded. "Then I can see why the Satrap agreed."

He crouched on his heels and examined a clay pot. The copper ribbon rested on the iron rod sticking from the pot. "All this and you don't believe in the gods? What a strange man you are." Jarngard tilted his head thoughtfully. "So why do they call it ghost fire?"

"Wet your finger and touch it." Heron grinned impishly. "Go on, don't be afraid of such a tiny piece of pottery."

Spurred by the challenge, Jarngard stuck his finger in his mouth. When it was good and wet, he jammed it against the copper with force.

The pain was immediate and his arm froze like iron while his vision blanked. When he opened his eyes, he was lying on his back. A metallic taste lingered in his mouth.

Heron was staring curiously at him with a hand on his chin. "Strange, it didn't affect me so strongly. I wonder if you Northmen are filled with iron or you did something I didn't do."

When the inventor examined the clay pot, the hint of a grin formed on his lips. "Yes, I see it now. Thank you, Jarngard. Your barbarian ways unraveled the thread."

"I did?" he asked incredulously.

"Yes. I was worried the pots had lost their vigor, but it seems I need to clamp the copper to the iron more strongly. I shall fix that and then we have an errand. Could you fetch the horses and gather provisions for a brief journey?"

"Not a steam mechanical?" he asked despite himself. He had a ship to catch.

"Too obvious. We'll pass ourselves off as traders, or maybe merce-naries." Heron smiled.

"Where..." Jarngard sighed, "...are we going?"

"To Memphis. Home of the pyramid builders," said Heron.

Jarngard could only think of the *Nereid's Song*, but the inventor must have interpreted his silence for a question.

"If we're going to build a pyramid, we need to learn how they're made," said Heron, as if it were a perfectly sane thing to say.

Jarngard opened his mouth to tell Heron that he was leaving, but he couldn't quite muster the words. In the north, he could find a quiet vil-lage and relax, and maybe even find a wife suitable for a man like him. If he stayed with Heron in Alexandria, who knew what would happen? At the very least, he knew there would be a battle with Rome and one side had to lose, most likely Alexandria.

If he left now, he would have plenty of time to gather his things and take a slow ride to the docks to board the *Nereid's Song*. With fees he paid, he had access to the officer's mess. He could continue drinking while he waited, looking upon the Lighthouse of Pharos until they set sail.

But that was the danger, he realized. The Great Lighthouse had been made by a man, a man like Heron, one of flesh and blood and not a god at all. Jarngard touched the leather bag around his neck in reflex. In Alexandria, he could watch Heron build something like that Lighthouse, a wonder that stretched his mind. If ever there were gods, was this Heron like one, to meld stone and iron and wood into monstrosities that moved by the power of the elements?

Heron seemed to sense his hesitation. "Do you think me mad like

Agog does for such plans? He's given me leave to try, but expects me to soon fail and come running back to the safety of the walls."

His hands suddenly had no place to rest. Jarngard sighed, more than once, trying to gather the words. He was a man of war, or an adventurer at least. Not one to build pyramids. Or was he? Jarngard forced the words out before he lost his nerve.

"I am leaving Alexandria."

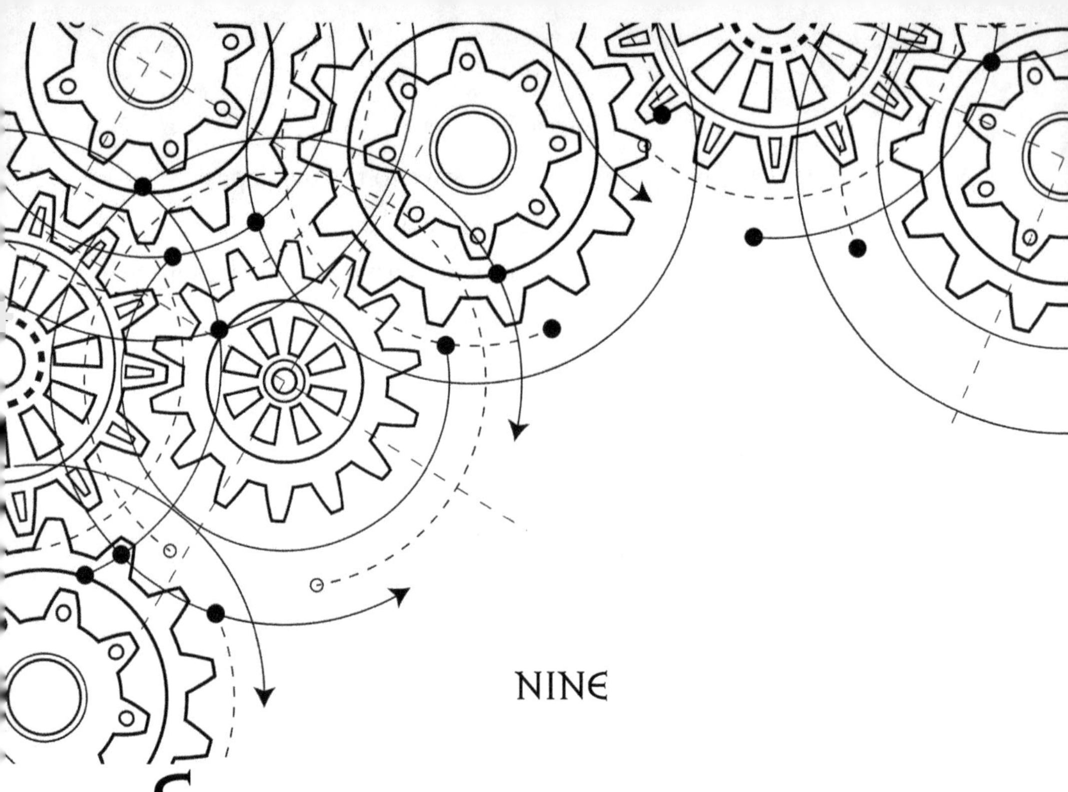

NINE

Scorpions skittered across the hardpack ahead of Heron. Her mount steadily carried her toward Memphis alone. Outside the city, she pulled back her hood, and let the wind sing through her hair.

On the road she entertained fantasies of riding past Memphis and exploring the world. Hoth had told her countless stories about his adventures, half of which she didn't believe, but knowing that didn't lessen their power.

The ride was bittersweet. Jarngard's absence burned a hole in her chest, a pain that even the quiet ride couldn't fully remedy. She hadn't seen his departure coming. Like Hoth, Jarngard's presence reminded her she was a woman beneath the man's tunic and restrictive bindings. She could imagine herself with one of the Northmen. They did not treat women like over-privileged slaves.

The sounds of the Parthian prince thrashing his wife still haunted her nights. That woman could be her, or Sepharia. Polyxena's flinching reaction had been no different than most Greek or Roman women. Heron imagined Polyxena had been beaten before in her homelands, probably by her father or brothers.

Which made Jarngard's abandonment even harder to take. Punt and Plutarch needed to stay with the statue of Ammon. The trip to Memphis was best taken by two. It was a three day ride and she would have enjoyed his company. Hoth was infuriating in his banter, while Jarngard was intriguing. His haunted blue eyes spoke of windswept desolate places that exuded a harsh beauty.

She shook her head, dismissing his image from her mind. Foolishness. Memphis was an ancient place, once the royal seat of the pharaohs. It was a city of builders under the protection of the god Ptah, the patron of craftsmen. When she'd told Punt about the trip, he'd had to hide his disappointment, but she could see it in his downcast gaze that he'd wished to see Memphis.

In the great Temple of Ptah, it was said the priests still contemplated the mysteries of building pyramids. The name of Heron was known there. She'd built miracles for their temple many years ago. She hoped that was enough to gain access to the builder's plans, for nothing in the Great Library explained their construction, though outlandish speculations filled hundreds of scrolls, including supposed eye witness accounts that a powerful sky people had built them.

Heron was so lost in her thoughts, she did not hear the rapid drum of hoof beats until the rider was upon her. Her fingers wrapped around the ivory cane at her waist, preparing to pull the dagger from the hidden sheath.

With her heartbeat thundering in her chest, Heron dismissed her fears as foolishness and decided the identity of the rider was most likely a messenger riding hard to receive a bonus for speed. A less probable but possible outcome was a Roman spy, but she'd been careful with whom she told she was leaving.

When the rider pulled up along side, she decided it was the latter. The blade whispered from the sheath and she held it to the rider's neck before the hood was drawn back.

"Pull that sword at your side and I'll let the desert taste your blood," said Heron.

There was a familiar chuckle from beneath the hood. "If you desire, I can return to Alexandria and arrange another ship, but I thought you'd prefer the company."

Using the tip of the blade, she pulled back his hood. "Jarngard?"

His salty stubble stretched wide in a grin. "Apologies, I should have warned you but I thought you would have recognized my horse as I approached. Or were you too busy planning miracles in that spacious head of yours?"

"The north will miss you," said Heron with a wide smile plastered on her face, "but better them than I. It is good to have company. Why did you stay?"

"It is not often that one gets to watch history in the making," said Jarngard.

"Watch history? I did not request a lazy foreman when I rescued you from the Palace, drunk and naked. I will push you as much as Alexander did his army, to the end of the world and back."

"And what do I get from this?" he grinned.

"A reason to not drown yourself in wine and the satisfaction of the job," she said. "But if you desire more, I will grant it, if it is in my power."

Jarngard spit in his palm and thrust out his hand. "An agreeable bargain. A future favor from the Machine Man could be quite valuable."

Heron was no stranger to deals and responded in kind.

"With that settled, I brought something," said Jarngard. "I stopped by the workshop to see if you had left and Plutarch gave me this. A messenger just delivered it."

The small handcrafted wooden box fit in the palm of her hand. Putting the reins in her teeth, she opened the box. Inside was a small, round red stone.

"I peeked into the box before I left. What is its meaning?" he asked.

"The end of an era. A message from old friends letting me know a deed is done." Heron thought briefly of the punishments inflicted by the Alabarch. "Something I would rather never think about again."

Heron dropped the box onto the road. The red stone catapulted out and rolled into a tuft of scrub bushes. Jarngard gave her a curious look and shrugged.

"I was considering riding past Memphis and forgetting about my instant of madness," Heron confided. "The wide world is quite enticing."

"I'm partial to such thinking. It will hurt my feelings but for the length of a sigh," he said.

Heron patted the horse's neck. "If only I could bring my workshop with me, then I would have the best of both worlds."

"I think Punt would agree to that as well. Your blacksmith is normally quite unreadable, but when I told him I was riding to join you, his shoulders slumped like a child being sent to bed early," said Jarngard.

"I tried to get him killed more than once on the journey from Old Babylon," said Heron. "His memory must be quite short."

"So is that why Hoth couldn't wait to get back to his ship?" laughed Jarngard.

"You'll wish the same in no time, I'm sure. But I won't have to worry about you sneaking off to the docks once we begin building the pyramid," she explained.

He raised an eyebrow. "Planning on chaining me to the stone?"

"In a manner of speaking. I won't be building the pyramid at Alexandria. The soil around Lake Mareotis is too soft and filled with clay.

There's a site south of Alexandria, about fifty stadia. There's a nearby limestone quarry for stone. I expect you to lead the men at the mine to bring me material for construction."

Jarngard stared at the horizon. "I'm not your man Plutarch. I have no mind for directing men in such a manner."

Heron shrugged. "Leading men in battle or in building, it's the same."

"I can promise you that I will try but nothing more. If it fails to suit me, you'll have to find another fool." Jarngard paused and cocked his head at Heron. "Who are these men you speak of? I thought your workshop was busy with the statue?"

"It is, but the Queen is sending men to the pyramid site. The Kushites are skilled stonemasons. By the time we complete our journey and return to Alexandria, they will be on their way to join us. I'll bring Plutarch and a few steam chariots to get the camp started, but after that, it'll be up to you."

Jarngard seemed to weigh her words carefully. He squinted into the distance. "How long will we toil at this construction?"

"Are you familiar with numbers?" she asked.

Jarngard shook his head. "Enough for battle, no more. Beyond the number fifty my head spins."

"Probably a good thing. The number of blocks we shall have to pull from the earth would shatter you then. I shall try and explain it another way. The ancient Egyptians took twenty years to build the largest pyramid—" Jarngard's jaw dropped. "—the one they name for Pharaoh Khufu, using a huge team of builders. I plan to build this pyramid in one year."

They rode in silence except for soft hoof beats. Jarngard glanced at Heron a time or two. Eventually he spoke, "You are as mad as Agog says you are and I'm mad to want to help you. How can you even believe that such a thing can be done by so few?"

"Alexander set off from Macedonia with the goal of conquering the world. Such a thing had never been considered and most thought it mad," said Heron. "The historians may look back upon this project and call it the Folly of Heron, and may deride my name for attempting the impossible, but unless I attempt it, I will already know they are right because I let my cowardice control me. If I am to truly change the world, then let madness consume me."

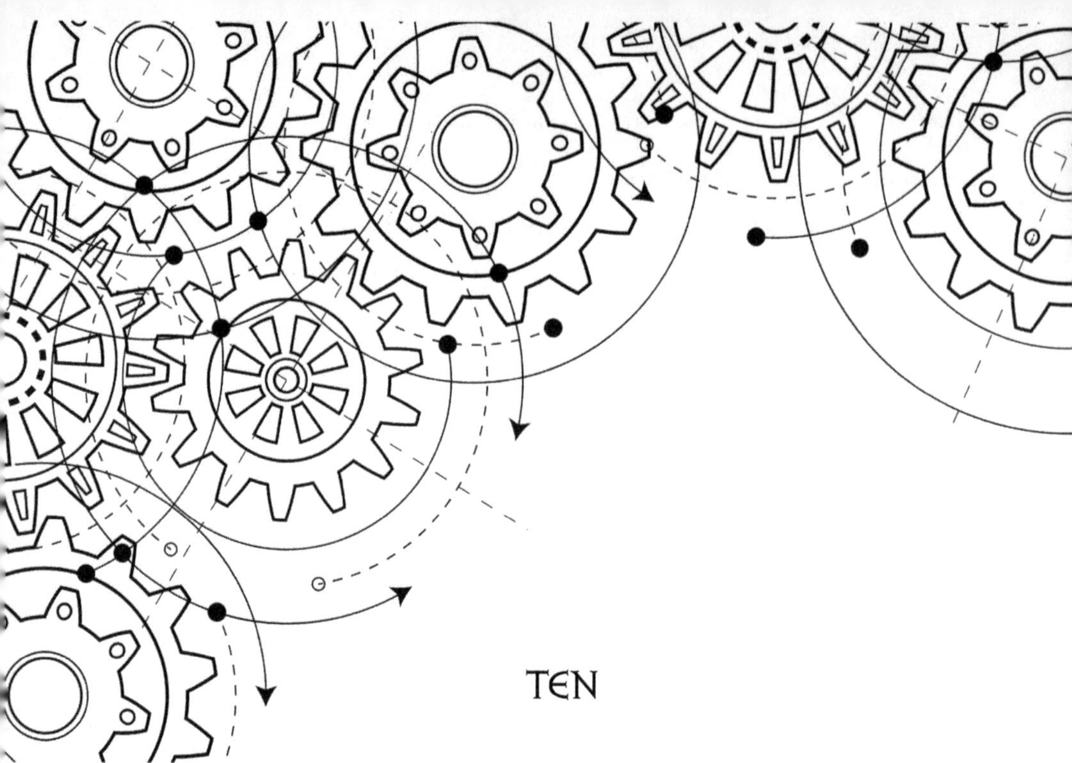

TEN

Prancing across the sands, the Gaul named Dracis waved to the crowd, his long hair bouncing across his back. Alexandrians cheered for the young steam chariot pilot. The crowd loved his every motion, rising to his arm thrusts and calling his name like a desperate lover.

Sepharia admired his naked chest, gleaming in the warm sun. Nearby, the Satrap and the Parthian prince compared notes on the pilots.

"He looks the part of the victor for this final race," said Vima, squeezing the railing eagerly. The prince looked ready to jump down and take the steerage of a steam chariot. "Ten talents on the Gaul. A confident man always wins."

Agog slapped his thigh with an open palm. "Done. I'll take Agnar, he's due for a win with three seconds this week."

The tall Northman climbed into his steam chariot, giving the crowd a terse wave. He was a grim pilot and the crowd did not love him.

The other nobles cast their bets. Most bet on Dracis, either in homage to the prince or because the pilot had won a fair number of races already. The bets ran heavy because it was the last race of the day and twice the length of the others.

Sepharia stood to the side. The royal balcony held strong, recent memories. She sipped her wine and studied the chariots.

"Maker's daughter."

She looked up to find Vima addressing her. His handsome gaze sent a chill through her heart. His smile contained hidden daggers.

"Yes, Prince?"

"Who do you favor? I hear the Machine Man's daughter is supposed to be a clever woman. Which is like saying she's the smartest oxen in the field," said Vima.

The laughter of the nobles cut her. She steeled her face from reacting. Agog watched passively.

"I have no coin to bet." She hid her trembling hands behind her back.

"A woman like you has a different coin. The one between your legs. Ten talents versus that bald smile between your legs." The prince grabbed his cock beneath his tunic.

A prince like Vima could not be refused and he was already cross with her family because of the incident in the workshop. Sepharia looked back to the pilots.

"The Egyptian. The one they call Apis." She pointed even though everyone knew the man.

"Him? I'll have you know this is a steam chariot race, not a wrestling match. Not that I mind, I don't think I've ever bedded a scholar's daughter," said Vima.

"Then you'll give me three to one," said Sepharia without thinking.

There was nervous laughter. Her father Heron was well loved, but the nobles knew Alexandria needed the Parthians against Rome. The whispers that followed weren't complimentary.

"By the gods, I'll give you five to one. And if Apis loses, I'll even lick your sandals," boasted Vima. His countrymen laughed louder than the others.

"Deal," she said, vividly remembering the way he'd beaten his wife in the workshop.

Agog glanced at her, his forehead hunched in concern. Sepharia knew she'd gone too far with the bet, especially because she believed she would win.

The crowd jeered Apis as he climbed into the chariot. His thick legs were as big as trees and arms barely reached the steerage. Sepharia was glad he hadn't donned a plumed helm like the others. He looked ridiculous enough without it.

Polyxena appeared, a strong hand cupping Sepharia's elbow. "Why didn't you choose Agnar or one of the others? Apis hasn't won a race all week."

"I know what I'm doing," she said.

"Do you really?" Polyxena whispered. "He got the name Vima the Viper because when he strikes, he strikes viciously. Just like he did with his wife and we haven't seen her since that day."

Sepharia turned her head so no one but Polyxena could hear. "I didn't like what he did to her. Nor to my father."

"Your father sent himself from the city. Not Agog. He has some mad dream in the desert to attend to," growled Polyxena. "And remember your place. We cannot let our pride get in the way of our fledgling empire."

"It's not pride—"

"It's foolishness." Polyxena's fingers dug into her arm.

Sepharia yanked it away.

"Girl, there are ways to do this, but not like this. You cannot play the man's game and win. Even if you win here, you lose," said Polyxena.

"You'll wish you'd listened to me and taken a man to your bed before Vima gets you."

Their conversation paused while the announcer yelled out the names of each pilot before the starting flag. Since the coliseum had been repaired, steam chariot races had kept the stands full, even bringing visitors from farther away. Alexandrians flocked to the races and even the workshops had gotten involved, sending newer steam chariot designs as they were made.

The resting steam chariots sounded like a pride of lions fighting over the last antelope. As the flag was thrown, the growl rose and the steam chariots burst from the line. Dracis got off to an early lead with Agnar in close pursuit.

Apis failed to engage his mechanical immediately and listed off the line like a hesitant mule. Laughter followed the steam chariot as it chugged around the arena.

"Friends, I think I know why sweet Sepharia bet on that sorry pilot," said Vima loudly, pausing long enough to catch everyone's attention. "She wishes to bed me and was too shy to ask."

More laughter followed. Sepharia hunched over the railing. The prince was not done, he drank deeply from his cup, dark liquid spilling onto the stone.

"I'm not called the Viper for only my prowess on the battlefield." Vima thrust his hips forward and took another drink.

Sepharia stayed quiet and the prince grew bored, returning to the rail to watch the race. He clasped Agog on the shoulder.

"You should give the pilots spears and let them at each other during the race," said Vima. "If it were my city, it's how I would do it."

"But it's not," said Agog, a little too forcefully. "Apologies, Prince, I know you grow restless here. Fortunately for us, the early winter has delayed the Romans and they cannot cross the mountains to attack by spring. We might not see their armies for a year, giving us ample time to prepare."

Vima swayed slightly and shrugged away the comment. "We have not yet signed an agreement, Satrap. Remember, my brother treats with the Romans and my father waits in Susa for word of the better deal. In truth, your steam chariots and automatas interest me, but if we side with the Romans then you will surely lose and I can have them anyway. The workshops will work for whoever owns the city."

The jovial mood dimmed. Agog watched the Prince with half-lidded eyes, his thick arms crossed and meaty fingers crackling as he flexed them. Even Vima's companions sipped nervously at their cups. The sounds of the race - growling steam engines, shouts and cheers, baritone voice of the announcer - provided an odd backdrop to the tension.

"So my boredom is dangerous for you and your city," said Vima like a cat lazily pawing at an injured mouse. "I'm less inclined to make this decision based on the chances of you winning this war, and more on how entertained I was while I was your guest."

The Prince's broad smile was not intimidated one bit by the bear-like Agog. The Satrap eventually uncrossed his arms and nodded.

"We shall make your visit a wonder of delights," said Agog with surprising congeniality.

Vima turned back to the race. "Excellent. Already my cock grows hard in anticipation of the delights." The Prince glanced menacingly toward her. "How goes your pilot, Sepharia? As his chances diminish, do you grow wetter?"

"The race is long and far from over," she sung.

Polyxena squeezed her arm. "Do not be rude to our guest."

Vima waved his cup, sloshing wine onto the stone. "No, let her speak. She entertains me." The smile plastered on his face did not extend to his eyes.

The Prince indicated the lead steam chariot with an outstretched arm. The Gaul pilot deftly leaned back and scooped more fuel into his fire chamber. Black smoke drifted in a haze above the speeding chariots.

"See! Dracis in the lead by half a stadia, nearly passing Apis in his sloth. My eyes are keen and see what other men cannot see. What a dreadful notion to think that a woman could bet with a man. I was wrong to call you a smart oxen. Maybe an average milk cow. You women are blessed to be ruled by men. The gods were right to give us strength and you a belly for babies, otherwise we'd have no need of you. When I attend the temples this evening, I shall lay a coin down for you, that you may one day have a spark of intelligent thought."

"Do you wish to double your bet?" She kept her voice calm despite the thunder of her heartbeat.

Vima snickered. "By what rights? I already own that wetness between your legs. What else can you give me?"

Sepharia glanced back to the race, confirming once again what her eyes had told her. She prayed she was not wrong.

"Your body slave for a month. Whatever you want," she said.

Polyxena whispered harshly. "You don't know what you ask."

"But I don't want coin in return." She paused, carefully choosing her words so she didn't offend. "We women are creatures of gossip and we miss the opportunity to trade words with your wife Zenobia and hear about the wonders of your distant land. If Apis wins, then we would like her to join us in the woman's wing so we can speak about simple things at leisure."

After a brief narrowing of his eyes, he shrugged. "Just like a woman to choose another's company rather than gold. I win either way in this bet."

Polyxena gave her a nervous glance. Sepharia tried to ignore the welling of nausea in her gut, focusing on the sands of the arena instead.

The race was down to the last laps and Sepharia began to wonder if she'd miscalculated.

Apis' steam chariot was showing some signs of accelerating, but Dracis' lead seemed quite insurmountable. Sepharia wondered if Apis would even catch Agnar, who was trailing as a distant second.

The bull-shaped Egyptian quickly dumped more fuel into the fire chamber. The steam chariot surged with unexpected power.

Sepharia stole a glance toward Vima. The Prince drank his wine confidently, speaking in quieter tones with the Satrap.

If he'd been a kindly man, his earlier comment that she was throwing the race to sleep with him might have been true. But the beating of his wife told her otherwise. His crisp blue eyes were cruel, not kindly.

The crowd had been lulled into a calm by the seemingly inevitable final result of the race, but when Apis passed his first chariot, they cheered. Dracis leaned into his fuel box, scooping up pitiful dust. Sparks flew from the fire chamber when he flung it in. The drumming of his chariot's pistons slowed.

"What did you see to make such a bet?" asked Polyxena, her eyes clearly searching the arena floor for clues.

"Fuel boxes," she said quietly. "To give the crowd something different, they lengthened the final race of the day. The racers are loath to add additional weight and I did not think the other competitors adjusted properly and put enough fuel into their chariots."

Polyxena nodded. "I see Dracis slowing. Will you have time?"

"Only the gods know."

The lead steam chariot slowed considerably, while Apis thundered around the track. He was gaining rapidly and would soon pass another chariot.

A flag for the final lap was thrown onto the track. A heavy weight settled on Sepharia's chest. Apis' chariot skidded around the track while

Dracis seemed to move with torpor as if his wheels churned through mud. The long-haired Gaul kept glancing behind him, and seemed to be pushing on the steerage, willing it to move faster.

Apis passed Agnar, who punched the metal shielding in frustration. Sepharia sighed heavily. If there'd been one more lap more, then Apis would have caught Dracis, but there was not. Dracis puttered down the final stretch while Apis was only coming around the corner. There wasn't enough track to catch up.

Sepharia sunk her face into her hands. Polyxena patted her back. The crowd cheered with vigor, probably for the well-loved Dracis as he crossed the finish line. The nobles hooted like commoners and a fateful dread sunk into her bones.

Suddenly, the Parthian Prince was in her face. Fingers dug into her arm and sour wine-soaked breath washed over her. He grimaced, almost as if he was in pain.

"It doesn't matter," he said forcefully, spittle flinging from his lips. "I'll have you eventually, in any way I desire. Or maybe I'll make you my wife as a part of the deal with the Satrap. Then you'll be mine as long as I want."

Prince Vima marched down the stone steps, his companions following close behind, glancing in her direction. Their glances felt like burning whips across the face.

Sepharia spun and looked down to the track. Dracis' chariot was dead on the track only a length away from the finish line. Apis rode victoriously around the track with his stubby arm raised.

"I won," she whispered to herself, "I think."

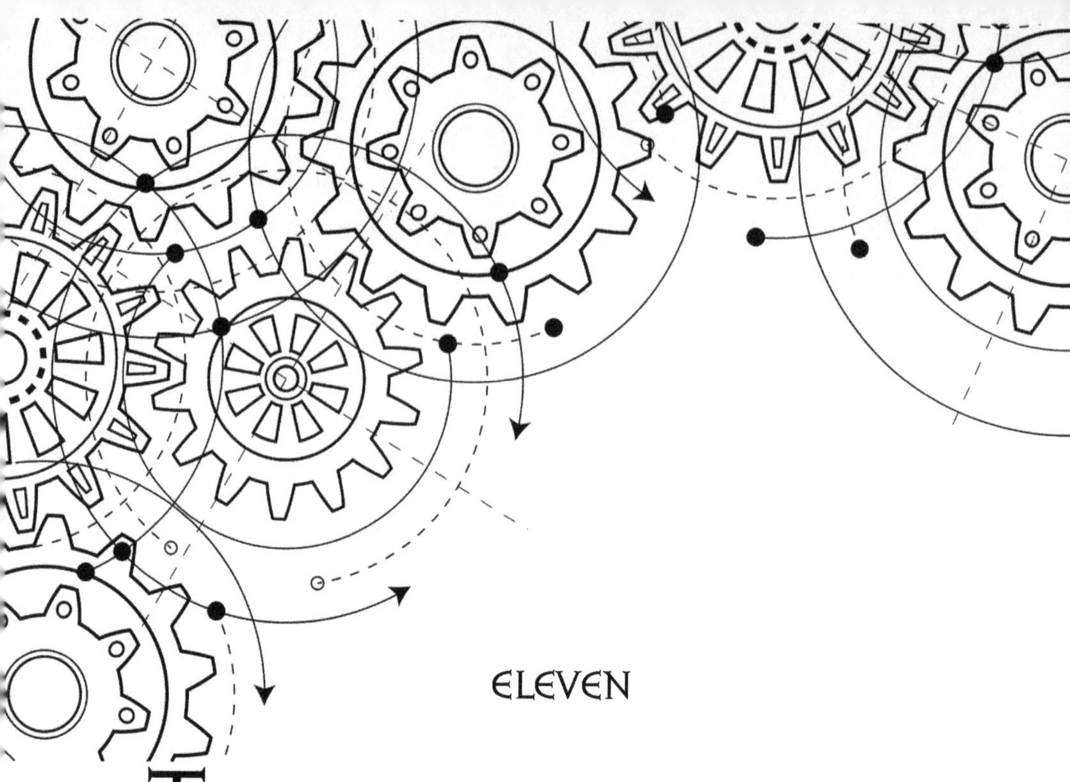

ELEVEN

The sun shone brightly against the white stones of Memphis. Their horses sauntered through the city. Bronze-skinned children often pointed at the Northman before skittering away. Old women beat the dust from colorful rugs, eyeing them lazily as they went about their tasks.

"This city is nothing but old women and children," said Jarngard. "Had they a plague on their men?"

"No," said Heron. "The men are at the temples. It's a city of priests these days."

"Was it always?" he asked.

Heron patted the neck of her mount. "No. This is an ancient city. Ancient even before Old Babylon rose and fell. Once it was the capitol of the pharaohs and maybe the center of the world. It's an old and proud and bitter place. Dangerous in its own way. If you noticed when we reached the edge of the city, there were no walls. A city with the might of Memphis did not need them."

Heron paused, enjoying the easy sway of the horse and attentiveness of the Northman. He was markedly different than Hoth and his waters ran deep. He nodded occasionally to let her know he was listening but otherwise seemed to be inwardly considering the implications of her words. She took a drink and continued speaking, "The pharaohs ruled for millennia. The city's many names tell the tale of its history. Djed-Sut, the Everlasting Palace. Mennefer, Enduring and Beautiful. Ankh-Tawy, Life of the Two Lands. Hut-ka-Ptah, Enclosure of the ka of Ptah. Others called it the Fortress of the White Walls. The white walls they speak of are from the Temple of Ptah. Our destination."

Jarngard put his hand to the leather bag around his neck, bringing a quiet smile to Heron's lips. She could see deep scars in the man, but not how they came to pass.

"This Ptah. Will you be able to petition him to build your pyramid? For now that I have laid my eyes on them, I cannot believe that they were made by the hands of man."

"Ptah is the patron of craftsmen. The god of creation. It was his priests that oversaw the construction of the pyramids. If anyone can understand the mysteries of their creation, it's these men," said Heron.

She pointed to a painted statue on the next street over. "There is the god Ptah." The legs were mummified and the skin faded green. The statue of Ptah held an upright staff. On the tip of the staff, the symbols for *ankh*, *djed*, and *was* were combined. Heron noted the wear on the statue and the dullness of its colors.

"He has other guises," she continued, "but that is most common. The mummified man with the green skin."

"His skin does not look green any longer. Maybe a dusty white," mused Jarngard.

"Yes," she said. "I see it too. There's a rot on these walls and buildings. This city has seen better days."

"Let's hope there's not a rot in your priests." Heron nodded and they rode on.

Later, Jarngard took a long draw from his water pouch. "Does this city never end? We've been riding through it since daybreak."

"We near our destination. Beyond those necropolis and sacred tombs, we'll find the temple," she said.

Over the next hill, they reined in their horses and observed the endless walls of the Great Temple of Ptah. A colossal statue of the pharaoh Ramses, large enough to ride a horse between its legs and not duck, guarded the road leading to the temple. Further down, a trio of priests chanted at a stone sphinx. The entranceway was guarded by bronze statues at least a third the height of the Ramses statue.

"They should call it Fortress of the Gray Walls now," said Jarngard.

"Quietly, Northman," she said. "We don't want to anger them."

He shrugged. "I see no priests nor guards that make me worry. This city is dying."

She could not deny his words. Ignore as she tried, the evidence of a city in decline was plain to see. The statue of Ramses seemed to lean forward and Heron estimated it might fall in the coming years.

"Leave your horse, we'll walk from here," said Heron.

"No worries for thieves?"

Heron tied a rope to a nearby tree. "Not so near the temple. We are being watched, anyway. They can watch our mounts as well."

Jarngard hesitated, putting his hand to his forehead and squinting into the distance. "We passed those pyramids this morning, and still they fill the horizon. This city makes me feel like a grain of sand on a beach."

"That is why they needed no walls," said Heron. "The power of their creations dulled men to passivity."

"Until your city of wonders came along," said Jarngard.

Heron shushed him. "Bridle your tongue. The rise of Alexandria began the slow decline of Memphis. The priests still remember. I hope my service to their temple still holds water, but we must tread carefully."

At the great gate, a bald priest greeted them. His beard was wrapped in gold wire and extended from his chin the length of a hand. His eyes were painted, dark, and merciless. The priest appeared as hospitable as a river full of crocodiles.

"Heron of Alexandria," said the bald priest in halting Greek, "have you finally come to beg forgiveness to the almighty Ptah?"

Heron kept her movements deliberate and bowed her head. "Priest Hotep. The white walls of your temple fill me with inspiration and though I labor far from here, I labor in the service of the god of creation."

Though the priest was only as tall as Heron and considerably shorter than Jarngard, he looked down upon the both of them. "If that was so then the temple of Ptah in Alexandria would be a grand place full of miracles, automata dancing his praises, and new works christened in his name at every season. The only god you seem to serve these days is that fat Northman."

The priest squinted at Jarngard, the skin of his nose wrinkling up like a dog bearing its teeth. Heron tensed, holding her breath tightly in her chest.

Jarngard kept his face neutral as if the priest had said nothing. The priest snorted disappointedly when he realized the Northman could not be rattled. A litany of retorts ran through her head, spoken in Hoth's voice. Heron was very glad that Hoth the Black sailed the seas and it was Jarngard by her side.

She cleared her throat gently to draw the priests attention back to her. "Good Hotep, door warden of the temple of Ptah, I have served this temple before, providing automata for your great hall. I come to ask a small favor, a question of building that only the wise priests of Ptah can answer."

Hotep made a noise somewhere between contempt and disgust. "If it were up to me, I would bar you from these halls, but the circle has spoken and you are to be allowed in." He held up a stiff finger. "We promise no answers."

She moved to follow when Hotep held up his hand. "The barbarian may not enter. He must return beyond the statue of Ramses. These Northmen do not create, only destroy. They are not welcome."

Jarngard gave her a look which she interpreted as a check on her safety. She gave him a nod and he left the white stone gate. Hotep seemed disappointed by Jarngard's easy departure. She guessed he was looking for a reason to refuse her entry.

The priest led her through the temple, which she believed was as big as the Rhakotis District in Alexandria. Past the entrance, a wide hall filled with numerous brightly painted pylons made her dizzy with color, even faded and worn as they were. A bronze Apis bull, the embodiment of the god Ptah, hunched in front of the next doorway looking ready to charge. Guards with ceremonial swords squinted questioningly at her, even after Hotep waved his hand, gesturing that she was to be let through. It was clear to her that foreigners were not typical. A cloud of incense created a light haze amid the hieroglyphics etched into the upper stoneworks. Distant voices chanting echoed from hallways they crossed. Heron got the sense of endless rooms.

A short distance away, there was a strange statue. A man with a missing hand and leg. The stone was worn with age and the features of the man appeared smoothed. The statue's appearance and odd location made her realize it was older than the temple itself. But as knowledgeable as she was on the comings and goings of the gods, she did not recognize this statue. Heron found herself standing before it and as she reached out to touch it, a brief shock traveled up her arm, keeping her fingers away. Hotep cleared his throat, a clear reproach for her wandering and he led her back onto the path.

Hotep stopped at a stone arch and motioned her through. Heron expected him to follow, but he spoke to her back. "Let them show you the way back or find it yourself, either way, I care not."

His angry, shuffling footsteps receded and Heron found herself in a scroll room. It was similar size to one in the Great Library. A deep, melodic voice called to her from behind the racks.

"Heron of Alexandria, it is an honor to have your busy hands within the Great Temple of Ptah." The priest appeared from between the racks. He was a short, chubby man in a simple tunic without a trace of jewelry. His pleasant smile was one she expected to see on an innkeeper, not a priest.

He laughed lightly. "I am not what you thought I would look like, eh? It is not uncommon, though I meet new faces less often these days. The temple is a dusty, unused place." His eyes widened slightly as she opened her mouth. "My name? Yes, you would want that. Most here call me the Keeper of Records, or the Keeper, but I see you are a less formal man. I was called Xan-Ra when I was a young priest here, or Little Ra by my friends when I roamed the streets throwing dirt clods at young girls. Now, the Ra of my name seems unwieldy, and overwrought, so Xan will do."

"Greetings, Xan, it is an honor to walk beneath your halls," she said.

"The honor is all ours. The temple has become stiff and unyielding. Our priests craft nothing and do nothing but guard the relics of history, arguing about who was the greatest of our craftsmen." Xan sighed heavily. "If it were not for my oaths and the burden of the scrolls, I would sorely love to visit your city."

"We could make it an official visit. A trade of scrolls, perhaps? The Great Library thirsts for knowledge."

His hand hovered over a scroll rack. His eyes sparkled with thought.

"Let us speak of other things, lest I grow maudlin. The temple does not look fondly on your Great Library." The crease of his smile was sad.

"Might we speak of the labors of your ancients, then?" Heron asked hopefully.

"You wish to know about our pyramids and how they came to be built," said Xan.

"And more," said Heron. "I offer my hand in collaboration. I seek to build a great pyramid near Alexandria. It would be a monument of Egyptian power as we ready to ward off the Romans. It would be right to build such a wonder with the good priests of Ptah at my side. The knowledge of the Egyptian ancients combined with the science of Alexandria."

His eyes grew hard and hope drained from her. "The building of pyramids is strictly forbidden by the temple. The last one was built by Aperanat over fifteen hundred years ago and they will not be built again until Egypt rises."

Earlier, the tone of his voice had seemed buoyant. Now his words seemed as dry and brittle as the papyrus scrolls stacked on the racks.

"Alexandria is Egypt. Egypt is Alexandria. Egypt rises and the Great Temple of Ptah should rise with it," she said.

"The circle has spoken through me," said Xan, "and there is nothing more to be said. If you have another question, I might be able to answer it, unless it involves the pyramids."

Heron blew a hot breath out her nostrils. "Then why did you bring me all the way here, if you were going to deny my request? If the circle has spoken then you already guessed at my request before I arrived."

A flicker of emotion crossed Xan's face. She sensed he was holding something back. "It was my curiosity that brought you here." He squinted at her, trying to convey a message. "I wanted to see the fabled Machine Man with my eyes."

She could not fathom what he was trying to say. "Well, now you have seen me. If you cannot help, then I am done here. I will build my pyramid in my own way." The words came out more forcefully than she had planned. She did not want to antagonize the temple.

"A guard will show you out." Xan clapped his hands. A guard appeared from behind a wall. Xan turned his back and returned to the rows of scrolls.

The guard pushed her shoulder insistently. "I'm going."

Heron walked back through the temple, barely noticing the colorful details she saw on the way in. Her mind was trying to decipher what Xan was trying to tell her. He'd been so friendly at first, almost fawning, but mention of the pyramids had turned him resolute.

Ejected from the temple, Heron found Jarngard on the hill, chewing a piece of grass. His mischievous smile brought warmth to her face.

"Gah, you Northmen are all the same."

His eyebrow rose. "That's no way to talk to a treasured companion. How was your visit? It seemed quite short."

"A waste," she said dejectedly. "They rot in their stone walls. And I am in no mood for banter."

"Banter?" Jarngard chuckled. "Don't confuse me with Hoth. He runs his mouth like a delator."

"Delator? You've stretched the boundaries of your Latin." She squinted at him. "Why are you so smug? Did something happen while I was in the temple?"

Jarngard spit out the piece of grass. "Maybe."

She squinted at him. "What?"

"An Egyptian boy came up here to sell me worthless trinkets," he said. "After I ran him off, I found he'd dropped this piece of papyrus."

Jarngard patted the ground next to him. He handed her the chunky parchment. The Temple's papyrus was not well made and the grains of the paper smudged the neat lines of the hieroglyphics. Heron was not well versed in the written language of the Egyptians, but she knew enough from her studies in the Great Library.

Once she translated the symbols, Xan's cagey behavior became transparent. He disagreed with the temple elders, but could not voice his opinion because there were listeners nearby.

"What does it mean?" asked Jarngard.

"We're to meet him in the Temple of Sobek on the western edge of the city at the dark of the moon."

TWELVE

inding the temple took them until late evening when the moon teetered on the edge of the horizon. Memphis was filled with temples and its boundaries stretched for leagues. The area around the temple had been abandoned for years. It was built on a reedy pond. Insects tickled her ear. They left the horses in an alleyway.

"I've seen bigger temples worshiping a goat's ass," said Jarngard.

"The crocodile god Sobek is not well loved in Memphis. You have to go further south to Arsinoe to find its priests."

Jarngard snorted. "Why follow such a horrific beast? We do not worship bears in the north even though they're deadly killers."

Heron glanced over the short wall into the temple commons. The pond was nothing more than an overgrown puddle, mostly mud. The reeds had become choked and half-dead.

"The Nile is the giver of life in Egypt and the crocodile guards its waters. Any Egyptian who lives on the river fears the crocodile. Some even consider Sobek to be the god of creation because he crawled out of the waters of eternity first and this is why he's fallen out of favor in Memphis."

Jarngard glanced around, keeping his hand to his hilt. "Where is this priest of yours? Are you sure we can trust him?"

"I'm not a good judge of people," she admitted, "but he seemed honest enough. I could sense a real dissatisfaction with his temple."

"He could be playing on your expectations." The Northman slid his sword out of its sheath halfway. "It's much too quiet, too secluded here. A great place for an ambush."

A small splash came from the pond. The tips of the reeds wavered in the dwindling moonlight. The night air brought gooseflesh to her skin. She rubbed her forearms reflexively and thought about retrieving her ivory cane from its niche on the saddle.

"Why would a priest of Ptah meet us at a temple of his rival?" asked Jarngard.

"They may not be rivals. The religions of Egypt are unlike most others. Their gods have been worshiped for thousands of years and in that time their roles have changed numerous times. The city of Arsinoe, also called Crocodopolis, is known for the Labyrinth, a structure that Herodotus said rivaled the pyramids though I have not laid my eyes upon its intricate walls. For a time, it seemed the god of crafting labored in Arsinoe, or that's how their priests see it."

"A Labyrinth?" asked Jarngard. "I'm not familiar with this word."

"Like a maze, but not intended to confuse." Heron smiled fondly as moonlight faded, remembering the maze beneath the Temple of Alexandria.

"So not like a scholar," said Jarngard.

Heron did not reward him with a smile though his quip humored her. She went on explaining, "The Labyrinth contained the bones of kings and sacred crocodiles. Herodotus described the place as baffling in its endless passages and galleries and courtyards."

"Then like a scho—"

The half pulled sword revealed itself to the moonlight as Jarngard spun about. There was a shuffling of feet from the next building over.

A voice called out, "I have seen the Labyrinth and it *is* quite astonishing."

A man in a worker's tunic and cloak appeared. He flipped his hood back. It was Xan, the Keeper of Records. His smiling eyes studied Jarngard.

"So this is a man of the North," said Xan. "Are you all this big?"

Jarngard chuckled lightly, shoving the glinting blade back into his sheath. "Bigger and meaner. A few too many of our ancestors got drunk enough to sleep with a giantess."

Xan squinted, as if he didn't believe Jarngard. "Hrmph."

"I gather you risk much in coming to meet us," said Heron. "We should not argue the dangers of drinking in the North while your absence may bring trouble for you."

"Well said. It is true that there is more danger than you might have guessed in your visit," said Xan. "Some of the circle argued that we should sacrifice you to the bull god, so that Alexandria would not have its favored son and that we might steal your magics through your blood."

A shiver went down her spine. She had not realized how perilous her visit was. "I assume I should thank you for being a voice for the other side."

"That and reason. Some argued that killing a maker such as yourself might anger Ptah and bring destruction upon the temple," said Xan. "And while the immediate danger has passed, know that some like the door warden Hotep, might act alone. Keep a wary eye while you travel around Memphis."

"A strange reasoning in this temple of yours, but I will take the advice. We leave Memphis this night," said Heron. "Speak quickly, then."

The moon had fallen below the horizon and distant clouds reflected light. Everything was shaded in silver. A night animal cried in the distance.

"I came for two reasons," said Xan. "The first was to warn you not to come to the temple again, for reasons I have already given. They may not make the same decision the next time. The second is to give you this scroll."

He handed it over. She tucked it into her cloak. The light was not strong enough to read by.

"Unfortunately," Xan continued, "it does not tell you what you came to Memphis for, the method of constructing the pyramids."

"And why not?" she asked.

The priest seemed to wrestle with internal thought. "Because the Temple of Ptah lost the knowledge."

There were many things that Heron expected Xan to say, but this was not one of them. Pyramid building was the greatest of the Egyptian technologies.

"Yes, I see the same thoughts on your face as when I learned this," said Xan. "How could we lose it? The truth is lost to the ages, but I believe it was purposefully done by the last builders. The records seem too neatly culled. I've even investigated the areas around the pyramids. There are no signs of the villages that had to exist to help build them. This is another reason why the Temple of Ptah was not happy to welcome you to its walls. This is a secret that burns in the heart of the temple. The greatest labors of our people and no one knows how they are done."

"But why not try?" asked Heron. "The Romans have built massive structures since then. The Coliseum. Aqueduct structures spanning great distances. The world has changed. There are newer technologies."

"They are afraid to fail. Failure would bring shame to Ptah and further lessen the importance of Memphis and its Great Temple," said Xan regretfully.

She touched the papyrus at her side. "Then what is this?"

Xan shrugged. "A fragment. Maybe a clue. It may be nothing, or it might help you with the pyramid. It pained me to give you nothing, so I brought this."

Dogs barking in the distance hushed them to quiet. Flickering torches moved through the streets toward them.

"Someone is coming," said Xan. "Over the wall."

The wall was short enough to hop over. Mud squished onto her sandals. The three of them hunched behind, peering carefully over the edge.

After a couple of minutes, the riders moved close enough for them to hear.

"...that old woman said they were seen riding in this direction."

Heron recognized the voice. Crouched next to her, Xan whispered, "Hotep."

Two priests and five guards, all on horseback, rode into view. Heron heard the rustling of reeds, but was too focused on Hotep to check.

Jarngard held his sword. His lips were pulled back in a grim line.

The horses sauntered to a stop. The torch-bearers held them high. Orangish light cast dreadful shadows across the reedy temple pond. Heron stayed firmly behind the wall and hoped their horses would not be discovered in the nearby alley.

"If they've ridden this far west, they might have just left the city," said the second priest.

"I think not," said Hotep. "They came out here to meet someone and I have my suspicions who."

The second priest made an amused noise. "Care to share your

guess?"

"Not now," said Hotep.

There was a long pause and Heron imagined the guards creeping toward their hiding place. She once again wished to be holding her ivory cane with the hidden dagger.

"We should have killed the Machine Man when we had the chance," said Hotep. "His blood would have been a good offering to Ptah."

"I saw him in the upper gallery," said the second priest. "What a stiff and unremarkable man. It's a wonder that such miracles in Alexandria could be attributed to him. Maybe if we would have cut him, we would have found nothing but iron dust. A Machine Man in total."

Heron's shoulder blades itched in anticipation. She felt like the two priests knew they were hiding behind the wall and were speaking directly to her.

The sounds of horses moved away from them and Heron dared a peek. Hotep and his party were moving north, torch light flickering against abandoned white stone buildings. Once the light had passed well out of range, Heron felt it was safe to speak again.

"Are you in danger, friend Xan?" she asked.

"No more than I was already," he said. "The temple is rife with intrigue. There are factions within factions and I am a part of the minority."

A glimmer of movement caught her eye near the reeds. Something dull and pale in the moonlight.

"I dislike this temple." Heron climbed out and the other two followed.

"We should part ways," said Xan. "I must return to the temple before I am missed and you should range far from Memphis before stopping again."

Jarngard gathered the horses from their hidden location and they left, riding harder than before. The chill night air blew through her tunic. They rode without light, using the remaining reflected moonlight to guide them until it grew so black they were forced to stop. When only the stygian darkness above was their companion on the desert sands, they camped and slept, though Heron slept uneasily as she had dreams of a great crocodile tramping through the darkness, its jaws hanging open and jewels reflecting from its bumpy snout. She woke once from the sound of a desert animal dying and did not sleep again.

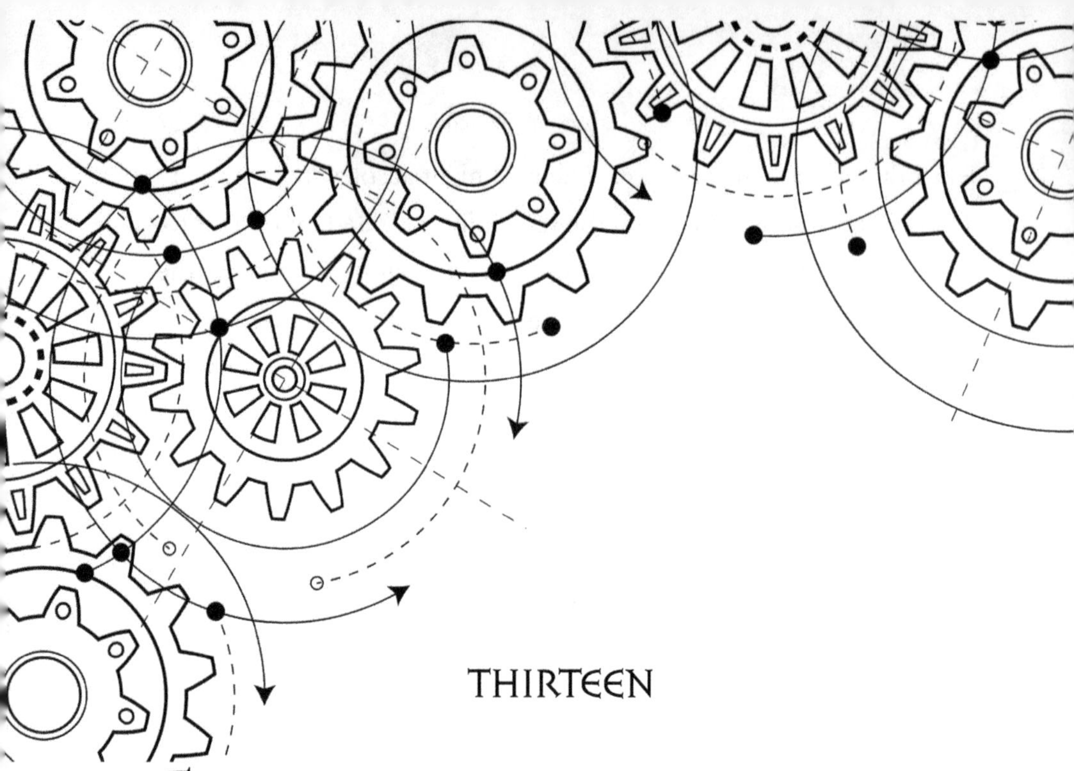

THIRTEEN

Sepharia was sipping spiced tea and eating honey cakes on the balcony when the snakes were dumped into her bed. Mist claimed the harbor and white sails moved through it like pale sharks. Water beaded onto the iron railing, occasionally breaking free and dripping onto the white marble. The stone was cool against her bare feet.

Seeing the city draped in white put Sepharia in an introspective mood. The legends of Cleopatra meant different things to her, now. Before, the queen seemed adventurous, a woman of myths in which every danger was met with a cunning smile. Sepharia's turbulent year, starting with the moment she revealed herself to Lysimachus, the deceptions of the exile Ramses, and now the menace of the Parthian Prince Vima; each of these had taught her that Cleopatra had not been adventurous, but merely surviving.

Sepharia had heard Polyxena enter her apartment. She'd grown used to the Macedonian woman's footsteps. They were patient shuffling, like a priestess dutifully attending to a sacrifice.

She'd expected to have Polyxena join her on the balcony. They ate together often, speaking quietly of the various comings and goings of the Palace. They learned much from the Prince's first wife Zenobia, though Polyxena cautioned Sepharia not to trust the woman too much. The Parthians could end up as enemies of Alexandria and even a beaten woman was bound to her country's fate.

A drawstring unloosed and the heavy slump of weight hit her bed. Sepharia looked over her shoulder to see Polyxena standing next to it, an empty sack in her hands, and movement in the blankets.

Sepharia was about to ask *'Are you mad?'* when she saw the serious glint in Polyxena's eyes. The petite woman wore a simple aqua chiton, accented with gold and turquoise. Sepharia joined her.

The snakes, at least a dozen, slithered listlessly across her bed. They seemed sluggish. Some were greenish and others brown. Polyxena wore her brooch, the one with the sunburst and the snakes.

"I am not a devout of the twice-born, Dionysus," said Sepharia curiously.

Polyxena picked up a long, green snake and stroked its head. The tail wrapped around her arm. Polyxena's blue and green eyes flickered with deep thought. "I do not expect you to join us, though it may serve you to appear so as some practices are quite practical."

"To sleep with snakes?" Sepharia took a step back from the bed as a curious reptile stuck its head from the edge of the blanket.

"It takes some mastering of fear at first though these snakes are quite docile. They're used to sleeping next to my warm body and will not bite, assuming you do not thrash around in bed," said Polyxena. "Pick one up, gently. They've just eaten so are easily handled."

A brown snake with diamond patterns along its back was picking its way through the folds of her blankets. Her face flushed as she thought about grabbing the snake.

"But why?"

Polyxena radiated a serene calmness as she held her snake, looking almost like a goddess carved in lifelike stone. "The snake first and then we talk. If you cannot handle one, then there is no point in relaying my secrets."

The brown snake's head was sticking from a fold. Its tongue tasted the air. Sepharia started to reach her hand, but as it neared the snake, she reflexively jerked it back.

"You sleep with them?" she asked, already knowing the answer.

"Behind every ritual, there is purpose. Pick one up. These are not poisonous and they will not bite unless startled," said Polyxena.

It hurt like an ache in her arm every time she tried to reach forward. "I don't know if I can."

Disappointment leaked out of Polyxena in a quiet sigh. "Then I will take them back."

The way the older woman's eyes creased with sadness spurred Sepharia to action. She grasped the snake by the middle, lifting it from the blankets. The snake undulated, its head reaching up toward her arm.

"Gently, Sepharia," said Polyxena, a faint smile lingering on her lips. "Support the snake and do not grip him so tightly."

The tiny scales of the reptile scrapped against her palm. She put her hand under the snake's head and it seemed to relax, slightly.

"Good. Learning to handle snakes will help you in other endeavors." The Macedonian woman had a secret smile and Sepharia knew better than to ask.

The brown snake slithered onto her arm. Its head bumped against her shoulder.

"Breathe," said Polyxena. "They will be easier to handle if you aren't so tense."

Her chest was tight with fear. She exhaled and refilled her lungs.

The snake seemed to relax and curled its head toward Polyxena, slipping its tiny forked tongue out more slowly now.

"Yes, my baby," said Polyxena, "she'll care for you as I would."

"Does it have a name?"

"No, but you may name them if you'd like. If it helps you handle them," said Polyxena.

"It might help me more if I knew why," Sepharia said.

Polyxena gently set her green snake back onto the bed. It coiled and stuck its head into the blanket.

"A bed full of snakes to protect you from a bigger, more dangerous Viper," said Polyxena.

"But I have a guard at my door," said Sepharia. "The Parthian Prince would not bother me, would he?"

The Prince's words came back to her in the silence after. There was yellowish blotch on her forearm where he'd bruised her. She recalled the way he'd dug his fingers into her arm. She almost rubbed the location, but for the snake perched there.

"Zenobia told me in secret that he plans on visiting you soon, maybe even after he returns from his fasting in the Temple of Zeus. When a man of royalty decides he wants something, no mere guard will stop him."

Sepharia put her hand on the lelathon cabinet near the bed. She pushed the molding and the side opened, revealing a hidden knife. "I keep a knife at the ready. Can I not defend myself?"

"What an intriguing container," said Polyxena. "But no, you cannot think like them. A woman must never appear to be resisting, or *competing*. Our methods must be..." A pause. "What is the name of that cabinet?"

"A lelathon cabinet," said Sepharia.

"Yes, like a lelathon cabinet, what a fitting name. You must appear beautiful, accessible, and useful, but hold hidden dangers. But yours can never be the hand that wields the dagger." Polyxena serenely stroked the snake's head.

"Will the Satrap do anything?" she asked.

"Not if he wants him as a future ally," said Polyxena. "You heard the Prince. He'll base his decision on how much he enjoys his stay in Alexandria. Agog would have me sleep with the Prince if that's what it took."

Sepharia gasped. "Would you do it?"

"I would have no choice," said Polyxena, "but I have been with men like him. I know what he wants and it would not be so bad. But for you, he's not looking for sex, though it'll appear that way. You started a competition with him and bested him at the races. He'll want to best you in bed and he won't be gentle."

Sepharia sat on the corner of the bed, forgetting about the mass of snakes lying there or the one on her arm.

Polyxena spoke quietly, "The Satrap has kept our guest quite entertained these last few weeks with slave battles, steam chariot races, and lion hunts, but he cannot keep him occupied forever. When he comes for you, the snakes will give him pause."

"But he is called The Viper," she said.

"For his quick striking ruthlessness. I doubt he's ever handled a snake before unless it was dead on the end of his sword." Polyxena came to Sepharia and put a hand on her shoulder. "When he comes to your bed, and he will, let him find a bed full of snakes. A man such as him will not know if they are poisonous or not, and to a man like that, a woman who sleeps with snakes is a dangerous creature herself. Let him wonder, let him think that the gods are with you, or that Dionysus himself protects you. Vima is a godly man, he makes offerings at every temple he passes, hoping to catch favor as Alexander did. This trust in the gods will serve you well. Cloak myth around yourself like armor."

She nodded, feeling bolder by the second. "Yes, I can do that. I will cloak myself in myth. Like Cleopatra."

"Good." Polyxena moved to the door. "There is one other thing that you must learn. This lesson you will find more pleasant."

She barely had time to open her mouth to ask when the Kushite princess Bani marched into the room in a translucent gossamer gown. The dark skin of the woman glowed and her eyes sparkled with purpose. She wore a heady perfume that made Sepharia dizzy.

"If Cleopatra is your muse then you should learn all of her arts, especially the ones she used to capture Caesar in her grasp," said Polyxena before leaving.

Bani slyly removed the snake from Sepharia's arm. She grasped her hands and pulled her standing. Electricity trickled up her arms.

"Now you must earn your womanly armor and sword," said Bani. "These weapons will protect you when others fail."

Nimble fingers untied the strings that held her chiton. Her belt was slipped off. The gown clinging to Bani's body slipped around her shoulders, exposing straining nipples.

The Kushite woman kissed her. Warmth flooded her body. Sepharia leaned into her, letting confident arms capture her and pull her gently to the couch.

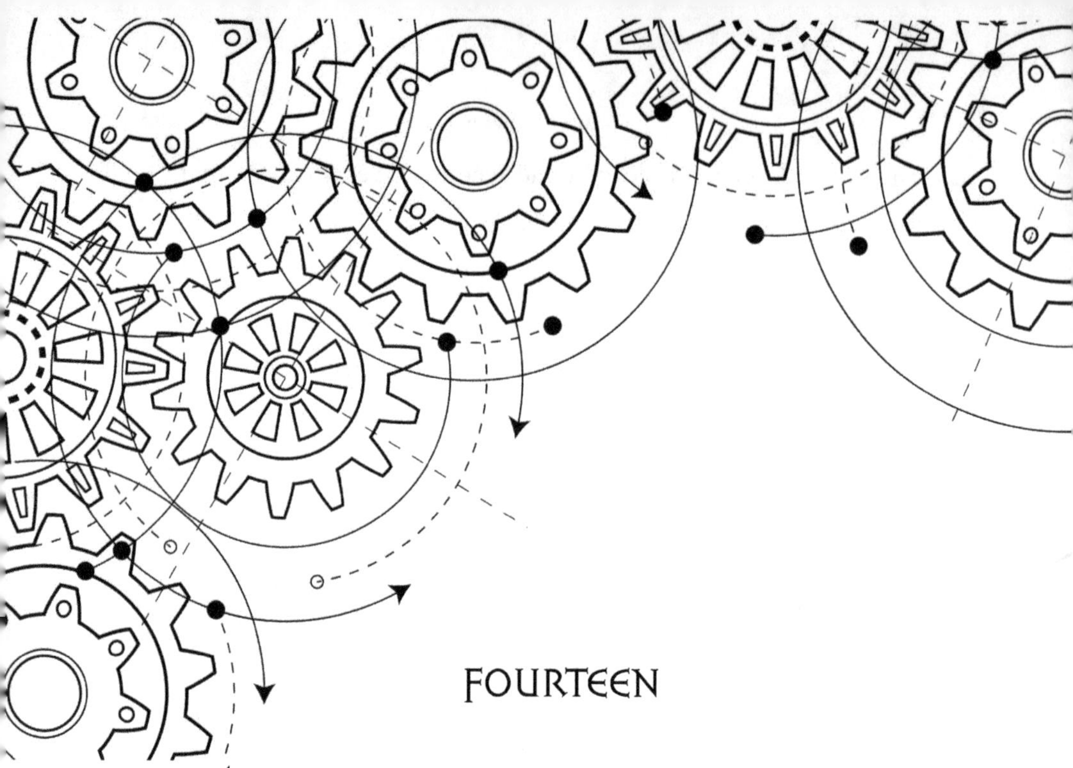

FOURTEEN

"**G**et your back into it! One and two and pull!" Jarngard shouted over the thundering steam mechanicals. Sweat rolled into his eyes as the rough bark ropes in his grip crackled.

The stone block strained against the ropes. Heron hadn't sent enough steam mechanicals to lift the blocks out of the quarry on their own, so the Kushite workers attached secondary ropes and assisted. They formed two long parallel lines.

Ergamenes, the Kushite engineer, was lying on his belly at the edge of the cliff. His back was littered with scars. The story of their origin was unknown to Jarngard.

"It is stuck on a jagged section of rock halfway up the cliff," said Ergamenes. "It will not come any further no matter how much we pull."

Jarngard wanted to curse, but he didn't want the workers to see him worried. He left the ropes and joined Ergamenes.

"Are you sure it's stuck?" he asked.

Ergamenes was nearly unreadable as he slowly blinked. "You can see for yourself. It is stuck."

He ground his teeth and glanced back to the struggling workers. Above him, the pulleys whined with effort.

"How do we get the stone back down?" asked Jarngard.

"In this configuration, the steam mechanicals are only set up to pull, not to let down. If our pullers loose the ropes the mechanicals will get pulled into the pit."

He saw that Ergamenes was right. The men couldn't support the ropes forever.

"Freda's frigid tits, we need that block. We're a week behind schedule and we haven't sent Heron even one tiny stone." Jarngard paced between the cliff and the ropes. It wasn't just the block, Jarngard had been desperate to prove that he deserved to lead the quarry crew. He was a warrior and not trained for construction projects.

The stonecutters had made quick work of the block, but they'd struggled in trying to get the block out of the quarry. He couldn't imagine how they were going to get the blocks to the site, over ten stadia away, when they couldn't even get it out of a hole.

"We need more mechanicals," said Jarngard. "They could pull it up."

Ergamenes shook his head. "More won't work and the men can't hold the block much longer."

"What if we cut the rope and let it fall? I don't want to give up this block, but we can always make more," said Jarngard.

"Only if you cut them all at the same time." Ergamenes was kneeling in the dirt, chalky dust smeared across his belly. "Otherwise whatever is left supporting the stone will be pulled into the quarry."

Jarngard crossed his arms and stared into the pit. The stone was only halfway up the cliff. Ergamenes waited patiently for the new direction, his hands resting on his thighs.

The Kushite engineer had been nothing but helpful. He offered sage advice when asked and pointed out potential problems when they arose. But Jarngard also sensed a distance. The Kushite engineer seemed to be constantly studying him. Jarngard cursed Heron for ever putting him in charge when the Kushite was clearly more qualified.

The decision to bring the stone up today had been Jarngard's. Ergamenes had offered a better design on their pulling mechanisms, a scaffolding that would move the pulleys further out so the block would stay away from the cliff wall as it was lifted, but it would take another week to build properly. They needed iron rods for support and a steam chariot would have to retrieve them from Alexandria.

Jarngard had thought the steam mechanicals, combined with the raw strength of the workers, would be enough to get the block out. He was desperate to send a block to Heron and was paying for his impatience.

Leaning over the edge, he could see the jagged section of rock keeping the block from moving higher. It wasn't much, something even he could break free with the right tools.

A groan from the rope line worried him. They couldn't hold forever, maybe not even another five minutes. If they let go, the steam mechanicals would go with it and that would set them back weeks. Jarngard had sent a request for three more mechanicals, but he didn't know when or if they would arrive.

"What shall we do?" asked Ergamenes.

"Get me a hammer and chisel," said Jarngard.

While Ergamenes retrieved them, Jarngard rubbed his hands in the chalky dirt. He didn't want sweaty palms to cause him to fall on his climb down to the stone.

The tools felt small in his hands. He was used to a sword hilt or shield grip. He tucked them in his belt and started over the edge.

Climbing was careful work. He focused on the handholds and wedging his feet into the cracks in the rock. He'd left his sandals above and used his toes to wedge. Working his way down the wall brought back memories of mountain raids, climbing up cliffs their enemies thought impassable. He remembered surprising a troublesome Gaul village that way.

When Agog's army had arrived, the Gauls catapulted buckets of shit into the ranks from their high mountain fortress. Agog had been furious and ordered his best men to scale the cliff wall at night. Jarngard volunteered. They lost four on the—

A piece of rock broke under his grip. He swung away from the wall, holding on with only one hand. A gnarl of rock cut him under the arm. He jammed his other fist into a hole and pulled himself back. After a few tense moments, he was able to regain his footholds.

He pushed himself against the wall. His knuckles were bleeding. He sucked the wound dry, tasting coppery blood and wiped his hand on his tunic. The blood came back quickly. He had no way to bind it. He would just have to break frequently to keep it dry.

While he was resting his arms, the bark ropes on either side groaned. The block sunk lower.

Ergamenes voice floated down from above, "Hurry! The men are getting weak. If we can't move it soon, they won't have strength left to lift the block."

Ignoring the ache in his hands, Jarngard continued moving downward. Rather than finding the best hold, he reached for the first one available, even when his fingers or toes found little purchase.

As he moved, he realized that if the men failed and let go of the rope, the steam mechanicals would get yanked off their platform and come crashing down on him. He could move out of the ropes, but then he wouldn't have the safety of the stone block beneath him if he fell.

Jarngard checked below. With another couple of handholds, he could jump down onto the stone. He reached his right foot toward an almost non-existent crevice. He jammed his toes in, feeling the stone squeeze around them. His left hand found a perfect piece of rock to grip. He stretched to the left.

When he shifted his weight, the rock in his left hand crumbled. His balance was too spread and he pawed at the cliff as he fell. Terror spread through his limbs as he flew through the air.

He hit the stone block with such force, the air was knocked from his lungs. He heard a crack in his chest and lay stunned for a long moment.

Peeking over the edge of the cliff, Ergamenes waved. "Are you well?"

Jarngard coughed, struggling to his hands and knees. The block shifted slightly knocking him off balance. He probed his side with his fingertips. He'd broken at least one rib, maybe two, on his right side. Swinging the hammer would be difficult and climbing back up impossible.

He reached back to retrieve his tools to find the chisel had slipped out when he fell. Up close, the stone that he needed to break was much larger than it appeared from above.

Grimacing, he shifted the hammer to his left hand and swung. Shards of rock exploded over his legs, hitting him in the chest and forcing him to hold his hand beneath his face. Jarngard carefully removed a sliver of rock from his thigh. Blood trickled from the wound.

He was readying a good curse when the bark ropes screamed and the block shifted. Jarngard reached for the cliff wall. Agony shot through his middle.

"Hurry!" shouted Ergamenes.

"Hurry?" Jarngard muttered to himself. "I am perfectly aware that the gods are laughing at me right now. I could have let this block go over on its own, but no, I had to come down and free it. Why again did I let Heron talk me into such cursed labors?"

Jarngard tore his tunic, freeing a piece of cloth large enough to tie around his eyes. He buried his face into the crook of his injured arm for added protection, despite the pain of his broken ribs.

The first swing of the hammer nearly took his breath away. Between the shards of rock piercing his legs and chest, and the broken ribs, Jarngard wanted to stop, but he knew if he gave in, he might not be able to start again. So he kept swinging, even though every impact of the hammer against stone was a new set of pains.

Before long, it felt like his chest and legs were raw meat. A sharp stone had sliced his chin and he could feel blood dripping liberally from it. He kept swinging. He was certain the bones in his ribs were grinding together. Every swing was a punch in the side.

When he couldn't swing again, Jarngard slumped to his knees. He pulled the cloth from his eyes. The protrusion of stone was smaller. He didn't know if the block could slide past it, but he had no more to give. Jarngard limply waved to Ergamenes.

Jarngard couldn't tell what was happening above. For all he knew, it was too late, and after his efforts he would still ride the stone block to the quarry floor.

Using his good hand, he started picking rock from his chest. He was a bloody mess. The blood was mixed with rock and dirt and his chest was slicked in dark fluid.

The block lurched, sending a knife of pain into his side. Jarngard dropped the hammer and grabbed one of the ropes. He couldn't swing it if he wanted to.

The block pitched to the side. Jarngard tensed against the rope to keep it from throwing him over.

"Careful up there," he muttered, "I'm not riding a stone bull."

On the third lurch, the block finally started to move upward. It immediately came in contact with the now reduced stone protrusion. Jarngard thought he hadn't done enough when the block stopped there.

He was about to spit on it when a piece of the cliff wall broke free and the stone block continued moving upward.

Using the rope, Jarngard pulled himself standing. The stone block sheered the cliff, breaking rocks and dust off and onto him. He spit the dust from his mouth. The edge of the block was ragged with wear. Heron had requested smooth blocks to fit together. They would have to stop the work and build Ergamenes' scaffolding before they brought more stone up.

When it reached the top, Jarngard gingerly stepped off with Ergamenes' help. The Kushite's eyes were wide.

"It looks worse than it is," said Jarngard, speaking through the pain. He limped away from the cliff so they could pull the block onto land.

Jarngard found a bucket of water to clean himself while they finished the work. Ergamenes found him once the stone block was secure.

"I think we'll have to wrap you in one big bandage," said Ergamenes with amusement in his voice.

Jarngard leaned against the wagon. He probed his chest for more imbedded rocks. Smiling weakly he said, "I think I'll listen to your advice next time."

Ergamenes shrugged half-heartedly with that hint of amusement still lurking on his lips. "It is always up to you, I am just your engineer."

"You knew that block would get stuck on the wall," said Jarngard.

"Know? Only the gods know for certain and even that is a question for philosophers. But it was a possibility, yes, one which I informed you of."

The keen eyes of the Kushite engineer studied him. Why did all these men of thinking have such belittling stares? Jarngard felt more comfortable staring down six men with swords rather than one righteous engineer. He felt the same way around Heron.

"You wanted me to fail so I would rely on you more," said Jarngard.

There was no more amusement, only a calculating stare. "I did not want you to die."

"No, that was my hubris. But if I had listened to you, then things would have gone more smoothly."

Ergamenes shrugged. "One never knows. The gods are fickle."

Jarngard paused, wincing as he held back a cough. "The lesson is well received. I'll listen more carefully to your counsel next time."

The corner of Ergamenes' lip tugged upward. "That is always up to you."

Jarngard's knee gave out and he slumped down. Ergamenes moved to catch him. "Start building that scaffolding of yours while I go to my tent and try not to die."

"A wise choice," chuckled Ergamenes, "I'll send a healer to your tent with a wagonload of bandages." He paused, looking Jarngard over. "It is said that the difference between bravery and foolishness is success. I am glad that today you were successful."

When Ergamenes left him to retrieve the healer, Jarngard watched him stride back to the quarry. He could sense the Kushite engineer still didn't trust him and Jarngard wasn't sure he trusted himself after the day, but at least he'd earned the man's respect. It was a start, anyway.

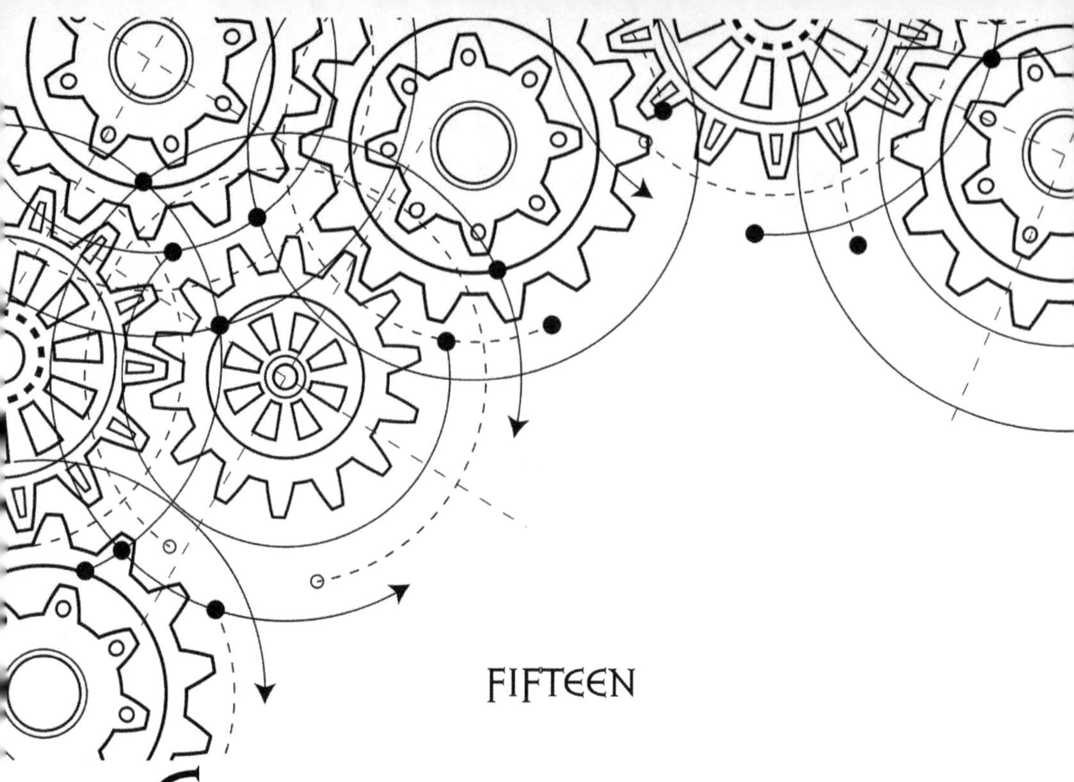

FIFTEEN

Colorful, billowing tents spread across the hardpack like mushrooms after a hard rain. The voices of Kushite workers speaking in their lyrical tongue carried over the snapping cloth, ebbing and flowing with each gust. The dry, sandy air left a layer of dust across Heron's face. Each time she wiped it away, she was sure a new layer formed.

True to her word, Queen Amanitore had sent a huge force of workers to her aid, including a trio of excellent engineers. She'd sent the best one with Jarngard for the mines and kept the others for herself.

She dipped the ladle into the bucket and poured it over her mouth, not caring if it spilled into the dirt. The Kushites had brought herds of cattle and wagons upon wagons of equipment. Many had brought their wives and families.

They'd spent the first few weeks preparing the site. Beyond the tents, ropes outlined the vast square that would form the base of the pyramid. When the requested stones never came, she set to building up her infrastructure. A stone millhouse kept them supplied in fresh bread.

The last word she'd received from Jarngard was that they were delayed waiting for a large enough steam barge to haul the stone block to the site. Heron had resisted every urge to ride west to the quarry and take command of his problems, but if she did, Jarngard would send for help every time there was a minor flare up. And Ergamenes seemed highly competent, though she had only spoken with him briefly. If he couldn't help the Northman, then she doubted she could. It was the same in her workshop. She gave Punt and Plutarch latitude to figure out most problems themselves lest she be mired in details.

Shouts echoed from the north side of the camp. Without significant work, most of the workers had been drinking or playing ball games in the open areas. They were paid by the Queen if they built a pyramid or not, though Heron supposed her sponsor would disappear unless there was progress, both here and back in the workshop on the Colossus.

The hair on the back of her neck tingled. Someone was watching her. Out of the corner of her eye, she caught a glimpse of a brown-faced boy. He disappeared as soon as her eyes had moved in his direction. An orphan or street-beggar, she assumed. While the smaller rats had stayed in Alexandria's sewers, the larger ones, like the boy that had been spying on her, had come to her little camp.

The Kushites were calling the area City-of-Stone-Mountain. Heron wasn't sure if they mocked her since the huge space next to the camp was barren and the camp was hardly a city. She'd picked the site because of the plentiful bedrock and the flatness. There were sections that were uneven, but they were shaving them down using modified plows. The work was slow due to the oxen. A plow pulled by a steam chariot would do the work in a tenth of the time, but she couldn't spare one.

She caught the Egyptian boy spying from a different location a few moments later. His black hair sticking around the edge of the tent gave him away.

"I'm not a machine," she called out, guessing his purpose. "Just flesh and blood."

Even the Kushites had been surprised to find her whole and not made of bronze or iron. Gebel, the second engineer, had grabbed her arm and squeezed when they first met, just to make sure.

She heard the sounds of little feet rapidly retreating. Heron dumped another ladle over her face. She wanted nothing more than to dunk herself in the nearby oasis, but she could never chance being discovered. Baths were wet rags in her tent and even there she didn't feel safe. The Kushites had few notions of privacy and came barging into her tent frequently.

Dust from her hair ran into her eyes along with the water. She'd have to get the foreman Teriqas to move the cattle pens further south so the dust they kicked up didn't descend on the camp, choking everything in it.

The sound of soft footsteps alerted her. "Plato have pity, I'm not a machine. Now go away."

A familiar voice said, "Then I shall take your stone block back to the quarry."

"Plutarch?" she said before she was able to open her eyes. When she saw him, she resisted every urge to throw her arms around him.

He bowed with a flourish. "Greetings. It is I, your savior, here with a very substantial gift."

Heron stood, knocking the dust from her tunic. She gave her trusted foreman a quick once over. "How do you not have a speck of dust upon you? I seem to collect it, along with ample bugs and mites."

His aquamarine toga was fit for a summer party. He gave a mischievous grin. "I gave a proper tithe to the dust gods."

"Dust gods?" She chuckled. "I sorely missed you, my friend."

"The workshop misses you, as well. The Colossus proceeds, but it seems hollow without your presence," he said in a lilting voice.

"The plating?" she asked, inquiring about the clay pots.

"It's magic to my eyes. The gold adheres faster than I would have dreamed." He paused. "Did the Queen not send satisfactory foremen?"

She grinned. "More than, but I am particular to the quirks of the ones I frequently employ."

"Quirks? What are these that you speak of?" He crossed his arms in a surly manner. "I am faultless."

"Enough talk, please tell me you've brought me a stone block," she asked.

The skin around his eyes creased. "No. I have not brought you a stone block, but let us go look anyway."

Her heart wanted to deflate, but she was too tired to bother. "Lead on, then."

"While we walk, you must tell me who thinks you are a machine," he said seriously.

Heron sighed. "The myths around my name grow too large. Every other Kushite that meets me wants to confirm that I'm not made of bronze. I'm afraid some fool might stab me with a spear expecting my flesh to easily repel it. There was an Egyptian boy here a moment ago, I gather trying to get a glimpse of my machineness. And the Kushites, though generous of spirit, treat me as a mechanical, giving me no privacy and thinking I do not sleep and have answers to every problem as if I were an oracle."

Plutarch smirked. "That sounds like the Heron I know."

"Leave your jesting to these supposed gods," she said.

"Careful, these supposed gods feed and clothe us."

Heron cleared her ear with a fingertip, it came back sooty black. "Men with coin feed and clothe us, but I would gladly believe in any god for a luxurious bath. I swear I have dirt and sand in every crevice."

"And for keeping me in the workshop, I thank you," said Plutarch, "though I suppose Punt might like to be here. He collects dirt like a Gaul on a dirt farm."

Heron snickered lightly. "I missed you, Plutarch. I miss all of you. The Kushites work as hard as any man in my workshop and are skillful with hammer and chisel and every other tool, but as I said before, they treat me like a machine."

"Are you not?" Plutarch smiled.

"I feel that way at times and others a slave to my work, even though it is work of my devising. Honestly, Plutarch, there are times that I wonder if something is missing in my life that I go on like this, never stopping and chasing the ghosts of Alexandria's ancestors," said Heron.

Plutarch paused and studied her. She hoped the warmth in her cheeks was hidden by the grime. He seemed to be coming to some thought, and sighed heavily. "Forgive me if I overstep my bounds, but I have never heard you speak as thus, so I suppose it is one of those times we can speak honestly."

Heron glanced around to confirm no one was nearby. They stood in an open area between the tents. The wind pitched through the spaces, blowing hair into her face. She nodded for him to continue.

"I've often wondered why you do not take a wife, or even just a lover. The lies you tell the others about women are obvious to me, though I know the others believe them. But I also know you do not have interest in men, as I. So I've often wondered if you have no desire at all. Maybe you funnel your desire into your work and that is the piece that you believe you are missing," he said.

"I have desire, Plutarch, just no one to share it with," she said.

"As the *Michanikos* of Alexandria, I'm sure you could get any woman you wanted," he said.

Memories of Bani kissing her on the Lighthouse returned. She smiled. "It's more complicated than that. And let us leave it there, I want to see what you've brought me since you failed to bring me one single block."

He narrowed his gaze briefly before smiling. "I will show you. Come."

They cut through the tents. The cheering of the Kushites grew louder and Heron began to realize they weren't playing games as she thought.

A crowd of workers bunched around what appeared to be a low riding steam barge. Heron didn't see them at first because their chalky sides blended into the sky. Lined up behind the steam mechanical was a train of six blocks.

"I did not bring just one single block," said Plutarch.

Heron clapped her hands, ignoring the puff of dust as they impacted. "I feel refreshed already! Why did not Jarngard come?"

"The quarry miners were making great progress and he wanted to bury you in blocks. The steam barge can pull six at a time and make multiple trips a day," he said.

She inspected the barge. The iron-reinforced platforms had multiple sets of small wheels on either side. The weight would be distributed across each one.

Plutarch explained as she circled the craft. "If the ground wasn't so flat between here and the mine, this would never work, the wheels won't go over bumps bigger than a small rock, but the wind keeps the way clear and the mechanical should make quick deliveries."

"You are the best foreman the city of Alexandria has ever known," she said. "My apologies, Plutarch, for not heaping gold on you regularly for your excellent work."

"It is not gold that excites me," he said impishly.

"Well said," she laughed.

"Jarngard sent me a message," said Plutarch. "He wanted to know how many blocks your pyramid would need."

"Just tell him on your way back to keep sending them," she said. "I'll let him know when we get close."

Plutarch tilted his head. "Won't Agog need him when the Romans move to attack?"

"Not until after next summer, I understand, and I hope by then, Agog has persuaded the Parthian Prince to join his side. With the might of his Empire, Alexandria may not need go to war," she said hopefully, though that hope fled as Plutarch glanced away.

"What, friend? What has happened? Has the Prince aligned against us?" she asked.

"Not yet," he said, "but the Prince bleeds us for entertainment, mocking Alexandrians in his games and hunts, withholding his support unless he has been properly and sadistically amused."

"And the Satrap allows this?" As soon as she said the words, she knew the answer. Agog would do anything to keep his empire. Plutarch nodded.

She dreaded her next question, "And Sepharia, how is she?"

Plutarch stared at his feet. Her heart raced to full.

"She bested Vima on a bet on the races," he said.

The implications were clear to Heron. She stared regretfully to the north in the direction of Alexandria. There were distant clouds and the air was dusty, or she might have seen the red glow of the Lighthouse on the horizon.

"Be careful, Sepharia," she whispered.

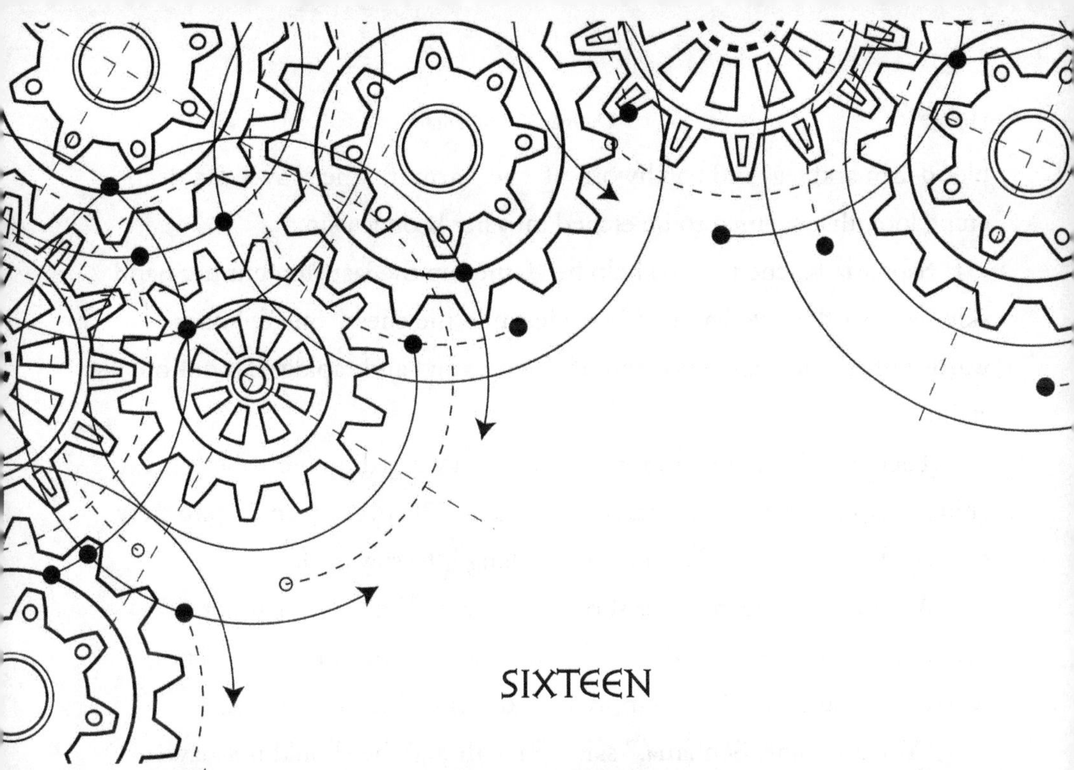

SIXTEEN

Sepharia stood at the apex of a golden pyramid that scraped the sky. Grasping winds turned her robes into crimson streamers. Distant lands could be seen as districts in the surrounding city. Armies the size of ants marched across winding roads. The dream felt impossibly real, as vivid and stark as running her finger across the edge of a blade.

Black clouds hung over the white city below. *Her city*, she thought, and though she could not see inside their walls, she could feel the industry within, like seeing an ant mound and knowing the labors going on beneath the surface. The hazy black clouds spread east and west and north and south, growing as the fires in the endless workshops blistered and sparked.

There was a clacking coming up the side of the pyramid. Bronze limbs moving with machine-like efficiency, glimmering in the summer air. An automata with a human head.

When it got closer, she gasped, "Heron."

Sepharia unconsciously took a step away. Heron had one flesh and blood arm and leg, and patchwork of chest armor. She scowled, a deepening look that seemed to be etched into her bronze skin.

Sepharia reached out to help her father up the last step but her hand skipped past the pale hand and hit Heron in the chest. She fell backwards hitting the angled portion of the pyramid and rapidly slid out of sight.

There was little time to react. The wind yanked on her robes, threatening to rip them away and leave her naked. The eyes of an empire were on her. Sepharia swiped at the wind, telling it to stay back.

A cold hand touched her shoulder. Prince Vima stood at her side, his face, holed through with rot. He leaned forward to kiss her. The scarred lips became a black empty hole devoid of teeth or tongue.

"You are mine, Sepharia," said Vima, though he should not have been able to speak with no tongue.

She tried to scream or push him away, but her arms were leaden. Vima leaned closer. Fetid breath gagged her. She...

—snapped awake in bed.

There was someone in her room. He stood near her bed just past the corner post. His face was hidden by the gauzy embroidered cloth that hung from the canopy, but she knew him by his tall, lean frame. She'd seen him throwing spears from his steam chariot too many times.

"Sepharia," whispered Vima, her name a promise threaded through with intent.

She kept her eyes half-lidded, in case he hadn't seen her wake. Her arms were folded across her chest. The feeling had fled from them. Sepharia was sure that if she tried to run from the room, her legs would crumple when she tried to get up. Vima would catch her anyway. She'd seen him running after frightened slaves, eager grin on his lips. She sensed that grin in the dark.

He moved up the bed toward her. The bed was wide and deep and she slept in the center. The nights were cold and she kept the blankets pulled high.

Vima gingerly put his knee on the bed. The way he took care, told her that he thought she was asleep. Her heart was caught in her throat.

Faint shouts came from the window. Her apartment faced the Great Harbor. A new ship must be arriving, drawn by the red glow of the Lighthouse.

The bed barely moved as he put his weight on his knee, balancing himself with outstretched fingers. She wished she slept with a knife at her side, but it was too late. And could she use it? If she killed the Prince, the Parthians would side with the Romans. Her friends and family would surely die.

All her lessons from Bani seemed irrelevant now. She didn't think Vima had come for that slow delicious dance. Otherwise he wouldn't have snuck into her room.

It'd been an Alexandrian guard at her door, not a Northman as usual. He'd probably bribed or threatened the man to let him pass. A worse thought entered her mind. That the Satrap had sanctioned Vima's entrance to her room. It was possible, she realized. His empire was fragile.

Vima pulled away the covers revealing her naked chest. The chill air stiffened her traitorous nipples. He grunted appreciatively.

The Prince leaned over, reaching out a hand toward her belly. Sepharia did everything she could not to react. Once he touched her, she would have to wake, but for now it seemed safer to feign slumber.

His calloused hand rested on her belly. Sepharia allowed herself a faint gasp, as if she was slowly waking. She gradually opened her eyes, steeling herself from grimacing. With his other hand he was fondling himself beneath his tunic. She forced herself to smile.

"I knew you wanted me, you stupid bitch," he said.

Vima grabbed her by the midsection as his other hand closed around her throat. Sepharia gasped for breath. She tried to push him away but he was too strong. His fingernails cut into her neck and her windpipe felt near collapse. Spots formed in her eyes as he pulled her closer, positioning himself between her legs. Sepharia almost preferred to pass out.

He was away in a start, screaming as he went, throwing something back onto the bed as he scrambled off it, nearly falling onto the marble floor. Men came running into the room with swords drawn, bringing light with them.

Sepharia pulled the covers back over her exposed body. Awakened by the commotion, her bedtime companions slithered across the covers. Even the guards seemed repulsed by their presence. Vima gave her a murderous glance and fled the room, his guards following close on his heels.

She stayed in the dark holding the sheet to her chin. The snakes resettled themselves relatively quickly, but she found sleep distant. He'll be back again, she knew. It was only a matter of time.

SEVENTEEN

The one-thousandth block was placed that morning right after the brief dust storm that had swirled through the camp. Heron ended the day's work and gave the workers the next day off. A party was planned in celebration that night. Word was sent to the quarry.

Heron stood on the edge of the vast plain holding a battered papyrus. From a distance, the blocks looked like toys left by a careless god. She'd set one at each corner and the rest in the center. Each block was as tall and wide and long as Heron from outstretched fingertips to toes. The Kushites had thought it a good omen when she'd demonstrated that her body fit the block's dimensions.

"Rest, Machine Man, it is a time of rest," said Gebel, coming up from behind.

"For the workers yes, for you, if you so choose," said Heron, "but I cannot. There are too many questions left unanswered. I must stay ten steps ahead of the workers or this pyramid will fail."

"I know, Machine Man, I know," he said.

The shirtless Gebel stood near the rope boundary, his hand shielding his eyes from the setting sun. He had pale, nearly colorless eyes, and a chipped tooth, third on the right from the middle. He smiled almost ritually, but his eyes always said something different.

"But even the sun needs rest," he said, nodding toward the horizon. "I find solutions usually come when I've stopped thinking about them. A sword pressed too hard against a whetstone will dull the edge."

"I rest every night," she said.

Gebel smirked. "When I wrap my sheet around me and say a prayer to the goddess of dreams, I look through the gap in my tent to see yours. The light always glows with your lantern."

"As I said, and have said before, I must stay ten steps ahead. We are not merely stacking stones. We must carefully build up the pyramid level by level, leaving the path for new stones clear or we will lose our way. I do not want to waste time rebuilding sections we have to tear down."

She crossed her arms hoping that would show him she was done talking about it, but part of her knew that wouldn't do it. His everlasting grin matched his questions. She would have sent him to the quarry to trade with Ergamenes, but Gebel was an excellent machine builder.

Even with the power of the steam mechanical, moving the blocks was unwieldy. Gebel had built a leveler that pushed the blocks together, rolling them into place before dropping them in the exact spot they needed to go. It wouldn't work once they started building the second level, but Gebel claimed he knew how they would maneuver the blocks then.

"Does that scroll you always carry have the answer you seek?" mocked Gebel.

Heron had thought about burning the scroll from the Temple of Ptah more than once. The text was so incomprehensible, she often wondered if Xan had really been working against her, using the scroll to lead her astray. It mostly spoke of honoring the gods and how Ptah had blessed them with the proper tools to construct their pyramids. The words were mostly invocations, barely above the drivel she'd heard a thousand times in the Alexandrian temples as she installed their miracles. The oddest part of the scroll was a middle section filled with what appeared to be an Egyptian love poem. The words were imprinted into her mind, as useless as they were:

> *The four sides of my love, point to the Ra of your heart.*
> *My love is strong, we are as two blocks, cast together.*
> *My heart burns like a volcano mixed with your white lips.*
> *You are twice my heart, one more, one more.*
> *Together we sink in liquid abandon.*
> *Together we rise; stronger, forever Bayuda.*
> *Piece by piece we climb, the heavens beckon onward.*
> *How the gods must be jealous to limit us.*
> *Stern Khufu marks the boundary of the sky and that is not enough.*
> *I will climb higher and steal the secrets from the gods.*
> *But until then, believe I wish no limit to our love.*

The poem seemed utterly useless, despite Xan-Ra's suggestions, but it stayed with her regardless, bubbling up in her mind at awkward times.

"Not the problem laid out before me," sighed Heron, dismissing her thoughts. "The construction of the pyramid progresses, but it carries a traitorous error that will doom it before we can finish the last block."

"You are the Machine Man, can you not consult the gods of gears and sprockets and fix this error?" asked Gebel.

She glanced askew, wondering if he was mocking her. His gaze was earnest though his grin crooked.

"If I am a machine, then why do you encourage me to rest?"

Gebel stared back. "Apologies, I know not the workings of your kind."

Heron sighed and continued, "The error that vexes me is one so small I cannot see it with my eyes. Only when I take a survey of averages on the dimensions of the blocks does the error become clear."

The angle of the setting sun turned the nearby oasis into a brilliant blaze of light. Arms raised to shield the eyes until it passed. Heron retrieved another scroll from her knapsack and handed it to Gebel. He used the remaining light to read her calculations.

After a time, the smile on his lips faded. "The blocks are not square enough. Our stone smiths have failed us."

"No." She shook her head. "Your people are renown for their superior work, but what I ask is impossible for their patient hands. If we toiled at a pyramid half this size, we would not notice the error for another couple of hundred years. But my pyramid will almost be twice as tall as the Great Lighthouse. The interior passages would be misshapen and the outer angles slumped like wet mud. The flatness required of each block lies beyond the capabilities of simple hand work."

"Can you devise a machine that will cut them cleaner?"

She took the scroll from him. "I might ask the same of you. The conundrum rolls around in my head without an answer."

Gebel left when she was done with him.

She stared at the distant blocks. She should have known better than to embark on such a foolish project with such little preparation. At first, constructing the pyramid had felt like Alexander's quest to conquer the world, now it felt they were stalled before they'd even gotten started.

Heron joined the party. Torch light bathed the dusty tents. Laughter flooded the desert. Walking through the people, she was surprised at the number of Alexandrians that had joined her camp.

Drinks and laughter were passed between the party goers as easy coin. Workers bowed as she passed, smiling and sometimes reaching out to touch her. A few women with wine-soaked breath sidled up to her and made promises and invitations that would have lured other men to their tents. Heron politely refused and thanked them.

She wandered aimlessly, carrying a cup of untouched wine, looking for Jarngard. She had not seen him since the first days at the quarry. Both had been too busy to even cross the few miles between the two sites. Most nights, Heron fell onto the cot in her tent after planning the next day's construction. She ached for his easy companionship.

Unlike her workshop, she felt a distance between herself and the pyramid workers. Occasionally she saw familiar faces, sub-foreman or skilled stone workers who she'd spoken with before, but they seemed little interested in speaking with her and knew nothing about the whereabouts of the Northman.

A beautiful Egyptian woman captured her hand as she tried to pass a ring of tents. The woman's toga was nearly translucent and firelight cast seductive shadows across her chest. Heron was struck by a thick, heady scent as the woman leaned close.

"Machine Man, my tent is not far," she said in a strangely accented Greek as she nibbled on Heron's ear, "let me take you inside and prove you are just flesh and bone."

The woman tried to reach under her tunic. Heron fended her off and shrugged away her advances.

"I am not a machine," said Heron, perturbed.

"Prove it." The woman pulled at her arm. "I will sing your graces to the heavens."

"I am filthy from work," said Heron, "you would not want me in your tent."

"Your oils are sweet perfume," replied the woman as she tried to seduce Heron with her eyes.

The seduction felt comical, given the circumstances, and Heron let out a short laugh. The woman recoiled as if struck.

"No man refuse me before," she said, huffing out each word in her strange accent. "Maybe you are machine."

She pressed against Heron again, moving close to kiss. Heron shoved her backwards. The woman fell onto her rear, and let loose a volley of curses in her native tongue.

When she climbed to her feet, she thrust her hip out, stamping her hand on it. Heron resisted every urge to laugh again.

"By the balls of Ptah, you *are* a machine." She retreated into the darkness, away from the tents.

Heron went another way, giving up her quest to find Jarngard. He clearly had not come to the tent city. Heron wiped away the ring of dirt around her neck, wishing for a bath, a real one, not a wet rag that would never truly wash her clean.

She remembered the small oasis that they got their water from. Everyone would be at the party and the oasis was some distance from the camp. If she snuck away, she might have an opportunity for a real bath. Even if some drunken revelers came to the oasis, she would be sure to hear them before they reached it.

Heron jogged to her tent, ignoring the ache in her knees, moved to hurry by the lure of a soothing bath. She grabbed a knapsack and headed to the oasis, curling far away from the party to reach it.

She hopped over the rope line, making her way across the flat, dusty plain. The quartered moon gave her enough light to avoid the scorpions and other night creatures that crept across the hardpack.

In the hollow of the oasis, the air grew cool. A grove of trees sipped at the edge of the water, while the other sides were covered in reeds. Heron left her knapsack in a space between the roots. She carefully tucked the fake wooden genitalia away before folding up her tunic, leaving it on a pile of moss.

She hesitated before wading into the oasis, thinking of crocodiles along the Nile. But this oasis was far from the Nile and she'd seen it many times in the day. The only danger was discovery.

The water slipped around her as she moved forward, its cool caress making her gasp. She sunk neck deep, then further, the water embracing her, breaking the dirt and grime away from her skin.

Heron floated on her back, letting her smallish breasts peek out of the water. The moon cast a delirious silver light upon her and the water around her ears reflected her heartbeat. She let all the frustrations of the day spill into the oasis.

When the clock in her head told her she'd stayed too long, Heron moved to the shallows. Her toes dug into the cool mud. She reached down and pulled out a blackish handful. The hunk smelled of rich earth.

Impishly, Heron lobbed a blob of mud at the shore. It splattered against a slab of rock. She threw another and it clung to the rock next to the first.

She was about to throw a third when something about the mud on the rock gave her pause. She stared for a good long while, wet mud dripping through her fingers, making plopping noises beside her.

The love poem rose up in her mind like a soft wind. It tickled her thoughts as a cloud passed over the moon, covering her in darkness.

A noise from outside the oasis jarred her aware. Men were coming. They sounded drunk and slow. Torch light bobbed in the distance. She had time to dress and escape if she hurried, though part of her wanted to stay in the water and continue staring at the mud. Her revelation would have to wait.

Heron washed her hands in the water and climbed to the shore on the thirsty roots of the trees. She was about to pick up her neatly folded tunic when she heard a noise, the crackling of reeds. This sound was near, just beyond the grove.

A shape melded out of the darkness, stepping onto the mossy soil. She froze, water dripping from her hair. A weapon hung menacingly from the man's hand. She was trapped against the water's edge with no way to sprint past him to escape. She could not see his face, but the cut of his Egyptian style tunic told her enough. The blade rose and Heron prepared to leap into the water.

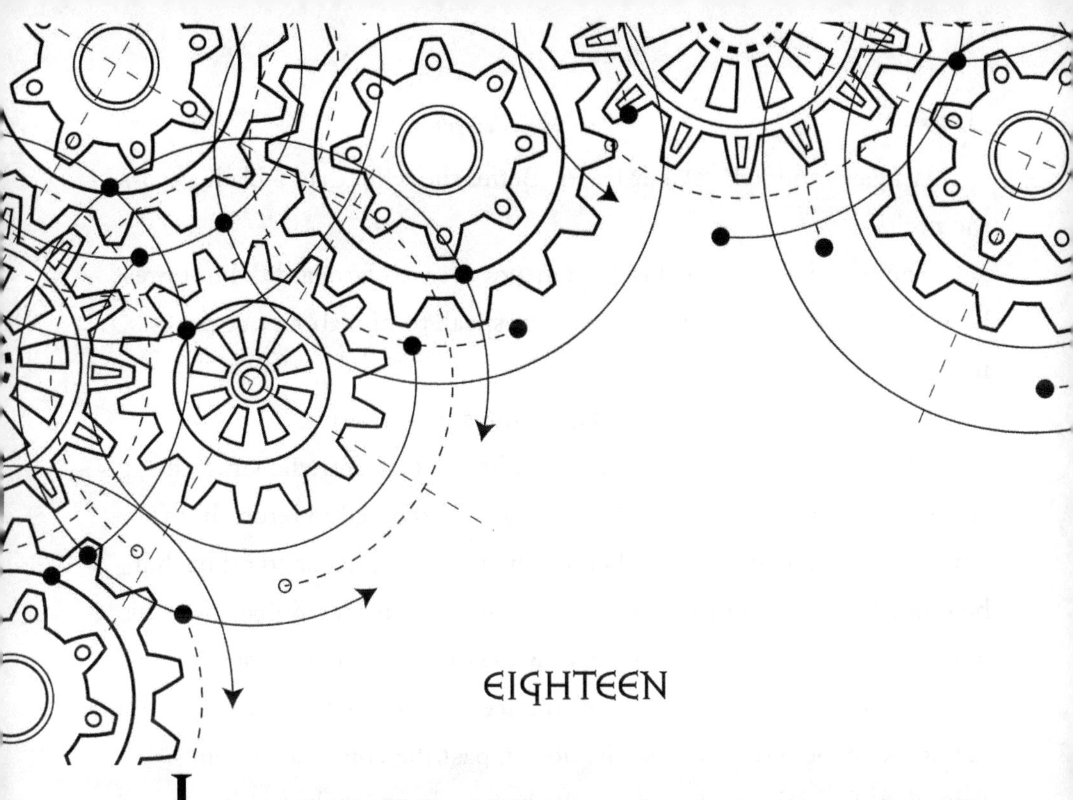

EIGHTEEN

Jarngard arrived at the impromptu celebration late. He joined Ergamenes for a cup of strong wine, gulping it greedily. The Kushite's lustrous dark skin glowed in the fire light.

"Has work with me in the quarry been so troubling that you need to erase the memories?" Ergamenes teased.

"No, friend. Quite the opposite. I fear I have tortured you with my ignorance," said Jarngard.

Ergamenes refilled Jarngard's cup. "Tortured? No, only a light flaying. The men love you, though. I've never inspired such dedication on any of my projects."

"How did you get those scars on your back?" asked Jarngard as the wine soothed his tired limbs.

Ergamenes stared into his cup. His smiling eyes flickered with remorse. "The Queen's men caught me stealing gold from the construction I was in charge of. If I wasn't a valuable engineer, I would have been beheaded."

Jarngard nodded. "A fair trade. Better the whip than a blade across the neck."

The remorse deepened in Ergamenes eyes, so Jarngard did not press him. "Have you seen Heron? I wish to speak to him about our progress."

Ergamenes shrugged. "Probably in his tent working."

Jarngard shared another drink with his friend before he left. The area around Heron's tent was dark. Jarngard prepared to return but for a flash of movement skulking behind the tents. With a hand on his hilt, he moved to the entrance. He saw no one and considered that it was his imagination. He'd had a few cups of wine on an empty stomach.

Before he could leave, he circled once. It was only a flicker, but he saw it. A shape moved across the desert, past the construction lines. Faint light from the moon turned the hardpack into a silvery lake.

Jarngard followed, partially out of curiosity, partially out of concern. He kept low so not to draw attention. Passing the stone blocks that marked the fledgling pyramid, he lost the trail.

The desert was flat and moonlight spread thin. Pulling himself on top of a stone block, Jarngard surveyed the area. He thought he saw movement near the reedy oasis, maybe more than one person if his eyes weren't deceiving him. Sighing, Jarngard glanced to the camp.

He wasn't quite sure what he was doing padding through the desert. He'd only come to see Heron and tell him that he would return to Alexandria soon. The work had been cathartic, but he was a man of war. Ergamenes didn't need him anyway. The Kushite engineer was overqualified for the quarry.

It was early spring. The Roman army wouldn't arrive until the fall, but he knew that Agog could use his talents in training his troops. Especially if they'd allied themselves with the Parthians. Better to crush Rome once and for all rather than bleed it out slowly.

Jarngard climbed from the block and started back toward the camp. Whoever was sneaking through the dark didn't need him following. He made it halfway back to the edge of the tent camp before his stomach ached with concern. He looked back to the oasis. It was a short jog away.

He knew if he didn't go investigate, he'd never be able to enjoy himself. Too many campaigns had bred distrust into his bones. One well placed spy or assassin could unravel the most water-tight plans.

If he hurried, he could make it back to the celebration. He'd seen a number of dark-skinned women he'd like to bed.

The oasis seemed more foreboding up close. He approached from the south. Thick grasses hid the pond. He saw no one.

His shoulder blades tingled with worry. Something in the oasis felt wrong. Standing still, he calmed his beating heart and listened carefully. *Snap.* On the far side, he heard a reed bend just enough to pop.

A cloud passed over the moon. Someone splashed in the center of the pond. A woman rose from the water. She'd been lying on her back and he hadn't seen her. Faint light illuminated her glistening body.

The woman moved to the water's edge, throwing mud onto the shore. The impact echoed in the cool hollow.

The breeze shifted and the sounds of laughing voices drifted over. A group of revelers headed toward the oasis, torches held high and bobbing. Jarngard smiled at the drunken laughter. Maybe when they arrived he would join them. He heard women's voices.

Glancing back, he saw a shape moving around the water's edge toward the woman in the water. She was climbing out, masking the intruder's careful splashing with her own. Sensing danger, Jarngard moved through the reeds as he slid his blade out.

The woman froze. The shape behind her fled. He was about to speak when the moonlight returned, coating the woman's face in silver.

"Heron?" The words left his lips as his mind reeled with confusion. The face was as expected, but below the chin was the body of a woman.

Her naked body dripped with water. She stood silently, fists clenched at her side, brow wracked with concern. The tuft of hair between her legs was unmistakable. Her perky breasts defied his expectations.

He forgot about the sword, half-drawn in his hand. The revelers grew near, voices growing louder by the second.

"I cannot be discovered," Heron pleaded.

He grabbed her hand as she scooped up her knapsack and clothes. They splashed through the shallows and pushed into the thickest section of reeds.

He pushed her down as the torch light flooded into the oasis. The space they'd created in the reeds gave little room for maneuvering. He laid on her, wet skin soaking his tunic.

The workers threw their torches onto the mossy bank and tumbled into the water like laughing children. There were a half-dozen men and an equal number of women. Their dark naked bodies shown in the moonlight.

The revelation that Heron was really a woman hit him. Jarngard thought back to every moment with her. The short hair and man's tunic had fooled him.

Heron maneuvered onto her back, head lying on the knapsack. She covered her chest with a draped arm and lower half with her tunic. Jarngard's leg was draped over hers awkwardly.

She leaned into his ear and whispered, "I have to know, will you keep my secret?"

Jarngard paused. In the North, women had more rights, though they were not the equal of men. The Romans treated women more severely. Even though Agog held Alexandria, the morals of the people had not changed. Revealing her secret would put her in grave danger from both the temples and the nobles.

"I will," he whispered.

"Thank you."

Not far from their location, a couple lay on the muddy shore and made love. The oasis revelers had split off into pairs. Jarngard could not see them, but their eager noises were unmistakable.

Lying on Heron's nearly naked body made him acutely aware of her femininity. Their faces were only inches apart as they listened to the nearby grunting.

He looked down to find she was touching the leather bag around his neck. It was hard to get the image of Heron the man out of his head. Through the reeds, the dappled moonlight played tricks with his mind.

Jarngard was about to speak when she pressed her lips forcefully against his. His mind spun, the two Herons revolving like spinning coins.

She pulled away. "Am I not?"

He felt her soft belly under his callused hand, strong thighs beneath his own, smelled her clean skin. He was slightly intoxicated and his groin ached with need.

He kissed her firmly, cupping her breast and grinding himself onto her leg. She tugged on his hair and matched his intensity.

After a time, they paused to catch their breath. The couple beyond the reeds still grunted, the woman making high wailing noises. Their lust fueled his.

"My horse is back at the camp," he whispered.

They sprinted away from the oasis, ignoring the cries of surprise from the nearby couple. A distance away, she threw on her tunic. They hurried back to the party, silently, avoiding the fire light. Shared glances kept their need taut between them.

Jarngard saddled the horse and she climbed on behind him, holding his midsection and pressing her lips against his neck. The ride back to his tent at the quarry took eons and went by faster than the snap of his fingers.

They tumbled into his tent, Heron pushing him down. Clothes pushed off just enough for frenzied coupling. Heron rode him ferociously, her hips rising and falling like pistons, her breath as steam in the cool night air.

Heron attacked him like she did everything. Her thrusts slapped against his thighs in a perpetual beat. Fingers clawed. When he released, she gave him a brief respite then returned, never resting in her deep moans. Long dark nights in the North were a canvas for endless love-making and Jarngard had stamina to match, but Heron mechanically wore him down.

During the frenzy of grunting and thrusting, Jarngard thought he heard Heron call out, not in moans, but in words. She seemed to be speaking in a thick Greek dialect and he couldn't tell what she was saying and he wasn't sure he cared.

When sleep finally came, the sun shown through the cloth tent. Jarngard lapsed into a deep slumber, feeling as he did after a long battle.

He woke once and saw her sitting at the little table, sketching notes on a stray piece of papyrus. She straddled the table and he was aware of the way her breasts pushed out her tunic. She must wear some binding device that keeps them covered, he realized.

Sometime later, when the sun beat on the desert and he was covered in a light sweat, he woke to an empty tent. He lay on his cot and briefly wondered if his night had been a dream until he noticed deep scratches across his chest.

Sitting outside his tent sipping tepid water he watched Ergamenes ride up. The day had passed into afternoon and men were returning in ones and twos from the little city near the pyramid.

"A good evening, I see?" smiled Ergamenes.

Jarngard touched the tender scratches. "What I can remember."

"'Tis a shame, it looks like it was a good time."

Jarngard sucked on his water pouch. The wetness briefly dispelled the desert in his mouth.

"Are you well enough to ride?" asked the engineer.

"Always."

"Good," said Ergamenes. "Heron wishes to see us as soon as possible. Says he must change our plans, that the blocks aren't working."

Jarngard ran a hand through his hair. Was Heron going to send him back to Alexandria since he knew her secret? Or had she been unhappy with their progress the whole time? Only the day before, Jarngard had been considering returning to Alexandria, but after the previous night, that option seemed less interesting.

He groaned as he stood up, feeling how sore his thighs and hips were. Ergamenes laughed from his horse. Jarngard threw on his tunic and climbed on his mount, suppressing the groans he wanted to make as he stretched his legs. He'd never felt so cursedly sore before.

As they prepared to leave, Ergamenes said, "You know what is rather sad?"

Jarngard raised an eyebrow while he ignored the ache in his groin. "What is that, my friend?" He took a drink from his pouch.

"While we vagrants were having a good time last night, our Heron was in his tent drawing up new plans for us to work from," said Ergamenes. "That poor man works too hard."

Jarngard tried not to spit out his water. He coughed into the crook of his elbow.

When Ergamenes gave him a strange look, Jarngard raised his pouch. "To Heron!"

The Kushite engineer nodded and they pointed their mounts toward the pyramid construction site. The whole ride over, Jarngard wondered how Heron would receive him.

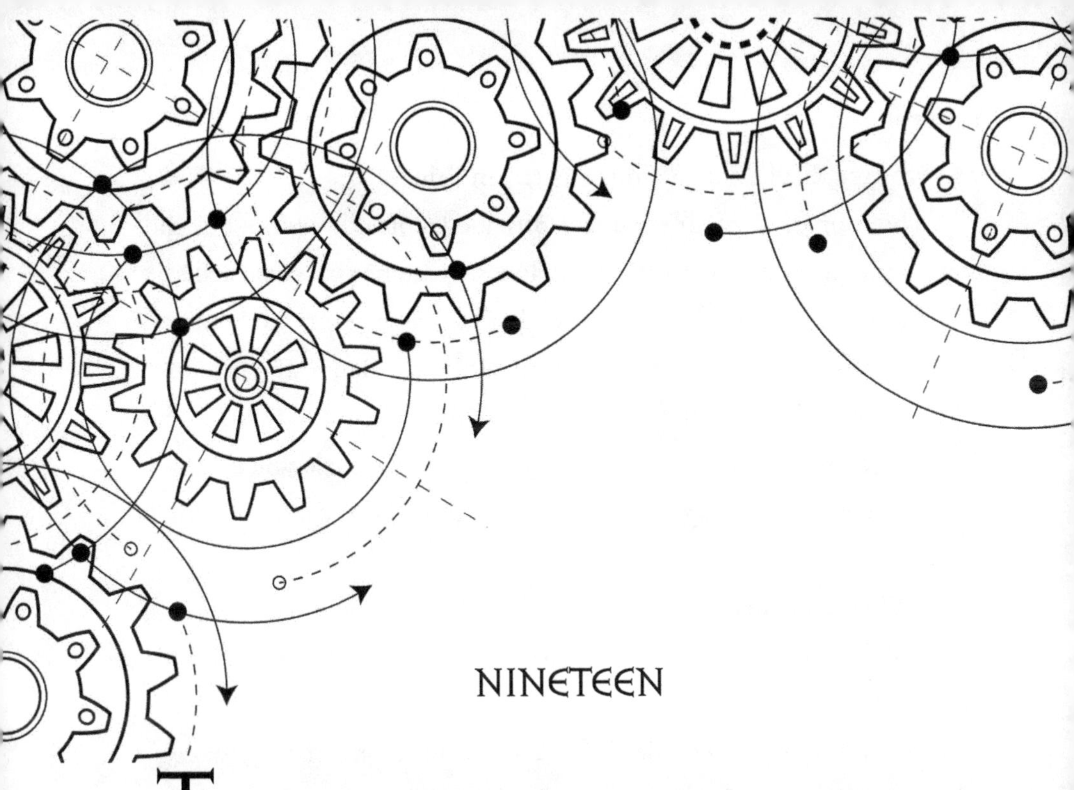

NINETEEN

The eastern breeze brought a mix of building pitch and human sweat. Sepharia could hear the crowds in the Emporium, jostling and bartering for textiles and foods.

Sitting atop the Antirhodos, or Star Chamber, Sepharia surveyed the city. The high stone roof was one of the tallest on the Royal Pier which was above the quartered city. Only the Lighthouse stood taller.

The streets of the city ran straight and true with the wide avenues of Canopic and Transversal crossing in center near the great canal. Sepharia had been disappointed the first time she'd learned about the layout of the city. The structured streets and avenues left no mystery, no sense of wonder. When she was young and learning to read, the tales of Babylon had inspired her imagination. A traveler in the great city could wander for days, stumbling upon hidden bazaars or strange temples. The streets of Alexander were as boring and predictable as Heron's tools.

She pushed the hair back out of her eyes and readied herself to leave. Bani promised a trip to the merchant district as a distraction. It was growing difficult to avoid the Parthian Prince.

The roof of the Star Chamber provided a nice diversion, but she could only sit up on the stone for so long before her backside ached. Bani complained whenever she asked her to massage out the knots.

She was about to move to the iron ladder that led to the balcony when she heard voices drifting up through the hole in the ceiling. Her heart seized with fear when she recognized the first male voice.

"I received a message from your father," said the voice she didn't know.

"What does that dying old man want?" asked Vima.

"He wants to know why you haven't concluded negotiations with the Alexandrians."

She was able to recognize the second man as one of the Prince's advisors. Vonones, if she recalled correctly. A heavy musky perfume drifted up through the hole. She wrinkled her nose in disgust.

"I haven't even started, but don't tell that withered cackle."

Vonones cleared his throat and spoke tenderly, "Prince of Princes, I do not presume to tell you what to do, but your father will become very cross if you do not finish your work here."

"Don't worry Vonones, I won't take out my frustration with my father on you. I understand your difficult position. But if I finish my work, I won't be able to keep myself amused anymore. The Satrap dances to my every wish for fear of me fleeing back to my father without his hand in alliance."

"Thank you, Prince Vima," said Vonones. "I'm humbled by your generosity."

Vima snorted. "Now don't get all simpering on me. You know my feeling on lackeys. I have enough of them. I desire challenge and despite the wondrous inventions of their workshops, these supposed heirs of Alexander have disappointed me so far."

"Does that mean you'll suggest the Romans as allies?"

Sepharia was in a crouched position. Her calves burned but she was afraid to move. She leaned toward the hole to hear the answer.

"Before we left, the counsel I gave my father was to let the Romans and Alexandrians knock each other senseless and then destroy the victor while they're recovering. My father, the weak minded fool, said that would be too risky. He said, why commit our empire to failure when we could ally and choose the winner and our rewards?"

She could hear the Prince as he moved to the balcony. The ladder rattled and for a briefly terrifying moment, she thought he would ascend.

The Prince continued speaking in a hard and earnest manner. "It is not negotiations that I wish but glory. Alexander the Macedonian's name will live in eternity for what he did. No one will remember my name for a well fought negotiation. It's strength of arms and cleverness in battle that the historians remember. Not men like my father."

Though she could not see him, she imagined Vima standing with his hands on the railing, hands gripping the stone tightly above the watery figures carved into each post, staring into the harbor. He was a handsome man, long and lean and hard in all the right places. His nose tilted slightly to the left, probably broken once in battle. If she'd only heard this one speech, she would have been quite moved to love him, or at least lust. But she knew the true man and shivered. He was vain not bold.

"You could still do that," said Vonones. "Ally with one and turn on them both at the height of battle."

Vima chuckled. "I like your thinking, but I have a different idea."

"Will your father approve?"

"In a way, he will, but I have things to plan first."

Vonones responded eagerly, "Shall I ready your entourage to return to Susa?"

"Not yet," said Vima. "I'm not done playing with the Satrap. There are some things I would like to collect before I leave. I do not like to leave challenges unmet."

Sepharia's hands went cold. Her calves screamed in agony so she readjusted before she fell over. The pad of her sandal scuffed against the stone.

"Did you hear something?" asked Vonones.

The iron ladder rattled again. This time Sepharia was sure someone was climbing it. She looked to the lawn beneath the Star Chamber. She was too far to jump. The ladder stopped rattling.

"Nothing," said Vima. "Maybe it was a sea bird."

With a breath caught in her chest, she listened as the two men left the Star Chamber. She waited until she was dizzy before letting it out.

When she finally got the nerve to leave, her hands shook as she climbed the ladder. She crept around corners to make sure they hadn't just moved to the lower level. It was empty.

Sepharia scurried into the hallways, her sandals clicking against the marble stone. She went straight to Bani's chamber, the Prince's words still ringing in her ears.

She swept in, nearly colliding with Bani. The Kushite princess was wearing a robe around her shoulders, but nothing else. Bani collected Sepharia in her arms.

"Sepharia, dearest, are you flush with anticipation? I was just lying on our bed dreaming of you." Bani kissed Sepharia softly.

"Not now," said Sepharia. "We must talk."

Bani pushed away, pouting as she pulled the robe tightly around her. She scooped up a cup and drained it.

"Apologies, Bani. I don't mean to push you away, but I need your help."

"Is my bed not enough?" said Bani sweetly. "A safe place from the Viper."

"It's him I need to speak about. I overheard him in the Star Chamber."

"Spying on him?" Bani raised an eyebrow.

"It was an accident," said Sepharia. "But what I heard was important."

"This isn't like when you first met Polyxena," said Bani, smiling coyly. "Lips say one thing and ears hear another, in bed and in palace politics."

"I know. And I know that you only want my lips to do one thing right now." Sepharia tenderly ran her finger along the curve of Bani's breast. "But please, listen, and when I'm done, you can have my fullest attentions."

Bani stretched a little and moved to the couch. She patted the space next to her playfully. Sepharia joined her and explained everything she'd heard from Vima. Finished, Bani asked a few questions, her demeanor wrought with concern, the robe cinched around her naked body.

"He means to get his revenge," said Bani, tapping on her cup with a fingernail.

"That's what it sounded like to me."

Bani cupped Sepharia's chin in her hand tenderly. She leaned into the caress. "What will you do?"

"I have an idea," said Sepharia. "But it will take time and resources. I have to be ready for whatever he decides to do."

Bani nodded. "Tell me your plans and I will help you make it happen." The Kushite princess grinned deviously. "Remember, I have a whole kingdom at my disposal."

TWENTY

Jarngard hesitated before he followed Ergamenes into the tent. He touched the leather pouch around his neck for guidance. The previous night felt like a distant dream.

He pushed back the double flap and entered. Heron was speaking to Gebel at a wide table. He noticed that he'd, no *she'd* - the gender tripped up in his mind - expanded her tent. Implements and scrolls and inkwells littered the two wide tables. Jarngard nearly tripped over a knapsack filled with blank papyrus. The noise brought a brief, unremarkable glance from Heron.

"...the machine should lift the buckets to the higher levels and be expandable as we build upwards," said Heron.

The papyrus beneath her slender fingertips was filled with notes and random sketchings. An older frayed sheet was pinned down on the top side of the desk. He recognized the Egyptian hieroglyphics. Beside it was a document with the wax seal of the Satrap.

Gebel shook his head, tapping his finger at the calculations on the paper. "I cannot! The weight will be too much. I cannot bring up that much of your mixture that fast."

As Jarngard stared at Heron, part of him found it hard to believe he'd never seen it before, but he also understood. Her delicate wrists did not hang limply like the women of the Palace, sipping cups of watered-down wine. She tapped on the papyrus confidently, demanding excellence from her engineers. Her eyes, brown with flecks of gold, keenly observed the reluctant Gebel. Soft musical words were filled with steel. The parallels to their lovemaking were apparent, bringing heat to his loins. She was a soft, beautiful woman in his tent, and attacked him like a machine with a never-ending supply of fuel.

He was content to stay silent, but Ergamenes, ever the inquisitive one, spoke up, "Tell us your troubles, friends, maybe we can help."

Gebel was not pleased and paced away from the table. Heron let him go, pulling the Egyptian papyrus to the edge. Her gaze flickered to Jarngard, but there was no hint of the previous night. He found it odd that he was disappointed. While it'd been more energetic than even he was used to, he'd slept with countless women before with no expectations of the next day. Usually he was moving on to the next village by then.

"Is that the scroll Xan gave us?" asked Jarngard, suddenly recognizing it.

Heron nodded. "I believe it holds the secret of pyramid building."

He wrinkled his face in confusion. "I thought you said it was an Egyptian love poem?"

"I thought it was until I had a moment of alchemical inspiration last night," she said.

He tried to hide his recognition, but enough came through that Ergamenes glanced curiously at him. He recalled the moment when she was speaking. At the time he'd thought it'd been a result of their lovemaking. And maybe it was.

"What were the fruits of your inspiration?" asked Ergamenes.

"This line," Heron poked the open papyrus, "right here, the ones about 'two blocks, cast together'. It's telling us how to make the pyramid. The documents detailing the construction of the pyramids were destroyed by jealous priests at the temple of Ptah. Someone must have hid the methodology in this poem."

Ergamenes furrowed his brow, frowning. He seemed unconvinced.

"Are you saying the pyramids were poured in place? I don't know if I can agree with that," said Ergamenes.

Heron nodded reluctantly. "I found it hard to believe at first, but it must be true. How else could they get those blocks so square and true? No stonecutter can cut that close and for that many blocks, unless the ancients had knowledge that we don't possess. And pouring them in place makes the materials easier to transport. Expecting them to move such massive blocks without machine help is a feat for the gods and these were just simple men."

Ergamenes clearly couldn't believe what she was saying. Jarngard had to go on faith that Ergamenes' disbelief was well anchored in his knowledge.

She indicated the notes on the second papyrus. "The ratios are correct. Early in my thoughts, I had considered using Roman concrete, but it wouldn't hold up under so much weight. I don't want the center of the structure to crumble from within. And that is where the next part of the poem comes in. Bayuda is a nearby volcano, which must mean volcanic ash."

Heron paused and tapped her chin. "The white lips of the poem confused me until I realized it means quicklime. When miners work a limestone mine, they come out with white, chalky lips. Then the poet gives us the formula: 'you are twice my heart, one more, one more'. The addition of the volcanic ash must make the stone stronger. The water pounded from it when it's drying. A machine can do it efficiently as well as bring the mixture to be poured."

"It seems plausible, but I don't like it. You just want us to crush the limestone and send it as broken stone? What elegance is there in that?" said Ergamenes, disgusted.

Heron patted him on the shoulder. "Don't worry, my friend. There will be ample opportunity to exercise your elegant solutions. My work-shop is secretly building five more steam mechanicals. We'll use them to make this operation efficient, once we figure out the proper machines to utilize."

The engineer Gebel, who'd been pacing in the center of the tent, scoffed. "So easy for you to say. Make a machine to lift blocks. I do. Make another machine to set them in place. I do! Now make a new ma-chine, ignoring all the hard work that Gebel has done, that lifts dust and rock and water hundreds of feet. And make sure you can move it and scale it at a moment's notice!"

Heron chuckled lightly. "Now you're understanding what I want. Don't worry, good Gebel, I will give you time enough to design this ma-chine. A day or two is enough, right?"

Gebel's eyes went wide and he prepared a retort, until he saw Heron smiling mischievously.

"I thought when I volunteered for this crazy project that I would be getting out of any war preparations. I did not want to die." He shook his head as he left the tent. "Maybe I was wrong!"

They shared a laugh after Gebel was gone.

"He's a good engineer," said Heron. "I hope that I do not push him too hard."

"This is not how we do things in Kush," said Ergamenes. "There we are given tasks that do not stray from previous expectations. A slightly bigger statue. A barely longer bridge. These are knowable things. But normally we are tasked by the Queen and she does not know what is possible, only what has been done."

"Only when we accept the impossible can we begin to do real work," said Heron.

"I am listening, but it will take time for my heart to understand. It is a rigid heart, beating time with the drum beats of old," said Ergamenes. "I will go talk to Gebel and help him find his heart. Once he prays to his gods and sleeps, he will see your wisdom."

Heron gave him leave and Jarngard was left with her alone. She glanced at the tent flap before her gaze traveled up his chest to look him in the eyes.

"Impossible things come easily to you," said Jarngard.

"I have no choice," she said softly.

"I see the Satrap has forgiven you." He indicated the sealed letter with his eyes.

Her brow hunched. "Have you read it? The seal is not broken."

"For Agog, if he is not speaking to you, that is your warning that he's unhappy. Once he can speak to you again, no matter the words or the tone, he has forgiven you. I'd wager much on this."

"Your dice?" The dusty wrinkles around her eyes creased.

He touched the bag. "You wouldn't want them. They're cursed."

"The northern or the southern gods?"

Jarngard ignored her. "Are you going to read his missive?"

Heron sighed heavily. "Maybe later. I have other things on my mind. I did not call you here just for talk of the pyramids."

"Oh?"

She wet her lips and pushed a strand of hair from her eyes. Jarngard wondered what she would look like with longer hair. Heron turned slightly and Jarngard stepped forward to see what she was doing.

Turning back, she bumped into him. The awkward recoil made him step away.

"I didn't see you standing there," she said.

"Apologies," he mumbled.

"Here," she said holding a papyrus, "read this. If you can read Greek, that is."

He grabbed the scroll and his hand brushed hers. A tingle went up his arm. Jarngard frowned at it and handed it back.

"Just tell me what it says."

"It's a message from Xan-Ra, the Records Keeper in the Temple of Ptah."

Jarngard nodded. "I remember him. What does it say?"

"A warning. They sent a woman to poison me while I slept, dripping the liquid into my sleeping mouth. He described her quite well. I remember her. She tried to take me to her tent," said Heron, gaze looking into the past.

"Of course, you would not go."

Heron smiled coyly. He resisted the urge to pull her close and kiss her, but he did not want to appear foolish if she rebuked him.

"He said they would try again if this one failed. They fear my construction will tarnish their legacy," said Heron. "But I think they have tarnished their own by doing nothing."

A streak of fierceness came through her words. There was a fire in her eyes, one that seemed to light something within himself.

"I..." He cleared his throat. "Do you need a guard? Should we tell Gebel and Ergamenes?"

"That's why I brought you here. Well, among other things." A deep thought cross her face. "I wanted your counsel. I'm afraid if the Satrap hears this he'll want to drag me back to the safety of Alexandria."

"I could change camps. Stay here as your personal guard," he said.

"I...I'm sure you would like that," she said and when Jarngard frowned, "I would like that as well."

"I hear the 'but' in your words," he said.

"But I cannot be discovered." Her gaze was resolute.

"I don't understand."

She paced away from him, glancing at him two or three times before mustering the words. "I want you. Even right now, I want to strip you down and feel you between my legs. It took all my self control not to tackle you when you came into the tent with Ergamenes."

Her bluntness left him stunned. "Then why should I not protect you?"

Her gaze blazed with need. "Because I want you. I would surely be discovered and I cannot have that. They would take everything from me."

"Agog does not believe as these southerners do. What do you fear?" he asked.

She grew hard and cold. "You do not see it because you're a man. I may pretend to be one, but I still have the eyes and heart of a woman. Think upon your time in Alexandria. How many women have you seen beaten, just for disobeying their husband or father? The city would rebel against him for allowing me to taint them and Rome would use it against us. I cannot be a tool for them."

Jarngard crossed his arms. "What then? Surely the Temple will send more as Xan-Ra says."

"I will keep my eyes and ears open," she said.

"One set of eyes is not enough. Let me tell Ergamenes and Gebel. Maybe the Kushites can keep watch for the assassin," he said.

She nodded reluctantly. "Go then. But send me a message explaining what it is they will do."

It hurt more than he cared to admit that she wanted a message sent, rather than telling her in person.

"Understood." He bowed and prepared to leave, pushing the heavy tent flap with an outstretched arm. It wasn't a long ride to the quarry, but he had much to do. He imagined he and Ergamenes would stay up late discussing the new direction.

"Wait."

She smashed against him, attacking his mouth with her own, fingers digging into his hair. She bit his lip, tugged at his shoulders and slipped her hand beneath his tunic. A fire burned deep.

She stepped away abruptly, dirt smeared across her cheek. Her eyes blazed like a thousand suns. She moved to the desk and picked up a quill.

"I will send for you at a later date," Heron said without looking over.

TWENTY ONE

The season was spent creating the base of the pyramid. In the days after, they began work on the sides. Steam chariots drove wagons onto the base. They used Gebel's clever machine to lift the dry concrete and water mixture, dumping it into the forms. The tamping mechanical had proved troublesome, so the workers spent hours pounding water from the mixture as it hardened using thick flat steel connected to a post.

The crews kept up with the flow of material from the quarry. Heron sent for woodworkers and sent her stone smiths to the quarry to speed up production. In another month, she expected to have two more crews casting blocks.

They worked on opposite sides of the pyramid. They would raise a small section about ten blocks in diameter to the height of five blocks. She wanted to test the construction methods while they were still closer to the ground and when failure was not as catastrophic.

There was a flurry of motion on Gebel's side. Heron watched quietly. Even from a distance, she could see Gebel pacing around the machine, dark skin against the pale stone, throwing his arms up in frustration. The gearing on the pulley system was not leveraged correctly. Gebel was still trying to squeeze more power from the steam mechanical rather than adjusting his gear ratios. Heron tapped the Egyptian boy on the shoulder and pointed across the base of the pyramid to Gebel's side. "Adjo, tell my friend to increase the ratio on the bottom gearing by a third."

"Yes, *Michanikos*!"

The boy, Adjo, hopped up and took off sprinting toward the other side. He was the boy that had been spying on her during the early days of camp. She befriended him and gave him a job as a camp runner.

Reaching into the knapsack to retrieve her plumb guide, she found the dice Jarngard carved for her. Crouching on her heels, squinting away the sun, Heron rolled them across her hand. The note he sent was in nearly illegible Greek. After a few reads, she finally figured out that the dice were meant to tell the future, but he couldn't write the secret of their use on papyrus, so he'd have to tell her in person.

Heron smiled, thinking of him. She hadn't seen him since the day after the party. She'd thought about sending for him or going to the quarry to check on progress, but she knew it was too dangerous. The only reason they'd gotten away with their frenzied lovemaking in his tent was that no one was in camp.

There was no privacy living in tents. A young couple near her location fornicated nightly. It made her loins ache whenever she heard it.

She smelled the bone dice and rubbed the smooth edges. It'd probably taken weeks for him to carve them. She wondered what he told the others when they asked what he was doing. Careful not to roll them, she set the dice back into the knapsack next to the ornate box and a thin silver spoon.

A trail of dust signaled the approach of a small caravan in the distance. It was coming from the direction of Alexandria. Behind the dust plume, the beacon of the Lighthouse could be seen, though a hazy mirage made the base disappear.

As the vehicles neared, she realized it was a larger caravan than she first thought. Her first concern was that something was wrong, something had happened in Alexandria. Her thoughts flitted to Sepharia, who she had heard little from during the construction.

The royal steam barge was unmistakable once she saw the reflections of its bronze molded carapace. The banners of Alexandria fluttered amid the black smoke emitted from the whirling steam mechanical. A guard of lightly armored Northmen rode with the Satrap.

Agog climbed from the barge, looking fitter than she'd seen in months. His beard was clipped short and the tunic hung loosely on him. He was less a mountain and more an impossibly tall cliff. The hair knot he wore when he first came to Alexandria had returned. He marched onto the pyramid and her workers wisely set their tools down and headed to Gebel's side. Even from a distance, she could see the thundercloud brewing in his eyes.

Heron made him climb the ramps. She stood waiting with her arms crossed.

Even before he'd made it up the final ramp, he barked out, "You haven't answered even one letter I've sent you. I've got better things to do than to track down errant engineers. Vestalis thought I should have just had you brought back in a cage."

Heron matched his furious gaze. "A cage would have been fitting for what you think of me. Nothing more than a pet to pull out now and then for tricks."

Her retort gave him a moment's pause before his brow knotted and his fury returned. "What mortal foolishness is this? I've given you gold and resources for your inventions. Would you rather have the Romans in

Alexandria? You seemed to be doing quite well under their thumb before I came along."

"At least they did not lie about their nature," said Heron. "Did you come all this way to give me a lecture?"

Agog paced across the white stone block. "I came here to bring you back to Alexandria. I need you and I need Jarngard."

He glanced around as if he expected to see his former companion standing nearby.

"He's away in Kushite getting more supplies. He won't be back for days," she lied. He was at the quarry with Ergamenes turning lime rock into dust for concrete.

"No matter, but when he returns, send him to Alexandria. I need him for the coming war. And I need you as well, once I solidify my alliance with the Parthians," said Agog.

"I'm not coming."

The words hung in the air. He casually blinked them away. "It's not a request. I am your Satrap."

"Then bring that cage and haul me back as your pet," she said, trying to hold back the fury from her voice. "You promised to make Alexandria a city free of slavery. Once you have met your side of the bargain, I will return. But even then I will expect progress on my pyramid."

He narrowed his gaze. "I've indulged your fantasies because you are without peer, but now is the time to put away such follies and return to Alexandria. Without my protection and resources, there will be no pyramid."

"Apologies, Satrap, but the pyramid was not your commission. You've had no hand in it. My work for the Kushite Queen has made this possible."

He raised an eyebrow. "I've known you for hubris, but this is madness. While you toil away on stone and dust, my patrols have kept the Temple of Ptah from interfering with your project." He paused and crossed his arms. "Yes, I see you are surprised. I told you before you're too valuable. Did you think I just let you wander in the desert alone? What would the people of Alexandria think if I let the *Michanikos* die, blood leaking into the sand?"

"It does not matter," she said, her anger less frothy in her voice. She glanced to the horizon as if she could see those patrols.

Agog peered at her carefully. "I know madness afflicts you."

Heron turned as if slapped. "I am not mad. I wield the tools of science."

"A different god." He shrugged. "But I can accept your madness because it brings great creation. Plutarch told me as much and about the powder and the long, sleepless nights."

"This is not madness."

"The warlocks of my lands make similar claims. Yet they imbibe strange mixtures and stare into the smokes of their hide-covered tents and go on for days until they are awoken by a great vision. Tell me you don't have a great vision?"

Heron stepped toward the edge. "It's not the same. That's magic and superstition. This is knowledge and learning and industry."

"Is it? Yes, your pyramid is a manmade construction of stone and sweat, but the reasons for its existence are magic and superstition. Your pyramid will not change the way the world works." His intense green eyes studied her carefully.

"How is this different than the quest you sent me upon? The heir of Alexander," she replied.

"Political maneuvering," he said. "And I have been proved correct by the presence of the Parthian Prince. Though I desire to see the day his backside is fading away from Alexandria. He's a vain and petty man, but once I have secured an alliance with his father, I will not need to entertain him any longer."

"I cannot come back," she said. "Not now. There are too many problems ahead. The pyramid will languish without my presence and probably remain a collection of stones lost in the sands."

He seemed unsurprised by her comment. "Then I will remove my protections from your little camp. I need those patrols heading north." He paused and a dark cloud passed through his green eyes. The color reminded her of the sea before a storm. "If I were a smart man I would have you killed for insubordination and to keep your technologies from the Romans. But, I owe you a debt. My kingdom would not exist but for your inventions. And I know your stubbornness would only vex them so the only thing I have to fear is your death."

She met his gaze. "I accept this arrangement."

"I'm not entirely sure you do. This means you renounce your holdings in Alexandria. Your workshop. Everything."

"How...who would run it? And the colossus for Kush?"

"I would give it to Nektam. He seems to understand his responsibilities as the Chief Engineer, unlike my previous one. As for the colossus, its construction continues based on your plans. Plutarch is an inspired foreman."

A tightness formed in her chest. "Give it to Plutarch instead." Agog raised an eyebrow. "The workers respect Nektam but love Plutarch, he would get the most out of them. If it's industry you want, Plutarch would turn the workshop into the most industrious of Alexandria."

He seemed to shrug with his eyes. "I will consider your advice." And shook his head regretfully. "Do you not see this madness? As I stand here it is clear as the pale blue sky. How you could renounce your holdings, the ones you worked so hard for, to build this monument of stone?"

"Everyone thought Alexander a fool when he left Greece to conquer the world," she said.

"Did I infect you with his sickness when I sent you on that quest? I would think you believed yourself his heir the way you act."

She was glad he was looking toward the horizon in that instant, because the truth was betrayed by her face. She *was* Alexander's heir. She did feel infected by his madness. Maybe Agog was right. She was mad, but she could not let go.

"My mind will not change."

He nodded, slowly. "I will ensure that the Queen keeps her bargain with you, but otherwise, you and I have no ties."

"What about Sepharia?"

A flicker of thought passed his bearded face. "Polyxena seems to enjoy her company. The girl is of age and has dug herself into Palace politics. She's no longer yours to decide."

A brief coldness invaded her bones. "I see."

Agog began walking down the ramp. "Send a message to Jarngard. I expect him in Alexandria by morning. He should be able to wrap up his work in the quarry quickly."

He'd seen through her lie or already knew where Jarngard was located. There were probably spies in the camp for the Satrap. She shouldn't have been so single-minded or naïve to think he would not keep watch on her. She was, after all, a valuable property.

Heron watched the caravan fade to the north. The beacon could no longer be seen. Its fires quenched by a haze. She felt empty and hollow.

"What an honor to have the Satrap visit your pyramid," said Gebel who had come up while she stared into the distance. "Will you have to return to Alexandria?"

She shook her head softly. The fading light tingled against her skin like a dream. "But Jarngard must return. Send for a rider."

TWENTY TWO

Flames danced against the stone of the Temple of Poseidon. Far above them on the island of Pharos, the glow of the Lighthouse beacon reflected against the clouds. Nobles gathered, drinking and milling around the lawn near the pier. Laughter was laden with heaviness and often left shortened with furtive glances.

Sepharia lounged on the cushioned divan with Bani. The princess wore a crimson lined toga and gold earrings. Her lustrously dark feet lay comfortably across Sepharia's lap.

"He parades for you," said Bani. "Preening himself like a peacock."

Sepharia looked up from her cup of wine. "What do you mean?"

"Vima. Look at him down there. I see him glancing frequently in your direction," said Bani.

"I would prefer it otherwise," she said, "but Polyxena expected me to come."

Bani sighed and swirled the wine in her goblet before gulping it down. A splash of wine spilled across her ebony skin. She slurped it off.

"Vima the Viper is a dangerous enemy."

"Don't I know. I haven't been able to sleep in my own bed for weeks," said Sepharia.

Bani put a hand to her chest in faux injury. "Am I such a horrible bed mate?"

Sepharia blushed and sipped her wine. "Apologies. I don't mean that. I just feel trapped. Like a pawn again."

"Again? When were you not?" said Bani, amused.

Sepharia glanced into the throng of nobles pensively. "You're right. But if we're careful, I don't have to stay one. I don't want to end up like her."

They both looked to Zenobia, his wife. They'd stopped inviting her to their womanly discussions. After the first few sessions, she started showing up with a bruised face. When Vima broke her arm, they stopped sending the chariot to retrieve her.

"You could go to him," suggested Bani. "You're quite the student under the sheets. Men think with that snake between their legs. Convince it to love you and maybe he might, too."

She shook her head lightly. "Not him. I can see it in his eyes when he looks at me. He wants to humiliate me, hurt me. Just like when he showed up in my room."

Bani made noises of agreement. "You're probably right. But what will you do?"

"The gods have not yet seen fit to ruin our plans," she said, idly massaging Bani's calf. "He means to enact his revenge and when he does, I hope I am ready for it. And maybe I'll learn the truth of his convictions for the defense of Alexandria. His words in the Star Chamber haunt my dreams nightly."

"All men scheme," said Bani, "and this Vima is no different. There is opportunity ahead if you're bold."

"And death and misery as well," said Sepharia, still watching Zenobia. The Parthian woman stared vacantly at the crackling fire. Even when she'd joined Polyxena's gatherings, the Parthian woman said little. She seemed a shell of a woman.

"Sepharia!" The Satrap's booming voice bellowed her name. The noble men were gathered around Agog and Vima. A bare-chested slave held a quiver of javelins.

Before Sepharia left the divan, Bani squeezed her hand. "Be careful."

She nodded and moved to the men, holding her toga up carefully. "Yes, Your Grace. How may I serve?"

Agog rested his hand along his belly which was not as large as it had been in previous months. Sepharia had seen him breaking swords with his men in the courtyard frequently. His mouth smiled but his eyes did not.

"Our treasured guest asked for your help," said Agog. "We were about to wager on a contest of throws but he demanded you as judge."

She glanced to Vima, who leaned confidently on a javelin. He had a cock-sure grin that she didn't trust. She bowed, holding up the hem of her toga.

"I would be honored."

Vima examined the shaft of his javelin. He tossed it to Sepharia, who caught it. "Of course you would. You seem to believe yourself equal to a man."

She swallowed her retort and answered as sweetly as she could, "I would never presume."

Agog cleared his throat. "Words are wind, let us prove ourselves at a game of skill. There are gourds on the lawn."

The Prince strolled to the quiver and deftly pulled another javelin. "Yes, let us prove ourselves. Sepharia and I, a contest of skill."

She tried to decline but Agog cut her off. "It would not be a fair contest. You're Parthia's greatest warrior. She's just a foolish girl."

Silence spread across the lawn. Even those out of earshot, sipped their cups lightly and watched events unfold. It took her complete self-control not to run from the Temple grounds. Sepharia was acutely aware of the statue of Poseidon looming over them with his trident pointed toward the sea. When a log in the fire popped, she flinched.

"See, Vima. Just a girl, frightened of a loud log," said Agog.

Vima replied simply, "A contest."

Realizing that the Satrap would lose honor if he had to argue on her behalf Sepharia spoke up, "If the Prince wishes a contest, I will join, though the Satrap speaks wisely, I am just a girl."

"Eager, isn't she?" Vima smirked. "Not a man here besides the Satrap would dare challenge me to a javelin contest and yet you accept. How filled with hubris you are, girl. The gods should see fit to punish you."

"That is not my intent." She knew he didn't care, he was just playing with her.

The Prince seemed to get bored by the verbal sparring and moved near the throwing line. "See that gourd out there, along the sea wall. Closest to it wins the first round. You first."

When she moved to the line, murmuring erupted from the assembled. Agog seemed to be shaking her off with his eyes, but it was too late, she was at the line.

She took a deep breath and hefted the javelin. She was no stranger to its use, though she was hardly skilled with it. Growing up in the workshop had given her ample time to play with the assorted weaponry. She'd spent sunny afternoons throwing javelins into the testing wall in the courtyard with Plutarch when there wasn't much else to do.

With her free hand, she held up her toga. Bets on the distance she would throw whispered through the crowd. Most figured she'd barely make it past the fire pit. The nobles in the path backed away carefully. Vima chuckled while Agog gravely stared into the distance.

She leaned back and rocked forward, snapping her arm and releasing the javelin at the highest point. It sailed through the air, well past the fire and landed shaft up in the grass. It was well short of the gourd but the noises of surprise told her she out threw even the most conservative guesses.

Vima applauded softly, a predator's grin on his lips. "Well done. If you were a man, maybe you would have been able to throw it as far as the gourd. Pity it was short."

Without hesitation, Vima stepped to the line and launched the javelin. Cries of astonishment followed his throw. Sepharia lost the projectile in the starry night sky. Waves slapping against the seawall swallowed the javelin's splash.

"By the gods, my throw has entered Poseidon's lair. It seems you have won the first round." The Prince's words sent a chill down her spine.

"Enough games," said Agog. "Let's you and I compete. Your throw was three times as far as hers."

"But hers was closer to the gourd. She won." He smiled. "But I'm feeling good about the second round. Shall we?"

Sepharia retrieved a javelin from the quiver. "What is our test?"

He wrinkled his nose at her. "One of accuracy, but this time from a short distance."

Vima snapped his fingers at a slave. The boy ran up and Vima whispered in his ear. There was the slightest hesitation before the slave ran to pick up a gourd. Even before he reached it, a tremor formed in her arm.

The boy held his arm out with the head-sized gourd balanced on his palm. He had tears in his eyes.

"You first," said Vima, patting her on the rear with the shaft of his javelin. "After all, you won the first round."

There were no bets passing through the crowd this time. Only the waves crashing against the breakwall could be heard above her beating heart. She took one, two, three cleansing breaths.

She threw the javelin. It flew limply toward the gourd. It landed to the right, short and wide. The slave boy sighed heavily.

"What a timid throw," said Vima with his back to the boy.

True to his name, Vima whipped around and launched the javelin. The crowd gasped. Sepharia's whole body tensed with anticipation.

The gourd fell to the ground. The slave boy followed, falling to his knees. The javelin had flown straight through the gourd and into the lawn behind. Everyone clapped, relieved not to have to watch a boy die, even if he was a slave.

Vima held his hands to the sky. "And round two to me. What would my father say if he saw me here, racked in a contest with not even a woman, but a fledgling whore, who barely has hair between her legs."

Agog spoke up, "I presume your father would say that you're wasting your time. Let me take her place if it's a challenge you want."

The barbarian pulled a javelin out. The weapon looked like a toothpick in his hand. Sepharia suspected he could throw it over the Temple if he wanted.

"But I am amused," said Vima, grinning, "and that's all I've asked of you." He glanced up at the Satrap, the threat clear in his clenched teeth. "And who's to say you'd be a challenge?"

Sepharia almost expected the javelin to snap in Agog's fist. "You're right," he said eventually. "I prefer to cleave my foes in two on the battlefield. Throwing sticks are for infantry and women."

The threat was left unanswered. Vima collected a pair of javelins, handed one to Sepharia and walked back near the fire.

"Come, my darling Zenobia, I have need of you."

The woman dutifully hopped up and scurried to his side. He whispered in her ear and she ran onto the lawn. While everyone watched, Vima spoke again, "Call your...friend. We'll need her this round."

Bani appeared from the covered divan looking every bit the Kushite princess. She strolled to Sepharia's side and held her hand. Her presence filled Sepharia with resolve.

Zenobia returned with two gourds, favoring her good arm. The other had just healed enough to have the bandages removed. She ran past her husband and gave one to Bani. The Parthian woman kept her gaze lowered. Up close, Sepharia could see makeup on the woman's exposed chest hiding a deep bruise. Bani glanced at the gourd suspiciously and squeezed Sepharia's hand again.

"Explain the third contest." Agog frowned and glanced meaningfully toward the south, almost distracted by a sudden thought. Sepharia could see a deeper conflict in his gaze.

"Of course, my future ally." Vima bowed. "The first one to hit their gourd wins. Almost the same as the second round."

Agog narrowed his eyes. "Almost?"

"This time my beautiful wife Zenobia holds my gourd, while Bani holds hers," he said. "And because she's a woman, I'll let her throw first. Last round. If she hits it, she wins. If not, I throw while she holds the gourd."

The Satrap seemed to growl internally. "I cannot allow it. Bani is under my protection."

"I offer my support of your alliance with the Parthian Empire as reward. If she wins, I will leave at once and return, securing the ties between our two great empires. Rome will fall in a year." The Prince grinned with aplomb, his eyes daring Agog to refuse.

Sepharia found she was holding her breath when Agog finally spoke. "I cannot. Her life is not mine to risk."

"But it is mine," said Bani, stepping forward. Sepharia implored her with her eyes to step back.

"I accept the role of gourd holder," Bani finished.

Agog sighed. "It is your right, but first we must know what the penalty for losing is."

"Nothing."

"Nothing?" asked Agog.

Vima shrugged. "I've been quite entertained by your little city. Though small, to fight beside the might of its workshops is quite enticing. On the other hand, the Roman army is ten times your size, maybe more. And it fights with discipline. The Roman Empire has endured for untold centuries for a reason. Even combined, the fighting would be terrible and the losses colossal. It's growing near the time that I should decide. My father requested me to leave my decision until I returned to Susa, unless—" Vima held up a finger. "—the choice was so clear that I could recommend one path or the other. He trusts my judgment in all things. So I offer that quick choice for a moment of diversion. Either way, I leave in four days."

Agog looked to Bani. Sepharia silently hoped for her to say no. Bani nodded, dark brown eyes reflecting the raging bonfire.

"Well then," said Vima, looking quite pleased with himself. "Let us begin."

TWENTY THREE

From the ruins of the ancient settlement, the priest watched the chariots turn and head north. He sensed their leaving was different. Their single-minded sprint back toward Alexandria said much to his keen eyes.

He scooted to the edge of the roof and prepared to scramble down. With his good hand supporting, he edged over. A rock in the wall shifted, unbalancing him and he reached out with his stump. Ghostly fingers grasped for purchase. The stump skipped off the wall, tearing the wrap, and moving him far enough away his other hand could hold no longer.

The priest fell and slammed into the dirt. He lay in the dust gasping for air, his arms wheeling above him like a dying beetle. Breath came haltingly. He coughed and checked his bandages. The raw pink skin was torn, exposing whitish puss. The stench of rot made him turn away.

Using the catcher staff, he climbed to his feet. The noose-like ending tickled the side of his face. He leaned the staff against the back of the wagon and began untying the tarp with his good hand.

"Low and go, the crocodiles lurk," he sang under his breath. "Chomp!" The priest giggled, a high tittering sound.

The knots were tricky. His knuckles were swollen and red, the jagged ends of his fingernails chipped. "Tooth and jaw, the crocodiles snap."

Busy with the knots, he almost forgot the end of the stanza. "Chomp," he said, surprised, almost if the word had come from someone else.

The priest gathered his supplies. The wrapping of cooked meat was covered in flies. He waved them off and inspected his meal. The lower half would need to be cut off and thrown away. Mold had claimed that side.

He picked up the clay pot, pushing it against his elbow with his good hand, and levering it up. Water swished around the bottom. He had a few swallows left. He hadn't expected this visit to last so long.

"Spin and turn, the crocodiles roll. Chomp!"

As he set the pot into the wagon, a quick-tailed lizard streaked across faded planking, leapt onto the priest's leg, and scampered across the hard-pack to disappear into a crevasse in the wall behind a tuft of green scrub.

"An omen," he whispered, "all glory to you, Sobek."

He pulled a small stone carving from a hidden pocket. A tiny, painted stone crocodile peered back at him with dead eyes. He kissed it on the snout before pushing it back into the folds.

The priest finished his preparations, humming the children's song as he worked, with the occasional "Chomp!" slipping from his lips.

His black and green robes were dirty and torn. Sobk and Sobki, his teachers in the ways of the crocodile god would have never allowed their garments to become soiled. The priest knew he was in the right. The Nile was full of mud and dirty water and great snapping teeth. What fitting homage to He Who Dwelleth Amid Terrors.

Nor had they given themselves to Sobek like he. They were whole and perfect, not fitting celebrants for the beasts of the earth. After leaving the temple, he had lived on the banks of the Nile, watching the crocodiles. Every one had scars or limbs missing, snapped off or damaged in the frenzy of eating.

Like the crocodiles, he nourished himself in the Nile, eating bugs and slimy things that lurked in the mud. The great beasts did not bother him, even when he waded into the shallows within striking distance of waiting mouths. He knew then he belonged to Sobek.

"Snap and rip, the crocodiles feast. Chomp!"

He set off toward the little oasis. The light faded and by the time he reached it, only the thin sliver of a moon would be in the sky. The crocodile's moon.

The little surefooted pony stepped lightly across the desert. Here were the flatlands. Sand raced across the surface, blown by the winds to finally rest in some far off southern dune. The stinging sand forced the priest to cover his head.

His face creased in remembrance as he thought of his teachers in the darkness beneath the temple. Sobk and Sobki. They were most helpful, explaining the use of the iron implements, even though he was well acquainted with their function.

Each scream was an acknowledgement of his skill. In a previous life, he reveled in such sounds, feeding his vanity. In the temple of reeds, he offered those sounds to his god Sobek, knowing those tumultuous noises derived from his time on the mossy slab.

"Chomp!" he tittered, ignoring the sand blowing into his mouth.

The threat of a sand storm was brewing in the west. The priest knew the signs and deep in his heart, he knew it was Sobek's storm. The crocodile god had made a bargain with Set.

He reached the oasis and hid the pony and wagon behind the bank of reeds. The catcher staff rested comfortably in his grip, the excess length tucked beneath his armpit. A quick tug on the rope sticking from the center would cinch the noose.

The priest pulled a bag of oats from the wagon and set it before the pony. It pushed its muzzle into the sack and began chewing hungrily. He stroked its matted and mite-ridden fur. Once he returned to the temple, he would give the pony to Petsuchos. He would never need to leave the temple walls again. And then he would take that lying woman into the darkness beneath the reeds and teach her the hymns of He Who Dwelleth Amid Terrors. The priest reset the catcher staff and squared his shoulders toward the torch-lit camp at the edge of the pyramid. The winds rose and wailed, long tusks of thick clouds racing across the river of stars, hiding the crocodile moon. The priest waited in the darkness.

TWENTY FOUR

Sepharia stared into the starry sky. The great bonfire spit sparks into the stygian darkness. Even from a distance, the heat flushed her face. A storm lurked in the south, but it would not come quick enough to change her fate.

When Sepharia looked back down, Zenobia was across from her, about ten paces. The gourd was held not on an outstretched hand like the boy-slave, but like a platter near her head. The woman stared blankly into the distance, not even appearing to care.

Sepharia glanced to Bani, but regretted it. Seeing her friend only reminded her of the stakes. As she tested her javelin for balance, the crowd moved back and away.

"Throw strong, throw true," whispered Bani.

She took a deep breath.

"You may throw when you like," said Vima. "I will wait until the javelin is in the air."

She closed her eyes once, just for balance. The gourd seemed so small even though it was nearly the size of Zenobia's head. She swallowed and wiped her sweaty palm on her toga, holding the hem up with her other hand.

"Wait. Wait," said Vima. "We cannot have this."

Sepharia lost her breath, thinking that he was stopping the contest, relief flooded into her limbs. Vima pointed to her legs.

"How unfair for her to have to throw in that thing. Someone cut the bottom from her toga so that she may throw freely," he said.

While she waited for the hem to be cut clean, she closed her eyes a few times. Vima stared, a faint smirk on his lips. He clearly relished her discomfort. For a moment, she entertained the idea of throwing the javelin at him instead of the gourd in Zenobia's hand, but that would only result in her death by his men who waited nearby. Retribution would be swift.

The tugging on her toga ended and Vima indicated with his hand that she could begin. Sepharia pulled her arm back and thought about throwing wide. There would be no penalty for failure. She could miss and the Satrap might still forge an alliance with the Parthians.

However, if she hit the mark, she could save the city in one throw. It wasn't a difficult task. She'd made many just like it. The difference was the woman's head, a handbreadth away from the target.

Vima chuckled. As he spoke, he speared her in his sights, each word a blow to her breast. "See how she hesitates? This is the difference between a man and a woman. A man can be ruthless when so much is at stake while a woman is essentially a coward. Barely worthy of our attention. She hesitates because she is weak. She won the bet because she was lucky. Even the roll of a dice could have picked that chariot. But this? This is skill. A test of a man's resolve, his speed and strength, and his will to accomplish difficult tasks."

Before the nerve could leave her, she raised the javelin back further and launched it forward, trying to hit the edge of the gourd, away from Zenobia's head. The javelin left her fingers and she closed her eyes as she saw Vima spring into action.

Next to her, Bani screamed. Screams of the noble women followed. Her stomach leapt into her throat. Someone grabbed her shoulder. She feared Bani dead.

A familiar touch slipped into her hand. As Sepharia opened her eyes, Bani pulled her close. "It's okay. He made you do it."

There was a crowd near Vima. He watched her with a smirk. Sepharia glanced behind to see Bani's gourd impaled into the ground a ways back by the javelin. Eventually, her focus returned to Vima's side. Part of her could not accept it.

Agog was speaking to Vima. The Prince nodded slowly and the pair left. One of the Zenobia's handmaidens was sobbing. The crowd split and someone looked back to her with a murderous glare. Zenobia was stretched upon the lawn with a javelin sticking from her neck. The guts of the gourd were spilled across the lawn, broken from the fall.

TWENTY FIVE

He'd burned the note in the embers of the cooking fire. Jarngard saddled his horse while the words ricocheted through his head.

"The Machine Man is a hard master to make you ride with a sand storm coming." Ergamenes lounged by the fire, gnawing on a hunk of charred goose. He nodded toward the gathering clouds. As if summoned, a wind gust slapped at the edges of the tent.

Jarngard acknowledged him with a grunt and a nod.

"Now is the time to be fixing tents and preparing the camp, not riding," said Ergamenes. "That note must have said something important."

Hunks of red wax were stuck in his fingernails. Heron had hid her words within successive layers of security. The note had been written in his language. The words chosen carefully.

"The Satrap wants me back in Alexandria. Heron has final instructions," he said.

Ergamenes tilted his head. He seemed to be looking through Jarngard. "Can't it wait until after the storm? It's not like you can ride to

Alexandria tonight."

"I'm just following orders," he said, though he didn't expect that the Kushite engineer believed him by his penetrating gaze.

Ergamenes finally shrugged. "If it's important you'll come by and let me know before you leave us."

Jarngard met Ergamenes and clasped forearms. "Of course, my friend. I would not leave without saying farewell to you and the team. It's been an honor to work with you."

"You're not bad for a pink-skinned Northman." Ergamenes grinned.

The wind stung him with sand on the ride to the pyramid camp. He repeated the words of the note in his mind.

J, Agog demands your presence in Alexandria for war efforts. Come to me, I need you. —H

Those last three words rung like a mantra. *I need you.* He could taste her hot, hungry breath. Feel her slick thighs wrapped around him.

To the gods with Alexandria and the war with Rome. She could never be a woman in these lands. He would convince her to ride south, past the Kushites, follow the Nile and live as nomads. Sleeping in tents and making love under the stars.

He left his horse in the timbered pen. He marched to her tent, feeling a hotness in his chest. Camp workers tied secondary ropes to the tents, securing them from the rising winds. Greetings were lost amid the shuttering fabrics.

Jarngard thrust his arm through the tent flap, preparing to gather Heron in his arms. The tent was empty. A dim lantern illuminated the inside. A note with her seal waited on the desk.

Jarngard ripped it open. He devoured the words written in his language. She was on the pyramid. Taken a tent and bedroll, a place for them to ride out the storm.

His face grew flush with desire. The warm light from the lantern spread thinly in the dark. In his haste, Jarngard missed the ramp and circled back around. He smiled thinking about her preparations. Moving them away from the camp would free them from discovery and the storm would hide their frenzied cries.

The construction area was littered with tools and buckets. Jarngard briefly wondered if the lifting mechanism would get damaged in the storm, but the pyramid wasn't his to care about much longer.

He assumed she'd hidden the tent amid the blocks, so they would be protected from the storm by the pyramid. The construction rose to a height of five blocks. He climbed ladders to move higher.

The area was empty. A form had been abandoned, wooden planks forming the outline of the concrete block. A bucket full of tamping hammers reflected his light.

Jarngard paced across the stone before he remembered there were two construction areas on the pyramid. Matching his thoughts, a light appeared on the other side. It fluttered to life briefly and then was quenched. A signal, he assumed.

He climbed down carefully after dimming his lantern. Halfway across, the lantern bloomed to life again. Jarngard shouted but the wind swallowed his words. She seemed to be looking for him. He leaned over to brighten his lantern when he thought he saw a flicker of movement on the pyramid with Heron. Jarngard broke into a sprint.

TWENTY SIX

Mallets thudded against wood, as two servants wedged a shutter against the window. Winds howled outside, a sand storm approached the city. Bani squeezed Sepharia's hand as Polyxena paced across the room.

"Not even the most addle minded noble would dare involve themselves in such a display with our treasured guest," fumed Polyxena, her words rising in inflection.

"I was told to do whatever the Prince desired. He wanted entertainment," she said.

Polyxena wheeled around. "Killing his wife is entertainment? You common fool. Our city hangs in the balance of his decision. We cannot defeat the Roman or Parthian armies separately. Together we would be crushed."

Bani cleared her throat. "The Prince nudged his wife into the javelin's path. I saw it. Everyone else was looking at Sepharia."

"I scarcely believe that your eyes were wide open as the Prince prepared to throw," said Polyxena. "You imagined this in her defense."

"I saw it, I—"

"Silence!" Polyxena's face was blotched with fury. "You could have ended that foolishness by declining. If he would have killed you, your mother would have ended ties with us. That was a game that should have never been played. I would send you back to Kush except I don't want your mother to get ideas on turning her back on us."

Bani retreated, crossing her arms and bowing her head. A servant brought a pitcher of wine into the room. When the servant moved to pour Sepharia's glass, Polyxena knocked it out of his hand. The brass pitcher bounced, splashing wine across the marble.

When the servant moved to clean it with a rag, Polyxena shouted, "Leave it!"

The servant skittered out of the room. Sepharia retrieved the rag and began cleaning the spilled wine.

"How like a common girl to be cleaning," said Polyxena. "Maybe I should make you my servant."

"My father would not like that."

Polyxena gave her a cold smile. Her insides knotted with worry.

"Your father has renounced his ties to the city. Agog spoke to him today. That pyramid madness is more important to him than the city." She paused with a smirk on her face. "Or you."

Sepharia rose slowly to her feet. Wine dripped from the rag. She shared a glance with Bani.

"The Satrap needs my father. His inventions will beat the Romans, or the Parthians."

"Hush, girl," said Polyxena. "The Satrap is negotiating the terms of the alliance as we speak. Do not further damage our chances with loose words."

"The Prince is just playing us. He wants to be like Alexander," she said.

Polyxena scoffed. "Every man born wants to be Alexander."

"I overheard him. He doesn't want an alliance. He wants glory. A negotiation will not get him that."

"He can have glory on the battlefield against Rome," said Polyxena.

"Better that my father could help rather than the Parthians. His inventions will not turn on the Satrap."

"I said before. Your father is not of this city. He's mad with pyramid building and you're lucky the Satrap did not kill him to keep the Romans from stealing him. Only his stubbornness stayed his hand."

The rag dripped sopped wine. What had happened to drive such a wedge between Heron and Agog? Was it madness as Polyxena suggested? Once an idea wedged itself in Heron's mind, it could not be dislodged.

"I could speak to my father," said Sepharia, "on behalf of the Satrap."

Polyxena glanced dismissively as she sipped her wine. "You will do no such thing. Your fate is on the scales tonight already. And we do not need the great Machine Man anymore. The new Chief Engineer has doubled the city's output and created iron boats to rule the seas with. The old one was a fool."

The way the name Machine Man passed cynically across Polyxena's lips was a spear in Sepharia's side.

"That is my father you speak of," said Sepharia. "His tireless efforts gave the city to the Satrap. Without him, there would be no freed Alexandria and you would still be a spy for the League of Corinth."

As soon as the words flew her lips, she knew she had erred. Sepharia ducked as the goblet sailed past her head and shattered on the wall.

"Seize her!" Polyxena commanded the guards.

Callused hands grabbed her. Sepharia was forced over the divan.

Bani watched with wide eyes.

Polyxena searched around the room frantically. There was a piece of planking left from the shuttering. She grabbed it and marched to Sepharia. With both hands she swatted Sepharia on the back of the legs. The wood bit into her flesh, but she did not cry out.

The blows came one after another until Sepharia's whole backside was enflamed with agony. When no more blows came, Sepharia cautiously looked back.

One of the Satrap's advisors, a man in a crimson toga, spoke quietly to Polyxena in the doorway. Words stayed low and they spoke for a while. When they both glanced at Sepharia, her heart jumped.

The guards were commanded to release her and Sepharia stood. Her legs shook, but she did not lean against the divan. She bit her lower lip.

Polyxena approached, eyes hard with purpose. "The negotiation is complete. My future husband has secured the alliance with Parthian. Vima leaves after the storm to return to his father and begin preparations for the war with Rome."

Biting back tears, Sepharia bowed her head. "That's wonderful news."

"Since the Prince is without his latest wife." Polyxena stared back coldly. "The Satrap has given him your hand in marriage."

Sepharia dared a glance with Bani. "How can that be? I am but a common girl."

"Indeed." Polyxena blew heat from her nostrils. "The Prince was quite insistent that he take you back to Susa. To further the alliance, tying our two empires together, the Satrap has requested that I adopt you since we are both Macedonian."

This news was unexpected. "But you're not married yet. The wedding isn't for another month."

Polyxena soured. "Tomorrow, before the Parthian caravan leaves, there shall be two marriages, so the alliance can be solidified."

"Apologies," said Sepharia timidly. "I did not want this to happen. It was not my intent to usurp your wedding."

The future Queen wandered to the shutters and stayed the rattling wood. The wind pummeled the Palace. "How could you know?" she said regretfully.

Sepharia dared another glance with Bani. Polyxena seemed to catch it the second time. She paused, looking back and forth between them. With a sudden start, she sent the guards from the room.

"What are you two scheming at? Tell me now, or I'll bring the guards back to flay the truth from your rears," said Polyxena.

"Nothing," said Bani, too quickly.

Sepharia put a hand to her tender bottom. "We are, Your Grace."

Bani tried to shake her off, but Sepharia shrugged. "She should know. Maybe she can help."

"What is it that you two are doing? Hide nothing."

"Vima has threatened me more than once that he would make me his wife just to punish me. Bani and I have been preparing for this eventuality, though we never envisioned that I would kill Zenobia in a game of javelins, or that it was you that would adopt me. We thought the Satrap might give me to one of his nobles."

Polyxena frowned precipitously. "That is the danger of Vima the Viper, he is unpredictable. I wish you would have come to me sooner. Tell me what you plan so that I may help."

"Apologies. I would prefer to keep our secrets. But know that I keep Alexandria's interests first. While I know you don't approve, I am not convinced that the Viper fully intends to ally with us," said Sepharia.

"Dangerous words, girl. I might feel the same, but his father is an honorable man. Once we have his blessing then we will be secure."

Polyxena held a finger up. "But until then, a careful ear would not be unwise. I'll send along personal attendants so we will have a way to pass messages."

"Thank you."

"If there is anything else I can do, speak now. Your freedom nears an end."

A tightness formed in her chest when she thought about the coming days. "There is one thing."

After she was done explaining, Polyxena grimly nodded. She left to begin preparations. Sepharia pulled Bani into her arms, pressing their cheeks together and shifting her weight forward to take the pressure from her aching backside.

"I could be a Queen," whispered Sepharia breathlessly.

"Yes, but a third wife, and married to a man who hates you and might be the enemy of your past and future fathers," responded Bani.

"It's a start." Sepharia squeezed her eyes shut, hugging Bani tightly. "Even Cleopatra slept with her enemy to get what she wanted."

Bani pulled away, slightly. Her wide luminous eyes were brimming with concern. "Do not invoke Cleopatra's name. She died in the end."

"As we all do," said Sepharia. "But better to live boldly and be remembered for hubris rather than cowardice. Tomorrow I join the lineage of Alexander the Macedonian. A fitting beginning to this escapade."

Bani's face pinched. "Do not take this Vima lightly. He killed his wife just so he could get back at you."

A brief shudder passed through Sepharia's midsection. "That is my biggest concern. That I have overestimated my cunning and our plans are too few."

"Plans." Bani kissed her lightly. "Tomorrow comes too soon and there is still work to be done."

Sepharia let her go. She limped to the shutters. The storm buffeted the Palace. When she left the marbled halls, her life would begin anew. Sepharia sat tenderly at the desk and penned a letter to Heron. Her father would not understand, nor could she explain in the letter. In their scheming, she and Bani had agreed not to leave any evidence of their plans on paper, but she needed one thing from Heron, one thing that would be critical if Sepharia was to survive the next few months with Prince Vima. One thing that she knew only her father could do for her. She made her request as carefully as she could, couching it in neutral language, to hide the true meaning.

Inside the papyrus, she placed a second one with sketchings Heron would understand. After dripping a candle and pressing her seal into the warm wax, Sepharia kissed the papyrus. Heron would not learn the truth of her plans unless she was successful. And even then it might cost her life. Sepharia planned to kill the Parthian Prince.

TWENTY SEVEN

The stone blocks and half-built wooden form provided a break from the wind. The travel tent fit cozily in the space. Heron unrolled the sleeping mat, listening to the wind howl outside.

Her heart jumped at every noise. The lifting mechanical rattled in the wind. Gears and chains clanged. It would take them a few days to fix the damage before they could begin work again, but it would not deter them.

Inside her knapsack were the implements of her stolen gender: the molded genitalia, stained worker's tunic, and chest bindings. She wore a hastily wrapped verdant chiton and touched it constantly to make sure it hung on her frame right.

Heron stroked the handle of the lantern, wondering when Jarngard would arrive. She'd sent the note hours ago.

The chiton rode up on her hips. She pushed it down, the loose fabrics filling her with unease. It felt strange not to wear the molded genitalia. The smooth wooden attachment was her armor. Heron reached between her legs, rubbing the inside of her thighs. Hair had been stripped clean from years of wearing the harness.

Every movement brushed fabric against her nipples. They ached with stiffness. Unlike the man's tunic, which hung orderly on her frame, the chiton was bunched and moved like a hundred soft fingertips caressing her skin.

The earlier argument with Agog came back to her as she sat cross-legged. A wave of anxiety passed through her. Had she gone mad? Renouncing her workshop and everything she'd built in Alexandria for the pyramid? Had she ever cared what the other workshops thought, she might have died in shame, because she knew they would speak harshly of her.

What would Archimedes or Aristotle say of her decision? It was their opinion that mattered most. She suspected they would think this project foolish.

Heron picked at the calluses on her fingertips, earned from measuring the flatness of stone. Her pyramid would not stand if the blocks contained even the smallest of errors. Much in the way, in her eyes, that society could not stand with the error of slavery, or the crimes against women.

Maybe when the pyramid was complete, she would cast off her disguise and show the world her true gender. The pyramid would be a shining example of what women can accomplish. It was fitting that the Kushite Queen was her benefactor. That way, no man could claim credit.

She suspected that Jarngard would tempt her with leaving Egypt, to travel to faraway lands, and be as man and woman, traveling together. She would like that, but then it would be an opportunity lost.

Heat rose to her chest and she desired Jarngard right then. In the quiet time after, she would command him to take no chances in the war against Rome. He would not listen, but she would make her heart known.

Concerned that Jarngard could not locate her in the storm, Heron wrapped a cloak around her and ventured out of the tent with the lantern. She stood on the edge of the block. Visibility was low and growing dimmer.

The lantern snuffed out. Heron returned to the tent to relight the lantern. After a few tries, she got the oil burning again and made sure the slats were tight.

Outside the tent, she held the cloak around her face and the lantern high. Sand stung against her shins. A bucket crashed against stone behind her. The wind must have curled around the barrier and thrown it.

The stone platform was wider than the other side. She'd had many a debate with Gebel about the proper way to construct the pyramid. Without resolving the argument, they decided to each try their methodology. Heron preferred hers because it gave more room to maneuver and prepare the next block. She knew Gebel chose his because his side stood taller, and he was a competitive man. Her height would surpass his when work lagged because they didn't have enough room.

A shadow moved near the form and behind her tent. Either something large, like a tarp or piece of planking, flew through the storm, or someone had climbed upon the pyramid.

"Jarngard?" Her words were swallowed by the wind. She tried again, this time louder. "Jarngard?"

Unease shivered down her spine. If it were Jarngard, he would have shown himself. Heron slid over, keeping the edge to her back. The Satrap's words about keeping the Temple of Ptah at bay felt more real as she searched the stinging darkness.

"Jarngard," she said, not as loud as she wanted. She hugged the cloak around her. The real sand storm was nearing. If Jarngard didn't arrive soon, she'd be stuck in the storm without him.

In the space between the two mini-pyramids of stone, a dim light flickered. "Jarngard," she breathed to herself. Feeling exposed suddenly, she moved to the ramp. Better to meet him halfway than wait up top while something lurked.

The darkness rose up against her. Something flashed by her head. Heron dropped the lantern and ran. Oil flame splattered behind, briefly illuminating the stone. Halfway down the ramp, something caught her heel and she tripped, slamming into the hard surface, ripping the skin from her knuckles. She rolled to the next level.

The cloak whipped from her back, sailing into the storm. The chiton covered nothing. She buried her face in the crook of her arm and took off running in the direction of the ramp. Someone grunted behind her.

The ground fell away. She flailed through the air, hitting the stone feet first. Momentum slammed her forward. She brought her arms up in time to save her face, but she heard a bone crack from the impact.

Using her good arm, she struggled to her feet, disoriented by the fall and the storm. The flash from the broken lantern still bloomed in her vision. Heron wheeled around.

She edged frontward, holding her broken arm and tentatively stepping so she did not fall again. She found the edge and slid to the left, feeling like whatever was following her was very near. Only the darkness kept her safe.

When her foot touched the next ramp, something brushed her ear. She reflexively ducked, feeling a scratchy object touch her head. Between the darkness and squinting, Heron could barely see. Whoever was behind did not mean her well.

Knowing the ramp headed straight down, Heron scrambled in that direction, praying she didn't veer too much left or right and fall again. When she hit the ground, she stumbled to her knees.

Heron shot up, sprinting into the storm, oblivious to any dangers ahead. She pictured the layout in her head. If she veered slightly to the left, she could make the little oasis. It would keep her safe from whoever was following her and the storm. If she missed it, she'd wander the desert until the sand storm stripped the flesh from her bones.

The howling winds swallowed her footsteps. Heron could feel the storm's power growing. Its fury had not yet reached her. She stumbled through the darkness until she found herself surrounded by reeds.

Heron pushed through the stiff plants, ignoring the ache in her arm. She moved until her toes found water. At the oasis, it seemed even darker. The verdant hollow swallowed whatever light had reflected through the storm. Heron was blind.

She gently splashed through the water until she found a good hiding spot. Crouching on her heels, Heron waited in the reeds. Her breath labored in her ears, heartbeats thudding like drums.

Safe. She was safe as long as she stayed in the reedy oasis. Nothing could find her here and the reeds would protect her from the sand if she crouched further in.

With a moment of respite, Heron thought of Jarngard. Had he found the empty tent? Would he assume someone had attacked her by the broken lantern? She hoped he did not injure himself looking for her in the storm. Prudence would eventually force him into the tent, she hoped.

Heron thought she heard a splash. It was hard to tell over the wind noise. The reeds rattled with fury. Cradling her broken arm, she craned her head, listening.

It could have been something falling into the water, a broken reed tip, perhaps. Maybe a small animal driven by the storm. There was no way anyone could have followed her to the oasis. Only she knew the area enough to make that frenzied dash across the hardpack in near darkness.

Or it was her imagination. Conceivably, she should not be able to hear anything over the storm and the rattling reeds. She was not fond of places like the oasis. She'd visited the Nile before and watched the great crocodiles break the backs of antelope trying to cross the river.

There were no crocodiles in the oasis, but her mind worked against her, using the canvas of the darkness to draw in these thoughts.

There was a second splash. She was sure of it. She rose a little further, straining to hear or see anything. Heron considered moving, finding a different hiding spot. She moved to take a step, catching her foot on a root, while reeds scrapped and clawed at her back. The winds rose in a crescendo and the air itself seethed with electricity. The hair on the back of her neck shuttered with anticipation. The storm sighed momentarily and the reeds stood tall like spears and it seemed she could see into the shuddering darkness and there was a shape, like a hole in the night. Something waited for her in the reeds. She reached out to slap it away. The hole crumpled, her fingers wrapped around the cloth. It was a section of tarp, thrown by the winds and caught by the reeds. Heron sighed and prepared to crouch once more into the reeds when a noose slipped around her neck.

TWENTY EIGHT

East of Alexandria, on the trade road to Tyre, the Parthian caravan encamped near the hill town of Mithrapolis. The town was nothing but a walled temple on a high hill, like a thumb upthrust from the lowlands, ringed by walls and cliffs on all sides but one.

Below on the plains, the camp bustled with fire light and men, gathering supplies and filling drinking cups. In the center of the camp, a great tent filled with luxurious carpets, bedding, and a small dining area was set up for the royal couple.

Sepharia, with help from a handmaiden named Pheme, fixed her makeup. Another handmaiden, Carme, set her hair, using ivory combs to turn it into a waterfall of flaxen curls. She applied a perfume to her neck and between her breasts, letting the potent aroma tickle her nose, reminding her of nights in Bani's arms.

The arrival of the men in the camp could be heard. Vima had gone to the nearby temple to sacrifice a bull for their marriage. The town had been named for the god Mithras. It was said a waterfall ran through the center of the temple, fed from a high rocky spring. Sepharia pushed the handmaidens away and adjusted the gossamer gown.

"Pheme. Carme. I will have need of you later." The handmaidens were gifts from Polyxena. Dark-haired girls who would serve as her link to Alexandria.

Sepharia glanced around the tent. It was more luxurious than her room in the Palace. The third wife of the Parthian prince lived better on the road than even an Alexandrian noble. She caressed the exquisite cabinets that held her clothes and other important items.

A bare-chested Vima pushed through the tent flap. His hair was pulled back into a handsome ponytail and his hands were covered with bandages, dark with blood on the palms. Her pulse quickened.

"*Mithras ma gas.*" Sepharia invoked the greeting she had been told to use when the Prince returned. She understood it to mean 'welcome home beloved son of Mithras'.

"Greetings, Beloved," said Vima without a trace of previous animosities.

Sepharia brought him a goblet of wine. He finished it, wiped his mouth with a forearm, and handed the goblet back. Sepharia retrieved the flask to refill.

After giving him a second, she gathered up a bronze bowl filled with water and a rag. While he drank his second cup of wine, she wiped the dust from his chest with the damp cloth. He tried to appear uninterested in her attentions, but his gaze followed her as she worked.

"May I clean the wounds on your hands?" she asked.

He narrowed his gaze. "Only Mithras may heal these wounds."

Though she was not supposed to, Sepharia knew from her work with her father that the followers of Mithras cut the palms of their hands to mix with the blood of the bull. Even if there was no bull sacrifice, they would cut their hands and leave their blood on the bull horns of the god's representation.

Vima paused, stared into his cup with his brow knotted and then after coming to an internal conclusion, handed the cup to her. "Finish it."

The wine was strong and tasted of raspberries. She drank it in one long gulp.

He had a wry, small, smile. His eyes were full of thought. "Did you bring your snakes?"

The question caught her unaware. She let a shyness blush onto her lips and cheeks. "Beloved. They are my guardians from the twice-born." An anger grew in him like coals blown with fresh breath. "For you just as much as I. Dionysus has blessed me with a gift. But those gifts cannot be taken until the moon is full."

The lie hung in the air. His mouth hung open like a predator. He turned away, sudden, swiftly. "Your mother told me as much. Snake-born. Dream-stealer. I do not like this Dionysus."

"I would worship your Mithras, if it pleased you."

When the words left her lips, she knew she had erred. The anger bloomed to flame, and just as quickly, was quenched. "Beloved. Mithras is only served by men who rule. I would cut off your feet if you entered his temple."

"Apologies." Sepharia busied herself with pouring him another cup of wine. Hands trembled at the touch of the pitcher, she put a second cup next to his and filled them both.

Vima stood at an open cabinet. He gestured to the vials and jars set along the bottom, some filled with liquids, others leafy clumps.

"What is this?" he asked accusingly.

"Herbs and potions for my nighttime companions. It keeps them healthy along with ample mice and insects."

"Are these poisonous?"

"No." She shook her head. "That jar by your finger is mint. The liquid behind it is vinegar and sycamore extract.”

Vima picked up the vinegar jar and held it up to a candle. He frowned.

“Drink some.” He offered the jar.

Sepharia walked confidently over, took the jar, unhinged the top and took a sip. She shuddered at its bitterness. “Is that enough, Beloved?”

He pulled out some mint and sniffed it, gingerly placing his tongue against the green leaf, before withdrawing it. Sepharia was reminded of his nickname, the Viper.

While she watched, Vima continued to poke through her belongings, investigating each one as if it were a dangerous object. He knocked once on the chest of snakes before giving her a stern glance and continuing on.

Finished, Vima stood in the center of the tent, drinking his wine, surveying the room. Sepharia let the gossamer robe slip open, revealing her chest, and moved to him. She gently pulled the cup away and pressed her lips against his.

The contrast to Bani was immediate. His lips were soldiers. Facial hair scratched at her chin. Her neck craned upward and she stood on her toes.

Yet, it was not unpleasant. She sucked on his lower lip, as Bani had taught her, until his mouth returned her eager kiss. She snaked her hand along his chest, feeling the hard muscles, the rope-like scar tissue across his chest from a sword swipe. Kissing him was what she thought flying might feel like. A heady, terrifying rush.

Sepharia had never allowed Polyxena to bring her a man. She’d never been ready. Cautions about the first time made her wary.

Those cautions fled and she moved to untie his loincloth. Rough hands grabbed hers. He pushed her away, narrowed gaze questioning.

“Do you wish to curse me? Your new mother made certain I understood the danger," said Vima. "And I do not disregard the wishes of the gods."

"There are other things we can do," she said shyly.

Vima snorted derisively. "The full moon is a week away. I will wait. Tonight I drink with my men. I will have a separate tent set up."

He left her frustrated. In time, she would send for her handmaidens, but for now she wanted to think. She drained the wine cup and returned to the cabinets, setting the vials and jars in their proper places.

A light pressure in the correct spots, revealed a secret compartment on the larger cabinet. As soon as she'd started preparing for this eventuality, she'd sent a request to Plutarch for a lelathon cabinet with specific instructions on the opening mechanism and the size of the hidden compartment. The secret latch required a light touch, something she knew Vima was not capable of, even if he knew where to press.

She peered briefly into the opening before closing it. Not even her handmaidens knew the true nature of the cabinet. Its secrets were insurance against the troubles that she knew lay ahead.

Bani had secured a vial of the exile Ramses' poison. It was odorless and tasteless and dissolved in wine quickly. It would be easy to kill Prince Vima with it, but they would immediately blame her. She needed the Romans to blame and she couldn't do that without Heron's help. She hoped her father was busy working on her part of the plan, otherwise she was sure the Parthians would turn on Alexandria and then there was no way any of them would survive.

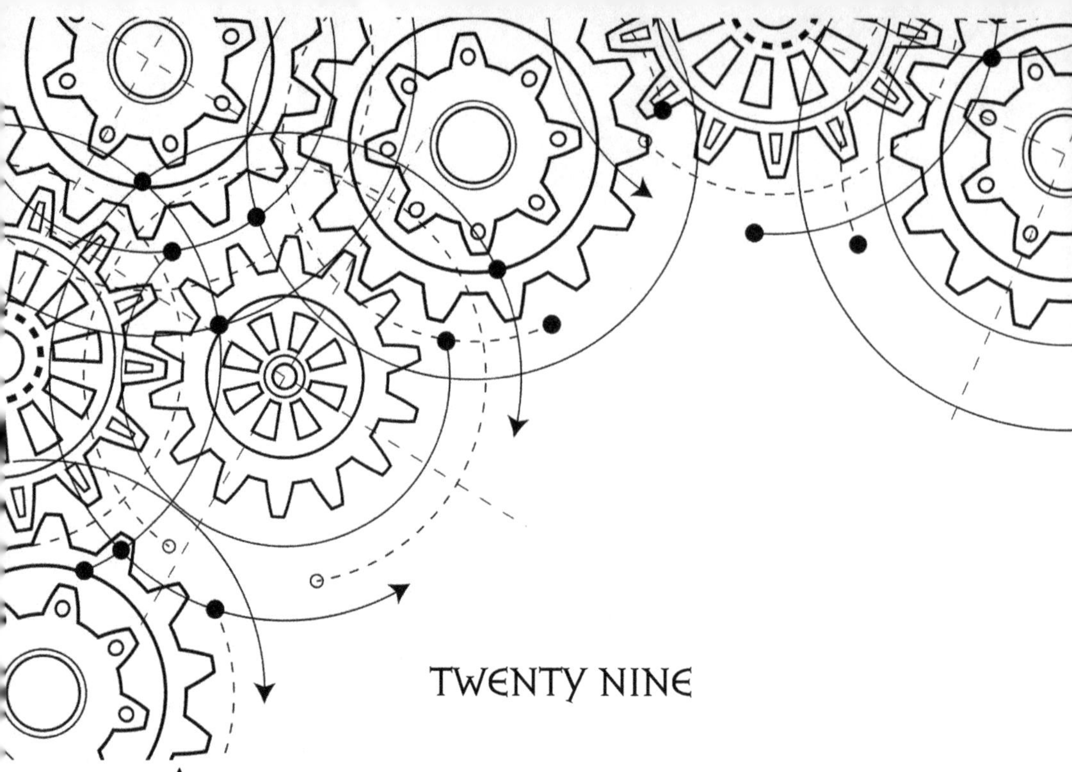

TWENTY NINE

A regiment of soldiers screamed energetically as they ran forward, gladii raised for killing blows. Listless thuds of their sandaled feet played a scattered rhythm. The battle dummies quivered with the slapping impacts of the sword blows.

Jarngard wearily climbed the observation scaffolding. His feet were iron bars. Agog stood atop watching his soldiers practice. In the distance, the dust plumes of steam chariots performing maneuvers across the hardpack rose in the sky like miniature clouds.

"Freya's frozen tits, this army fights like a pack of dogs chasing a squirrel." Agog spoke over his shoulder. "You're two days late. I will not defeat the Romans with such insolence in my own captains. If you were going to leave, you should have left on the *Nereid's Song*."

Jarngard coughed, his throat raw from breathing sand and dust. If he'd left on the *Nereid's Song* so many months ago, he'd never have learned the truth about Heron.

Agog turned. "You look like camel dung, Jarngard. Did you try to swim through a sand dune?"

"He's gone." He almost said *'she's gone'.* Would it matter now if he did?

"Of course, I know that. Your ship left months ago," Agog growled.

"No," said Jarngard. "Heron."

Agog turned. "He left?"

"Taken. Right before the storm. I tried to follow, but it nearly killed me."

Agog narrowed his brow. "I didn't know the inventor had earned such loyalty from you."

"And I didn't know how easily you threw people away once you were done using them," replied Jarngard.

Agog took a step closer. "I did not throw Heron away. He left. It was his choice." A pause with reflection. "I would prefer for him to be here. Do you know who took him?"

"I thought the Temple of Ptah. When I could not find a trace, I rode to Memphis and spoke to a friend. He claimed the temple was not involved."

"Then it was the Romans, I should have dragged him back here in chains." Agog punched the wooden railing, the structure shuddered.

"Not them, I think. I found this afterwards." He handed over the tiny stone crocodile.

"That is good news," said Agog, "after our last discussion, I thought he might be mad enough to join Rome against me."

"Good news? Are you addled? If it were Rome, we could at least bargain with them for the inventor's life." Jarngard pointed to the stone totem. "I fear this means grave things for Heron. We must find...him."

"The *Michanikos* has had a strange effect on you." His gaze was searching, reflective. "You and I have lost many friends in battle, killed or taken prisoner. Brothers even, and I have not seen such loyalty before."

Jarngard moved away to the railing. "I felt purpose in his service."

"Tragic as it may be, the *Michanikos* is lost to us. When we have our victory against Rome, I shall erect a statue to him, rivaling even the one being made in his workshop. But now we must focus on squeezing discipline from this army and figuring out how to best use our steam chariots and other war machines. I expect you to make up your delay in arrival."

Jarngard spun. "Lost? Heron is not lost. That stone crocodile in your hand may lead us to him. To save Heron before fate pulls his thread."

"This?" Agog soured. "If I truly thought I could help him, I would. But this? Maybe he might find truth hidden in the stone, but he cannot help us find him."

"What about his daughter?" countered Jarngard desperately. "She is clever like him."

"Gone," said Agog. "Married to the Parthian Prince as part of the alliance arrangement. She rides to Susa."

Jarngard gripped the railing with both hands. "By the jarl's cock, you'll do anything for your empire, won't you?"

Agog grew calm, dangerously calm. "I did not cause that. She invited his interest with her scheming mouth. Too clever for her own good. He would not leave without the promise of her hand."

"Is this the payment received for supporting your Empire? To be sold to another empire, or left to rot hither unknown, or squeezed for ideas or coin?" Jarngard grabbed the leather bag around his neck.

"One man, or girl, cannot weigh against the needs of the realm. I've given you each slack for your needs, only to find you tangled in the rope, choking. Rome laughs while we bicker amongst ourselves like children. Only through sacrifice, yes sacrifice, can we beat them. Not all will live in this clash of kingdoms."

Jarngard let a bitter smile tread across his lips. "Sacrifice. What a fitting word. You'll sacrifice us just like you sacrificed Aurinia against the Gauls."

Agog's hand was around Jarngard's throat before he had a chance to blink. The Satrap moved like lightning. Jarngard tried to push him away, but the grip was too strong. Spots formed in his eyes. He tried to reach for his dagger, but a second hand held his arm fast.

The big man's bearded face loomed in his vision. His green eyes reflected the stormy seas of the north. Jarngard punched his friend in the jaw. Agog barely flinched. He felt himself going under, being swept out to sea, drowning in the middle of a desert.

Jarngard didn't remember falling, but he found himself on the wooden planking, holding his throat, trying to force air past his swollen neck. A dreadful wracking cough overwhelmed him, loosing blood across his hands.

He struggled to his knees and found Agog looming once more over him. A finger appeared in his face.

"I need you. Forget about the *Michanikos* or anything else. My army needs discipline and you are my general. If you dare defy me, I'll have your corpse thrown into the ocean."

Agog left him on the scaffolding amid the shouts of troops training. Jarngard pushed himself onto his rear and the wind caught his hair as he sat upright. The wood was surprisingly smooth. Old timber, reused, and repurposed for a time of war. Maybe it'd been used for theater seating before, or an inn table, both happier employs. Either way, it would not stay in its current form long. War needed wood, and bronze, and steel, and men. And after, none of them would be the same.

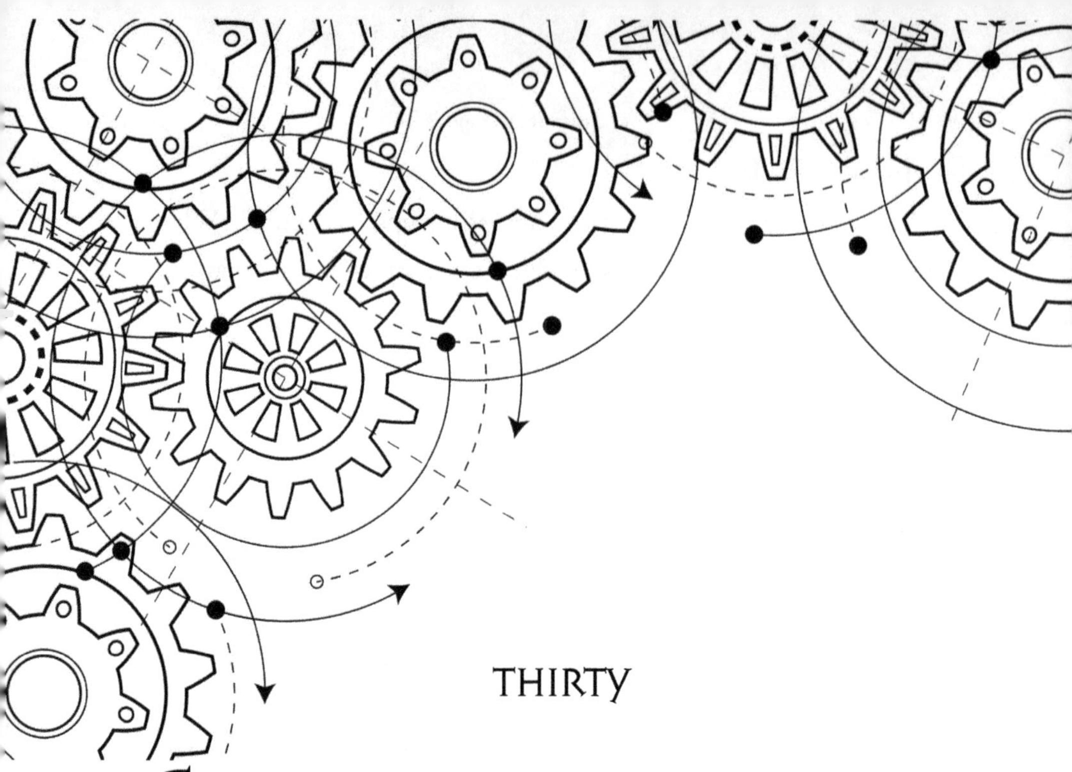

THIRTY

Sepharia rode toward Susa with Pheme and Carme, her hand-maidens from Polyxena, and Amitris, her Parthian handmaiden, in a steam barge finely decorated with silken curtains and a sunshade. The bronze shielding, hammered into the shape of a gryphon, kept the wind from battering them. The road was nearly smooth and the cups vibrated, dark liquid dancing, occasionally jumping from the lip.

The men rode horseback, along with the occasional elephant, and the pace was languid. The King of Alexandria, formerly the Satrap, Agog, had gifted them three steam chariots, in addition to the barge. Vima rode up and down the length of the caravan in his personal steam chariot encouraging his men on the journey. Amitris had explained they would travel north and east to Damascus to meet Vima's younger brother before circling down to Susa.

"Your Prince is quite handsome," said Pheme, lounging on the pillowed divan. A small table sat between them. Except for the thunderous noise of the steam mechanical and the smells of horse dung, she could have been in a room in the Palace.

Pheme was the younger of the two, though both were older than Sepharia by a year. She had a long, narrow face while Carme's was roundish. They each wore simple chitons with saffron highlights.

Vima rode by at that moment, wind whipping his hair like a banner. His skin soaked up the light. From a distance, he appeared to be someone she could love.

"He is," said Sepharia simply.

"You're very lucky," said Pheme. "From a commoner to a marriage with the handsome Prince of Parthia."

Sepharia did not take offense, Heron had long taught her the importance of acknowledging truth. But Amitris, who had been sitting quietly staring into the distance, leaned over and slapped Pheme across the jaw. The sound was deafening.

"Sepharia is the heir of Alexander the Macedonian. Not a common girl at all. The papers prove it. Never speak like that again, girl."

Amitris was only slightly older than the other two, but her weary gaze betrayed her burdensome experience. The handmaiden composed herself and the brief fury disappeared beneath featureless brown eyes.

"Apologies, Princess Sepharia," said Amitris in a fluent Greek. "If your Prince or one of his men heard that, they would probably cut out her tongue."

"Your wisdom is appreciated." Sepharia caught a murderous glance from Pheme. "Thank Amitris, she might have saved your life."

The youngest handmaiden murmured thanks while her eyes threw daggers. Sepharia sighed and watched the horses saunter alongside the barge. She realized she knew nothing about Parthia, other than a few hasty pieces of advice from Polyxena before she left.

Amitris resumed staring at the horizon and after the slap, the other two seemed less inclined to conversation. Sepharia studied the Parthian handmaiden. She had wide, brown, luminous eyes and soft features. Pheme and Carme's black hair was dull while Amitris' hair was lustrous.

She realized she needed to befriend Amitris. A task complicated by the fact that Sepharia had thrown the javelin that killed her former charge.

"Do you think Vima is handsome?" asked Sepharia.

The Parthian handmaiden regarded her soberly, glanced in the direction of the Prince, and looked back. "Of course he is." She returned to her study of the horizon.

"What about his younger brother? Khusra is his name?" asked Sepharia, hoping to draw her out.

"As well," said Amitris, keeping her gaze blank. "Khusra and Vima look similar though Khusra has a kinder smile."

"Have you heard how the Romans received him?" Sepharia asked carefully.

"It is not my place to say, Princess Sepharia. Ask your beloved Prince."

The quiet rebuke was clear enough that even Pheme and Carme understood. Though she was a Princess of Parthian now, she was not yet trusted.

To break the heavy mood, Sepharia tried a different tack. "Amitris, tell me about my Prince's companions, so that I might better serve him."

Sepharia thought she detected a hint of approval for her question. If a twitch to the lips could be interpreted as such. Amitris faced Sepharia, placing her hands in her lap.

"There are not many you need to know. The Prince's advisor is Vonones. He wears more gold than an Egyptian and you'll know him by the musky perfume he wears always. The Prince keeps his counsel with Vonones about all things. When you speak to Vonones, you speak to the Prince."

Mention of the musky perfume brought back memories of hiding on the Star Chamber. The man had suggested treachery against Alexandria. Sepharia made a mental note not to trust the man.

"And the others?"

"There is only one other you need to know. Pakur, the Prince's second. He has no hair on his head or face and he is said to be a fearsome warrior."

"I do not recall him."

Amitris made a strange face. "You would not know him. He has been on errands for the Prince since we arrived in Alexandria. They have been friends since they were boys. Vima has no fiercer protector. When they go into battle, it is said that Pakur turns to a raging spirit of vengeance, punishing all who try to strike at his friend. His fire is so hot it burns the hair from his body."

"The gods have known stranger things," said Sepharia, noting that Amitris spoke in a breathless, angry tone as she explained Pakur. "But I am curious to meet this Pakur."

"You will soon enough," said Amitris. "It is said that Pakur will meet us soon, near Jerusalem. The Prince plans a party to celebrate their rejoining."

"Are there others I should know?"

Amitris shook her head tightly. "Vonones and Pakur. Only them. The others fear to get too close, because those two are so protective."

"They fear their Prince?"

Amitris' eyes flashed with fire. "Yes, as we all should."

A deep breath was not enough to cleanse the worry from her bones. Sepharia poured a wine for her and Amitris over the protests of Pheme and Carme.

"Tell me about Parthia and Susa. Tell me everything."

The Parthian handmaiden narrowed her gaze before nodding. She got right to it, starting with the lineage of the king. Sepharia was used to sneaking into the Library dressed as a boy, and because her time was precious, she remembered almost everything she heard. Amitris spoke for the rest of the afternoon and well into night once they had camped. Sepharia only interrupted for questions or clarification, refilling the hand-maiden's glass to keep her speaking.

Afterwards, she curled up into bed with the three women. They fell asleep quickly, while Sepharia lie awake, thinking, and turning over the knowledge in her head. The Prince did not visit her that night, and even though clouds covered the night sky, she knew that in two days, the day of the party for Pakur near Jerusalem, it would be a full moon.

THIRTY ONE

"The goddess Artemis blesses your hunt this night," called out Vonones. Prince Vima, surrounded by his warriors, lifted his cup to Sepharia, who sat on pillowed benches with her handmaidens. The men whooped and hollered and drank with their Prince.

A *gosan*, court minstrel, had just finished reciting the romantic tale of *Vis and Ramin*. Amitris translated the meaning, but Sepharia almost preferred to listen to the lyrical language, even though she couldn't understand it. The emotional intonation was enough for her.

The silvery moonlight mixed with the ruddy campfire, casting conflicting shadows. The camp was placed away from the walls of Jerusalem. The city was still held by a Roman governor. Since the Parthians were still in negotiation with the Romans, an envoy was sent out to greet them, but no formal invitation into the city was given. Not that it had been expected.

A host of murmurs erupted behind the tents. A man entered the circle of firelight and the Prince rose to greet him. As the Prince was tall and lean, the newcomer was shorter and stockier with arms as large as other men's legs. Sepharia knew it was Pakur by the absence of hair on his head.

The two men embraced. Vima made room for Pakur and the two began chatting quietly. Vonones waited nearby, hands stuffed into the folds of his robes, golden chains around his neck reflecting the fire. Vonones did not join them. Their influence with the Prince must be separate, she decided.

Pheme was telling them about growing up in Macedonia. She had a touch of royal blood herself, which was why she'd been given the great honor of attending Polyxena. Sepharia barely listened, watching Vima and Pakur talk quietly. Pakur glanced in her direction twice. Sepharia could imagine the subject of Zenobia being brought up. The Prince left with one wife and returned with another. She would have to get used to such stares when she reached Susa.

Pakur appeared a few paces away, his face dripping in shadow. He pointed a finger and spoke to her in a thickly accented, broken Greek, "You are no Zenobia."

He left the ring of light and Prince Vima followed. His glance gave her a shiver. Amitris frowned and her hands dug further into her lap.

Sepharia opened her mouth to ask Amitris a question, when Vonones appeared. Jewelry rattled like faint chains. "Do not worry, Princess Sepharia, Pakur will come to accept you eventually. He loved Zenobia before she became Vima's third wife."

The robed advisor scrutinized the handmaiden Amitris as if he expected a response. Amitris' gaze flickered to Vonones once before returning to her lap.

"Thank you for your concern," said Sepharia. "But given the circumstances of my marriage to the Prince, I expect this will not be the first time I receive such hesitations."

The corner of his lip twitched upward at the choice of word 'hesitations'. He bowed his head slightly in her direction. "The Princess is quite wise and I should not be surprised given her pedigree. Alexander *and* the famed Machine Man, Heron. Few can boast such lineages."

The silkiness of his words were such that Sepharia could not detect if he was poking fun at the hasty nature of her adoption or if he was actually complimenting her. But he did seem to be currying favor. Sepharia guessed the relationship between himself and Pakur was tenuous.

"A word, Princess?"

She nodded. Amitris snapped her fingers at Pheme and Carme when they did not leave. The Macedonian girls hopped up and scurried after Amitris.

Sepharia motioned for Vonones to sit beside her. "A cup of wine?"

His hesitation indicated he did not trust her. While she'd had no hand in it, the poisoning of the Jewish Princess Shayna had been attributed to her. Ramses the Exile had done it, she was sure, but she'd pushed him over the railing at the coliseum, so he could never admit fault. That misappropriation suddenly became useful. Sepharia wondered if that was why the Prince had scoured her belongings, making her drink her potions and eat her herbs, thinking they were poisons.

"A word of warning," began Vonones after confirming no one stood near. "The Prince can be a volatile man. While I've counseled him that the alliance between Parthia and Alexandria depends on image just as much as written contract..."

He paused, clearly letting her comprehend his message. He was letting her know that the Prince's sober treatment of her was his doing.

"...the influence of Pakur on his mood can be quite strong."

Vonones glanced regretfully at the fat, silvery moon in the sky.

"Your kind words are much appreciated, good Vonones." She smiled and patted his arm.

Vonones moved to stand before hesitating. He gave her a sad, worn smile, as if the tale he was about to tell was heartbreaking to him. Sepharia knew better.

"Zenobia and Pakur were meant to be married before Vima took an interest. She was a minor noble from an insignificant family. When the Prince announced he was marrying Zenobia, Pakur rode away from the city. The next day he was at Vima's side as if nothing had happened and his loyalty to the Prince became fanatical."

His dark eyes were mesmerizing. He continued, his voice dropping even lower, so much she had to lean in to hear him.

"I was there on the night of Zenobia's death. I understand the *trage-dy*," said Vonones. "Pakur, however, will not."

The advisor left. Sepharia took a long drink and stared into the coals of the fire. Zenobia's reluctant participation in their womanly endeavors became clear. The woman's heart had been rended in two. Sepharia wondered if Zenobia had thrown herself in front of the javelin or she'd been pushed, as Bani claimed. Either way, this was a point that Vonones seemed to relish. It was clear Vonones did not like Pakur's influence on the Prince. The knowledge that Zenobia might have been murdered could drive a wedge between Vima and Pakur.

Pheme and Carme returned after a short time. Amitris had retired for the evening. The two handmaidens giggled about the hairless Pakur, keeping Sepharia from musing on the events of the evening.

Later, Amitris appeared bleary eyed, robe pulled tightly around. Doubt, or concern, weighed heavily on her shoulders.

"The Prince, he wishes to see you."

There was no point in waiting. Sepharia kissed her handmaidens and bid them a restful sleep.

She was nervous and she told herself she should be. And while she had yet to be with a man, Bani had taught her many things. She did not feel unprepared.

Parthian men spoke to her as she moved through the tents. She knew enough of their language to exchange greetings. It kept her mind off what would happen in the tent.

At the threshold, she reminded herself that a few days ago, she'd desired him, had encouraged his interest in her. Only the lie that Polyxena had told him kept him away from her, trading on his respect for the gods. The lie would ensure that, even if it did go poorly, he would only visit her for a few days every month.

Sepharia made a silent prayer to Cleopatra and entered the tent. Vima stood with his back to her, wearing only a loincloth, a bronze goblet in his hand. His bare back was rippled with muscles. A white scar trailed down the right shoulder blade.

"I am here, my beloved."

He turned his head, but did not speak. Sepharia moved to him, put a hand on his back. He flinched.

"Apologies, my beloved. My hand is cold."

He kept his face turned from her.

"Do you know why I asked for you?"

She swallowed. "No, but I was honored that you did so."

"Of course you were."

She kept her hand on his back. Vima gulped at his wine.

"If a man leaves nothing unconquered," he began, "then his enemies will know he is a man of his word, and his word is made of action."

Under the palm of her hand, his muscles rippled with effort. He was burning hot.

"These Alexandrians and Romans are fools. Even my father is a fool. Treaties and agreements don't win empires, only action. Vonones travels with a chest full of papyrus. Paper! I want no empire built on paper."

Vima turned and put a hand on her shoulder. His eyes were blood-shot like he'd been sitting in a smoky tent. He smelled like incense.

"Are you loyal?"

His gaze was horrific. Sepharia steeled herself from turning away.

"Of course, my beloved."

There was a half-grin on his face that could have been carved on a statue in the Temple of Sobek. His grip tightened.

"No one is loyal at first," he said calmly. "Just like the stories of the gods, they must be tested, time and time again, to prove themselves. Even dear Pakur was not loyal at first."

Sepharia tried to smile serenely. "I will be loyal. A good wife and a good Queen."

The expression on Vima's face changed suddenly. He slapped her hard. She spun onto the floor.

"A Queen? You will never be a Queen. To please my father and to ensure the *paper* link to Alexander the Macedonian, it could have been any girl. Just like our marriage is written in *paper*. It means nothing. I know the last words of Alexander. *To the Strongest!* I am the strongest. I will show that fat King of Alexandria, that so-called Emperor Claudius, and even my father. To the Strongest!"

Vima grabbed her by the hair and dragged her across the room, knocking over a table, spilling a fat candle. She was no match for his strength. She clawed at his hand. Vima threw her on the bed.

Sepharia had imagined that he might be rough, that he might even be aloof or cold when they had sex, those were the prices she would have to pay. Bani had warned her. Though in her heart, she believed she could seduce him just as Cleopatra had seduced Caesar.

But he wasn't interested in sex.

His violence surprised her. She froze. None of the scenarios she'd imagined had played out like this. He smacked her across the face, glowering over her. Blood ran from her nose.

He hit her again, moving like the viper for which he was named. Sepharia tried to fight back but he was too strong.

"You're not the strongest," she spat, which only enraged him further.

The fist connected with her forehead bringing stars to her eyes. He kept pummeling her around the midsection, knocking the air from her lungs. She clawed him in the shoulder, but for every one of her strikes, he hit her five times. He pushed his weight on her neck and before long unconsciousness claimed her.

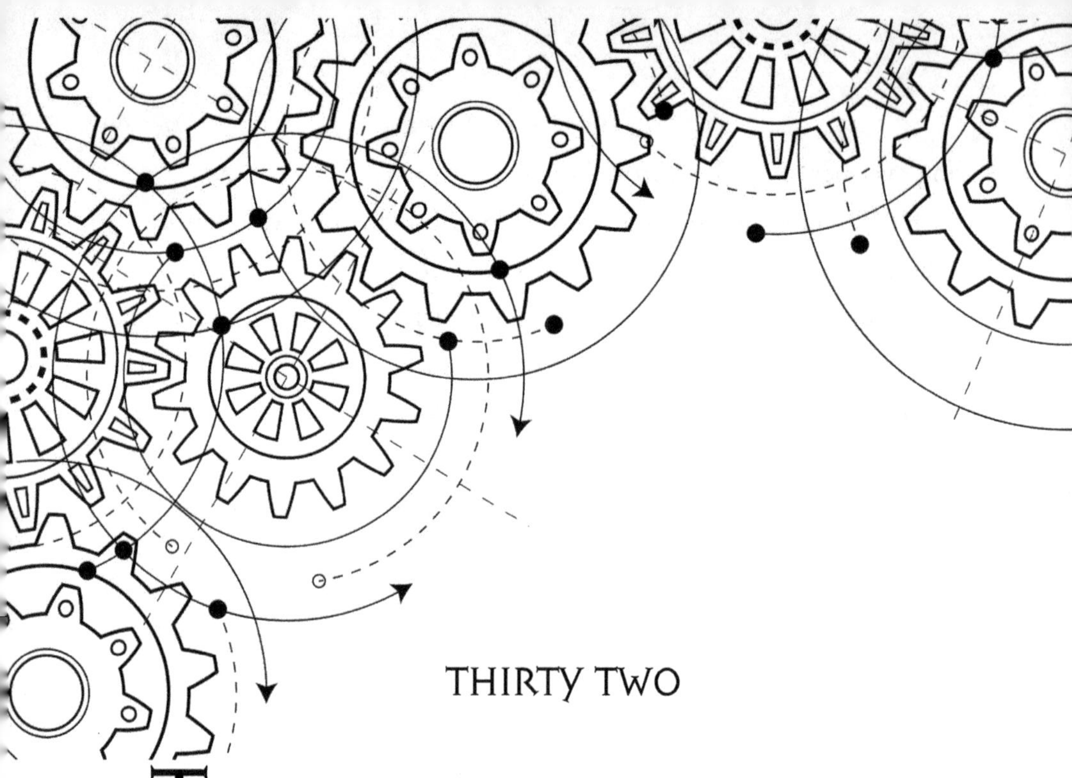

THIRTY TWO

The mottled walls of the temple room shimmered with soggy wetness. The stone was rough as if the space had been clawed open with bloody fingers and a primordial dripping kept time for Heron in the murky light.

The scaled throne chaffed against her bare legs. A millipede scrambled around her calf. Heron strained at the leather restraints, wrists pinned to the arm of the chair. The tiny insect disappeared beneath her and she thought she felt a bite.

Sweat beaded against her brow, brought on by the moist air. The chamber felt like the mouth of a great beast. To her right, hanging on the stone wall, deadly implements waited like traps.

Her inventive mind conjured uses for the items. Gears and springs actuated, the force was calculated, the pain imagined. Whoever had designed these torture devices knew their trade.

"...the crocodile rolls..."

The sing-song voice of the crocodile priest drifted down from the upper chamber. He would visit her soon, she knew. He had yet to use the implements on her, but she knew that time would come soon. Maybe even this time.

On previous visits, he'd fed her and cared for the wounds from her capture. There was no talking in his presence. The first time he brought food, she had asked him a question. He shook his head, the crocodile mask shifting slightly, gaze eager, and left.

The second time she stayed quiet and ate the nearly raw meat he fed her. She ignored the bloodiness and choked down the meal.

Though she had been in the temple for a week, a length of time she guessed from her slumbers and the nearly perfect time of the dripping water, she knew little about her captor. The crocodile priest left few clues. He was missing a hand, and part of his foot, based on a limp and the way he put his hand against the wall when he descended the stone steps.

His verdant robes were plain, devoid of the gems or jewelry she expected to see in the temples of Alexandria. His mask, while perfectly kept, was ancient. She was familiar with the Sobek Temples and the style: simple lines, closed mouth, ovoid eye slots, and marked it against the opulent artifacts of the other temples.

This was a simple temple. Heron thought she knew where that placed her. Once the priest had captured her, he'd driven the wagon through the whipping winds. She lay in back, hands and feet bound to the planks, face exposed to the stinging sands. Somehow, the priest found an abandoned settlement with broken walls. He drove into it and threw a tarp over them both.

After the storm passed, they drove for three days. The tarp stayed over the wagon, covering her. They passed caravans on more than one occasion. The tarp muffled the voices. She never heard the name of their destination, but she knew the trade routes around the city and the location of pyramid construction sites. There was only one place she thought they could be: Arsinoe, or commonly called Crocodopolis.

But why had the Temple of Sobek taken her? The priest gave no indication. Had she wronged them in some way? Were they co-conspirators with the cult of Ur? Or the goddess Nanna? Of all the gods, Sobek was the most solitary. Sobek was feared by the other temples. They did not have a tangible presence in the world like Sobek. No toothy green monsters lurking in the murky water taking even bony children who had wandered too close to the river's edge.

The priest seemed unsurprised by her gender. He'd given her a tunic, which only covered her upper half. The torn lower hem rested against her upper thigh and she caught him staring at the space between her legs. Strangely, she did not see sexual desire in those beady eyes, maybe he was a eunuch or had lost other parts, and that left thoughts she feared to consider.

A door opened above. The walls seemed to shrink from the light. Uneven footsteps announced his entrance.

He was singing again, in Egyptian, "...spin and turn, the crocodiles roll. Chomp!"

At the word, '*Chomp*!' she heard a hop in his step. He seemed in a buoyant mood. Her stomach rolled.

"Snap and rip, the crocodiles feast. Chomp!"

He giggled and then he was there, standing before her scaly throne, hand and stump leaning against the armrests, so close to her fingers. He studied her from behind the mask, the snout invading her space, rancid breath emanating from the tiny air hole at the end.

"Are thee well?"

He spoke in fluent Greek and she thought she recognized it, but the mask distorted the tone. A shadow of a memory waiting like ravens in high trees. And that was when she realized he was not Egyptian. His hair was dark, but not that lightless ebony that the Egyptians seemed to have.

The crocodile priest seemed to remember something. "Oh," he tittered, "you may speak now. I wish to converse."

"You come from Alexandria," she said.

He drew his words out, "Of course you would figure that, but do you know who I am?"

She blinked and searched her memory. It seemed she should know him. "No," she said eventually.

The pink, cracked stump of his arm poked from the robes. He rubbed it across the back of her hand. She could sense him smiling beneath the mask.

"What do you want?" she asked.

"Ahhh...a negotiation? Is that what you think this is?"

She glanced to the wall of torture devices. "No," she said sadly.

He nodded approvingly, "Then you understand why you are here."

"No," she said. "I understand what will happen, but not why. What have I ever done to the Temple of Sobek? I made miracles for the temple in Alexandria, successful ones, I remember."

Amused, he stepped away. He touched the device with a huge metal jaw in the shape of a crocodile's mouth, hooked to a gear which could be turned by a handle. Turning it would slowly close the mouth.

"Do not worry. Today is not a day of worship for He Who Dwelleth Amid Terrors. Today, we are getting to know each other."

"And tomorrow you will put me to those devices," she said defiantly. "Why wait?"

He turned to her. "I honor the temple of Sobek and the priest and priestess who came before me. They taught me the way of the crocodile god, much as I will teach you. Eventually you will come to love him as I do."

"I do not believe in the gods," she said. "Only in the cruelty of men."

The crocodile priest tilted his head. "It doesn't matter if you believe in them. They believe in you."

His voice was tantalizingly familiar. She wanted to scream. "Who are you?"

He put his mask into her face, the snout grazing her chin. His beady eyes drank her in.

"*Lex Talionis*," he whispered.

Her jaw went slack. He laughed.

"The red stone," she said.

"Yes, your little message. When I strapped my teachers to the chair, I showed them things even they had not thought of. They gave up their secrets easily."

His name was a wound on her tongue, "Lysimachus."

The crocodile mask fell away. He held his stump before her.

"*Lex Talionis.*"

THIRTY THREE

Sepharia lifted the delicate hammer, measured the distance with an astute eye, and smacked it against the medallion. With only a few more strokes she would be complete and it would be ready for Heron's inspection.

Only she couldn't find the needle press and the etching had to be just right, or she wouldn't be able...

What? She couldn't remember. That was fine, she was sure she would remember, eventually. There was always more work, more work, and more work. She had all she wanted in the workshop.

The hammer was smooth and solid and when she lifted it—

"Where is my hammer?" she asked, staring acrimoniously at the piece of footwear in her hand. "This is a sandal. Who took my hammer?"

A voice answered her, but the words flowed past her, not understood. Why was this person speaking in another language? Sepharia ignored it and went back to searching for the hammer. How she got a hammer and a sandal confused she would never know. Maybe she'd been working too hard. She had a lot to do, but—

"Where's my hammer? Who took it?"

A hand grabbed her arm. A face loomed in her vision. Someone was shaking her.

"You must listen to me now," said the slightly familiar voice, "take off that man's tunic before Prince Vima sees you. I beg of you, take it off."

"But my hammer, I need it," she told the voice. Why didn't it understand? Her work would not be complete without it. That, and the needle press, she needed that, too.

"Princess Sepharia."

The name seemed to be hers, especially that second part. But Princess? Surely that had to be a dream?

"Princess Sepharia, if Vima sees you in this man's tunic..." The voice paused, maybe it didn't know what it wanted to say, "...then you'll wish he'd killed you."

The face seemed familiar. "Amitris?" she asked it.

"Yes, it's me, Amitris. I serve you. Help you, like I couldn't help Zenobia."

"Zenobia, yes, I remember her," said Sepharia.

Except she didn't want to. She remembered throwing the javelin and melons spilled against the grass and the eye of the Lighthouse, watching, unapproving. What had she done?

"Let me get this off you and clean this up. You're bleeding again." Amitris tugged the tunic over her head. The gooseflesh spread across her skin like waves. She shivered.

"Yes," said Sepharia listlessly, "I think the hammer slipped."

A hand grabbed her chin. "No, listen to me. It was Prince Vima. The Prince. I won't let you do what Zenobia did. It was all my fault.

You cannot go away, even if you want to."

Sepharia cinched her arms around her midsection. The tent was so cold. "Can I have a blanket?"

"First, let me clean you up."

Amitris wiped the dried blood off her face, scrubbing vigorously when it wouldn't budge. Sepharia shivered the whole time until the cold, wet rag was away and a blanket was wrapped around her shoulders.

"I'm not in the workshop, am I?" asked Sepharia.

The color from Amitris' lips fled as she smashed them together. A tight shake of the head. "No. You are married to Prince Vima. Do you understand?"

"Yes," said Sepharia sadly, "I understand."

The Parthian handmaiden led her to the bed, each step was a minor agony, and gave her a cup of watered-down wine. "Drink this, it will help you sleep."

"Give me water, instead. I think I've slept enough, haven't I? I thought I was in the workshop. I dreamt it," after a pause, "or wanted to."

Amitris handed her an opaque glass filled with water. The sparkling water soothed her lips and throat.

"Why are you helping me?" asked Sepharia.

Amitris stared into her lap. "Because I failed Zenobia."

Realizing the sandal was still in her hand, Sepharia set it down, staring at it cautiously. Part of her still remembered it'd been a hammer.

"How did you fail her?" she asked, still keeping an eye on the sandal so it wouldn't turn into a hammer again.

Amitris whispered, "When Zenobia was first married to him, even though she was a third wife, she was happy. He's a handsome man and looks the part of a hero from times past legend. But the Prince is nothing like his father or brother. He's a cruel, small man. Once she got to know him, she was unhappy, and I thought I would help. Women in the Parthian court sometimes have paramours and I found one for her as handmaidens do. She seemed happy."

"Pakur," said Sepharia.

"Yes, that's right, but the Prince must have absolute loyalty," said Amitris.

"I understand. And now he wants to control me completely."

Amitris frowned regretfully, making a tiny shrug with her eyes. "I do not know the mind of a Prince, especially this one. I only knew Zenobia and she was kind to me."

Sepharia put a hand to her forehead. "And I killed her."

There was a flicker of accusation, but it quickly turned to sadness.

"No," said Amitris, "I was there. I saw her lean into the javelin. It was not you."

"I did it. I threw the javelin."

"But you didn't kill her," said Amitris. "She was dead inside. Like you will..."

The beautiful Parthian handmaiden gave her a sad, poignant glance, almost apologetic. For whatever reason, the depth of that reflected pain woke Sepharia.

"I won't," she said, hearing the resolve tighten in her own voice. She'd come with a plan, though what she and Bani had planned was not enough. After the night with Vima, her efforts at scheming seemed feeble. She still had the poison, buried in the hidden compartment in the lelathon cabinet. She could kill him in revenge, but without the Romans to pin it on, they'd kill her and she'd ruin the alliance with Alexandria, if there'd ever really been one in the first place.

Amitris seemed to sense the change in Sepharia. "Do not act rashly. Zenobia tried to run away once. He dragged her behind his horse until she passed out."

"Do not worry. I won't be rash," said Sepharia.

The handmaiden studied her face. Sepharia sensed the woman didn't believe her. She wanted to trust her, but trust was a foolish endeavor. She didn't even trust her Macedonian handmaidens and they were a gift from Polyxena. She just hoped they could pass messages safely when the time came, which could be soon.

"Thank you, Amitris."

Sepharia leaned forward to kiss the woman on the cheek when Amitris recoiled in horror.

"You're bleeding again! This will not do. Stay here, I must fetch the physician."

The handmaiden left the tent, pushing through the flap, leaving Sepharia alone. She sighed and kicked the traitorous sandal away.

Not long after, Vonones appeared in a white, gold-fringed robe. His cheeks were rosy.

"I came at once, are you well?" he asked.

Sepharia pulled the blanket over her lap. "Where's the physician?"

The smile spread across his face. "It is me. The Prince must trust the person attending to his bodily needs." He glanced over his shoulder. "And Amitris is fetching me some bandages."

"I'm sorry, it's just..."

"I understand. But I promise I can help." He placed a hand on her arm and nodded reassuringly. "Amitris told me what the Prince did. I'm very sorry that I could not calm his rages."

"No," she shook her head, "you warned me. I thought I might overcome my earlier—" A pause. "—struggles, and find a way to make him love me."

"It's difficult to be a woman in his court. His brother Khusra is kinder and people find their love for him easier, but he is not his brother. He is Vima the Viper," he told her.

"Thank you for your kindness, Vonones. I feel I have few friends here," she said.

He nodded. "In time, they will get to know and love you. You are a beautiful woman and the daughter of the great *Michanikos*. You will bear him wonderful children."

Her stomach rolled at the thought, but she kept her little smile propped up. Amitris appeared with bandages and a bucket of clean water, saving her from further discussions about Vima.

"Let me examine you," he said. "I will be as gentle as my practice allows."

She reluctantly let him pull away the blanket and did not protest when he carefully examined the bruises on her ribs. After a brief and uncomfortable examination, he stood.

"You are still bleeding. I will have Amitris bring you some poppy's sap to put in your wine to help with the pain and more bandages."

She nodded and Amitris left. While they were waiting, a messenger appeared. He seemed to have important news. Vonones apologized and stepped outside with the messenger.

She could hear the murmur of their voices, but not the clarity of their words. Despite the pain, Sepharia wanted to hear what was being said. She pulled the blanket around her waist and hobbled toward the entrance. She had to be careful. If he came back in quickly, her eavesdropping would be obvious.

The tent ruffled and Sepharia nearly fell over herself trying to scramble back to the bed. It seemed they were moving to the back of the tent, away from the bed. With ginger steps, she followed. A brief glance showed her sudden movement had brought more blood, filled with thick black congealed lumps.

The voices were still unclear so she got on her knees and put her ear to the bottom edge. Blond curls fell into her face, tickling her nose.

"...and there is one more thing," said the messenger in halting Latin.

"Get on with it," growled Vonones in a hushed tone. Sepharia pressed her ear to the gap.

"Arsaces, King of Kings, is displeased with his son. He was not authorized to sign treaties in his father's place."

"Please explain to the revered *Dikaios*, King of Kings, that as his son's advisor, I could not persuade him otherwise. I humbly remind him that his son is willful," said Vonones.

"And he anticipated you would say that and he reminds you that you serve his son with his permission," said the messenger. "You can be replaced."

The messenger cleared his throat. "Excuse me, this foreign tongue hurts my ears."

Vonones responded in a different language, the lyrical growling speech she heard from the soldiers in the caravan. She stayed long enough to hear the names of cities: Susa, Damascus, and Haran. The importance of those locations was lost on her and she did not linger, taking the time to hobble back to the bed.

She reached the bed when Amitris arrived. The handmaiden gave her a curious glance. There was a blood trail leading to the back of the tent, but Amitris did not acknowledge it.

The blood was thick and sticky against her hip. Amitris cleaned her again. Then she made Sepharia a cup of tea with drops of poppy. She dutifully drank and let Amitris put her to bed.

"Good Amitris, would you send for Carme when you are finished?" she asked sleepily.

The woman wrinkled her forehead. "If you desire something, tell me," said Amitris, "I am your servant."

"I need Carme," she said as gently as possible, "because I do not want to sleep alone and I would ask you, but I have another errand for you."

"What do you need? If you promise you won't put on any more men's tunics, I will gladly fetch it for you," said Amitris.

"A map," said Sepharia. "I wish to know the lands of my new people and the routes between it and Alexandria. It will help keep my mind occupied."

"It may be difficult to acquire, but if it will help, I will retrieve it." Amitris squinted. "I assume I should keep this map secret."

Sepharia nodded. "I do not think my husband would like me showing signs of learnedness, though I would surely love to learn your language so I can listen to those wonderful stories each night."

"I can teach you. I will go now. I will find you a map and maybe tomorrow when you are feeling better, I can start teaching you our language," said Amitris.

Sepharia laid her head on the pillows. The poppy tea drained away her strength. "Don't forget Carme."

Amitris left.

The weight of sleep pulled heavily on her lids, but she resisted. When Carme arrived she needed to give her a message. Agog had to know that the treaty they signed was not valid. If that was true and the Parthians sided with Rome, then she would be on the wrong side of the war and the poison in her cabinet might be her only way out.

THIRTY FOUR

Time kept miserable friends in the darkness. There was something almost worse about the between times. The *before* and *after* of the crocodile priest. Lysimachus.

A muscle in her neck throbbed. She strained momentarily at the bonds, not too long, she didn't want to waste her energy. She would need it for later, when he returned. How long that would be, she didn't know. It felt like every time she closed her eyes, he showed up to teach her the usage of a new device.

Teaching. That was the worst part. She couldn't help but admire the efficiency of the devices and each one spawned new inventions for her workshop. But those ideas would die in the darkness, locked in a damp hole beneath the Temple of Sobek.

Though her voice was raw from screaming, it was the knowledge that these ideas would never reach the light that hurt most. A pair of coiled wires pushing two plates that crushed her arm between them could help smooth the steam chariots rattling. When Lysimachus easily turned a handle, the gears multiplied that inevitable force to push a long barbed needle through her thigh.

When she did sleep, she dreamt of Alexandria. Not her Alexandria, but one unslipped from the bonds of slavery. One where her inventions had been allowed to multiply, like ants or scarab beetles. Strange machines scurried through the sky, beating bronze wings. An endless serpentine machine snaked into the distance carrying men and materials (driven by the gearing of the needle device.) If the Romans could spread their law by the force of the legions and speed of the roads, she could do the same with an interconnected network of machines.

This future Alexandria chaffed at the sky, leaving the Lighthouse in its shadow to chase birds. Iron boats as big as a kraken were lifted out of the harbor using massive cranes that dwarfed Archimedes' designs. At the center of this *Pax Alexandria* her golden pyramid glittered in the sun, not a tomb, but a monument to human creativity.

Heron stared regretfully at the bonds around her wrist. Then she flinched, even before she realized she heard the tittering laughter of the crocodile priest. It was easier to think of him that way. The name Lysimachus seemed like a misused label. The customs man she knew in Alexandria was changed.

She kept her gaze drilled into her lap as Lysimachus approached. He did not wear the mask any longer, though she would prefer it. His skin was tallow white and his eyes were dark rocks pushed into flame-wet wax.

Each time he held up his stump, the cracked pink flesh, always with one scab or another from him bumping into rough objects, the words *Lex Talionis* formed in her mind like a beacon.

"Have we thought on the lessons from our last session?" he asked as calmly and with the same erudite passionless demeanor as one would expect from a scholar in the Great Library.

"No," she said honestly. "I can't even remember what we discussed."

He did not get mad as she thought he would. "An excellent sign. There is nothing explicit about He Who Dwelleth Amid Terrors. Nothing to truly *learn* or remember. Sobek is the primal fear, the original source that drives all other endeavors. He is the font of creation."

She glanced to the wall of implements. Lysimachus required the airing of opinions, as he liked to call them. He was more likely to put her hand in a vice if she stayed silent, but she was too tired to parse her thoughts and let them flow out unimpeded.

"There is nothing vital to your Sobek. A rational, but misplaced fear of death, assigned to the great crocodiles of the Nile," she said.

"Oh, this makes me so happy." He giggled. "You are the perfect tool for Sobek. You will become his greatest priestess and they will flock to his temples because they will see that if you love him, so should they."

"I will never."

Lysimachus let his stump rest on her arm. His thigh set against her calf. "But you already have. When I was the Alabarch, did your debts not drive you to creativity? Without fear, would you have worked so hard and so long? Humanity is inherently lazy. Without the primal terrors of Sobek, man, or woman in your case, would grow fat and dumb."

"Creating machines and dissecting the gears that run the world drives me, regardless," she said. "I must assume each person has their calling. This is the way of the Great Library."

"Cover it in reeds, however you like," said Lysimachus, "but it is terror that keeps us together, it is terror that is the first force. Even Rome knows this."

"Rome runs on its legions and roads and laws," she replied, knowing he would respond again. It was like this each day (or what she conceived of days), the back and forth, until he moved to the wall and the true pain began.

His beady, black eyes flickered with amusement. "Rome runs on terror. Those roads and legions and laws bring that terror to all who disobey. Laws work because men fear them. It is in their nature to hurt and destroy, like crocodiles at a feast. Have you ever watched them? They'll snap off a foot of a fellow crocodile in the frenzy to eat."

"It doesn't have to be that way. Knowledge will overcome fear. Your implements put to better use could relieve the ordinary pains of man. Hiding them down here is an affront to their possibilities."

Lysimachus traced the stump along her arm. The half-broken scab felt like a fingernail. "I knew you would like these devices. Appreciate their workings. Even when you are screaming, I can see your mind working to understand how they work, which only proves my point. He Who Dwelleth Amid Terrors brings the drive to create. Without him, we would still be beasts in the wild. He created man, fashioned us out of mud on the banks of the Nile. Why should we begrudge him a few wayward children? But these are things you will understand in time, as I have. And when I'm done with you, you'll either be his greatest priestess, or I'll feed you to Petsuchos one limb at a time."

He studied her carefully and she assumed he saw something he liked, because he made a noise of pleasure. Despite her exhaustion, Heron stared back.

"Tomorrow, I begin your training," he explained. "What you have experienced so far was just the beginning. To help you understand the scope of what Sobek has to teach. I promise you, you will in time come to love my attentions. As agonizing as they will be, they will pale against the terrors inflicted in the intervening times. And all the lies you tell yourself will be exposed. Be ready, I come for you tomorrow."

A flickering candle had always been left for her, to view the implements of torture on the wall, she assumed. This time, Lysimachus blew out the candle on the nearby table. The darkness was suffocating. She heard the door close after a while.

In a short time, images played across her vision on the canvas of the darkness. The subterranean dripping sounded like patient steps of some watery beast. When those steps turned to what sounded like claws against stone, Heron froze. She was sure the noise was her imagination until she heard a snort, not but a few lengths from her scaly throne. Heron sucked in a breath and tried to hold it, knowing that eventually she would have to let it out. When something heavy bumped into her bare foot, she tried not to scream.

THIRTY FIVE

All the lies you tell yourself will be exposed. The words haunted her mind like a desolate wind through canyons. Lysimachus was right about the intervening times, the times between, those were the worst.

Between, the darkness was a waking dream. Without light to know the end of a dream and the beginning of the real, Heron was afraid to sleep. She dug fingernails into her palm, or bit her lip until she tasted coppery blood to keep from slumber.

Once, a mouth full of teeth swallowed her leg, digging into her calf. Heron screamed and kicked it away with her other foot, feeling the scaly underside of the beast. When it was gone, she wasn't sure she hadn't imagined it.

Other things came to her in the darkness. Jarngard met her in that voidless place. Always she saw him from a distance, holding a red light and when he neared, his face was bloody and raw from the sand storm. He reached out to touch her with bony fingers, hunks of skin hanging loosely from the knuckles. This was the least of her nightmares.

Sometimes she woke in the middle of a teaching. Lysimachus stood over her with the iron vise already around her kneecap. The pain of bones grinding together and ligaments nearly snapping caused her to cry out until she felt bereft of her sanity.

Heron was dozing, head nodding against the throne, waking each time she bumped against it. It hadn't been long since his last visit, or so she hoped. Heron hoped to find a stretch of sleep in the darkness. Hoped that he would give her time to rest, time to recover. When the candle flame sparked into brightness, she recoiled, squinting away the light, and cursed the day she ever left the safety of the camp.

Lysimachus sat across from her. The table had been pulled near. How long he had been like that perturbed her. She never heard him in the darkness. Couldn't figure out how he snuck up, noiseless and lightless. The table had to weigh one hundred stones and he only had one hand.

"He Who Dwelleth Amid Terrors revels in your offerings," said Lysimachus. "Your fear feeds him and brings you one step closer to him."

"Never," she said. "Your crocodile god is a farce."

Undaunted, Lysimachus produced a barbed hook from the table. A tan, waxy bag connected to thin strings sat next to a stumpy candle and next to the candle was a papyrus and inkwell with a quill sticking from it. The writing equipment was a curious addition.

He set the hook in his lap. It was the type of hook she'd seen on the docks of Alexandria, the kind they caught whales with, but thinner and without a barb.

Heron knew this game. He wanted her to look upon it and feel terror before he began torturing her. He might do it right away, or he might wait a while, or maybe not even use it and bring it back another time, or not at all.

"Have I told you about my hand?" he asked.

Heron shook her head.

"How do you think I lost it?"

"I really don't care," she said. "Use your hook and get it over with. All these games are just like the miracles I made for the temples. They're designed to confuse and convert the masses. And though the pain and terror is real, I'm not one of those people. I will not succumb. Get it over with."

Lysimachus tilted his head. His eyebrow raised slightly. "If all women were like you, maybe you would not be considered the weaker sex. Still, I will break you all the same. As the Alabarch, I was a mediocre teacher of pain. Sobek, Teeth of the World, has given me extraordinary powers."

"Every priest in every temple feels the same way," said Heron, summoning her resolve. "You were a failed customs collector and now you're a failed priest."

If she was lucky, he would get angry and kill her quickly. Eventually everyone broke, she would be no exception. In moments of weakness, when the pain had her in its grasp, she'd said things she didn't believe. For now.

But Lysimachus didn't react. He only studied her like a scholar studies his scrolls.

"My hand," he said eventually. "I offered it to the beast when they left me on the slab. Even now I question my sanity in that moment. Why would I willingly offer my hand to a crocodile? Yes, I see that look on your face. You hadn't expected that I gave it willingly, nor that I would not regret it, but this is the power of Sobek. I understand that now. I'm lucky that they had restrained me on the slab, or I would have willingly crawled into the beast's mouth."

The moment of reflection surprised Heron. She thought him taken by madness, but this sanity made her situation even more dangerous.

"The lies you tell yourself will be exposed," he said finally. "Fear is the original force and this session, I will show you the power of my god. You will design the implement of your pain. Sobek will provide the fear and you will create, marking your design on this papyrus."

He didn't wait for her to deny, or spit back a perfectly crafted barb. Instead, he reached forward with the hook, grabbed her left breast with one hand, squeezing and massaging it until the nipple popped out, and then slipped the hook through the base of the nipple. He repeated the insertion of a second hook with her other nipple. Blood leaked from the hooks as tears flowed down her face.

With the precision of a one-handed fisherman, Lysimachus tied string around the hooks and connected the string to the tan, waxy bag. When he noticed her watching, he remarked, "Breath of Sobek, this one is called."

Lysimachus lit the stumpy candle and held the bag over the flame. Heron was surprised how thin the bag seemed. She thought it was leather at first, but then she realized it was papyrus, modified in some way.

She expected the bag to burn when he put it over the flame. The thin material glowed with reddish-orange light. Eventually, the skin pressed outward and gently released from his fingertips. A webbing fell from the bottom of the bag and Lysimachus slipped the candle into the center of the crossing strings.

Slowly, the lighted bag climbed higher until it was pulling against the hook through her nipple. Enraptured by the curious invention, Heron barely felt the pain.

Lysimachus pushed the table against her chair and loosened the bonds around her right arm, giving her enough slack to reach the papyrus and quill.

"The pain is bearable," he said, "but that will change in time. I will add a second bag and the constant pressure and stiffness of your nipples will give you motivation."

What makes it rise? She wanted to ask him this question, but she knew his answer. *The will of the Sobek*, or some such nonsense. Despite the pain, she was fascinated by the floating bag.

He produced a second bag and performed the same trick. She grimaced as it tugged against her sore nipple.

His smile was altogether unpleasant. He motioned toward the quill. "Conjure an invention from that mighty mind of yours. Something future pupils of Sobek will fondly remember you by. Help me create it and I will gladly take these away."

Rather than answer, Heron stared at the floating bags. Lysimachus' gaze flickered between the quill and her hand.

"I am a patient man," he said.

When the pain made her dizzy, she closed her eyes. Bile rose in her throat. A deep breath tugged on the strings, bringing tears to her eyes.

"Sobek is the font of creation. Let him lead you to salvation," said Lysimachus. "I can see that mind working behind those eyes. Your lies will be exposed. Lift up that quill and begin drawing the next object of Sobek's worship. You cannot lie to me, I can see your mind working, despite your grimaces."

Heron looked away. He was right, her mind *was* whirling through designs, creating as those sharp hooks pulled painfully on her taut nipples. But it wasn't for him, or for Sobek. The candle fuelled bags scaled up in her mind, until they were as big as buildings and she rode beneath them, flying over the landscape like a bird.

Using an estimated size and weight she calculated how big it would need to be to carry a person, assuming that the scaling was linear. Experiments with the material would bring the best weight to air entrapment ratio. She assumed the heat lifted the bag, much in the same way the heat was worse at the tops of the scaffoldings in her workshop. The fuel source would be a problem, but once she had an idea, figuring out the details was trivial.

A fist slammed into the table. "Start sketching, now. I can practically see the design dancing across your eyes. Give back to Sobek what he has given you. He gave you the proper motivation, now draw."

Heron slowly shook her head, hoping to enrage him. He pushed himself away from the table and marched to the wall of torture implements. Quickly, she scanned the table for something to grab while his attention was elsewhere. A pile of candle stubs was in reach. There were also loose, clear stones, nearly flat. Her fingers were not as nimble as they used to be and she only had one hand to work with, but she was able to grab one. The smooth, round disc felt like glass beneath her fingertips. Before Lysimachus could turn around, she dropped it in her lap, let it slide down her thigh and scooted over it.

He pulled a metal box from the wall. It had gearing on the side, a lever on the back, and a hole the size of a fist in the front. The mouth of a crocodile was painted over the hole. She tried not to imagine what kind of pain it was capable of creating.

He dropped it onto the table with a thud. Lysimachus untethered her other hand and stuck it into the box. A clever binding held her wrist fast in the hole, reminding Heron of an invention she'd made years ago.

The lever was ebony, oiled to a fine sheen. The box, though metal, didn't have a particle of rust on it.

"Last chance for inspiration." And when she didn't reply. "Shall I explain the box? Yes, I see I must. When I turn this handle, the mouth opens."

Lysimachus, watching her with his beady eyes, turned the handle one revolution. It took some effort and when the handle made it around, she heard a heavy click, like metal on metal. There had to be a spring inside. Then she noticed a thick metal sheet poking from the top of the box.

The twin flames flickering above her head seemed to annoy Lysimachus. He produced a knife and cut the strings, tossing the bags on the table after he blew out the candles. The pressure on her nipples had reduced considerably, but now she was focused on the box.

He patted the square torture device. "This lever opens the mouth inside the box. At the bottom of that piece of metal sticking out the top is a razor sharp edge, sharper than a well-kept gladius. Each time I turn the handle, it pulls the edge higher. I keep going until you start sketching. If you don't ever start and I hit the top, then I'll hit the lever and let it come down on your hand, sheering it clean off."

"Your god creates nothing," she said. "He is a lie."

Lysimachus turned the crank once. It snapped into place. She wasn't sure how many times he could turn it before he would hit the lever, but it couldn't be many.

A linen wrap was produced from beneath the table. He tied it around her wrist until her fingers started to go numb. Next, he poured out a viscous liquid into a bowl and moved a candle near.

Then he waited, hand on the handle. He watched her and she stared back. She couldn't do it. When her inventions were misused, it pained her. To willingly make a device to torture others would pervert everything she believed in.

Another revolution and the blade clicked into place. It was halfway out of the box. There couldn't be much more room.

"You could be his greatest priestess," said Lysimachus. "Remember how you trapped me in your workshop. Lured me into the box and sent me here with them. Think of how that changed me. And now I have been sent to teach you. Bring you into Sobek's waiting mouth. He Who Dwelleth Amid Terrors can make you immortal. Greater than the pharaohs. You only need to lift the quill."

He turned the handle again. The click was an explosion in her ears.

She stared at the box. Her fingers were numb, tingling with a thousand tiny needles.

Click. She couldn't even see Lysimachus, standing there in his faded green robe. There was only the box.

The air seemed to tighten around her body. Water ticked faintly, like some far away place. It seemed she could hear the humming of the earth, like it was some great beast, awakened to take her back.

"*Lex Talionis.*"

Lysimachus pulled the handle.

THIRTY SIX

"The man-god Alexander stood on this spot and split the knot with his sword, completing the prophecy that he would rule the world," said Vima, standing before the statue of Alexander. They'd detoured to the walled town of Gerasa, south on the road to Damascus when he heard about the statue. The town was not even as big as the Dock District in Alexandria. The surrounding hills were filled with olive trees and the occasional grape vine.

Vima paced around the bronze figure in the center of the town square. Villagers watched from doorways, but did not venture near the ring of Parthians.

The statue gave the impression the bronze Alexander was swinging his sword downward into the lumpy knot on the wagon yoke. Since they'd stopped, Vima had been lecturing his men about Alexander and the story of the Gordian knot.

Sepharia found it worrisome that he spoke in Greek when few of his men spoke the language. She kept her eyes focused on her hands, clasped in front, even when he glanced meaningfully in her direction.

The bull-legged Pakur examined the stone Alexander. His face was pinched as if the statue reeked of sewer.

"I rather cut man in half than knot," he said.

Vima clasped his friend on the shoulder. "That is why you are my shield, my protector, my friend. A Prince must understand these things, he must know. That is why I wanted to see this place, to feel what he felt here."

Pakur frowned and poked the bronze Alexander with a stubby finger. The Prince circled the statue again, regarding it with a secret smile. He turned to his men with a grand flourish.

"Your Prince wishes he had such challenges as Alexander. I would best them just the same!"

Pakur shrugged. "No time for not-rope knots. Necks are good."

Sepharia bit her lower lip and tried to stay as small as possible. Her handmaidens were busy laying out her tent and she was alone.

"My Beloved Sepharia," said Vima.

She bowed her head. "Yes, my Beloved Prince, I await your command."

He gave her a wry smile. His eyes were hard, his chest swollen with swagger.

"Pakur does not seem to understand how important the Gordian knot was for Alexander. He is your ancestor. You can tell him so he understands. Make him understand."

She could hear the strain of annoyance in his voice. He was displeased with his friend Pakur, though the thick-legged warrior did not seem to understand. Vima's eyes flickered like a snake between them.

"I am only a girl," said Sepharia. "I do not wish to presume."

"Presume away." He laughed. "You seemed to enjoy it before."

"Tell me this knot," said Pakur with heavy lidded eyes.

Sepharia glanced to Vima and saw she would not be able to avoid the question. She cleared her throat and began cautiously, "In ancient times, before Alexander was a boy, an oracle gave a prophecy that the man who would one day cut the Gordian knot would rule Asia."

"And how does this knot help a man rule?" asked Pakur in complete sincerity.

"I am not one to know the mind of an oracle," said Sepharia, "but when he was in the land of Phrygia and cut the knot, his friends and enemies took that as a prophetic sign."

"Phrygia?" Vima stepped forward. "What lies do you speak of? Here is the place he cut the knot. Why else would they put a statue here? Of course, this is the place of the Gordian knot."

"It is not my place to say," replied Sepharia.

Vima snorted derisively. "Did you hear that, my loyal friend Pakur? She said 'say'. A true and proper wife would have said 'know'. There are still rebellious thoughts behind those downcast eyes. She thinks she knows better than I, the Prince. Do not think I am fooled. Out with it, wife."

She shook her head. "Apologies for the incorrect word. I'm sure this is the location. I misspoke when I said it was in Phrygia."

Contrary to his name, Vima strolled to her as slowly and deliberately as possible. He put a finger under her chin and lifted it up until she was forced to stare directly into his gaze. The scattered laughter died like the wind.

"Do not lie to me," he said. "You are just a third wife. Do not think you can know better. Tell me the thoughts behind those pretty eyes or I'll cut them out with a horse tooth."

Despite her fears, she answered him, keeping her tone as level as possible. "Many towns claim the Gordian knot. It brings visitors, especially to a town like this off the main trade roads. It gives them a reason to lie, even though the real town is named in the *Alexandrian Romances*."

He searched her face for many, long immeasurable breaths. He seemed to be deciding. Finally, he strolled back to the statue.

Vima cupped his hands around his mouth and yelled, "Citizens of Gerasa. My lowly third wife, the beautiful but iron-headed Sepharia, claims your statue of Alexander and the knot is a lie. Unless you can send someone out to refute her, I will pull down your statue and have it melted into slag!"

A knot formed in her stomach. She did not begrudge the town for luring visitors for trade, nor did she want to be the cause of its destruction.

Vima spun around, looking for anyone to come out. He yelled again, "If even one person can tell me she is wrong, I will punish her for her lying mouth."

He winked and her palms grew cold. Out the corner of her eye, Sepharia saw doors close. The common born were not foolish enough to get involved with the royalty of any nation, especially when even his small traveling band could decimate the town.

Vima shrugged and called for a horse and rope. As the horse was being led to the town square, Vonones appeared with Pheme and Carme trailing behind. When he adjusted his dark robes, he appeared to be a raven settling onto a branch. Neither handmaiden would meet her gaze. The coldness in her palms spread to her arms and chest.

After a spate of quiet discussion, during which Vonones looked in her direction multiple times, Vima turned to address her.

"What message did you try to send to Alexandria?"

She tried to hide her swallow. "I sent no message."

"Are you saying my trusted advisor Vonones is a liar? This seems to be a common thing for you, girl. Are we all liars to you? Only you may dispense your wisdom to the world? Tell me the truth. What message did you send to Alexandria? Tell me now."

The contained fury in his voice made her knees tremble. She lifted her chin and stared back. "I sent no message."

"Fine," he said disgusted. "Pheme. Carme. Only one of you will live much longer. The first one to tell me what message you were given to send will earn a longer life."

The two handmaiden's glanced at each other. Pheme bit down on her lower lip, eyes wracked with internal decisions. Carme took one look at her fellow handmaiden and the words spilled from her mouth as fast as she could get them out:

"The message said, 'the father voids the treaty, change the plan to Mithrapolis.'"

The handmaiden Pheme pulled away from Vonones grasp and ran away, holding her chiton up around her thighs. Vima whistled and a soldier tossed him a javelin. She didn't make it past the first building before he stuck it in her back with a grunting hurl.

Tears fled from Carme's eyes. She started to scream, but Vima slapped her. The tears turned to sobs.

"Traitorous women," said Vima. "Bring me her things. All of them, especially the furniture."

A pair of Parthian soldiers moved near but did not touch her. Sepharia waited, staring blankly into the dust.

"Did you think you could out think me?" asked Vima. "Vonones bet me that you wouldn't betray me until Susa. I said Damascus. He owes me ten talents."

Vonones handed over a leather pouch, eyes twinkling with mirth. In that moment, she realized the messenger had been a fake, or maybe the messenger had been real, but he'd purposely given her the opportunity to overhear the conversation. She shouldn't have trusted any thing said in Greek.

Her things, including the lelathon cabinet, were brought to the town square. The soldiers tore her things apart, ripping sheets and cloaks, smashing vials. The chest of snakes was dumped onto the dirt and the creatures chopped into pieces.

When a soldier put his foot through the back of the lelathon cabinet, gearing snapped and brass shone from the jagged hole. Vima stopped the man from continuing and moved to investigate. He borrowed an axe and chopped the back from the cabinet, eventually revealing the hidden compartment. When he pulled the vial of poison from the hole, she thought about running.

His gaze narrowed before a dangerous grin spread across his face. He motioned for Carme to be brought to him.

"Drink this," he said.

She only delayed for a moment, still blurry-eyed and sobbing, and let the vial of liquid run down her throat. Vima held Carme's arm while he stared at Sepharia.

After a minute, Carme began to gag, holding her hands to her throat. Then she coughed, and blood splattered onto her hands. She doubled onto her knees.

Sepharia could not help but watch Carme die. She'd never been her favorite handmaiden, hadn't really liked her at all, but she felt responsible for the girl's death, just the same.

"I guess the town gets to keep their statue after all. For how can I believe a lying woman like you?" asked Vima, and much to her surprise, he walked out of the village square, leaving her standing there.

Stricken with confusion, Sepharia stayed perfectly still until Vonones approached. It was almost a relief to know that she would meet her fate soon. She just wished she'd gotten the word back to Alexandria to warn them.

Vonones loomed over her. "You are no longer his wife. The marriage is voided. You're my property now, a slave. Obey and you might live to see Susa. Give me even one reason and I'll have you chopped up piece by piece and fed to the dogs while you watch."

THIRTY SEVEN

"Fetch me a drink, girl, and be quick about it," said Vonones as he scribbled on a papyrus, half-melted candles surrounding him. The advisor worked late each night sending messages and reading the ones brought to him at all times of the night.

Sepharia had been curled up at the base of his cot, wrapped in a thin sheet when the tent flap was pulled aside. Vonones was a light sleeper and rose immediately.

She slipped into the camp, rubbing her arms as the chill night brought goose-flesh. The Parthian soldier outside the tent nodded as she lifted the empty wine carafe.

The camp was on the edge of the Syrian desert. They were headed northeast toward the major trade town of Rutba. She found the camp supply wagon and woke the sleeping form in the back. The woman muttered something and Sepharia recognized the voice.

"Amitris?"

The dark-haired woman rose from the blankets, rubbing a knuckle in her eye. "Sepharia? What are you doing?"

She held up the carafe. "A messenger came for Vonones. He's thirsty. What are you doing?"

"Without a Princess to serve, I was sent to the supply wagons," said the woman through a faint yawn.

"Apologies, Amitris. I have wrecked your position," said Sepharia.

Amitris shrugged. "When I return to Susa, they will give me to another noble woman. My life will be okay." Her gaze turned dark. "You should be careful."

"Thank you, Amitris." Sepharia paused, thinking carefully. "I miss our language lessons."

"You are a quick learner. It was a pleasure to teach you," replied Amitris.

"I must get back. Vonones will be waiting." Sepharia handed the carafe over and Amitris filled it.

Before Sepharia left, she asked, "Do you think they would let you teach me?"

Amitris stared into the darkness between the tents. "When you come back next time, I'll have a scroll for you. As tender of the supplies, I must keep records. I can write a few words for you each time and you can learn them."

The flickering flame of a guard neared. Sepharia knew she had delayed long. "Thank you, Amitris. You are kind."

The bittersweet smile on Amitris' lips made Sepharia wonder what had befallen the handmaiden before. Sepharia headed toward the tent, but was too busy thinking about Amitris and got turned around in the camp.

She came out on the side near the horses and steam chariots. Agog had gifted the Prince three of their precious vehicles to take back to Susa: one for the father, one for the brother and one for Vima.

Before she turned back to find Vonones' tent, she realized, in the light of distant fires, the middle steam chariot was familiar. Sepharia moved closer to find it was the original steam chariot her father and Agog had driven to the Oracle of Siwa.

Sepharia hadn't noticed before since Vima rode the newer version. She supposed this one would be given to the brother. A wagon attached to the back of the steam chariot was filled with black fuel rock. Sepharia recognized the wagon, as well. It came from Heron's workshop.

Before she could move closer to investigate, a guard appeared. He spoke roughly and quickly and she understood nothing.

"I got lost in the dark," she said, knowing he wouldn't understand.

The guard grabbed her arm, digging his fingernails into the crook of her elbow, and dragged her toward the center of the camp. As they neared Vonones tent, she shook him off, spilling a bit of wine in the process, and marched into the tent.

Vonones was waiting for her. The guard followed her in.

"Where have you been?" he asked.

Sepharia considered lying briefly before telling the truth. "Amitris tends the supply wagon. I spoke briefly with her before returning, but I got lost in the camp."

Vonones exchanged a few words with the guard before dismissing him. "He confirms your story. Though I am curious why you wanted to see the steam chariots?"

"Apologies," she said, "I got lost, truthfully."

He pondered her words for a moment, tapping the table with his quill. He stood suddenly and strode to the other side of the tent.

"Pour my wine," he said. "I thirst. And pour one for yourself. I wish to speak to you, not as my body-servant, but as a daughter of Alexandria."

The Prince's advisor had been wearing a sleeping robe, hastily thrown over his shoulders when the messenger arrived. He removed the robe, revealing his naked backside, before donning a more formal garment.

As she poured the wine, she glanced at the words on the page, trying to memorize them for later. She knew Heron could know the whole page in a blink, but she lacked that gift. She could imprint the words into her mind if she only had more time.

When Vonones turned around, she held out his cup of wine. His dark gaze regarded her carefully.

"May the gods grant us long life," he said before taking a drink.

Sepharia matched him before asking, "What do you command of me?"

"Tell me about your father's workshop," he said. "Since you now know Parthia will side with Rome, tossing aside the agreement with Alexandria, I must know what other inventions your father might create for this war."

"I don't know," she replied. "I'd been in the Palace with Polyxena."

"Think hard," said Vonones. "Though you may be my slave now, I can make your life much more pleasant if you cooperate. Maybe you will even learn to enjoy serving me. I appreciate your mind as much as your beauty."

While she sipped at her wine and acted like she was thinking hard, he refilled both their cups. His gaze traveled the length of her form.

"Before I left," she began carefully, "my father was making plans to create an army of metal soldiers."

"Good," he said, leaning forward and pushing her flaxen hair from her shoulders, "tell me more."

"They would be able to fight without rest and would be nearly unkillable. Before I left, he made one that helped him kill the former Alabarch." She glanced to Vonones, hoping she'd filled her lies with enough truth to convince him. But she saw it wasn't her words that interested him at this moment.

Vonones stood near, his robes parted at the middle, exposing his chest. He leaned forward, wrapped his hand around her neck and pressed his lips against her.

She kept her lips hard and stiffened at his touch. Vonones pulled away, his eyes casting dangerous shadows.

"Apologies," she said, putting her hand against his chest. "I didn't want to spill my wine on your robes."

As he narrowed his eyes, she took their cups and set them on the table. Before turning around, she summoned her resolve. Cleopatra had once slept with Caesar to improve her position. How would this be any different?

Sepharia moved into his arms, pushing aside his robe and caressing his nipples with her fingertips. His tension melted away under her touch and she felt him stiffen against her belly. She softly pressed her lips against his neck and he moaned.

Bani had taught her ways to delay desire and let the excitement build, but Vonones was slightly drunk. She let him lead her to the bed and before long, amid a frenzy of kissing and scratching, he entered her.

Her ribs hurt from the beatings. Sepharia brought him to a quick climax and he tumbled asleep immediately.

His heavy snores were unlike his normal sleeping patterns. Sepharia carefully untangled herself, readying to slide back into bed should he awake, but he seemed to be sleeping heavier than other nights.

She made it to the table and after confirming Vonones was still asleep, she looked over the document he was working on. As she studied the page, Vonones gave a heavy snort, startling her. Sepharia thought about returning to the safety of his bed, should he catch her spying again, he was sure to be unmerciful. She stayed and continued memorizing the shapes of the words.

Near the bottom, she recognized a few words in their language: the word for 'king' and the word for the city Tyre. She carefully imprinted them into her mind. As she was finishing, she realized it had grown dreadfully quiet. Vonones was no longer snoring. She slowly turned. Vonones was still slumbering in bed. She let out a heavy sigh and crept back under the covers.

He awoke when she slid into his arms. He started to ask a question so she pressed her lips against his. Vonones replied eagerly and before long, he was inside of her again. This time, she made sure she finished along with him and afterwards, lay quietly amid the covers, staring at the faded underside of the wide tent, letting a plan form as Vonones snored.

THIRTY EIGHT

Flies feasted on the crusty stump at the end of her arm while the sun mercilessly assaulted her light-starved eyes. Heron squinted away the overwhelming whiteness and lifted her head to view her surroundings. Before tying her to the table, Lysimachus had let a scruffy dog loose into the walled courtyard.

The dog hesitantly approached the water's edge, ignorant of the dangers lurking as logs in the water. Past the reeds and the shallow waters, a great bulk rested on the sandy island. Something sparkled from the beast's scaly head.

"Dog," she called to it. "Come! Away from the water."

Her throat was raw and the dog ignored the command, patiently lapping at the water with its pink tongue.

"Come, dog!"

Then she switched to Egyptian.

"Come! Dog!"

The scruffy mutt raised its head. Shapes moved in the water towards the reedy edge.

"Dog, away!"

The water erupted with teeth and the dog was caught by a crocodile. The dog whined and bones crunched. Heron closed her eyes, but she could not close her ears. Eventually, the reedy temple returned to silence.

The sounds of children playing drifted into the swampy courtyard. Heron tugged on the bark ropes. The thick binding chaffed at her wrists and ankles.

An ache formed at the center of her forehead, brought by the light. She'd been in the darkness so long that she'd forgotten how bright it was outside. The aching of her missing hand, though seemingly months ago, burned under the searing sun.

Lysimachus had given her a tunic, though she could still see the scars and wounds along her arms and legs. The loss of her hand was a grievous wound. Though she knew she would probably never escape the Temple of Sobek, the absence of a hand was critical to an inventor. In the bowels of the temple, the visions of future inventions danced in her head, brought by the implements themselves that did the damage.

Those torture devices made the perversion of the 'miracles' in Alexandria a trifling abuse. Heron cursed the forces that kept these inventions hidden from the world, rotting in the dark, destroying humanity rather than lifting it up.

If she ever made it out of the temple, she would unleash these new ideas onto her workshop. Then she remembered she no longer had a workshop. She'd given it up for her work on the pyramid. Lying on the stone slab with one hand missing, she found it odd she felt no regret for that decision.

If she had returned to Alexandria at Agog's command, she would have her workshop and her hand and her freedom. But she would not have had those moments with Jarngard, nor felt as a woman, even for that brief time in his tent. The end, if it came at the hands of Lysimachus in the Temple of Sobek, would be a bitter one. She mourned not her death, but the loss of those ideas contained within her mind. Even if she had no workshop, the other owners would gladly take her ideas, which was all she ever wanted.

A heavy splash woke her from her thoughts. The crocodile called Petsuchos left the sandy island. Heron strained against the dry, crackling ropes to see if Lysimachus watched from the arched doorway.

Reeds cracked and bent as the monster tramped through the muck. The beast's head bobbed as it approached the stone slab. Heron pulled her limbs to the center as far as the ropes would allow.

Holding her breath, she listened as the beast grunted and snorted, circling her perch. Worried that she would not get another chance should the beast lunge to get onto the slab, Heron produced the piece of glass she'd stolen from Lysimachus.

In the darkness and between her sessions with Lysimachus, she'd examined the stone, feeling the round, fat middle and thin edges. She hoped the piece of glass was what she expected. Based on a particular implement on the wall, she assumed what pain the stones inflicted, but he'd never pulled it from the wall.

With Petsuchos circling around, Heron held the piece of glass out, angling it perpendicular to the sun. The rope did not allow much freedom, but she was able to lift her head and see the pinpoint of light focused from the piece of glass.

Heron angled the light toward the rope. The thick rope would not burn easily. After a time, the faint smell of burning bark tickled her nose.

The beast, called by the new smell or finished with its investigation, slammed its open, toothy maw onto the stone near her head. Attentive to the burning rope, she barely got her head out of the way.

Dead eyes gazed from lumpy, green mounds. Behind them, jewels sparkled in the sun. The stench of dead flesh was overwhelming. Bits of rot squished between its teeth. Heron could barely keep the light focused on the rope.

Should the beast lunge again, it could crush her. It waited with an open mouth. Heron could not imagine what madness drove Lysimachus to put his hand inside. Despite the regular torture, Heron clung to the ideas swirling through her head, rather than succumb to madness, though others might call that a form of lunacy.

Smoke swirled from the bark rope which seemed to incite the beast. It edged its mouth closer until Heron could pull no further away. A tooth nearly touched her forehead. Hot, swampy breath washed over her face. The mouth was a tomb of yellowish temples in a sea of pink rot.

When a flame erupted from the rope, it took all of Heron's restraint not to yank. The bark was not burnt completely through and she risked putting out the fire by moving too much.

Petsuchos snorted and the tooth bumped her hair. Trapped against the stone, the tooth could impale her with little effort. Heron watched the beast's eye loll toward the flame. Sensing another movement, she yanked on the rope. The blackened bark cracked and held, the flame winking out as she strained. Summoning a reserve of energy, Heron pulled against the rope, bumping her head into the beast's mouth, but snapping the brittle binding.

Incensed by her touch, Petsuchos thrashed forward, teetering onto the slab. Freed on one side, Heron was able to slide out of the way. The snapping mouth barely missed her shoulder. Without a hand, she was able to slide the other rope over her stump and immediately began tugging on the leg bindings.

The great beast was done being patient and scrambled onto the slab. Heron untied the bark ropes from her ankles, thanking her luck that the one-handed Lysimachus had made terrible knots.

She leapt from the stone a moment before the beast's belly came crashing down. She landed in the sucking mud and her legs, unused to holding her up, failed and she tumbled face first into the black muck.

Petsuchos snorted and the lesser crocodiles of the temple scurried away from the water's edge. Spitting out foul tasting mud, Heron pushed herself standing. The beast scrambled from the stone as Heron rushed away, pushing through the slapping reeds, trying to avoid the water, but running out of land.

The reedy pond ran right up to the wall, so Heron was forced to dive into the water, hoping no crocodiles lurked. With a missing hand, she slapped against the brackish water, bugs and mud swirling away from each thrust.

She heard the beast hit behind her and kicked harder, feeling teeth snapping onto her feet at any moment. Upon the sandy soil of the island, Heron crawled to her feet moments before Petsuchos surged out of the water.

A broken tree trunk on the backside of the island provided no protection, so Heron kept moving. She was able to leap over the pile of rocks in the center of the island which kept Petsuchos from pursuing her directly.

Hitting the water, she tripped over the tail of a crocodile hiding on the backside of the island. The water enveloped her. She sunk into the murky depth before she was able to kick upward.

Heron broke to the surface and tried to orient herself, looking for the wide limbed tree she'd seen at the back of the temple pond. Once she saw it, she thrust through the water, kicking madly.

Coming through the water, headed straight towards her, was a crocodile, its eyes barely above the surface. There was too much water between her and the edge. Heron froze, waiting for the inevitable snap of teeth.

Then the water exploded as Petsuchos launched itself from the shore, squarely on the smaller crocodile. Tangled, the beasts fought and Heron, choking, paddled toward the edge. Disoriented, she found herself on land, and before she could stand, vomited up a lungful.

Soaked, weakened, and dizzy, Heron made for the tree. She reached the base as the battle in the water ended. The smaller crocodile wisely swam away. Petsuchos was already climbing onto the muddy soil as she was grabbing the lowest limb.

Weak from hunger and torture, and with only one hand, Heron wasn't sure if she could pull herself into the tree. Whatever strength she had was almost gone. She would have one try to make it up and if not, the beast would have her.

She set her feet against the trunk, gripping the rough bark with a slippery hand, and leapt upward. She was able to wrap her forearm around the limb, holding fast with an elbow and used her toes to scramble up.

Her feet swung onto the limb moments before teeth snapped together beneath her. Heron wasn't given long to rest when Petsuchos began pushing its belly into the trunk and lifting its snout.

The limb was still within reach, so Heron climbed to her feet, woozy from the effort. She grabbed the upper branch and took a deep breath. If she could climb a little higher then she could escape the beast and maybe get help. Even Lysimachus would not be able to get her and he'd have to brave the crocodile to even try.

The promise of escape was tantalizingly near. Before the beast could lunge again, Heron wrapped her fingers around the bark, first wiping away the mud. Glancing down once for inspiration, she pushed off the limb and yanked upward.

Freedom was hers for one brief moment, until the upper branch snapped from her weight. She fell backwards, landing on the lower limb, her legs dangling beneath like hanging meat. She sensed a gathering primal force and before she could lift her legs out of the way, she felt the beast's mouth close around her right leg, teeth sheering skin and muscle and bone.

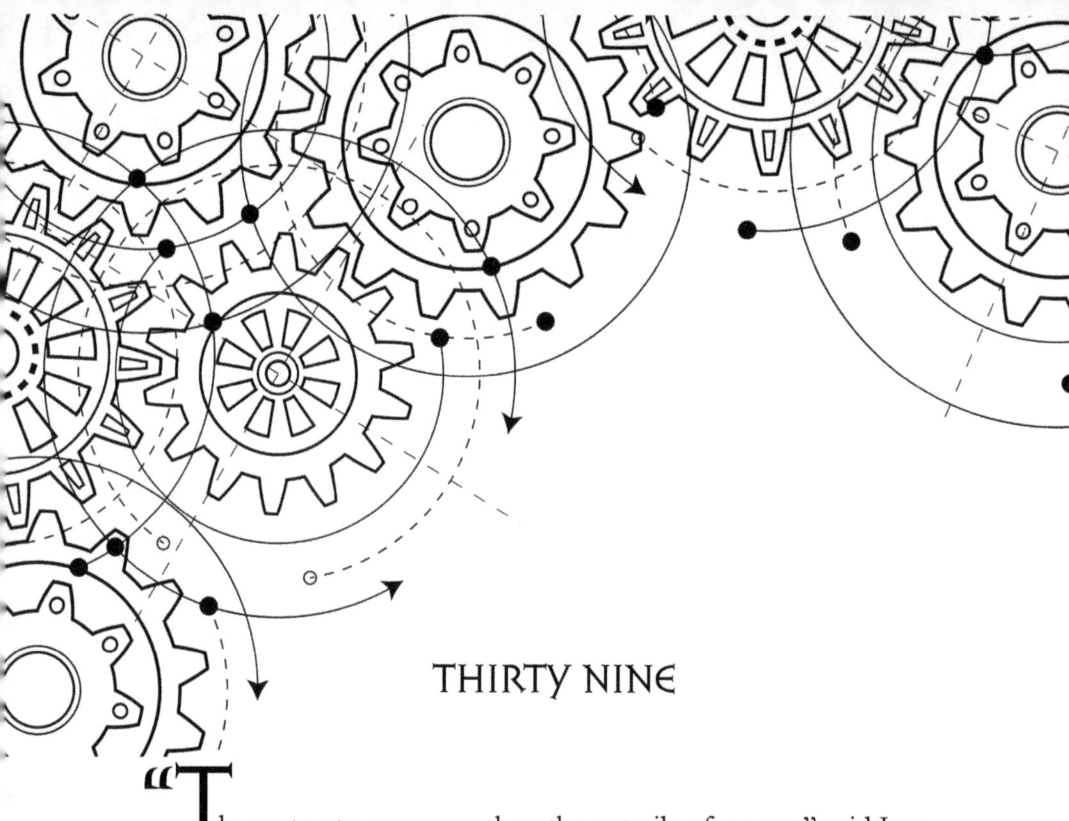

THIRTY NINE

"These streets are worse than the entrails of a goat," said Jarngard over the thundering pistons of the steam mechanical.

Punt nodded as he steered the craft through the torturous streets. A cluster of children followed them from a distance. The horseless wagon brought wide-eyed Egyptian children, brown skin soaking up the sun.

Tormod stamped his foot. "Let me put my axe to a few throats and we'll find your miracle worker. Drop me off at the next street and I'll sneak around and capture us a few of them boys for questions."

"These townsfolk don't want us here," said Jarngard, "let's not give them any reasons to keep us from searching for Heron."

Inside, he knew for certain that Heron was probably dead. Kidnappers usually made ransom requests and they'd received nothing. But he at least wanted to exact his revenge for her death and the trail had led them to Arsinoe and a one-handed priest of Sobek.

Further down the next street, Jarngard noticed a pair of loin clothed men with long spears watching. It wouldn't be long before there were more of them.

"What if Heron's in the walled part of the city?" asked Punt.

"Then we'll make them let us in," he replied, touching the bag around his neck.

They'd been searching the city for two days. Between training sessions with his troops, Jarngard had been questioning every trader that came through the Emporium asking about followers of Sobek, hoping the chance find of the stone crocodile meant something. A discussion with a trader from Thebes sent him to Arsinoe to find a one-handed priest. Followers of Sobek outside of Arsinoe weren't rare, but the timing was right after the sand storm.

"Circle back around," said Jarngard. "I want to talk to one of those children."

When Tormod reached for one of his axes, Jarngard held a hand up. "My way, brother. I want their help, not a city full of enemies."

There was a group of about ten children. As the steam mechanical circled around, the smaller ones disappeared like smoke in a brisk wind. Most of them were boys, though it was hard to tell. They were of a young age and either naked or in loincloth.

Jarngard directed Punt to slow the vehicle, disengaging the mechanical so he could hear himself think. The newer machines were quicker and could travel longer, but gave him a headache faster than Hoth.

After throwing a few ha'pennies into the dust, he cupped his hands around his mouth and yelled, "Have you seen the one-handed priest?"

Another child slipped behind the broken wall, leaving only two. Jarngard counted three more spear wielding men gathering. A few more and they'd have to leave the area.

He was about to yell again when Punt touched his arm. "They don't speak your language."

Jarngard cursed himself. Of course, he should have remembered that. "Please, Punt."

Punt did not cup his hands, instead, his booming voice traveled through the chalky white streets. One boy, a wary lad by his twitching, responded by yelling back, looking ready to leap over the stone wall and disappear at any moment.

After a brief exchange Punt engaged the mechanical and thunder resumed in Jarngard's ears. When the vehicle was steered the opposite direction, headed out of the city, he moved to Punt's side. Before Jarngard could speak, Punt pointed to another cluster of Egyptian men with spears.

"Had the boy seen the one-handed priest?"

Punt shook his head.

"Then why are we headed this way?" asked Jarngard.

"The boy said we should turn off our machine so he could talk to us."

Jarngard nodded. "A trap, eh? What have we done to them?"

Punt gave a brief shrug. "Pale men on a strange machine? Egypt is a strange land and Arsinoe the strangest of its cities. Do not judge Egypt by the Alexandrians you know."

"Then where do we go?"

Punt's head dipped slightly. The steam mechanical slowed until it stopped. "Heron must be dead. I do not want to believe it, but I cannot see it any other way. If it was a priest of Sobek, I find it hard to hope. And there are others that despise the *Michanikos* that would be worse. These thoughts shame me."

Jarngard put a hand on the man's shoulder. "Do not feel shame. I have these same thoughts. We search because to not search is to admit Heron is dead."

Tormod opened his mouth to speak, but Jarngard shook him off. The axe-wielding Northman tilted his head as if he heard far off sounds.

Jarngard turned his attention back to Punt. The blacksmith stared blankly at his open palms. "Without Heron, what use are these?" asked Punt. "The *Michanikos* is the greatest inventor the world has ever known. Greater than Archimedes. Greater than any of them. The city of Alexandria should feel shame for turning its back on Heron. I should have been there to protect. To my death, that will be my great shame."

Jarngard felt the words keenly. Despite the bright sun, the air was as dark as a thousand nights. To stop searching would allow the constrictor around his heart to finish its job.

"Search a while longer, friend Punt," said Jarngard. "Together we'll either find him or find the one-handed priest and finish what the gods clearly could not do."

They clasped forearms. Punt nodded grimly. "That's a promise I can make."

Though Jarngard had never fought with Punt, he felt a brotherhood with the thick-armed blacksmith as if they had. Punt was a man he could die next to on the field of battle and feel proud.

Tormod leaned into the middle of them. "I hear screaming."

As soon as the words were said, the sound of distant screaming soldered to his ears. The voice, even above the thrumming machine, brought images of terrible pain and fright. Jarngard knew that voice, one that had made joyful noises with him in his tent.

"Heron!"

He leapt from the steam chariot with swords drawn, sprinting toward the sound of her voice, looking in every direction to find her.

"Heron!" he shouted, not caring if it brought more spear-wielding men. He would slay them all if he had to.

The streets were a never-ending seas of whiteness. Jarngard stopped at a corner near a collection of stone buildings. Walls ran away from him and the echo of Heron's screaming tore through his soul.

A bronze-skinned naked boy ambled around the corner. His eyes grew wide and he fled. Jarngard took a step after him, hoping he might know the location of the screaming. He looked back to the steam mechanical. Punt was turning it around and Tormod was pointing to the next street over.

His legs churned, spitting up chalky dust, determined to stop whatever was causing her pain. When he found himself blocked by a stone wall, he sheathed his swords and began climbing.

Scrambling over the top, Jarngard was prepared to encounter just about anything. He imagined a man with a whip flaying the skin from Heron's flesh or a dreadful torture device crushing her chest or limbs, but when he landed in the muddy soil, producing his blades by the first step, he hesitated when he saw the jewel encrusted beast.

He'd seen a crocodile before. It was hard to escape the scaly beasts in the land of pharaohs and sand. But the beast before him was something out of legend. Its mouth could fit him whole and the teeth were as long as daggers.

Jarngard did not see Heron at first, until he realized the beast had something bloody in its jaws. Heron lay on a branch of the tree, blood dripping from her leg. She was no longer screaming, nor even moving, and the beast seemed to have her leg in its mouth. When her arms slipped from her chest and dangled loosely from the sides, he screamed, "For Heron!" and flew at the beast with whirling blades.

The battle nearly ended in the first pass as he misjudged his footing. The mossy earth looked solid but he stepped into foot-sucking muck and barely yanked himself out of the way when the beast snapped its jaws.

Jarngard rolled and gave the beast a vicious slice as he came to his feet. He didn't have long to admire his bladework when the tail whipped around and knocked him over again.

Retreating to the wall, Jarngard spied his cut and felt his balls cinch up to his groin as he saw the results of his strike. The blade had barely nicked the scaly armor.

Tramping toward him, the great crocodile opened its mouth. Jewels sparkled like a crown in the noon-day sun. Jarngard waited until the last moment before diving to the side.

The beast rammed the wall with a satisfying crunch. Jarngard did not hesitate, gaining his feet and then leaping onto the crocodile's back. Stabbing downward like a spear, he jabbed at the beast's eyes. The lumbering giant was too large to shake him from its back and still reeling from the impact. Jarngard gouged out an eye before he had to jump off.

Once again, the soil misled him, but this time, he couldn't recover. Before he could pull his feet free, the beast slammed its tail into Jarngard's back. He heard something snap and he knew the price would come later when the battle fury faded.

Mud sucked him down at each step. A growling snort alerted him to the beast's approach. Jarngard turned, knowing he could not outrun it. With a moment more, he might be able to climb the wall on his left, but Heron was bleeding to death in the tree. If he didn't kill the great crocodile soon, she'd be dead.

Preparing to receive a charge, Jarngard leaned forward, steeling his arms for impact. If he couldn't jam the blades into the tender portions of the beast's mouth, it would hew him in half.

The lumbering beast was a length away when the wall exploded, crashing over the crocodile. The beast's mouth missed closing upon him and instead a section of the wall slammed him in the chest, bending him backwards.

Tormod's leaping cry echoed over the steam chariot, bursting through the wall. The bronze shielding was bent like a giant had punched it. Punt followed the scar-faced Northman through the breech and they set upon the monster with blade and warhammer.

Leaving his blades and ignoring the broken ribs in his chest, Jarngard made his way to the tree, avoiding the mess of blood and flesh beneath its shade. He climbed onto the branch. Heron's eyes were closed and her mouth was open. Jarngard ripped the leather bag from his neck and prepared to throw it into the boggy pond in the temple courtyard when he saw the brief rising of Heron's chest.

Looking down, he found she'd tied a tourniquet around her knee before succumbing to blood loss. Crimson fluid dripped from the mangled flesh of her missing leg. She was not dead, but if he couldn't get her to a physician soon...

"Hand him down," said Punt from below.

Jarngard slid her from the branch into Tormod and Punt's waiting arms. They carried her from the temple, climbing carefully over the broken wall. The steam chariot looked like it would go no further.

They set her in the chalky street, tightening the bandages around her knee. Blood gathered in the dust and strange ideograms formed on the surface of the crimson pool.

"Heron lives," said Punt.

"But not much longer," whispered Jarngard.

Tormod pulled his axes free. "Men come. I see spears over the wall."

Jarngard glanced to the temple. His blades were inside, but he did not move to retrieve them. Warmth fled from her slender fingers. If Heron died, he wanted to be by her side.

"What soldiers are these?" asked Tormod.

When Jarngard glanced up, he immediately recognized the sigil of Ptah on the lightly armored soldiers. Short blades were drawn and spears set into the dust, pointed sunward.

Jarngard blocked the sun from his eyes with a raised arm. The priests of Ptah approached on horseback, hoof beats like cruel drums.

Tormod cracked his knuckles against his axe grip and Punt lifted his war-hammer. Jarngard was the last to stand.

Astride his horse, the bald priest of Ptah, the one called Hotep, motioned for a rider in the back to come forward. He turned to them, his gold-wrapped beard glowing in the sun and called out in a loud, clear voice, "We come for Heron of Alexandria."

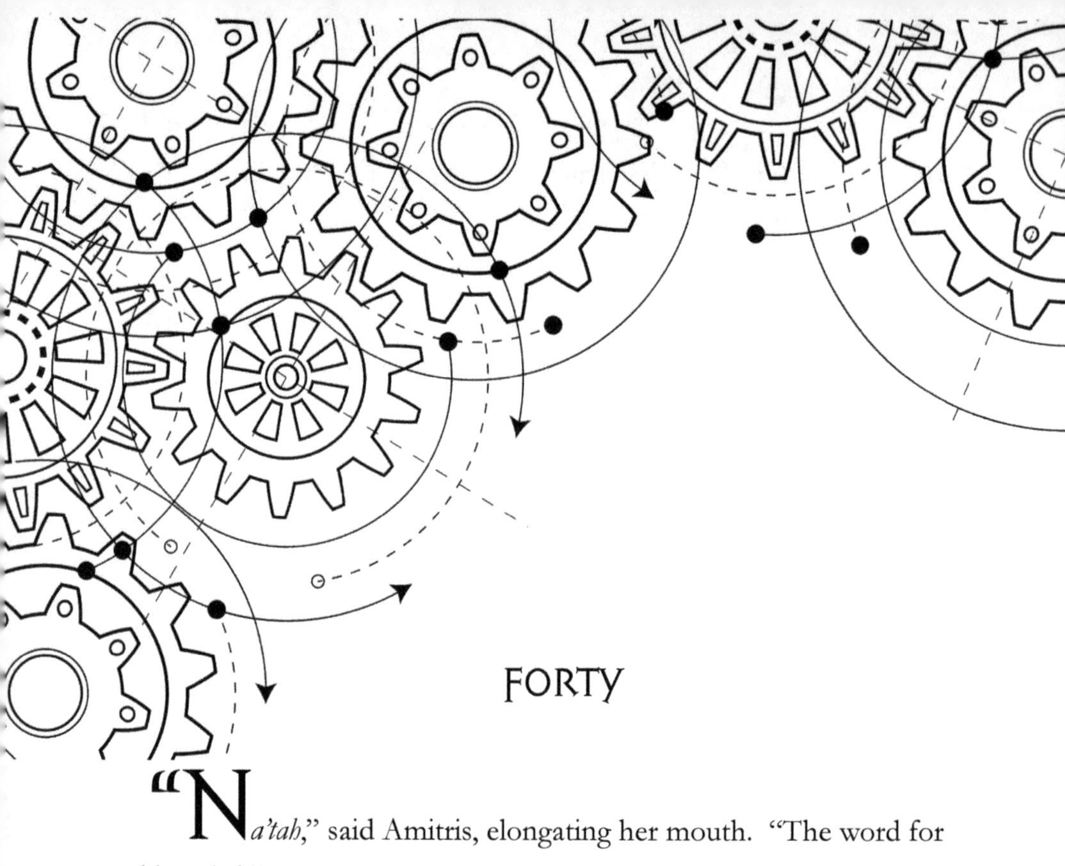

FORTY

"*N*a'*tah*," said Amitris, elongating her mouth. "The word for road is *na'tah*."

Sepharia took a deep breath and fixed the word in her mind. The cushion in the back of the supply wagon provided little comfort, but she blocked out the annoyance and copied the shape of Amitris' lips and said the word, "*Na'tah*."

The squint was as much a rebuke as she would receive from Amitris. Sepharia said the word a few more times until a faint smile appeared on Amitris' lips.

"You learn quickly," said Amitris, giving a rare compliment.

Sepharia shook her head. "I have the mind of a Cyclops. Even when I say it right, I don't know what I'm doing differently."

"In time," said Amitris, her eyes flickering to the soldier stationed not far from the wagon, "you will learn our language."

"I...yes...I suppose," said Sepharia wistfully.

"Vonones has been good to you?" asked Amitris.

"He has treated me fairly. Better than…well, he's treated me fairly," said Sepharia, lowering her voice.

"Yes," said Amitris, patting her hand, "and he lets you visit me to learn our language."

"So I may be more useful to him," said Sepharia, leaning against the wooden wall.

The Parthian handmaiden glanced to the soldier, standing a few paces away. The darkness in her eyes was distant, but seemed ready to rush forward. "We survive while we're useful."

"Do you enjoy it here?" asked Sepharia.

Amitris made a slight raising of one shoulder. "I survive."

The Parthian woman seemed so mysterious to Sepharia. She knew so little about her.

"Have you loved?" Sepharia asked.

Amitris sat up, quickly. "Have I loved?" She glanced out the back. "Everyone has loved. The question you should ask is 'have you been loved.'"

Her eyes were the color of an evening rainstorm. The muscle in her jaw pulsed.

"Have you been loved?" asked Sepharia.

"Ask someone else."

"I'm sorry," said Sepharia. "I'm not a very good companion. I come here for learning and bother you with stupid questions."

Amitris shrugged again. The brief gesture spoke volumes. She stared out the back, refusing to make eye contact.

"Apologies, Amitris. I'll go now."

Outside the wagon, Amitris said her name.

"The scroll," she said.

"The scroll?" Sepharia didn't remember bringing a scroll.

Amitris handed the rolled parchment over the back and spoke in her language, "Vonones' request."

Sepharia glanced to the soldier. "Oh yes, of course." She took the roll and hurried away. The soldier followed until she pushed her way into the tent.

She breathed a sigh of relief that Vonones wasn't in the tent. The Parthian caravan slowly moved toward Damascus, stopping for days at a time as messages came day and night. Vonones was probably meeting with Vima or another messenger. Something was happening and Sepharia was determined to find out.

Crouched into the corner of the tent, Sepharia unrolled the papyrus. It'd taken weeks to learn the shape of the markings and determine the words she'd seen in that message. Since then, Vonones had not left any documents for her to memorize, so she only had the one to go on.

There were a few words she didn't understand, but they were the most crucial. Without them, she couldn't decide what she needed to do next. Unfortunately, it'd been difficult to lead Amitris to explaining those words without knowing what they were or letting Amitris know what she was trying to do. The handmaiden just thought she was helping her read, not spying on the Prince's advisor.

The words she knew from Vonones' papyrus were: road, delay, dark moon, and Damascus. The moon would be hiding in a week. Whatever the messenger had told Vonones would happen then.

Sepharia glanced over the new scroll, the one Amitris had given her. Later, she could read the markings and learn from them, but for now she wanted to know what the message meant. She scanned the chunky paper, looking for familiar shapes. She'd gotten used to the swirling letters and thin slashes of ink.

When she saw the word, her heart leapt. Sepharia closed her eyes, picturing the document in her mind and made sure the markings were the same. It was the same technique she used when etching brooches.

Often times, she had to sneak into the Great Library and study the scrolls herself, but since she could not remove them from the racks, she had to fix them in the drawing space behind her eyes and recreate them later.

The word was the same. It was the word for 'king'. Focused on the papyrus, she didn't hear Vonones approach until he greeted the soldier outside the tent.

Sepharia shoved the papyrus under a pile of blankets and moved to the tent flap to greet him. The royal advisor ducked through the opening, worry lines gathering around his eyes. He smiled when he saw her.

"Sepharia," he said softly, "how my heart greets the sight of you."

She swept into his arms and shared a kiss. After a moment, he pulled back. "Does something trouble you?" he asked.

"Trouble? No," she said. "I finished my lessons and I was practicing in my head. Let me make it up to you."

She pressed her lips against his, this time more forcefully, grabbing the back of his neck and leaning her thigh into his crotch. He moaned hungrily and dug his fingers, almost painfully, into her shoulder.

He pulled away, eyes darted wildly. "Not now. My mind thickens with duty. I have letters to send."

"And I have lessons to practice, but the thought of you between my thighs will keep me from them."

Vonones entangled his hand in her hair, playfully flexing his fingers. His eyes were filled with heat and mirth. "What a fool the Prince was for throwing you away. Beautiful and intelligent and oh, so, wet between the sheets. Together we will be quite the force in Susa."

A thought crossed his eyes and the mirth fled, replaced by a darkness. His hand grew limp in her hair.

"Apologies," said Sepharia, "did I do something wrong?"

He shook his head. "Not you. The perils of my position I suppose. They weigh on me. Be thankful you are a woman and do not have to worry about such things."

She cupped his face in her hands. "Is there something I can help with? Unburden yourself to me."

She knew she said the wrong thing when his lips squeezed to whiteness. He stepped away, out of her arms.

"Do not mistake me. I feel great fondness for you. But I cannot trust you, either," he said.

Sepharia nodded. "This, I understand. I feel some measure of betrayal each time we fall into the sheets. I hope my father would understand."

He smiled at her revelation. "You will do well in Susa, beautiful Sepharia. It is the true mark of royal intrigue to balance these dangers while keeping your head. Eventually, we will come to trust each other completely, but for now, I think you understand."

Thoughts of the papyrus flickered in her head. "What is the king like? Will he like me?"

A dark cloud passed across Vonones' face. Some internal conflict battled across it. "He's a great man. When I was a young boy at scholarship, he brought me up and gave me my position. The father and the son are nothing alike, though the Prince is great in his ways. But don't worry, you will meet him soon enough."

The message from the papyrus became clear. The king was coming to Damascus and had been delayed. That explained their constant dallying as Vima rode off into the countryside on hunts and other activities. They weren't supposed to reach Damascus before the king, for what reason she could not guess, but they would be there in five days.

To allay suspicion, Sepharia twirled into his arms and slipped her fingers beneath his robe, caressing the soft flesh around his hip. She kissed his neck, smelling incense and musk. Vonones made a sharp intake of breath.

"Something bothers you," she said sweetly, her breath dancing off his chest. "Let us cleanse you of these worries so you may tackle the challenges of your position with a clear head."

Vonones kissed her and they fell into the blankets, arms and legs writhing like a kraken in the deep sea. And when they finished, Vonones did not return to his desk as she suspected he would. Together, entangled, they lay in each other's arms and for a few brief hours, Sepharia let the fear drain away to be replaced by a calm introspection.

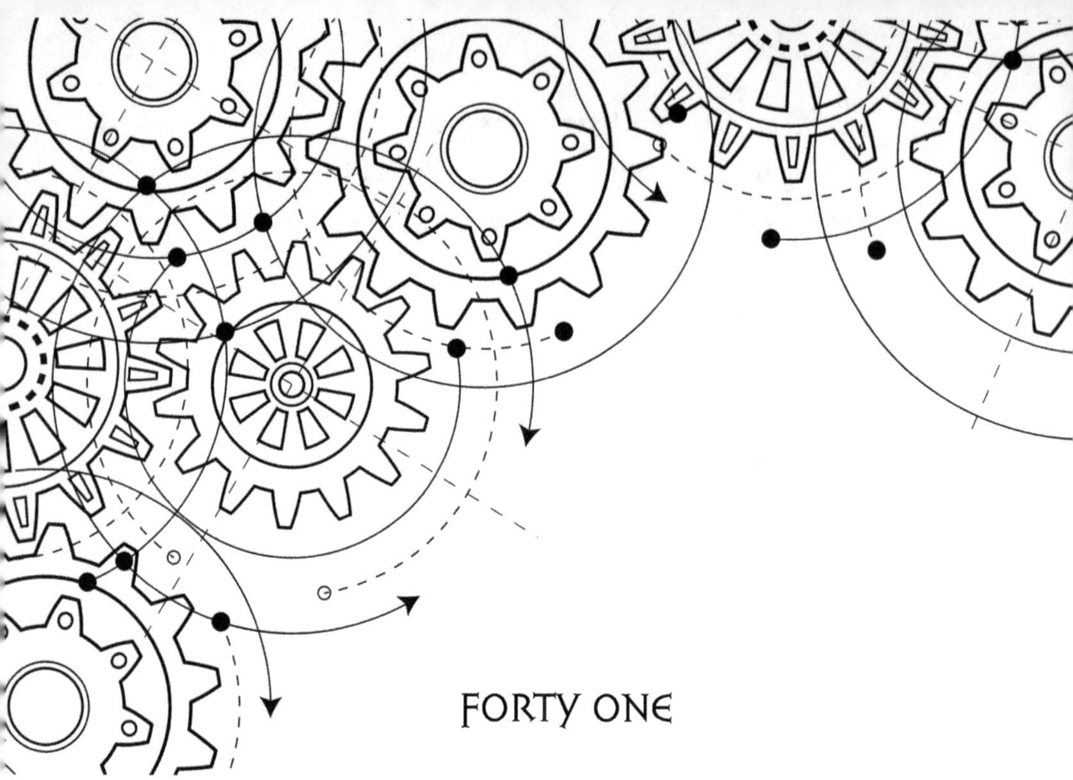

FORTY ONE

Agog watched the sleeping form of the great inventor, feeling the mass of guilt resting on his shoulders like the pyramid Heron had tried to build. A handless arm rested across the midsection and beneath that, the blankets lay smooth where a leg should be.

Sunlight shone on Heron's face and Agog marveled at the delicate features, fine black hair settled gently across a smooth brow; soft, feminine lips pursed in half-breath. How could this small man, with strength barely enough to lift a sword, change the world so effortlessly.

The Northman knew there'd been hundreds, or perhaps thousands, of warlords like him before, conquering the world with strength and stamina and sheer force of will. Of Heron's like, there had been few: Archimedes, Aristotle maybe, but not many others.

Agog felt the fool for risking so much by abandoning the miracle worker. The Northman leaned against the iron railing, the familiar thrum of hammers in the workshop shaking his great belly. The scents of warm bread wafted through the window, brought by southward breezes. Outside, above the din of cityfolk moving through the streets, a flag slapped against a bronze pole.

A deep in-breath and Heron stirred. Agog found his flint and a candle. A strike, and light flared into the room. When Heron's gaze fell upon him, he moved to the window, avoiding the sight of those luminous caves.

"I would have woken you earlier," said Agog, "but Plutarch threatened to toss me from the Lighthouse if I did."

Heron spent some time reviewing his injuries. The cracked pink stump seemed to cause less reaction than the empty blanket beneath his knee. After a sip from a mug, Heron asked with a weak voice, "How do I live?"

Agog looked out the high window, gazing to the north, thinking of the iron boat he'd sent with his friends on it. "Jarngard found you in Crocodopolis, in a temple of Sobek. Along with Punt and Tormod, they killed the beast that took your leg. Unfortunately, they never found the one-handed priest who kept you there."

"It was Lysimachus," she said eventually, the effects of the poppy's sap wavering through her voice.

This news surprised him, but answered many questions. "I thought he was dead."

"He escaped his captors and killed them, before coming for me. He'll come again. When they tortured him in the bowels of the temple, it drove him mad."

Heron grimaced, touching the empty place on the blanket where a leg should be. On his face lived pain and fear and something else.

"I see the scars..."

Heron narrowed his gaze, his voice, delicate and strong like spider silk. "And so you think I am mad like him? No, mad maybe, but not like him. I was a fool to believe that building a pyramid would solve our problems."

"It gained you friends in the Temple of Ptah," he said, watching Heron's reaction.

"Ptah? Surely, you jest," said Heron, the effort of speaking straining each word. "They would rather splash my blood across their altars."

"Maybe the pyramid persuaded them otherwise. I did not tell you the whole tale from your rescue. Even after Jarngard found you, you would have died had it not been for the temple. They came upon the scene right after the battle and their physicians kept you from bleeding to death," said Agog.

"For what reason?" asked Heron, eyes blinking slowly, deliberately.

"It's not for me to say, but the priest Xan-Ra is my guest in the Palace, waiting for your recovery. He asks each day when he can speak to you," said Agog. "I, for one, do not understand, because work on your pyramid stopped when you were taken. A small group stayed, but most returned to Kush."

Heron returned inward, touching his wounds carefully like a priest sanctifying holy objects. The physicians had kept Heron liberally under the poppy's influence, but Agog made them hold back on the dosage so he could speak to the inventor.

"What is it that you want?" asked Heron groggily, trying to sit up. "You did not come here to be my nursemaid."

"No," said Agog, "but I can get you more of the poppy's sap if it pains you. Your leg is still healing. It will take some time."

Heron shook his head drunkenly. He did not bother to tell Heron that the water he'd been drinking contained the sap. Knowing Heron, Agog figured he would not take the drug.

"Where is Sepharia?"

Agog turned back to the window. "I married her to the Prince."

"What madness is this? To that monster? You saw what he did to

Zenobia," said Heron.

"War *is* madness. I do not deny your claim, but circumstances required it, though certain things have changed since then," he said, almost apologetically. "A message from Sepharia arrived a week ago. It said, 'the father voids the treaty, change the plan, I will go to Mithrapolis.'"

"What plan?" asked Heron, clearly fighting through the effects of the poppy.

"That was what I said when I received the message. Then we found the message she left for you."

Agog produced the scroll and handed it over. Heron forced his eyes wide and read it, examining the detailed drawing.

"She believed Vima false all along and made plans ahead of time," said Heron. "Except, I wasn't there to make sure they were carried out."

"We received the message soon after Jarngard brought you back into the city," said Agog, growing quite frustrated. "She told us what to do, but not why or how it was going to help. Why did your daughter want the statue hooked to those clay pots of yours? First, Damascus, then Mithrapolis. What is it for? They went after her - Punt, Hoth, Jarngard - on one of those new iron boats. I wish you would have been awake. The fate of the known world teeters on your daughter's plans."

Heron did not answer and leaned his head back into the scroll. Agog moved near the bed and examined the drawing as well, even though he'd practically memorized the document. He'd been studying it since they found it. The statue on the drawing was the god Mithras with bull horns coming out the sides of his head. There was no lower half of his body, only a large rock. Plutarch had explained that Mithras was said to have been birthed from a rock. He was an ancient Parthian god and the workshop had done work for the temple in Alexandria.

Bronze rods connected the bull horns to the ghost fire jars hidden in the base of the statue. Plutarch had explained those, as well, but had no idea of what Sepharia was trying to do, or why.

"Did they make the statue?" asked Heron, squinting.

"Yes, but there was no time for a statue made of bronze. Jarngard cast it with your pyramid material. Except for the rods and the horns, those were left bronze, though no one would tell me why," said Agog. "I believe Jarngard still blames me for your injuries."

Mention of the pyramid brought the inventor upright in bed. Thoughts collected on the man's face, gathering until Agog could almost see them glowing through Heron's eyes.

"Sepharia means to kill the Prince with the pyramid," said Heron and then, "I mean, statue."

"How? And why?"

Heron pointed to the pots in the base of the statue, his finger weaving across the papyrus drunkenly. "These hold a secret fire to kill a man. She would know from the workshop and put them in the pyramid... statue."

Agog ignored the slurring and the misspoken word, admiring the ingenuity of the maker and his daughter. Despite the danger to Alexandria, Agog found himself impressed.

"But she requested it to be made before she left," said Agog.

Heron looked over the drawings again, his fingertip passing across the page until it rested on an inscription to be written along the base.

"To the Parthian Empire, from your friend and ally, Emperor Claudius," read Heron. "If this pyramid, I mean statue, kills the Prince, then the Parthians would surely side with Alexandria."

Agog leaned against the sides of the window and stared at the fire at the top of the Lighthouse. The implications of the statue reeled in his head. "First, I signed the treaty with Parthian, but then we receive a message from her saying the father has voided the treaty and now her statue might push them back into our arms. I do not know what to believe."

When Agog turned back, Heron's eyes were half-closed. The inventor was fighting against the poppy's effects.

Agog posed his question before the inventor drifted to slumber, "Will it work? This statue of hers and those strange pots?"

Heron shook his head, like a horse shaking off a biting fly, and nodded, but not in agreement. His eyes opened and closed and opened again. His lips began to move, but Agog couldn't hear anything so he moved closer.

Maybe he shouldn't have given him more poppy's sap until he received the answers he wanted, he realized. Agog placed his ear in front of Heron's mouth. The words were faint, but he could make them out:

"It's all wrong, it's not going to work, the rods in the statue, the rods in the statue..."

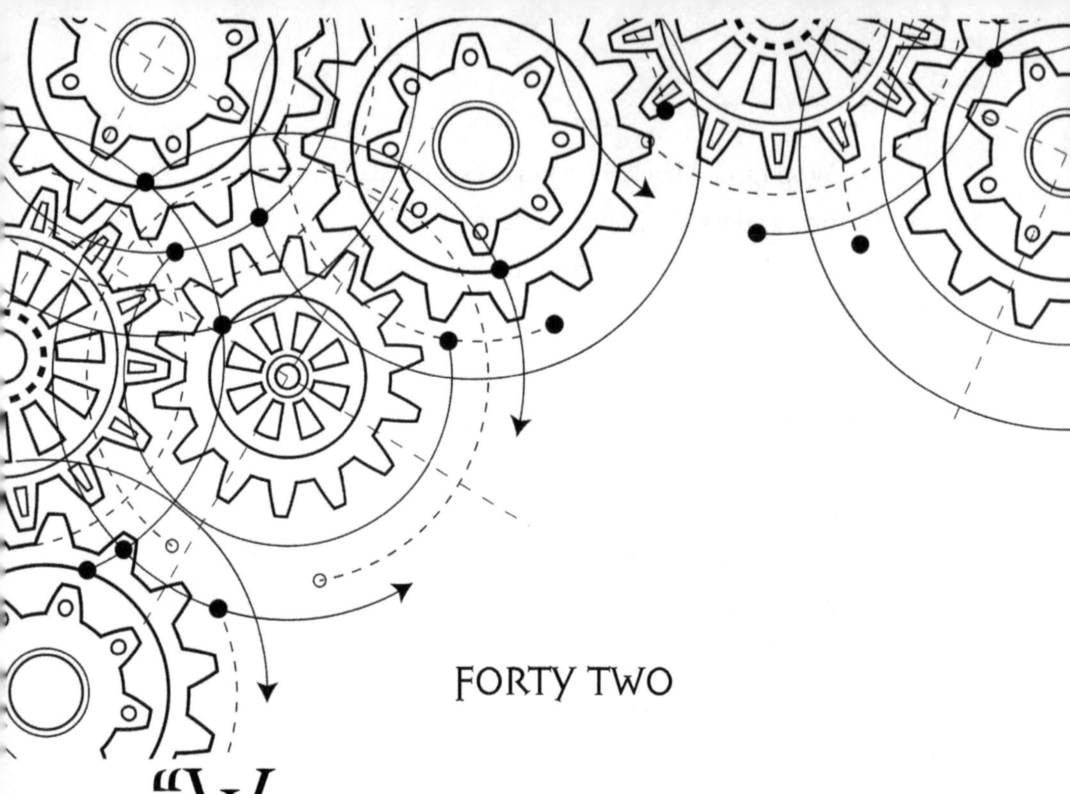

FORTY TWO

"With haste, Sepharia, with haste," said Amitris, wrapping the chlamys around the shoulders. "You cannot be late for King Arsaces."

Outside, the sounds of horse hooves passed the house. This was Damascus, not Alexandria, and Sepharia could tell by the stone echoes. Damascus was haphazardly built and the echoes were doubled and confused, rather than orderly as in Alexandria. They'd been given the house to use by the Roman governor.

Sepharia adjusted the belt, straightening the folds of the chiton at her midsection. Her hair had grown dusty and limp on the trail. Amitris noticed her fussing with it and slapped at her hands.

"No time," she said.

"I don't understand," said Sepharia. "Why does he want to see me? Will he kill me because of those messages I sent?"

Amitris faced her as she adjusted the fabric around the neck. Her eyes creased at the corners, followed by a twitch on the lips. "I cannot know the mind of a King," she paused, clearly considering her words, "but Arsaces, King of Kings, is from a long line of rulers. He is a proud and precarious man. However, if he wanted you dead, you would have been executed already."

"Then what does he want?"

Amitris hesitated, biting her lower lip, before putting a simple golden chain around Sepharia's neck, then said, "There are worse things than death, but know that I do not believe this is why he called you. Otherwise, Vonones would not have instructed me to give you this jewelry to wear." A jade bracelet was placed around her wrist. "We must go now."

A guard waited outside the stone house. The town of Damascus had greeted them like liberators, throwing fragrant flowers at the Prince as he rode down the center of the street. The guard led them away.

King Arsaces waited in the Mithras Temple. Unlike the Roman temples which displayed carved columns at the atrium, the Temple of Mithras appeared to be carved from a giant slab of granite. A bas relief of a bull was festooned on the imposing doors seemingly fitted for a tomb. Two soldiers in light mail and leather waist guards opened the way.

The King would be receiving her in the entrance chamber, the only place the uninitiated were allowed to tread. A partition painted with battle scenes separated the two chambers. Sepharia glanced around, expecting to see Vonones waiting, but the royal advisor was not present. Amitris gently herded Sepharia towards the side of the partition.

Amitris whispered, "Quickly, Sepharia, do not keep the King of Kings waiting."

"What do I do?" she whispered back.

The handmaiden blinked. "Apologies, you have never been in his presence. When you approach, you must stop five paces before him and fall prostrate to the floor in greeting. This is *proskynesis*. Only when he speaks can you stand. After that, be careful in your words. Less is more."

"I understand," said Sepharia, "and thank you, Amitris, for all you've done."

They shared the kiss of parting and Sepharia took a deep breath and gathered the fabric around her knees so she did not fall. The room was dim and full of incense. She smelled sage and musk and sycamore. Upon a simple wooden chair waited King Arsaces in a white robe and crimson sash. In him, Sepharia was impressed by his seemingly wise and kingly nature, unlike the barbarian Agog. King Arsaces was a figure out of the scrolls and Sepharia felt the burden of his line weighing on her. Sepharia measured her steps and when she reached the appointed distance, she bent knee and slipped carefully to the floor, touching her forehead to the tapestry.

"Rise, girl, and stand before me," said King Arsaces, in Greek, reaching out with jeweled fingers and pointing to a spot ahead. Sepharia took two steps closer and kept her eyes low, head slightly bowed.

"You are as beautiful as I was told," he said, and after a time, "but not as verbose as expected."

"Apologies," she said, "I was told only to speak when spoken to."

King Arsaces chuckled. He was older than she expected, his hair grayed by time. He rattled the golden bracelets around his wrist while stroking his well-kept beard.

"And more mannered, as well," he said. "How has my son treated you? No," he held his palm out and shook it, "do not answer that. I've already spoken to Vonones. Tell me instead about your father."

Sepharia clasped her hands in front of her, squeezing the shaking from them. "Agog is said to be..."

"No," said King Arsaces, "your *real* father. And don't make that face, of course, I know about the adoption to Alexander's heir, the Macedonian woman Polyxena. But your father, the *Michanikos*, he's the one that interests me. What is he like?"

The King leaned forward, an astute, but eager smile on his face. Sepharia was reminded of a kindly grandfather, though she knew from Amitris' warnings he could be a ruthless man. The son was proof enough of that.

"The scholars of the Great Library say he is unmatched in his inventions. He's contributed more knowledge to the scroll racks than anyone, save Archimedes, and one day he will surely pass him," she explained.

As the King narrowed his gaze, she realized he was interviewing her for a purpose, probably to learn more about the potential battles ahead. Sepharia chose her words carefully from then forward.

"He has made giant metal soldiers that can fight on their own," she continued, her words gathering momentum, "and steam chariots that can outrun any horse and keep going for hundreds times hundreds of stadia. It is said his steam chariots could circle Rome three times before Emperor Claudius even got out of bed."

King Arsaces smiled and Sepharia wondered if she'd gone too far. "These things I've heard, as well. But tell me about the nature of Heron the man."

Sepharia hid her smile behind a hand, feigning fixing her hair. He is no man at all, she wanted to say. "Apologies, Your Grace, what do you mean?"

King Arsaces made turning motions with his hand, like a gear winding. "How does he work? Does he sleep? What is he like? I am intrigued by a man who can stand up to my son. Does he truly believe his machines can replace slaves?"

Sepharia searched for the right words. "My father, he is always working. Either in our workshop, or helping another. His fingers are stained with ink and his latest sketchings can usually be found on his arm when he forgets his place in his work. His memory knows no match. It is said, and I have seen it, that he can memorize a page only by looking at it."

"Can you do this?" asked Arsaces, smiling.

She shook her head. "Apologies, no. But my father *does* believe his machines can change the world. That we do not need slaves. Only his machines."

King Arcases leaned into his chair. "I would like to meet this man, more than even the barbarian Satrap, as interesting as he sounds."

The words wanted to leap from her lips, but she saw the thoughts brewing behind his eyes, so she waited and watched, and maybe hoped a little. The faintest hint of a smile tugged at the corner of King Arcases' mouth.

"Is it true he builds a pyramid greater than those in Memphis?"

"Though it is many stadia south of Alexandria, it can be seen from the Great Lighthouse," said Sepharia softly.

King Arcases shook his head. "How can one city have so many of the great works of our world when my capitol has none?" He tapped his fingers on the armrest while his lips thinned.

He tilted his head and narrowed his eyes and Sepharia dreaded his question even before it'd left his lips. "If you were in my place, what would you do?"

Sepharia bowed her head and remembered Amitris' words. "It is not for me to know the mind of a king."

"Yet, I am asking," he said. "Indulge my royal desires." He chuckled and she found herself liking him.

She gave the question some thought, hoping he would indulge her with patience, as well. She was not a strategist, nor had she been at the discussions with Agog or Vestalis. But they were not here and he was asking her and as much as her gut worried it was a trap, she knew she could not be silent on the matter. She thought of Cleopatra and her negotiation with Caesar. King Arcases was much too old for her tastes and he did not seem the type for seduction. The grandfatherly impression came back and suddenly, Sepharia knew what she should say.

"Rome cares only for itself," she began carefully, mimicking the oration of the Great Library. "Caesar was proof of that. If you ally with Emperor Claudius and he takes Alexandria, he'll turn his new found steam mechanicals on Susa and your legacy will end then and there. Alexandria would not spend its blood and treasure on a pyramid if conquest was its desire. My father's pyramid is meant as a beacon of welcome to the world in the same way the Lighthouse of Pharos greets sailors on the long voyage across the Mediterranean. Alexandria has always shared its knowledge and would gladly share its technology."

While she spoke, his smile disappeared, and the gears behind those aged eyes churned with each word. Before she could take a breath, he fired back a question.

"What about the barbarian?" he asked. "He is not one of you, nor is he a scholar. Hasn't he come south to conquer? These brutes of snow and ice are well known for their savagery."

"Do savages take a city from Rome with only a handful of troops and then wisely name themselves the Satrap as not to anger the people?" she asked. The last part was something she'd heard Heron mention once. Her father had much admiration for the barbarian.

He tapped his chin with one finger. "Well said." He nodded. "You speak well for a woman, girl, I should say. Your thoughts mirror my own on the matter, though I have not shared them with anyone. Especially since we sit in a Roman city."

Flush with excitement, she glanced toward the entrance, almost expecting to see a Roman soldier. He shifted on his chair, silently chewing his thoughts.

"But Rome is the problem," he began. "Even with Alexandria by our side, Rome outnumbers us five to one. The legion is unmatched in battle."

"My father's inventions will tip the scales," she said hastily, regretting it when he frowned slightly, the mark of a silent rebuke.

King Arcases sighed, and it was not a sigh like other men. Sepharia could hear the weight of a nation in that out-breath. In that moment, she felt the ache and solitude of decision, and part of her wondered how such an introspective king could birth a monster as Vima the Viper.

"In the end, I am a vain man," said King Arcases. "If I side with Rome, history will not remember my place in quelling the barbarian uprising. But with Alexandria, I can help usher in a new age." He smiled softly. "And in truth, I desire to see this new pyramid and the nature of its building. And your father's workshop and the automata at every corner and all the miracles contained in the City of Wonders. If Rome wins, they might destroy it as punishment. I would not like that."

Sepharia could not believe his words. She bit down on her lower lip, to keep herself from saying more, lest she destroy the hope of a rejoined alliance.

"You have been sleeping in Vonones' tent, haven't you?" he asked.

"Oh, yes, he has been very kind to me," she said.

"After my son treated you so terribly," he continued. "He is a fearsome warrior, him and his body shield Pakur, but he is not a leader or a wielder of law."

King Arcases glanced toward the wall as if he could see a great distance. He nodded, a decision made.

"This marriage is useful, and I would like to claim a piece of Alexander in my future lineage." The King winked. "Henceforth, you will sleep in your own place. A grand and honored location next to mine and your handmaidens will be returned to you." He paused and smiled. "And your hair will be cleaned and brushed properly."

Sepharia reflexively touched a strand hanging limply near her cheek.

"I'm grateful for your kindness," she said, a great lump of dread filling her insides.

He clapped his hands. "Apologies," he said. "By my words, you must think I mean to keep you married to my son Vima. By Mithras, no, I mean to marry you to my son Khusra. He will know how to treat a woman such as yourself. He is learned and though he has a temper, he knows how to place his anger."

Stunned, Sepharia reached for something to grab onto and had to step back as not to fall. A great rush of heat and weight fled from her chest, as if a burning ember had been laying there and had just been taken off.

"Though he is the younger, I plan on giving the kingdom to him rather than Vima." King Arcases chuckled. "Assuming we survive the war against Rome. And that is where my son has been, treating with Rome, and though the negotiations went well, and he acquitted himself with cunning and honor, I will side with Alexandria."

"Oh, Your Grace, thank you." The words gushed out of her mouth and she resisted every urge to run up the dais steps and throw her arms around his neck.

"When Khusra reaches us, we will travel back to Alexandria to strengthen our bonds and make a proper alliance. The Parthian army travels from Susa as we speak," he said.

Spurred by a joyful buoyancy, Sepharia fell to the floor in *proskynesis*. King Arcases laughed a mirthful laugh and gave her permission to stand. Her eyes were brimming with tears, but she kept them back, though the smile on her face was irrepressible.

King Arcases tilted his head and his smile faltered, slightly. "My son Vima comes as I requested. There is more to speak about. I have plans upon plans and I need your expertise on the barbarian Agog, remember you will be on my side when we return to Alexandria." He winked again.

"Go around that vestibule over there and wait while I speak to my son. When I'm finished giving my instructions we can continue our conversation."

Sepharia practically skipped around the corner. She was not sure how much her argument had persuaded the king about siding with Alexandria, but it almost didn't matter. That she had been there at all made her flush and heat blossomed on her cheeks.

When Vima's rough voice cut through the hall, her smile lessened. She stood near an open window and below her was a hedge and she rubbed her arms, warding off the shivers she knew that would come.

Outside, the city of Damascus seemed a world different than Alexandria. No bronze spinning cups stuck from rooftops. Flags were listless and only the gray sky hung above the city, rather than the towering Lighthouse. The city draped itself in pale odors and even a hearty sniff brought only stale air. She would be glad to get back to Amitris and tell her all that had been said.

Another shout and Sepharia was brought back to the temple of Mithras. She could not hear what transpired between Vima and King Arcases, but the tone set her teeth on edge. Sepharia crept to the corner and put her ear to the stone wall.

"...it is not bravery but foolishness that you speak of," said King Arcases.

"There is no glory in ink and papyrus," shouted Vima. "Alexander carved his empire from the nations of his time. I do not wish to *ally* with that unwashed barbarian and his city of broken toys."

A baleful wrath rose in the King's voice: "It is not for you to decide. I am King Arcases, King of Kings. You are only a son with a future that might soon become dreadfully short."

When the whisper of steel cut through the room, Sepharia had to clamp down on her lip or let a noise out. She dug her fingers into her thigh, feeling nails cut skin.

"Do not dare your blade in my presence," shouted King Arcases.

"Or what, old man? Alexander said to his men when he died, 'to the strongest'. I am the strongest here and I'm going to take what I want," said Vima.

"Your brother will avenge me," said King Arcases, fear suddenly filling his voice.

Vima laughed a cold, biting laugh, and Sepharia shivered when he did. "My brother will side with me when I tell him that bitch Sepharia killed you. And then after we've wiped that cursed city from the sands, we'll turn on Rome and I'll cut Claudius' throat myself."

"You fool," said King Arcases, his voice resuming its towering authority. "You'll be the ruin of our kingdom."

There was no more said and a terrible gurgle cut through the room. Sepharia put a hand to her mouth and realized she had to get out of the city. Not only did Vima want to kill her, but the whole Parthian nation would as well when they heard of the slaying of King Arcases. Sepharia slipped from the window, landing in the bushes below, ignoring the cuts on her hands and legs. She had to get out of the city or find herself once more at the mercy of Vima the Viper.

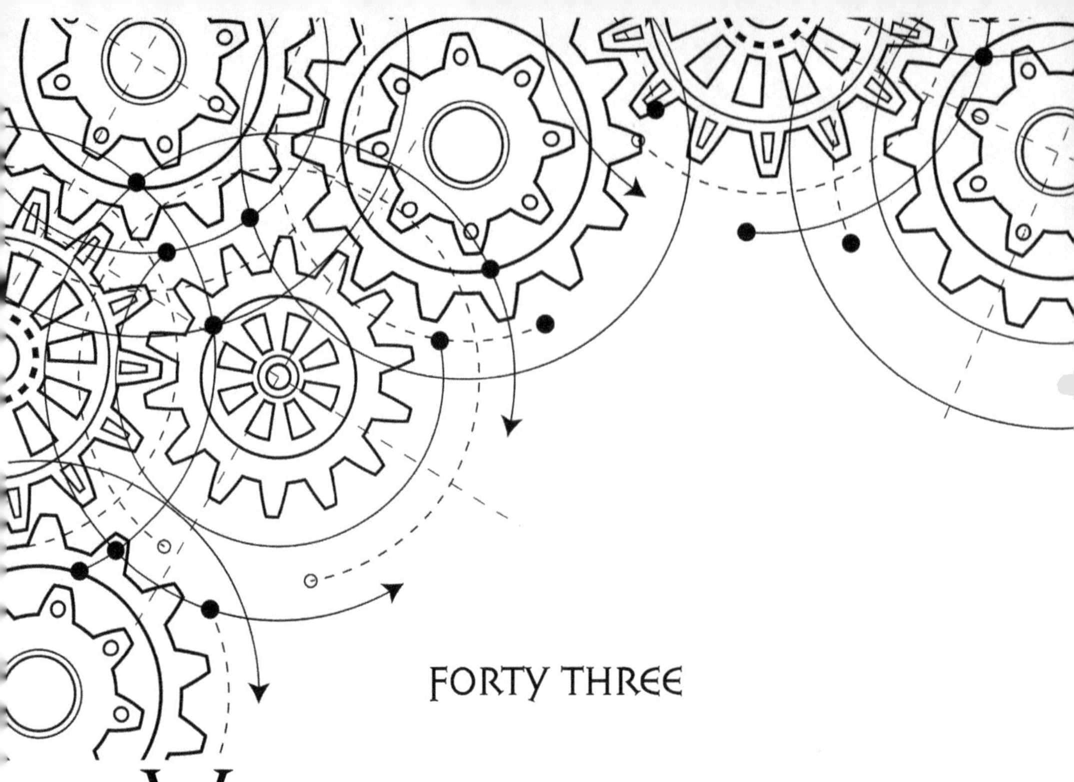

FORTY THREE

With his father dead, Vima carefully cleaned the blade on the white robes. Annoyed by the vacant, open-mouthed stare, Vima slapped the old man's corpse, knocking one eye closed.

"What a fool," he said, before strolling from the room. If he had to see his father again, it would only be to watch his corpse catch flame on the funeral pyre.

Vima gathered his rage before he stepped from the stone door. Before the first guard could even turn to greet him, Vima grabbed him by the neck.

"The King is dead! How could you not protect him?"

The soldier's look went from surprise to horror and then pleading. Vima cut his throat and turned on the second guard. He tried to pull his short sword out, but Vima grabbed his hand.

"Your punishment will be worse if you do not bring the king's advisor immediately."

The guard nodded and ran off, fear bubbling on the man's lips.

Vima paced before the stone bull, tearing at his clothes and hair. By the time the royal advisor ran up, with Vonones and others on heel, Vima had drawn blood from his face and arms and chest.

"My father is dead!" he told them on approach.

The royal advisor, a doddering fool nearly a decade older than his father, shook like leaves in a storm, and his bloodshot eyes glistened. "How can this be?"

Vima slapped the royal advisor, trying not to let them see how much he enjoyed it. "It's your fault for leaving him with such scant protection. I found him near dead, with a dagger wound in his chest."

Vonones stepped forward and put his arms around the king's advisor. "Did he say who killed him?"

The urge to smile nearly betrayed him, but he kept his rage, remembering the way the bitch's father had grabbed his arm when he was educating his stupid wife Zenobia, or when the girl's lucky chariot had won the race. She would be sitting in her room right now with Amitris. After this little play, they would march there and he would drag her from the house by her hair and cut off her fingers one by one.

"The Alexandrian bitch, Sepharia."

Vonones gasped and Vima laughed inside. His advisor had taken the girl into his tent, a weak gesture by a weak man. In the past, Vonones had given him good advice. Befriending the girl betrayed his lack of judgment. Maybe it was time to replace him with someone more cunning.

The royal advisor, keen to shift Vima's blame from himself, commanded a soldier to secure the house she had been staying in. The man ran off while Vima directed the frail royal advisor to attend to his father. He motioned for Vonones to follow, knowing he would enjoy the reaction from his former advisor as he punished the girl.

Before they reached the house, the first soldier ran to them, placed his fist against his chest, and said, "She's gone."

"Gone?" he said, feeling his rage unfold for real.

"The handmaiden said she never returned from the temple."

"Send men back to search. She might be hiding inside," he said.

"Send men to the camp and the city gates," said Vonones, "she might try to escape back to Alexandria."

Hiding his smirk before he turned, Vima wheeled on Vonones. "Did you have a hand in this? You'd grown awfully close to that girl since I disposed of her."

"No, my Prince," said Vonones, worry threading through his voice. "I'm loyal to the end. I only sought to keep her so your father could question her."

Vima slapped him. "Fool! And you let her kill him." He turned wildly. "You're all fools!"

"I swear I didn't think she would do this," said Vonones.

Vima placed his blade against Vonones' throat. "Then tell me where she is and you might live."

His advisor stammered out his response, "I swear I had no part in this. I loved your father. He treated me well. I would have killed her myself if I would have known what she was capable of."

"Then save yourself by telling me where she went," demanded Vima.

Vonones blinked hard and his mouth yawed open and close. A realization burst onto his face, and he spit the words out, "Mithrapolis! Remember the note: the father voids the treaty, change the plan to Mithrapolis. She's headed to Mithrapolis. The poisons you found were never for you, but for your father. The barbarian probably sent her as a spy and assassin."

"Mithrapolis, yes, probably," said Vima thoughtfully. "She probably has allies there ready to take her back to Alexandria."

"We can send soldiers there," said Vonones. "It's doubtful she could make it far."

The Prince turned back and forth, searching for the next step. He never intended for this to last very long. Kill his father, blame the girl, move on to the battles, and his eventual glory; that was the plan. And he wanted the enjoyment of taking her life. He couldn't let her get away.

"I'll take the soldiers myself along with Pakur," said Vima. "Keep a contingent in Damascus in case she's hidden here. Maybe she hasn't left at all."

Right then, a soldier ran up, out of breath. "Prince Vima, I checked the stables. Two horses are missing."

"She fled the city," said Vima. "I'll take the steam chariots and we'll catch her soon enough. Wake Pakur from his slumber and tell him we have a hunt today. She won't make it far on horseback when we have her father's steam chariots. Mithras smiles on me today."

FORTY FOUR

"Heave, blacksmith, unless you can hammer some legs on this statue and convince it to walk to that spot over there," said Hoth, wearing the scaled chestplate of a Roman soldier, pushing on the statue from atop the chariot.

Punt wiped the sweat from his smooth head and wrapped the rope around his hand, again. The statue of Mithras leaned precariously onto the timbers and Punt feared if he pulled too hard it could topple and break.

Acolytes in white robes watched from balconies. The sound of splashing on rocks from the spring fed waterfall only reminded Punt how much he wanted to soak his head in the chilly waters. The Roman armor was not made for laborious activities and he'd built a furnace in his chest from his efforts. At least there was a slight breeze, for the hilltop temple reached far above the rolling plains and the inner chamber of the temple was large enough to fit the steam chariot and have room enough to circle it back out.

Jarngard spoke from behind him, "Maybe if you actually pushed rather than preening like a peacock, we might actually move this hunk of rock."

"Less talk, more pulling, brother," smiled Hoth. "One and two and now!"

The rope cinched around Punt's hand as he leaned back and yanked, ignoring the burn in his back. The statue, frustratingly immobile, suddenly shifted and began to slide down the timbers, faster than expected. The head of the bull-horned god leaned toward the ground. Wide eyed, Punt pulled harder, shuffling backwards, trying to keep moving so the statue didn't fall and shatter into chunks of stone, ruining Sepharia's trap.

The statue of Mithras rattled down the timbers and slid across the floor into the place the high priest had designated for the gift. Punt let the rope fall slack and admired the statue.

From behind him, Hoth snorted. "Freya's frigid tits, this is why I have a crew. I ripped the skin from my first finger."

"If we hadn't brought your iron ship, maybe we would have had room for a crew," said Jarngard, sipping from a water pouch.

Hoth the Black laughed. "A ship that does not need a crew for rowing or pulling the lines is worth a rub on the finger. Nektam did well in his shipcraft, though it was smaller than I hoped. He promised me the next one will be bigger, with room for cheirobalistras that I can fit with fire charges."

"Not going to give the poor Romans a chance to take back the Mediterranean, eh?" chuckled Jarngard.

"You know well, I do not fight fair, brother," said Hoth.

"A lesson I learned all too well when you stole my wife while I lie in bed," replied Jarngard with a smile on his face.

Punt retrieved his water pouch while the two continued their banter. They'd gone on like this during the whole journey, and the ship wasn't large enough for the blacksmith to escape. At least the incense of the temple hid Hoth's perfumes.

A voice, one well worn by time, called down from the balcony. It was the high priest, a man Hoth had said reminded him of a grape left in the desert for a month. Despite the priest's age, his voice carried into open chamber.

"Riders come from the north," he said. "Your friends, I presume?"

Jarngard spoke for them. "May we come up and see for ourselves?"

The priest motioned toward an acolyte and after the sound of footsteps echoed through the walls, a hidden door opened. Punt followed the two Northmen and tried to ignore the chaffing of metal armor on his ribs. Before they left, they'd acquired Roman armor from the abandoned garrisons, but it'd been made for differently shaped men.

The priest led them up a winding staircase, stopping frequently to catch his breath. Knowing riders were approaching, Punt felt restrained by the languishing pace. They exited atop a bell tower, high above the small town.

Punt took a moment to survey the layout of the buildings. The temple took up the majority of the plateau on the upthrust hill. A smattering of houses, the living quarters of the priests and acolytes, fit in the space between the gate and the temple walls. Only the high priest lived in the temple and they'd passed his quarters on the way up the tower.

"Steam chariots," said Jarngard, indicating the trails of smoke in the distance with an outstretched arm, "three of them."

The Northman's eyes were better than his, but Punt saw the reflections of bronze shielding glinting off the sun. The three chariots, one of them with a wagon trailing behind, had surged ahead of a group of horsebacked riders, at least a dozen strong.

"I suspect that's Prince Vima, as promised," said Hoth the Black, "though I'm not sure how she did it."

The old priest perked up at the Prince's name. "Prince Vima? The Parthian? He's a generous man. Sacrificed a bull and gave ample tithe when he came through here, scant but a few weeks ago."

"Where is Sepharia?" asked Punt.

"Good question," said Jarngard, "but I'm sure she knows her place in this plan."

"I wish we knew ours," said Hoth, oddly sedate.

The old priest made a noise as if he was pleased with himself and headed down the stairs. "I must ready the acolytes for the Prince."

After he was gone, Jarngard crossed his arms. "What now?"

Hoth squinted at the steam chariots. "Remember the time with the Ugrian witch?"

"I'd rather not," said Jarngard, "I seem to remember getting stabbed by that guy dressed like a lizard."

Hoth scrunched his face up. "Oh, that was that place? Nevermind, it'd never work here."

"What about when we dressed Agog like a woman?" asked Jarngard. "You have the features for it."

Hoth chuckled sardonically. "But we don't have a dozen mules, nor a finely crafted *balbota* doll, so that would never work."

"Good point, brother," said Jarngard. "I wish I knew where Sepharia was. It might help us form our plan."

Hoth tilted his head. "What about the Saami priest?"

"Didn't we have to give him half the gold for his part in it? I don't think the high priest would approve. He seems smitten by the young Prince."

"We don't have to involve him," said Hoth and then he turned to Punt. "Do you know anything about Mithras rituals?"

The blacksmith recalled making a miracle for the temple in Alexandria. He'd been present during the unveiling, working the ropes from behind a painted screen. He nodded. When eager grins formed on the Northmen's faces, Punt knew he'd erred.

"Good," said Hoth the Black, "you get to be the high priest today."

Jarngard patted Punt on the back. "Let's get moving. We have to get the steam chariot hidden. The Prince and his men will be here within the hour. We'll explain your part once it's moved."

Punt tried to refuse but the two Northmen had already hurried down the winding wooden steps, footsteps echoing over what suspiciously sounded like laughter. The blacksmith glanced back to the trails of dust and the many riders and slowly shook his head. He moved to follow and though he was moving downward, it seemed each step weighed heavier than his journey to the top of the bell tower.

FORTY FIVE

When Sepharia was a child in the workshop, she'd crawled into a statue of Ares during the early morning hours when the workers had not yet arrived. The bronze belly made wonderful sounds as she babbled to herself or tapped on the walls like a drum and eventually, she grew tired and fell asleep. The statue was near complete and when the workers arrived, they fastened the last section over the body of the war god Ares.

The child Sepharia had woke in darkness in the belly of the god. Light could not penetrate the hollow space and Sepharia thought she'd gone blind. She beat her tiny fists on the walls, one more soft thumping added to the cacophony of wooden mallets beating pegs into scaffolding or fixing the shape of bronze moldings.

The futility of her cries for help were like acid on her bones and eventually, sobbing and exhausted, she quit. Heron was typically busy at work and no one noticed that Sepharia was missing until evening time when the workers had left. When she heard faint calls of her name, she beat upon the great bronze belly, her fear providing strength, and soon after she saw Plutarch's smiling face sticking through the reformed opening.

When Sepharia closed the hidden compartment on the wagon, those memories returned and her arms felt instantly weak as if a spell had been cast on them. The moment she'd seen the wagon connected to the gifted steam chariot, she knew she had a method to escape, if only things fell the right way, though she hoped she would not have to use it.

Closed into the darkness, King Arcases' feeble cries as Prince Vima stabbed him returned to Sepharia in full. For a brief time, Sepharia had hoped that Parthia would join Alexandria in fighting the Romans. With King Arcases dead, and his death firmly blamed on her, the Parthians would be enthusiastic foes of Alexandria.

Outside, she heard cries of alarm. She assumed they'd realized two horses were missing from the corral. Before she'd crawled into the wagon, she'd led them into the private stalls kept for royalty. Vima had ridden his steam chariot, so she hoped they wouldn't be found until later.

When the steam chariots rumbled to life, Sepharia made silent prayers to the gods. The wagon yanked forward and Sepharia breathed a sigh of relief, but not for long, as the first bump slammed her face directly into the wooden flooring. Her nose stung and she braced herself as the wagon bounced across the cobblestone streets.

She wasn't sure she'd be able to hold her position, arms and legs wedged to keep from being rattled around the hidden compartment like the hard beans in a *krotala* percussion instrument. Arms ached and a knot formed in her shoulder blade. Sepharia tried to turn, but the wagon bounced across something intractable and the side of her face rebounded across the bottom, bringing stars to her eyes.

The violent shuddering was unbearable and her teeth felt like they would come loose from her mouth at any moment. Sepharia wasn't sure she'd be able to survive the journey to Mithrapolis. Then the worst of the bouncing stopped and she realized the steam chariots had left the city and sped across smoother dirt roads.

Occasionally, the wagon would bounce, but she learned to keep her arm draped over her face to protect her nose. It was then the darkness seeped into her, but she reminded herself that she'd survived much worse and that she would get out of the wagon eventually.

With her arms recovered from the jarring traverse across the cobblestone streets of Damascus, Sepharia began her investigation of the opening mechanism. The lever was still sheared off from when they'd trapped the Alabarch in the wagon, but unlike the Alabarch, she understood the nature of its construction and had a knife to aid her in bypassing it. However, she had no plans to bring out the knife while the wagon was still moving, but she knew once the steam chariots stopped, she might have little time to escape, so she had to be ready.

Using her fingertips, she found the outline of the wooden handle, a bristling moon shape in the otherwise smooth wood. The jagged edge was rough against her fingers and she lamented the softness of her hands. The last few months in the Palace had deprived her skin of its toughness. Sepharia vowed to return to the workshop, should she escape the Parthians.

Once she memorized the construction of the release handle, Sepharia rolled onto her back, placed her arm across her face and tried to sleep. Rest came fitfully. It seemed each time she started to doze, the wagon would bounce and shake her awake from dreamland, which partially seemed safer, because she feared the dreams the gods would visit upon her for her role in these events.

The road between Damascus and Mithrapolis was relatively flat. The path rose and fell, but not sharply, and she slid to one end of the compartment or another, and waited for the road to level out. When it seemed the wagon was tilting backwards, farther and farther, until she felt like she was standing, she knew they'd reached Mithrapolis. The walled temple was built on an upthrust hill that seemed like a mountain lost from the northern Caucasus range.

Sepharia pulled her knife from the sheath when the rumbling steam mechanicals went silent. Outside, she heard men speaking, the sharp language of the Parthians, but she tried to ignore them and focus on the handle.

She thought she might be able to stick the knife end into the handle and slide the mechanism over, but quickly she realized the error of her thinking. The knife had no leverage. As the voices outside faded away, she tried wedging the blade edge into the gap around the sheered handle. Using her fingertips to steady it, she was able to wiggle it in, but the handle was stuck fast, even when she pushed hard enough to grunt.

The darkness felt tangible again and not because she feared the blankness, but that if she couldn't get free of the wagon, the Prince would eventually realize she wasn't in Mithrapolis and return to Damascus. Sepharia tried the handle again, pushing on the hilt and praying the blade wouldn't slip and flay her fingers to the bone. She was already weak from hunger and a deep enough cut would leave her to bleed to death trapped in the wagon.

The urge to kick wildly like a frenzied mule nearly overtook her, but then she remembered the futile pounding of the Alabarch. He was a bigger man and had kicked the door repeatedly. If she was going to get out, she needed to use her wits, not her strength, of which she had little.

Sepharia took a deep breath, and imagined the handle again. She heard voices and momentarily thought the Parthians had returned and she'd run out of time, but it was just the caws of birds flying over. Sepharia focused on the handle in the same way she concentrated her mental energies on a piece of jewelry when she was working. At those times, her fingers were not fingers, but extensions of her imagination. Rather than forcing the handle, Sepharia experimented, testing the leverage at differ-ent points until she thought she detected a weakness. When she thought she found the proper spot, she wedged her body into the space - and *pushed* - feeling the blade bend like a reed. The knife jumped and she was certain her fingers would be cut, but the wagon mechanism clicked and the door swung open, letting in a blinding white light.

Sepharia sheathed her knife and climbed from the wagon, almost expecting rough hands to grab her as she squeezed out. No soldiers, or people for that matter, were near the steam chariots. Only the occasion-al heavy snort from a saddled horse sounded. The grounds before the massive temple were empty, which Sepharia found odd.

She considered taking one of the horses or steam chariots, but she was not a skilled rider and if they saw her, she wouldn't make it far. The town was high above the plains and riders could be seen from a distance. She also thought about hiding in one of the houses, but she didn't know who might find her and if they would give her away. The Prince had visited this town a few weeks ago and they would be keen to help him.

The temple doors had been left wide. The opening in the stone wall was a cave into the temple and she could hear voices. Sepharia crept toward the opening, determined to understand her situation before she made the next move.

Standing at the entrance, she heard voices clearly, including one that seemed familiar, but why Punt was conversing with Prince Vima, she couldn't understand, even though she knew it'd been her note that had gotten him here. If Punt was inside the temple, then maybe others were lying in wait, readying themselves to ambush the Prince, or maybe they were negotiating the surrender, though she doubted the Prince would ever do that, and that still wouldn't explain why Punt was the spokesper-son. That would be like asking Agog to lecture on the mysterious arts of mummery.

Sepharia peered around the corner and did not see Punt at first, until she looked into the balcony and saw the bald, bronze head of the blacksmith, looking radiant in white robes. Despite the stammering of his words, on Punt, the robes seemed natural on his blocky frame.

Vima stood in the center of the temple in light mail and leathers, hands resting on his blades, Pakur by his side. Ahead of him, the statue of Mithras with bronze horns rose above, stone hands outstretched to receive an offering. Sepharia swallowed her excitement, seeing the statue inside the temple. *Where were the others?* She could not imagine that only Punt had been sent, and why did they not just leave the statue and be gone?

The Prince spoke in Greek, his voice clearly carrying above the splashing water of the little spring fed waterfall, "You say you've seen no sign of the Alexandrian girl, nor any others?"

Even Sepharia could hear the mistrust in his voice. Whatever stratagem her friends were planning was not going well.

"We have not," said Punt.

"And the high priest and the acolytes have been downed by this strange illness?" asked Vima.

"It's terrible," said Punt. "A greenish pus leaks from their ears and penises. Mithras punishes us for some misdeed, we can only assume. They lay moaning in the upper chamber."

"Why not keep them down here so you may easily fetch them water and help?" asked Vima.

There was a dreadful pause and Sepharia bit her lip, but Punt answered eventually, "The elevation seems to lessen the pus. Maybe they are closer to Mithras up here."

If the Prince accepted Punt's reasoning, she couldn't be sure, but Vima moved to the statue and put his hand on the stone belly. Sepharia found it curious the statue was stone, except for the bronze horns, when her design had been all bronze. She hoped the ghost fire jars in the base would still work.

"And this statue was delivered here?" asked Vima questioningly.

Punt cleared his throat. "Roman soldiers came and left not but a day ago. The illness came right after. Maybe Mithras has punished us for not making proper sacrifice to the gift."

"Mithras does not suffer fools," replied Vima. "Maybe he punishes you rightly."

The Prince spoke quietly to Pakur and she could not hear the exchange. Punt searched around, and she could see his unease. The Parthian soldiers with Vima touched their weapons and started glancing around as if expecting an ambush.

Punt cleared his throat again. "Prince Vima. Would you honor us by making that sacrifice and lifting this illness from our holy order?"

Vima grumbled and shook his head. She almost expected him to decline. He pulled out a dagger and drew the edge of the blade across the palms of both hands, murmuring incantations all the while. He spoke in a tongue she did not recognize.

When he stepped to the statue, her heart hung in her throat by a slender thread. Vima reached toward the bronze horns of the god Mithras. When his hands grabbed the curved surfaces, he shuddered and leapt backwards immediately.

"What magic is this, priest?" he yelled, and turned to Pakur and gave instructions in Parthian. The soldiers spread out and began knocking on the walls, clearly looking for the secret entrance. Sepharia punched her leg in frustration. The statue should have delivered its ghost fire into the Prince, killing him. Somehow, the trap had failed.

Punt seemed frozen, so Sepharia ran back to the steam chariots. She needed to do something to help. If it were only Punt, he was in trouble.

The coals were still glowing hot, so she was able to start the mechanical right away. She engaged the gearing as two soldiers came out to investigate the noise. The courtyard was wide enough to gain momentum and the soldiers had to jump out of the way to avoid the wheels.

As the steam chariot passed through the opening of the temple, shouts and sounds of battle could be heard from inside. Men fired bows into the upper chamber, the twang of bowstrings drowned beneath the battering echoes of the steam mechanical. Soldiers filed into an opening in the wall, the temple's hidden entrance, and Prince Vima stood before the statue, directing his men with swords drawn.

Sepharia planned to jump from the chariot once it'd gone through the opening. It was just meant as a distraction for Punt and the others, if there were others, so they could get away. But when she saw Vima standing there before the statue, Sepharia leaned into the steering mechanism and prepared for impact.

FORTY SIX

When the Parthians found the hidden entrance, Jarngard knew the time for trickery was over. Hoth the Black was closer to the hidden stairwell and moved to intercept with Punt right behind, shouldering his warhammer for battle. Arrows whistled past the balcony, forcing Jarngard to duck.

Screams followed by a rumbling cacophony filled the wide temple hall. A steam chariot shot through the entrance, bronze shielding momentarily reflecting the sunlight outside, casting a blinding glare before falling to dullness.

Piloting the chariot, Jarngard saw Sepharia, looking determined as she leaned into the steering mechanism, hair flowing past her shoulders on her brief flight. Prince Vima turned to leap, but the shielding caught him mid-jump, spinning him into the shallow pool. The impact shook the temple as the chariot slammed into the statue. Sepharia flew from the front, over the pond, and into the rocks.

Arrows flew past Jarngard's head. He ducked beneath the edge of the balcony and hustled to Punt's side, glancing below to see if Sepharia or the Prince survived.

A fit of rage erupted from below, like a hundred lions marking the hunt. Pakur stood above the fallen, motionless Prince Vima, half in and half out of the pool, whose face was a bloody wreck. The hairless Pakur snatched up his charge's weapon and leapt into the secret hallway. The advance of the Parthians surged forward, buoyed by Pakur's rage and soon it took both Hoth and Jarngard to keep from being overrun.

"Fall back to the upper chamber," said Hoth.

"Not the tower," said Jarngard, beating back a sword thrust, "we don't want to get trapped up there."

"Not there," said Hoth, "this whole upper temple is a maze of rooms."

Jarngard nodded and before they moved on, he glanced once more at the fallen form of Sepharia. There would be time enough for mourning later, if he survived to mourn.

Spurred by the retreat, the Parthians doubled their attacks. Pakur led them, his arms whirling with ferocity. It took both of them to keep up with the assault. Jarngard did not try to counterattack, for it served their purpose that Pakur blocked the others. No one man could keep swinging his arms for that long. While rage was useful in open battle, tight quarter fighting required patience and discipline. Hoth and Jarngard kept up their alternating defense while moving backwards, counting on the raging Pakur to tire.

"Through here," said Punt, standing at an open doorway.

Jarngard caught Hoth's eye and they nodded. Hoth made an unexpected attack to Pakur's legs. The Parthian warrior did not jump back and the blade cut across his thighs, spilling blood like a fountain. Jarngard expected Pakur to jump back and turned to slip through the doorway when the blade came for Hoth's head. Jarngard felt his blade come around too late and expected to see Hoth's face split wide when a war-hammer snuck through the gap and blocked the blow.

Punt shouldered between the two Northmen and hurled his war-hammer forward, hitting Pakur in the chest and entangling the Parthians in the hallway. The distraction provided time to escape through the doorway and slam it closed.

Jarngard found himself on a wide balcony. While Punt held the way with his body, Jarngard and Hoth hauled a stone table against the exit. Pounding came moments later, followed by an axe blade poking through the wooden slats.

"This won't keep them long," said Hoth.

Jarngard examined his surroundings. The balcony was on the back of the temple, high above the town, though not as high as the bell tower. Sunlight streamed through gray-white clouds and faint black smoke from distant villages curled and climbed the sky. Beauty in the unexpected moment caught breath in his throat and he ached for Heron to be by his side.

"Unless we can grow wings, I think we're trapped," said Hoth.

Jarngard shook free his thoughts and moved to the edge of the balcony and looked around the side. The hole in the door was growing wider. "You might be a fish and you're not a bird, but today let's be a tree frog."

Suddenly, Hoth looked like he was going to be ill. "I'm not going over that railing."

Jarngard glanced at the door, rapidly splintering. "Your choice, but I'm going this way."

The temple walls were made of stacked stone, filled in with mortar. Jarngard fit his fingers into the gaps and swung out around the corner. Punt, still wearing his temple finery, climbed over, taking to the wall easily.

Jarngard kept moving sideways, wondering what was on the other side. He hoped they would find a balcony and a way out safely. If the Parthians figured out what they were doing, they could quickly move to cut them off.

When Hoth swung around the corner, moving his hands and feet rapidly, Jarngard knew the door would be breached soon. The wall was nearly as wide as the temple and when they reached the halfway point, a head poked around the other side.

"By the jarl's balls, they cut us off. Quickly, down! Before they bring bows."

Moving downward, Jarngard kept his hands and feet moving, knuckles scraping stone, resisting the urge to rush. When he'd been moving sideways, he'd pretended he was only a few feet up. Headed toward the bottom of the building and the beginning of the cliff, it was hard not to notice it was a long way down.

They made the sliver of land between the building and the cliff edge when the arrows started whistling over their heads. A pair of archers leaned around each corner.

"We need to get out of their range or on the other side of that wall," said Jarngard.

Hoth moved around the other way and Jarngard followed, with Punt trailing. The wall curved around, blocking the archers, but the path disappeared into the thin air above the cliff.

With his back against the stone wall, Jarngard peered over the edge. The cliff was not vertical, but steep enough to make it more hand over hand climbing.

"We can go down or over to that window and try to fight our way out," said Jarngard.

"I don't think it's going to matter," said Punt, pointing to the north.

"By the gods, what is that?" said Hoth.

In the distance, a dust cloud rose into the sky and light glimmered like a thousand coins dropped into shallow waters. Jarngard imagined the thunderous noise of horses, covered in heavy scale, carrying the warriors astride them, and imagined the heavy musk of horse scent, and the thrill of battle passed through him.

"The Parthian cataphracts," said Jarngard heavily. "The brother comes from the north."

"Even if we climb down this cliff, we're still caught," said Hoth. "I think I might just stay here and take my chances with the brother."

A stone flew by their heads and all three looked up, just in time to dodge a second, larger rock hurling from above. There was a window high above them and someone was lobbing stones from it.

"Down it is," sighed Hoth the Black.

Punt grunted. "What about Sepharia?"

Jarngard paused and shook his head.

Punt nodded, a grim countenance on face. "I can't say I'm looking forward to the climb, either."

"Well, brothers," said Jarngard grimly as he moved to the edge, "last one down has to give the bad news to Heron."

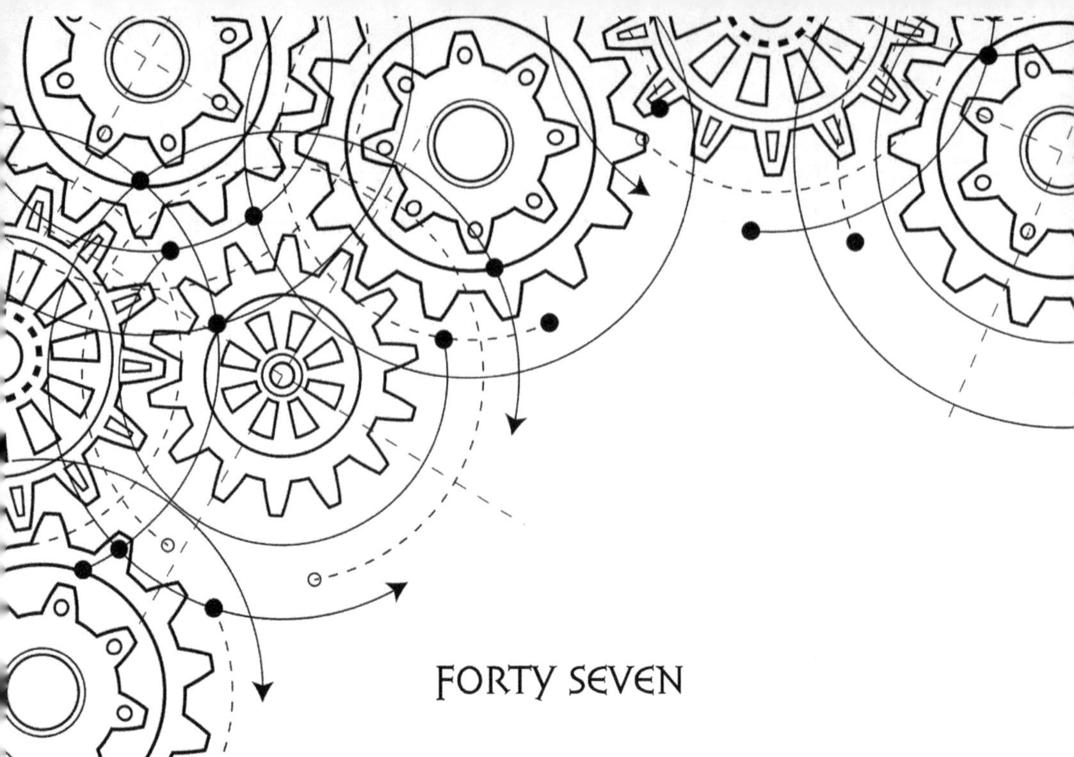

FORTY SEVEN

Blood pounded in her ears. Vertigo grabbed hold of Sepharia's world and whipped it around. Water, trickling over stone, tickled
her face, her fingers, her lips. She pushed upright and vomit rose in her
throat. She swallowed it back and tried to open her eyes again. Darkness
overtook.

The hall was silent, though distant battle echoed through the stone,
ringing the boulder-sized headache in the middle of her skull. She
managed to get one eye open without losing the meager contents of her
stomach.

The air stunk of burning cloth and hair. Broken stone littered the
ground. Sepharia pushed away from the rocks of the waterfall. A fire
burned at the center of a ruined tapestry, lit by the scattered burning
coals from the chariot impact.

The statue of Mithras had been sheared off at the base. The bronze
tops of the hidden ghost fire jars looked like the gray eggs of a stone
crocodile. One of the bronze rods that formed the horn was tangled

around the wheel, bent like a wet reed.

She wiped her face and came away with a bloody forearm. The metallic, salty taste in her mouth was fresh. She'd bitten her tongue, at least, maybe more.

Staggering to her feet, she surveyed the room. Then she heard a moan. Before trying to climb off the rocks, she checked herself for injuries. Except for the cut on her forehead, she could find no broken bones, though the tender probing brought tears to her eyes.

The doors to the temple were open. She could see horses and the other steam chariots. If she ran out the door, she could take a chariot and escape. Even if she drove until the fuel expired, she would at least be away from the high town, and Vima.

Sepharia glanced towards the balcony. She knew Punt wouldn't be there. The soldiers had gone after him. She could only assume that Jarngard was with him and maybe some others. She couldn't leave them. Maybe she would start the chariot and circle the courtyard, waiting for signs of Punt and the others.

It was a good enough plan for her rattled brain. Sepharia wiped a second forearm of blood and climbed down the rocks. Another moan cleared the air and caused her to momentarily freeze.

As she gingerly stepped around the chariot, she remembered what had happened. The chariot had crashed into the statue, throwing her over the side. The moaning she heard took shape as a man stood like a specter rising from the grave.

It was Vima.

His face was a bloody mess. A tooth hung by a thread of pink flesh, dangling from the side of his mouth. He saw her before she could move away.

He spoke and the words turned into a hissing blood splatter, "Bttccthh…"

Vima came after her. Sepharia fled up the wet rocks, feeling her way with slippery fingers. Vima grabbed her ankle, pulling her down.

Hands found her throat, nails digging into flesh. Red liquid dripped from the broken mess that was once his mouth. With bloodshot eyes enraged, he squeezed until black spots formed in her vision. Kicking upwards, she caught him in the groin and she could breathe once again.

The Prince made noises like a beast rutting and raving in the wilds. He punched her in the ribs, the mailed fist leaving an imprint of rings. Vima reared back and prepared to strike again. Sepharia grabbed a hunk of stone and struck him in the chest, skipping off his armor and thumping the soft flesh beneath his chin.

Vima stumbled backwards, somehow keeping his feet until he made the level ground. He tripped and fell unceremoniously into the pool of water, the fall nearly comical despite the circumstances.

Sepharia searched for a weapon and found it, lying near her head, almost sliding from the rocks. It was the second rod from the statue, still tipped with a bronze horn. Ignoring the vertigo and the weakness in her legs, Sepharia scrambled down the rocks with the horn-tipped rod held like a spear under her arm.

Right when the Prince staggered to his feet, still bent at the waist, Sepharia reached him. The overlapping straps of the leather loincloth parted and Sepharia shoved the horn tip between the gap.

The sharp bronze point penetrated the Prince and he screamed a soul rending scream. With the Prince impaled on the rod, Sepharia pushed, sending him stumbling forward until he landed chest first on a large rock.

Except it wasn't a rock. It was the base of the statue, the hidden location of the ghost fire jars. The Prince, soaking wet and covered in light mail, landed on the bronze pegs on top of the jars. When his body started convulsing, Sepharia realized what she'd done.

The smell of burnt flesh quickly filled the air and Sepharia carefully moved around the Prince's body until she could see his face. His blank stare was confirmation enough.

She was about to run out the front when she heard soldiers' voices. With no place to hide in the wide hall, Sepharia moved deeper into the temple. Three soldiers in mail jogged to the steam chariots and began readying them for travel by scooping new fuel into the furnace.

Cursing her slowness, Sepharia almost missed the hidden doorway in the cubby behind the waterfall. The inner hallway led deeper into the temple and Sepharia made her way through, taking turns at random, expecting to run into a soldier at any second.

She froze when she heard voices. She was standing in a stone hallway that had a window to the outside. When she realized they were one's she recognized, she tried to figure out where they were coming from. She stuck her head through the window and found her friends preparing to climb down the cliff.

"...last one down has to tell Heron about Sepharia," said Jarngard.

"Last one down has to tell Heron what about me?"

The men startled, Hoth grabbing the stone so he did not go over.

"By the gods girl, how did you survive?" asked Jarngard. "Nevermind, it doesn't matter. Are you well enough to climb?"

"I've never climbed before, except on the scaffolding," she said.

"No better time to learn," said Jarngard. "The wall makes for convenient hand holds. Come out the window and make your way to us. Below is a chimney, of sorts, you can climb above me and I'll catch you if you fall."

"Or take you with me when I do," she said, slipping out the window.

The yawning space beneath made her hesitate, but the fear in her veins was drained from the fight with Vima, so she moved out after Jarngard. Hoth and Punt already moved down the cliff, though she wondered at the wisdom of them going first. If she fell, it would mean death for the four of them.

Jarngard pulled her onto the thin slice of earth and started making his way down the stone chimney. When it was her turn, she edged over, keeping her fingers dug into the stone. The walls formed a nice crescent and she found frequent handholds, but the distance was so great she feared her arms and legs would tire before she reached bottom.

A quarter of the way down, she paused, wedging her legs into a little ledge and rested her arms. Jarngard called up from below, "No stopping. The Prince's brother brings his army to Mithrapolis."

"He's not the Prince's brother now. He's the Parthian King. Vima killed his father in Damascus and blamed it on me," she shouted down to him before moving downward again.

"That explains his mad rush to Mithrapolis," said Jarngard.

Sepharia did not speak again, instead focusing her energies on making it down the cliff safely. Maybe when the new king captured them, she could explain what Vima had done. Both Amitris and the old king had said Khusra was a kinder man, though most men were not kind when they had their enemies in hand.

As they neared the bottom, Punt cried from below. "A steam chariot approaches!"

Sepharia remembered the men readying the steam chariot above. Punt and the Northmen had left their weapons to focus on climbing. The rumble of horses could be felt through the stone. The lone steam chariot would keep them trapped until the others arrived. All her plans had been for naught.

Busy in her thoughts, Sepharia missed a handhold and felt the stone slip away from her fingers. She skidded down the wall and thoughts of careening through the air blew through her head. She fell for a length before thudding suddenly and unexpectantly heels first into the soil. She had only fallen a short, but startling distance. Sepharia heaved a sigh, steadied herself, and turned.

The glittering bronze shield of a steam chariot approached, thunderous pistons echoing off the cliff wall. Sepharia was preparing to grab a rock to throw when she saw the pilot of the craft.

"Heron!" she cried.

Her father stood awkwardly at the steerage, a strange metal object at the end of her arm, connected to the steering mechanism somehow. Plutarch rode on the back end of the chariot. It was a newer, larger design.

"Get on, quickly," cried Plutarch, "soldiers approach!"

They scrambled on and no sooner, Heron turned the chariot and fled south. Sepharia thought they were safe until a flood of cataphracts in their glimmering mail burst around the cliff, catching up to them like a roaring avalanche.

Suddenly men lunged with outstretched swords. Sepharia cast about for a weapon. Jarngard threw chunks of coals at the horsebacked riders.

"We're caught," screamed Sepharia into the wind.

Heron turned her head to speak, and Sepharia was stunned into silence by the haggard gaze of her father. Pinkish scar tissue threaded her neck and the eyes glowed bloodshot. Sepharia suddenly realized Heron was not standing on her own two feet. She was propped up, one leg on the ground, the other, a stump below the knee, leaning on the pedestal.

Heron spoke like graveyard stones grinding together, "To the gods with them, we fly on our own wind."

A lever engaged and the steam chariot lurched forward, pistons ascending a thrumming symphony. The horsebacked riders fell behind, javelins landing impotently in the grass. Soon, the waves of riders slowed as the steam chariot sped away from the Parthian army.

Wind and bugs slapped at her face. Sepharia smoothed a strand of hair away, pulling it from her mouth. Sepharia was struck by how smooth they traveled, despite the uneven ground.

She moved to Heron's side, the determined look almost terrifying in its intensity. Sepharia hovered a hand over the missing leg, too fearful to ask.

"How do we fly so fast and so smooth?" asked Sepharia, daring the only question she could.

The glance from Heron was burdened with an impossible weight. Heron's words sent a chill down Sepharia's spine: "I brought knowledge from the underworld."

Heron faced the front and the chariot flew south, running on a coal-fueled wind, back to Alexandria, back to home, where plans for the coming war with Rome and Parthia would come to a head. Sepharia settled in the back and dreamt of home and a dead-eyed Prince. She did not sleep well.

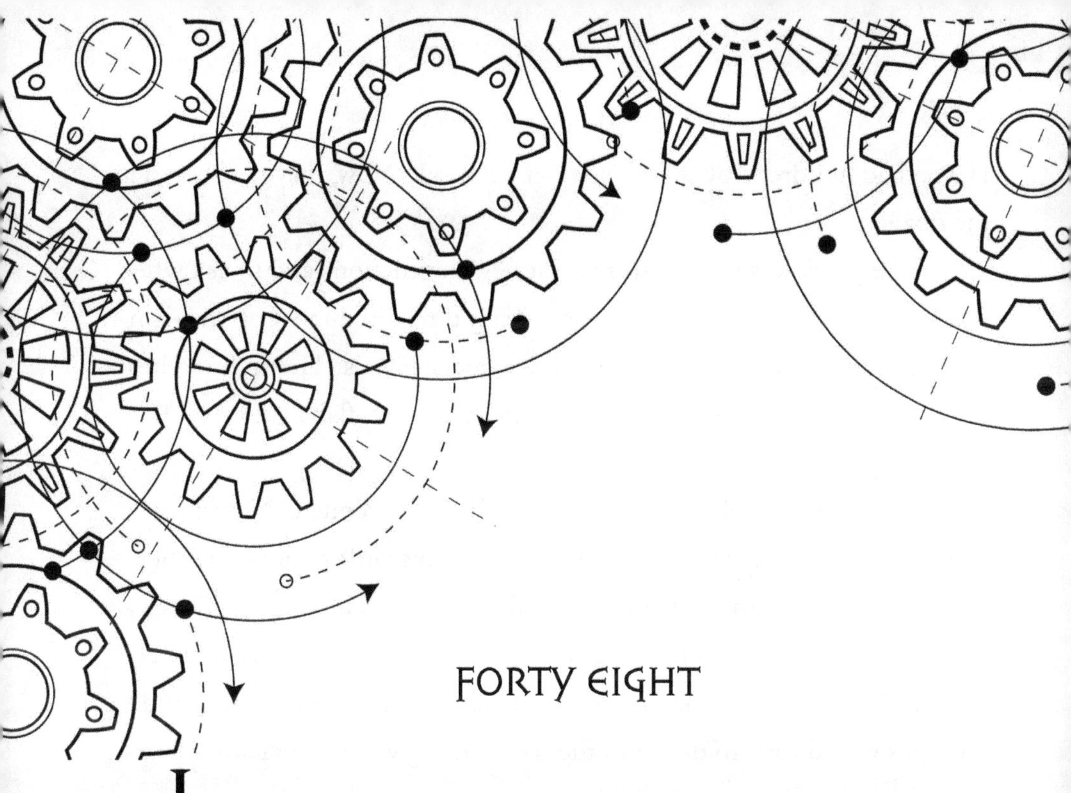

FORTY EIGHT

In the darkness of her room, Heron wrestled with sleep, forgoing the smothering embrace of the poppy so she might hold counsel with her thoughts. For too long since the temple she'd been wracked with pain and forced to rely on the drug.

Slipping from the cot, Heron crawled to her desk, ignoring her own lopsided wobble as she made her way there. Climbing into the chair, Heron made light and took a sniff of solace from the ornate wooden box. It did not hide her pain, but sharpened her thoughts after washing away the cumulative effects of the poppy.

Sighing, she read the papyrus on her desk once more. The script was in Ergamenes' neat scrawl. The markings as steady and organized as the man's machines. The Kushite Queen had called for the return of her workers so the pyramid site was abandoned. Additionally, the sand storm had damaged the machines and would take considerable rebuilding.

Despite the call from their Queen, the two engineers intended to stay and continue work, along with a small, but dedicated crew. Before,

Heron had hundreds of workers at her disposal. Now, they numbered in the dozens.

Ergamenes was writing to request new instructions and to ask when she could return to oversee the work. They'd repaired most of the damage from the sand storm but needed new mechanicals. Heron hung her head and rubbed the chunky edge of the document, flaking pieces off with a fingernail.

The pyramid could not be built. Not as she intended. Not in the scale of her visions. The poem had given her that information and her calculations since had confirmed what the ancients had known. There was a limit to the size of the pyramids if they were meant to last. The weight of the upper blocks would eventually crush the lower ones, and the sides would turn to dust and the whole thing would inevitably crumble. She was building a ruin.

She had not penned her reply to Ergamenes yet. She intended to tell him that the pyramid could not be built, including the calculations in her message, in case he did not understand. She valued his knowledge and loyalty, especially given that she'd been thought dead for quite some time, and didn't want him to think she was abandoning him.

When the iron staircase rattled heavily in its moorings, she knew the man who ascended. When he reached the top, he didn't have to turn sideways to exit the spiral, but his hips caught on the railings and he was momentarily stuck before pushing through with a grunt.

"I didn't ask for visitors," she told him.

"I'm not a visitor, I'm your King," said Agog.

"King now? When did you start that?" she asked.

Agog smoothed his tunic back. His normally shaggy hair was not so unkempt, though he still had a bit of wildness in him, despite the jewelry and lightly painted eyes.

"When I needed to signal to the world that I wasn't just an unruly city-state. That I meant to rule," he said. "King Wodanaz sounds more impressive than the Barbarian Satrap, or Agog."

"Was Agog ever your name?" she asked, suddenly curious.

He shrugged. "I have many names. It seemed a fitting joke at the time."

"Are we just a game to you?"

The big man paused, the candle light flickered across his normally green eyes, though in the dim light they appeared black.

"Of course not," he said, and made a heavy sigh, wandering to the window. He put his hands on the stone edge, leaning forward, looking out into the city. "I give you my heartfelt apology for what was said before."

"You should," she said.

He chuckled, shaking his head. "You're not an easy man to know, Heron of Alexandria."

"What do you want?" she asked. "You didn't come all this way just to apologize."

He turned to her. "Actually, I did. This war was never yours and I have treated you poorly. At every turn, you have met your obligations and I have misled you, time and time again."

"You did not come to me for more warmachines?"

"No," he said, "I come to offer my resources for your pyramid. If your workshop wishes to build a pyramid, I will support it."

"It's my workshop, again?"

He nodded. "No one truly wanted it and Plutarch only held it until you returned. He never doubted that you would."

"And you're not going to sell my daughter again?"

Agog momentarily bristled, before containing it beneath his regal appearance. "I did not sell her, but either way, the damage is done."

"At least she's given up the intrigue of the Palace and taken up her old room in the workshop. Her talents were wasted in your gilded halls," said Heron.

Agog chuckled, again. "Not entirely. My lovely wife Polyxena has told me numerous times that the girl was quite talented in the arts of deception. A bit raw and naïve at times, but talented. She could make a very effective and determined Queen someday."

"She's not of royal blood," she responded.

"She is now," he said sheepishly.

Heron sighed and glanced into the darkness of the stairwell.

"I will leave you now," said Agog. "But if you wish my resources, whatever they are, I offer them to you. Just say the word."

As the big man's hand touched the iron railing, she spoke: "I'm not going to build a pyramid."

He paused in half-step, and looked to her.

She continued, "It won't work. The ancients knew this, too. If I cannot build it as I wanted, I will not build it."

"This is unlike you to give up," he said.

"I'm not giving up," she said. "I'm just not building the pyramid. I have other things I need to do."

"And may I ask what those are?" He appeared worried.

"Warmachines," she said simply.

Confusion wracked his meaty face. "But I thought you did not want to make them?"

"I never said that," she said, "I only asked if you expected them. But no matter what you want. It's what I want. Through all of this, the pyramid, the crocodile priest, the Parthians, rescuing Sepharia, I've learned something."

"And what is that?"

"To the strongest."

He stared at her for a long moment before nodding. "I shudder for our enemies."

"I do, too."

The iron rattled again and Agog disappeared from her room, leaving her with the scrolls. She picked up the quill, dotted it with ink, and held it above the blank page. When the blackish liquid formed a bloated droplet, she put it back in the inkwell and blew out the candle. And in the darkness, she sat and thought, and when the stars rotated across the blanket of the sky, she had not moved, until the light came again and her room glowed with the day. Then, and only then, did she pick up her quill, dab it in the ink, and begin her return.

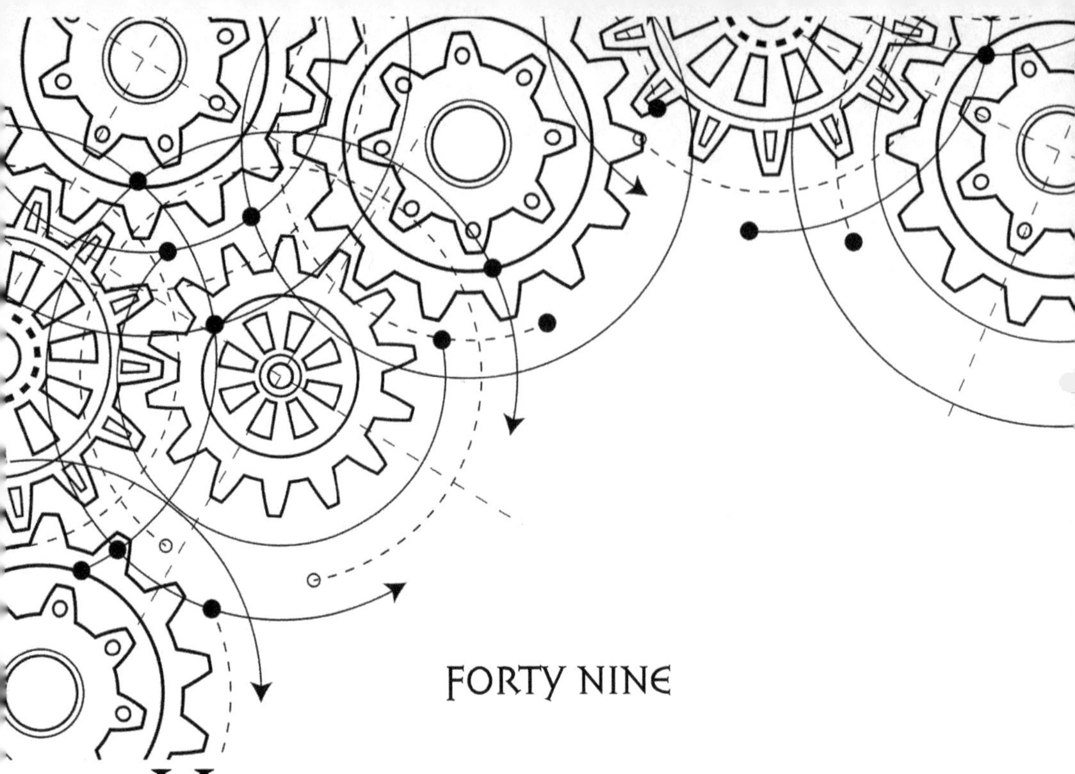

FORTY NINE

Heron piloted the steam chariot to the royal pier. It was a craft of her design, refined by the trip to Mithrapolis, and built for one. It'd been months since she'd been on the streets of Alexandria. The now familiar smell of burning coal was prevalent and she passed at least a dozen other steam chariots hauling supplies across the city. No longer did residents scurry away from the vehicles as if they were chariots of the gods. A work crew smoothed the cobblestone street near Canopic street, the King's orders she knew, though it was unnecessary. Her new spring design let the body of the craft float above the wheels, but it would take time to pass that technology to the other workshops and she had more important business first.

Thinking about the spring reminded her of the temple and what irked her was that Lysimachus had been there at the inception of the idea. If he were in Alexandria, the crocodile priest would lay claim to her invention, calling it a gift from Sobek, but she knew better. The priests and priestesses of Sobek had taken those wondrous inventions and warped them in the sucking, damp, dark of the temple.

Once she no longer needed the sap of the poppy, she instructed Plutarch to send men to the temple and take the torture devices Lysimachus had used on her, but when they got there, the temple was empty. Even the pond was free of crocodiles, only the mud and reeds and biting insects remained. She wondered about the whereabouts of the crocodiles though it could have been any temple that had rescued them and wasn't necessarily a sign that Lysimachus had moved.

When Plutarch returned, she thought about sending him back to raid other temples. Between them, the temples probably had as many inventions as the Curiosity Rooms, if her captive torture hall had been any measure. But inciting the high priests of Crocodopolis to war was not in her best interest, even if Alexandria could destroy the southern Egyptian city with a backhanded blow. Not when she needed to focus on beating Rome and Parthia on the battlefield, a task she now threw herself into with earnest.

When it came time to climb from the chariot, she paused. Eventually, she would have the leg of an automata and such simple tasks would not vex her so. She'd given the designs to Plutarch last week and her best craftsmen were assembling it, but until then a carved wooden leg and the ivory cane would have to do.

First, she closed her eyes, whispering a silent prayer to Aristotle. Getting off would be the hardest part. Using the cane to steady herself, Heron tipped herself from the seat and jammed her wooden foot down before she could sail over the side. The extension of her leg unbalanced her, and she teetered forward. Heron shuffled from the steam chariot and once her feet landed in the dirt, she was flung forward, landing on her forearms.

With eyes closed, she made a second prayer (a record for her), this time that no one had seen her inglorious dismount. She looked up to see a man in white and gold robes running toward her, loose fabric around his arms flapping like ungainly wings.

She recognized his chubby face as he approached. It was Xan-Ra, the priest of Ptah. Using her cane, she leveraged herself standing.

"Good Heron," said Xan, "are you injured?"

She stared back at him, unblinking. "Apologies, I have an appointment I must get to."

"All is well, I can walk with you." He paused. "If you don't mind."

The excitement on his face was nothing short of exuberant. Turning him away would only delay the inevitable. She sighed and motioned for him to walk with her.

"I've been needing to speak with you," he began.

"Recovering," she said simply, meaning as much about her health as the rescue of Sepharia.

"Of course," he said. "It's most wondrous that your daughter has been returned to you."

"Hardly returned, but she is home, never the less."

"Apologies again, I know I am taxing your patience. If you will only give me a moment to explain why I needed to see you, I can be gone and back in Memphis, if that's what you desire."

His rosy cheeks were pink and his kind eyes disarmed her. "It is I that should apologize," she said. "It was your temple that saved my life after the crocodile took my leg. Though I still wonder if it was only so Ptah could spill my blood on its altar rather than Sobek."

He lowered his eyes, nodding slightly. "You have every right to feel grieved. Hotep still regrets his rash actions of the day you visited our temple, but much has changed since then."

When he looked up at her, an inner glow shown through his eager eyes. She felt like she was staring down at a puppy begging for scraps.

"What has changed?"

"You, the pyramid, everything!" he said as if that would explain it.

"Words," said Heron, "I require more of them, hopefully including a few complete sentences."

He nodded enthusiastically. "At first, Hotep sent his men to harry your workers at the pyramid. He was convinced that you should be stopped. He went so far as to send in a woman to kill you."

"I remember her," she said.

"When that didn't work, he made his way there as a lone trader. When he finally saw the pyramid with his own eyes, he was converted."

"Converted to what?"

"Oh, he is still a follower of Ptah, but he came back to tell us that Heron the pyramid builder was the coming of the Broken One," he said. "His words carry much weight for the followers of Ptah."

She recoiled slightly, though he was so wide-eyed and slack jawed with wonder that she doubted he noticed. "What is this Broken One?" she asked with considerable trepidation.

"He is you," said Xan. "Our god Ptah is first a builder, a craftsmen. He fashioned us out of clay on the banks of the Nile. When he made the First Man, gifting him life with his wondrous breath, and set him on the river's edge, Sobek got jealous and sent a great crocodile from the waters and it wrapped its jaws around the First Man, shaking its head in deathly fury, and tossing him onto the shore. The First Man, missing his arm and leg, crawled back to the mud and refashioned his limbs, but he had not the magic of Ptah the builder and they stayed clay, though he could still use them. That is how he became the Broken One. Hotep said you saw the statue when you visited the temple."

The memory of that place rose up in her mind and suddenly she felt suspended from a great height with the world whirling around her. She recalled the eerie feeling she'd had when touching the statue on her way through the temple. That eerie feeling came back a thousand fold.

"It means nothing," she said.

"It means everything," Xan replied.

Heron ground her teeth. "Even if I am your Broken One, it means nothing. The pyramid building has stopped because of the war. There's no pyramid for you to worship now."

He didn't seem to be affected by the sting of her words. "We did not come to worship it, but to build it, with your guidance, of course."

The offer gave her pause. It felt like a trap, or a distortion of her beliefs.

She leaned on her cane, the ivory handle biting into her palm, and stared back at the city. Black smoke curled from distant buildings, drifting over the spinning bronze cups that had become as common as sunlight.

But what of the pyramid and the vision she shared with her ancestor, Alexander the Macedonian? That fury and conviction had been a sand storm in her head, obliterating everything else in its path. Now, she felt the winter of her wounds.

Xan, probably sensing her hesitation, moved back into her vision and began to speak again: "If only you could see the Temple of Ptah now, you would understand. You have awakened us and the halls teem with excitement. The craft halls sing with hammers, old makers dream new inventions as plentiful as sand, even our famed white walls gleam with an inner light. We are reborn by the work of the Broken One. How can you not look at your own wounds and know this is true? You saw the statue yourself. You must know it in your heart."

The statue in the Temple seemed such an odd coincidence. Part of her almost wondered if Lysimachus had been used to damage her in a way that would make her look like the Broken One, but she knew it could not be true. Lysimachus was truly mad now, a faith-filled and enthusiastic priest of the crocodile god.

Xan grabbed her forearm, right above the metal hand fitted on her stump. He was undaunted by the sharp look she gave him. "You were the one to unravel the poem I gave you, revealing the secrets of pyramid building."

"And in my hubris I did not calculate the true difficulties of building it. The first stanza gave the secret, but the second warned the limits of their pyramid craft. It cannot be done, the pyramid will fail if I try to build it that large."

Xan smiled as if he knew something she didn't. "You are the Broken One, we have faith that you will find the answer. The ancients did not have your machines or the cunning airs of your intellect."

An image of the pyramid formed in her mind, triggering another thought, one she'd had in the throes of her injuries, drowned in the sap of the poppy. Golden, glittering rods floated above the pyramid.

"See!" said Xan. "I can see your mind devising answers as we speak."

Heron shook her head, dismissing the dream. She stumbled towards the docks in a headlong rush to escape the priest of Ptah. "I cannot. It's dead. My pyramid is dead."

Xan followed her as far as the stairs that led to the docks. When he saw Jarngard standing on the deck of the iron boat, he gave her a little bow.

"Apologies, I've kept you from your duties," said Xan. "But I can see that we will have much to discuss soon. I shall wait in the Palace for my instructions."

Before she could tell him that waiting would be a waste of time, that she did not intend to give him any instructions, he fled back to the Palace, robes billowing from his haste.

Sighing all the way down to her bones, Heron looked down to Jarngard and then to the stairs. She wished he wasn't watching. At least there was a railing she could hold onto.

Hooking her elbow around the wooden shaft, she slid along it for balancing, stabbing the cane down on the next step, before attempting to place her wooden foot. The first five steps were traversed without trouble and she thought she might get down without incident. But when she hit the sixth step, the wooden foot skidded off the slick stone and she nearly toppled over and down the stairs. Swinging into the rail, Heron clung for life, splinters finding the soft spots in her underarm.

Once recovered, and warned of the danger, Heron made her way down the rest of the stair with only minor slips. Standing at the bottom, she collected herself and prepared to make her way to the iron boat.

And though she had tried to steel herself from this moment, when she looked up, now close enough to see the light stubble on his face, and the worn leather bag hanging from his neck, and his dark blue eyes, deep like the forests of the North, she had to resist every urge not to abandon her cane and try running into his arms.

She laughed quietly, realizing what a terrible sight that would be. Knowing she would probably fall on her face at the third step. Drained of her impulse, Heron set off across the dock and to the iron boat where Jarngard waited for her.

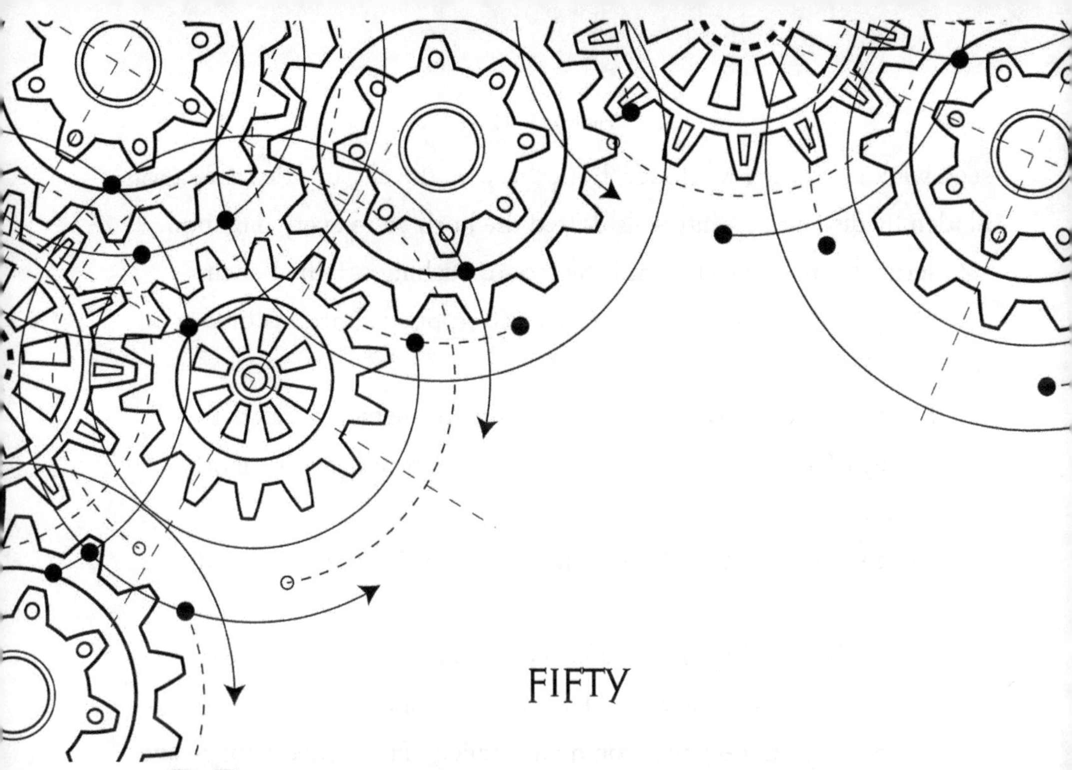

FIFTY

Heron sat in the middle of the iron boat, away from the edge, where the choppy waves splashed onto the deck. The clatter of the steam mechanical made odd rhythms with the slapping water as the craft pushed through the incoming waves.

She glanced behind them at the white froth and the smoothed waters where the boat had passed. How different from a trireme that cut through the water, riding with the wind.

Jarngard stood at the steerage, not so unlike her steam chariots. Nektam had used the base of her design and converted the energy into spinning blades on the back of the boat rather than wheels.

The muscles in his shoulders flexed as he turned the steering mechanism. Heron tried not to imagine nuzzling his neck, fingers kneading his chest. When she did, it only took one glance at her missing hand and wooden leg to banish the thoughts.

The thrum of the mechanical slowed until they fought the sea no longer and floated with the waves. The Lighthouse of Pharos could be seen winking in the low clouds, but otherwise the city of Alexandria was hidden by distance. White sails dotted the horizon in every direction.

Jarngard moved to her and she stood, pushing off the bench, expecting to feel his arms around her. He stopped short, his blue eyes searching her.

She looked back to the housing for the mechanical. "Soon they'll be as many of these iron boats in the sea as there are steam chariots in Alexandria."

"The world is changing," said Jarngard, "and you're the one that changed it."

"If the King," they shared a knowing smile, "wouldn't have come south for his revenge, this would have never happened."

"Without you, the King would have failed. He needed your steam mechanicals. Even now he needs you, more than ever," said Jarngard.

He was only an arm's length away and she could smell him: snowy pines, hearth fire, the tang of cold. When she looked into his eyes, she imagined the warm hut, wrapped in furs, naked and entangled.

"It's not for him," she said. "I do it for the city of Alexandria. I am nothing without the learnings of those that came before. Above all, I must protect the city, the Library. Rome let the city burn once, so they should not have it."

"Alexandria has never had a fiercer protector. The warrior-maiden Heron." His eyes had a mischievous cast and the corner of his lip was pulled upward.

She laughed, a bubble of tension in her chest popping. "It sounds ridiculous. They'd stone me if they knew."

"I think you underestimate your city. I do not deny that some might have words, but the rest would embrace you," he said.

"Is that why you brought me out here?" she asked. "To convince me to reveal my secret?"

He shook his head. "No. I did because you must hide it. I knew anywhere in the city, you would be Heron the inventor, the miracle maker, the *Michanikos*. Here, you could be Heron..."

He paused and tilted his head. "That was not your name before, was it?"

"Ada," she said, anticipating the question.

"Ada." He rolled her former name across his lips as if he were savoring a fine wine. "It suits you."

"It is my name no longer. I am Heron. It is all I can be now. And that's who Alexandria needs. Ada would only be a distraction."

He grinned as wide as the sea. "There is truth in that. I am distracted." He pulled her into his arms, and she stumbled on the decking, but was crushed against his chest before shame could take hold.

Lips were pressed against hers and she forgot about Ada, about Alexandria, about everything. Heron kissed him, feeling the warmth of his hand against her back, pressing, touching. She moved to stroke his head, and he winced, pulling away.

"Apologies," she said, stumbling backwards and landing unceremoniously onto the bench.

He rubbed his head absently. She'd forgotten about the metal hand.

"I can't," she said, cradling the metal hand against her chest.

Jarngard knelt before her, his knee right against her foot, his thigh hovering near the calf of her good leg. He gently pulled the metal hand away from her chest and set it in her lap. Then, with careful, determined fingers, he unfastened the buckles on the strap that held the hand to her stump. As the hand slipped off he caught it, as gently as one might an egg, and set it on the bench next to her.

She pulled the stump to her chest, hiding the pink, cracked skin beneath her other arm. Undeterred, Jarngard slid his hands beneath her tunic, pushing the fabric up until it kissed against her upper thigh. The buckles came loose under his patient fingers and the leg was away.

The cool sea air stung at first, a bit of salt spray landing on the mottled flesh, and she gasped. Jarngard rose and pulled a fur blanket from a sack and spread it on the deck. The boat rocked lazily from side to side, the seas having calmed from their ride.

Heron waited, thoughts for once not revolving around her inventions. With the spot set, he moved to her, and tugged at her tunic. She put a hand on his and he stopped.

"I can't," she said, peering up at him.

"If not now, then when?" he asked. "Soon, Alexandria goes to war, and I go with it. There might not be another time."

"I'm a cripple."

A calm smile rose to his lips. "It is the world that is crippled."

She stayed his reaching hand with fingertips. "I must know. Why? How? You knew me for a man until the night of the reeds and now I am deformed."

He pushed aside her protest. "It is not often one gets to make love to the greatest thinker of an age."

She laughed quietly, knowing that was not really his answer. If there was an answer, he gave it by loosening her belt and tugging her tunic over her head. The wind brought gooseflesh to her skin. Jarngard pulled a knife from his belt and slipped the edge of it underneath the wrapping that bound her chest. As the cloth ripped away, freeing her breasts, her nipples sprung out, and he brushed a thumb against one, smiling at her with his eyes.

Last, he slipped his fingers around the harness at her waist. He removed the wooden genitalia and set it gently on the deck. Jarngard helped her standing and she moved with him, but before he could stop her, Heron hit him in the chest with her good hand, knocking him onto his rear on the furs.

She fell onto him and began removing his clothing, not trying to be gentle. She took him into her and rode his hips, feeling him thrusting against her motion. The rising and falling of the boat sometimes accentuated their opposition and other times it pulled them apart, doubling the ache of need in her groin.

On top of him, she forgot she was a cripple and it felt like she was the sea, never ending, rolling on forever. She rode, and rode, and when the slapping matched the long counts of the waves against the boat's iron hull, she smiled as she felt the sea with her.

And when he came, shuddering and calling out her name, once Heron, and twice Ada, she gave him no respite and kept going. They made love for the afternoon, taking a break only to sip from a water pouch, before plunging back into the furs, hands probing and hips thrusting.

Afterwards, when Jarngard was asleep and the sun hovered above the horizon, a whale broke the surface next to the boat, spraying water onto her face. She smiled and crawled to the edge. The whale floated next to the boat, its great eye searching before it blew again and disappeared into the deeps.

When the night came, they used each other for warmth and ate figs and hard bread beneath the stars. She rode him twice more before he slept for good. Heron was awake and watched the warm glow of the Lighthouse through the gathering clouds.

Alexandria was her home, and muse, and light. But when she returned she would be Heron the inventor again, not, whoever she was with Jarngard, part Heron, part Ada, part something else. And though she thought long about it in the night, she could not unravel why she felt so strong with Jarngard when they were having sex. Was this how other women felt?

As Heron, she loved the smell of foundry fires and the clink of wooden mallets on bronze, of ink drying on papyrus, her ideas encoded to them. With Jarngard she felt strong, too, but in a way that was missing when she was Heron. It filled an ache she tried not to admit she had.

Was it the act of coupling together that made her strong in that moment? She could not help but envision Jarngard thrusting into her as a rod on her steam mechanical, and the thought made her flush with excitement. In the starlight, she looked at his sleeping face and wanted to press her lips against his and wake him, and she might, but not yet.

In his way, Jarngard seemed broken like her, though his wounds were carried on the inside. And having been surrounded by men most of her life, and privy to their actions and moods, she knew they were not so strong, either.

They needed women just as much, which made her angry that they were not treated as equal. Could men not see that apart they were not as strong? In sex, she needed his rod as much as he needed her. These dualities were a scientific inevitability. Like the piston and shaft for her mechanical, or that a foundry fire needed both fuel and air to make strong steel, or that her pyramid...

She sat upright, the thoughts lying tantalizingly against her tongue. The pyramid? Just like the pyramid, the way the stone needed rods to make it strong. The realization hit her right in the chest and she felt dizzy.

"Ada?" asked Jarngard, leaning on his elbows, blinking bleary-eyed. "Is something wrong?"

She kissed him. "No, nothing at all. In fact, it's wonderful."

"What is?"

Heron pushed him onto the furs. "This," she said, laughing. "Take me again so I cannot forget this moment."

She climbed on top and took him inside and before long the boat swayed against the waves. Triumphantly, they came together and afterwards, they sprawled across the deck, steam slipping from their glistening bodies, and when at last Heron slept, she dreamt of a great pyramid that reached the sky.

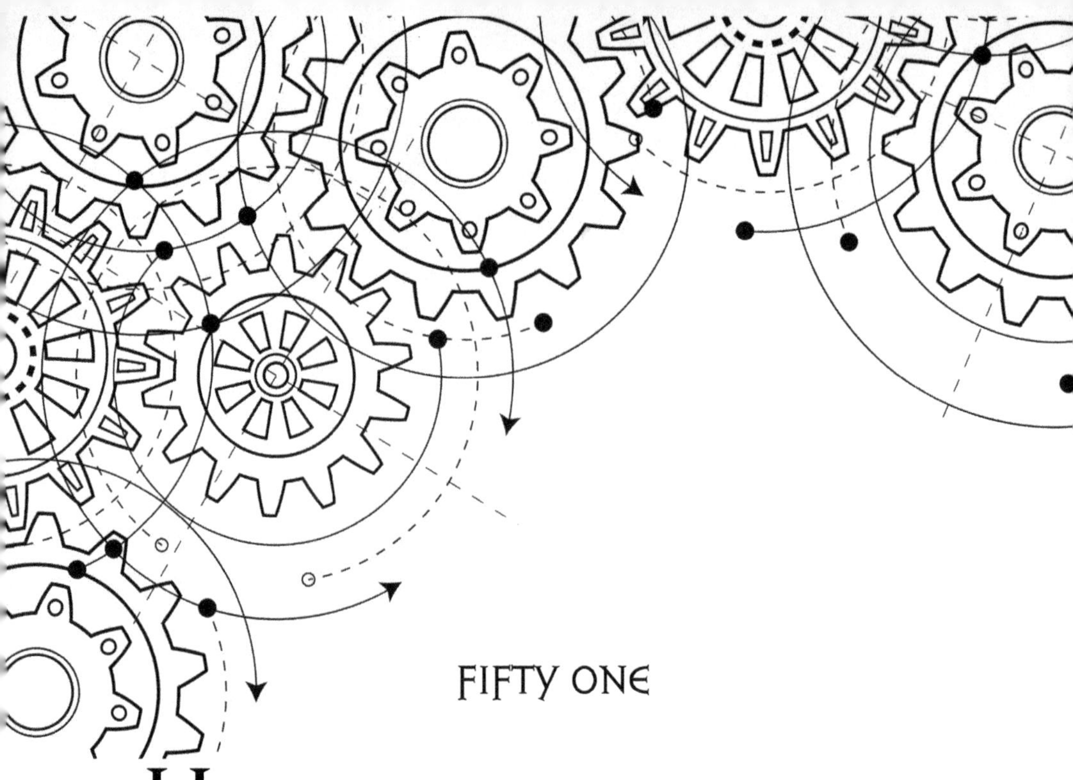

FIFTY ONE

Heron was sitting in her room sketching the last of her new
designs for the great pyramid, when she thought she heard voices from
below, but dismissed them out of hand. She had work to do. Once the
craftsmen from the Temple of Ptah had shown up at the pyramid site,
Ergamenes had sent for instructions. Heron had been at her desk, day
and night for the last week, sending at least a dozen scrolls a day, and
receiving back a similar number.

The rod and stone design, pioneered by Jarngard in the Mithras statue, would give the pyramid the strength to achieve the scale she wished.
They would need to remove a couple of the blocks already in place, but
after thorough calculations, she was convinced the rest could remain.

With everything happening, planning for the war effort, respond-
ing to Ergamenes and the Temple workers, she had no time to visit the
site and only had to go on the words of the messengers that a small city
had sprouted up next to her fledgling pyramid. The priests of Ptah had
brought a sizable portion of their temple.

Sepharia had returned to the workshop, but hadn't been seen, not that Heron had made it out of her room very often. The wooden leg made getting around difficult and she preferred to have her food and drinks brought up the spiral stairs rather than risk injury.

Heron glanced to the new table in her room, covered in implements, mostly steel, brushed clean of rust and dried blood. They were full of sharp edges and crushing plates, powered by gears and sockets, wound or sprung. A pile of scrolls next to the desk owed their existence to the torture devices from the Temple of Sobek.

Between answering the many questions about building the pyramid, Heron found inspiration from their designs. The latest had been an improvement in the steam catapult. Her earlier versions had failed to launch the stones much further than the length of her courtyard. With the geared latch and spring design, taken from the limb crushing implement, she was convinced she could launch a stone the size of bucket the length of the city.

She was contemplating the latest batch of questions, quill posed right above the papyrus with ink rapidly drying, when Plutarch broke up the stairs, wide-eyed and panting. The iron stairs settled their rattling while he took deep breaths.

"Good Plutarch, what is wrong?"

He glanced to the floor, and her heart seized with fear.

"Come downstairs, quickly if you can," he said.

The need in his voice forced her to set her quill down.

"Was there an accident?"

He shook his head. "Just come down."

Plutarch returned to the lower level, while Heron called after him, "Is it Sepharia? Or Rome? Has the siege started? Curse you, Plutarch, tell me."

Only slightly more adept with the wooden leg and cane, Heron hobbled to the iron stairs, thankful the railing made for easier descent. She set her hip against the spiraling curve and hopped down each step, cane ringing on steel.

As she made her way to the workshop, the possibilities of what was wrong careened through her head. Someone must have died, she decided. She couldn't keep packing up every time she thought Agog might die. If it was him, she'd just push one of the others to take his place. She was too deep in this now.

That only made her think of Jarngard, and her palms itched like a prickly cactus. Not Jarngard, and not Sepharia. Let it be anyone but them. Or Punt, let it not be Punt, either. She at least knew that it wasn't Plutarch. Or let it be that no one had died. But it had to be bad, whatever it was.

Rounding the corner as quickly as she could stab her cane onto the stone, and haul her wooden leg one step forward, Heron steeled herself for the worst. She almost wished for the siege to begin. There would be a catharsis in battle. But she knew the Roman army was still months away and Parthia was staying back, waiting for the full might of Rome.

When a crowd of waiting men and women shouted, "Ave!" Heron nearly fell over in her haste. Stunned into silence, she glanced at the familiar faces in the group: Jarngard, Sepharia, Hoth the Black, Punt, Plutarch, her workers and craftsmen, and even King Wodanaz. The last stood above the others like a mountain lording over the plains.

A thin flute of dark wine was thrust into her hand.

"Plato have pity, what is the meaning of this?" she asked.

Plutarch winked. "The great unveiling. Everyone wanted to be here."

"Your new limbs," said Jarngard.

"But why are you all here?" she asked, hearing her voice crack slightly.

"You've sacrificed much for us," said King Wodanaz. "We wanted to be here when the machines restored you whole."

"I won't be whole," she told them, and paused, while they stared at her grinning. "You all look like hyenas and I'm your favorite carcass, stinking with flies."

"Well, at least you got that right," said Hoth.

Sepharia wrinkled her nose. "Yes, father, are you going to ever wash? We can smell you from the workshop."

A wave of laughter passed through them, echoing in the cavernous workshop, and Heron heard her own laughter join theirs, though she couldn't remember the last time she had laughed. The muscles in her face felt weak and unused, and as it died down, she rubbed at the soreness she would surely feel tomorrow.

Plutarch, always the master of ceremonies for events like these, rolled a flat, wooden chest into the room. Odd paintings covered the sides and top, and Heron couldn't quite figure out what was on them.

When Plutarch turned it sideways, Heron realized white teeth had been painted there, and along the front. Green mottled skin covered the top, including two familiar dead eyes with jewels inset along the brow ridge. The chest was painted as the crocodile Petsuchos, the one that had taken her leg and that her friends had killed for her.

She laughed, smiling despite herself. "What friends you are to bring me such fanciful furniture. Next, should I ask for a dining table with Emperor Claudius' face on it?"

Hoth smirked. "Better Claudius than our own King Agog. There's not enough wood in the city for his face to fit."

A few of the workers in back started chanting, "Open it! Open it!"

"Open it," said Jarngard, a secret smile in his eyes. "The crocodile painting was a last minute addition from your daughter. The real prize is inside."

Using the cane for support, Heron hobbled to it. She couldn't both stand and open the chest, so Sepharia moved to support her.

The brass object inside gleamed in the sunlight coming through the upper windows when she opened it. Gears peeked through gaps between the polished, brass outer skin, and rods ran the length, fitting onto harnesses that she assumed went around her knee.

The whole contraption reminded her of the original harness that she'd designed when Lysimachus had hobbled her, and it bore a passing resemblance to the sketching she'd given Plutarch when she wanted something better than the wooden leg. But none of those descriptions quite matched what her eyes were seeing. If the aeolipile was the inspiration for her newest steam mechanicals, then the sketching she'd given them was comparable to the object inside the crocodile chest.

Agog cleared his throat. "Sepharia redesigned your leg. As much as I hate to admit it, her talents in the workshop outweigh her considerable talents in the Palace. It's almost a shame you'll probably step in horse shit with that piece of magnificent machinery."

The smile practically split her face wide open. "It's beautiful. I'll never have a better leg."

"Or hand," said Sepharia, pointing to the smaller brass and geared limb next to the mechanical leg.

Plutarch patted Sepharia's shoulder. "I don't think she's slept all week, tweaking the design. The workshop has poured every ounce of its creativity into it. Everyone leant a hand."

Heron rolled her eyes. "I'll try not to make you regret it by sticking my nose back into the workshop."

"We wouldn't have it any other way," said Punt.

"Put it on!" came the cheer from the back.

With considerable trepidation, and help from Sepharia, Heron fitted the leg on her stump. Thankfully, the crocodile had bitten below the knee, so her joints were still useable. As Sepharia adjusted the leg, Heron heard her daughter mumbling, clearly finding areas for improvement, though Heron could see none.

Punt took the wooden leg away and held it up high. "I'll burn this for you now."

"No, not yet," said Heron, "I might need a backup."

"We'll make you another one," said Sepharia. "But less about that. Let's see you walk."

Heron took a deep breath and took a step. Her first one was a stumble, not because the leg didn't perform, but because she was used to the wooden leg not being so supportive, so she overcompensated.

The second step was better. The brass mechanical leg ticked and hissed air as she bent her knee, springing forward to step. Heron was surprised by the smoothness. She'd expected a lurching movement.

Sepharia was frowning, scrunching her face up at the mechanical leg. "It's so loud. I'll have to work on that."

Plutarch held his hands up. "No, please, no. This way we can hear him when he comes into the workshop."

They laughed again and Heron took the distraction to take a few more steps without them staring at her. She still felt like she'd had one too many glasses of wine, but the leg performed beautifully.

Marching around the workshop, she felt her limbs surge with energy. Overwhelmed by the generosity of her workers, she could not keep the smile from her lips.

Sepharia held out the brass hand. Heron let her fit it on, the cushioned inside sliding over her stump, a thick guard went over her forearm, while a web of soft leather wrapped around her elbow.

"See these buttons in the palm?" asked Sepharia. "They actuate the gears to close your hand."

Sepharia pressed the one in the middle of the brass palm with a fingertip. The fingers curled into a grip, slowly closing further and further until they touched the palm.

"Springs inside this area," Sepharia tapped the guard on the back, "keep the fingers moving until they meet resistance, then they slowly close around it."

"How do I let go?" asked Heron.

"The button on the back." Sepharia pressed it and the fingers sprung open.

"It's a work of art," murmured Heron. "I'll gift it to the Library when I'm dead."

Sepharia raised an eyebrow. "You're not dead yet. And while you're alive, you might need these other buttons. They close the fingers in a different way, hopefully to give you a different grip should you need it."

Heron pulled Sepharia into her arms, and realized the girl was as tall as she. The assembled clapped and heat rose to Heron's cheeks.

"Plato have pity," she said to them, "we have work to do. Now that I'm mobile again, I can properly supervise you. Plutarch, up to my room, I have a pile of scrolls that need to be turned into working models by next week."

Grinning, Plutarch sprinted out of the workshop. The workers took their cue to return to work.

"You too, master blacksmith," said Heron. "Stoke those fires, we're going to need a lot of steel."

Punt snapped a dirty towel over his shoulder, gave her a graceful bow, one that surprised the Northmen in its elegancy, and returned to his foundry.

As she laid her eyes on him, the barbarian held his hands up. "I go, I go," said Agog, "before you put me to work."

"I'll send for you when I need something destroyed," she called after his massive shadow as he left.

Hoth, not to be outdone by the Egyptian blacksmith, gave her a flourishing bow so low, the dark streak in his hair dangled onto the stone floor. When he popped up, his impish grin was irrepressible and he left without another word.

Finally, Heron kissed Sepharia on the forehead. "Yes, I see it in your eyes, you wish to tinker with them. Back to your shop, I'll come by later after I've had a chance to use them. You can adjust the gearing then."

Sepharia skipped away after saying farewell to Jarngard, who was as still as a statue. Heron stepped near, near enough she could smell the mint leaves he must have been chewing earlier. She glanced to the workers, already onto the scaffoldings like ants, making the sweet music of her workshop.

"When will I get to see you again?" he whispered, his voice thick with need.

"After the war," she said. "I don't know when either of us will be able to get away."

His nod was filled with regrets and sadness. "When we were building the pyramid, after the time in the reeds, I had a desire to take you away from all this. Let us wander the lands as man and woman, headed east on a grand adventure, or west across the sea to find what's on the other side."

"I would like that." She paused. "Someday. But not now. I have too much to do. But after the war, after Rome. I would go with you, as man and woman."

He raised a mischievous eyebrow. "I get to be the man, right?"

"If I never have to wear this binding or harness again, I'll be the happiest woman in the world."

"Then it's a pact," said Jarngard, his sad blue eyes fixed on her. "After the war. We leave all this and see the rest of the world. As man and woman."

"It's a pact."

He gave her the smallest and slowest of bows, like a soft kiss, or an intimate glance. She returned a bow, and then he left, and a shiver went down her spine.

"After the war..."

§ § §

Continue Heron's adventure in Book Four of The Alexandrian Saga

WARMACHINES OF ALEXANDRIA

OTHER BOOKS BY THOMAS K. CARPENTER

The Hundred Halls Universe

SEASON ONE
THE HUNDRED HALLS
Trials of Magic
Web of Lies
Alchemy of Souls
Gathering of Shadows
City of Sorcery

THE RELUCTANT ASSASSIN
The Reluctant Assassin
The Sorcerous Spy
The Veiled Diplomat
Agent Unraveled
The Webs That Bind

GAMEMAKERS ONLINE
The Warped Forest
Gladiators of Warsong
Citadel of Broken Dreams
Enter the Daemonpits
Plane of Twilight

WANIMALIANS HALL
Wild Magic
Bane of the Hunter
Mark of the Phoenix
Arcane Mutations
Untamed Destiny

STONE SINGERS HALL
Song of Siren and Blood
House of Snake and Tome
Storm of Dragon and Stone
Sonata of Shadow and Thorn
Well of Demon and Bone

THE ORDER OF MERLIN
The Order of Merlin
Infernal Alliances
Tower of Horn and Blood

ABOUT THE AUTHOR

Thomas K. Carpenter resides in Colorado with his wife Rachel. When he's not busy writing his next book, he's hiking, skiing, and getting beat by his wife at cards. He keeps a regular blog at www.thomaskcarpenter.com and you can follow him on twitter @thomaskcarpente. If you want to learn when his next novel will be hitting the shelves and get free stories and occasional other goodies, please sign up for his mailing list by going to: http://tinyurl.com/thomaskcarpenter. Your email address will never be shared and you can unsubscribe at any time.